sc

here
we
lie

D0227829

Sophie McKenzie is the author of best-selling crime novels *Close My Eyes* and *Trust in Me* as well as over twenty books for children and teenagers including the multi-award winning *Girl, Missing* and *Split Second* series. She has twice been longlisted for the prestigious Carnegie Medal. *Here We Lie* is Sophie's third book for adults. She lives in London.

Find Sophie online at www.sophiemckenziebooks.com, on twitter at @sophiemckenzie_ and on facebook at www.facebook.com/sophiemckenzieauthor.

here
we
lie

Sophie
McKenzie

SIMON &
SCHUSTER

London · New York · Sydney · Toronto · New Delhi

A CBS COMPANY

Property of Stockton Borough Libraries

First published in Great Britain by Simon & Schuster UK Ltd, 2015
A CBS COMPANY

Copyright © Rosefire Ltd, 2015

This book is copyright under the Berne Convention.
No reproduction without permission.
® and © 1997 Simon & Schuster Inc. All rights reserved.

The right of Sophie McKenzie to be identified as author
of this work has been asserted in accordance with sections
77 and 78 of the Copyright, Designs and Patents Act, 1988.

3 5 7 9 10 8 6 4 2

Simon & Schuster UK Ltd
1st Floor
222 Gray's Inn Road
London WC1X 8HB

www.simonandschuster.co.uk

Simon & Schuster Australia, Sydney
Simon & Schuster India, New Delhi

A CIP catalogue record for this book
is available from the British Library

TPB ISBN: 978-1-47113-318-3
PB ISBN: 978-1-47113-319-0
EBOOK ISBN: 978-1-47113-320-6

This book is a work of fiction. Names, characters, places and
incidents are either a product of the author's imagination or are
used fictitiously. Any resemblance to actual people living or
dead, events or locales is entirely coincidental.

Typeset by M Rules
Printed and bound by CPI Group (UK) Ltd, Croydon, CR0 4YY

For Eoin

PART ONE

November 1992

Rose Campbell took a step closer to the door. The floor on the other side creaked again: the loose board right beside Mum's dressing table. Was someone inside, rifling through Mum's jewellery? It was probably just Mum herself, home early from work like Rose. Except if it was Mum, why hadn't she answered when Rose called? In fact, why had she shut the door in the first place? Mum *never* shut any doors.

Rose reached for the handle as the floor creaked yet again. She was tired. Too tired to think properly. She'd come home with a bad headache after one of the customers had been rude to her. Rose hated waitressing. And she hated how long it was taking to save the money she needed to go on the trip she had promised herself next spring. Gap year, they called it. A chance to explore the world before heading off to uni next autumn. So far all that Rose had explored was the grungy back room of The Bath Bun.

'Mum?' The word came out more softly than Rose meant it to. Her voice barely a croak. The floor had stopped creaking but now she could hear a thudding sound, as if the dressing table was being knocked against the wall. Surely there was no way a burglar would be making so much noise?

Rose reached into her handbag for her phone. Well, it wasn't hers ... it was her boss's state-of-the-art mobile. He had let her borrow it while he was abroad for a few days in case there was any kind of emergency at The Bath Bun. Neither of her parents seemed to realize how extraordinary this phone was – Mum in particular was totally gadget-phobic, refusing even to learn how to work the CD player – but Martin thought it was really cool and predicted everyone they knew would have one within the next couple of years. This seemed highly unlikely to Rose, but at least having the mobile with her right now meant she could call the police if there was a burglar without having to get to the house phone.

'Mum?' Rose whispered again. There was still no reply from inside the room. She lifted her hand to knock on the door, then dropped it again. If a burglar *was* in there, knocking would just alert him to her presence. Better to open the door swiftly, see who was there, then turn and run. She could call the police from outside. She gripped the handle. Pushed open the door.

It took a second to register what she was looking at. A woman – a stranger – with long, flame-red hair was bent over the dressing table, *Mum's* dressing table. She was sideways on to Rose, her skirt hitched up, her fingers clutching wildly at the edges of the table, her profiled mouth open in lipsticked ecstasy. Behind her was Rose's father, his trousers around his ankles, his right hand pressed lightly on the back of the woman's neck. He was watching himself in the mirror.

The woman turned her head and saw Rose. She froze, her look of triumph turning to horror. Necklaces and rings bounced silently to the carpet as Rose's father followed the woman's gaze to the door.

But Rose had already fled.

Sarah had suspected Iain was having another affair even before she found the long red hair on the dressing table. It was the usual story: late nights at the office, a sudden interest in Sarah's own timetable of nursing shifts, an inability to meet her gaze. But the hair was something tangible, something Iain surely wouldn't be able to explain away. Especially seeing as Sarah had found the hair in their own bedroom. And after all Iain's promises ... she couldn't bear it. She was going to talk to him. Now.

'Rose?' Sarah called up to her elder daughter. Rose was listening to pop in her room. Sarah wondered at her taste, all sugar-coated boy bands, no one who could play a proper instrument. When Sarah had been eighteen back in the early seventies, teenagers were into real musicians like Jimi Hendrix and Joan Baez.

'What?'

Sarah sighed. Of her three children Rose was the one she had always struggled with, right from the start when it had been such a battle to breast-feed.

'Come down here, please.'

There was a thump, then a loud sigh from the landing, and Rose trudged sullenly downstairs. Sarah watched her. What on earth was she wearing? Couldn't she see how revolting that fluorescent windcheater was? All hot pink and neon green, nothing of the natural world about it at all.

The other two had always been easier. Emily was the youngest, the sweetest of children, Sarah's angel, while Martin was her special, precious boy. In the deepest, most secret place of her heart, Sarah knew that Martin was the love of her life. It wasn't that she didn't love the others – or her husband – but she had fallen in love with Martin the second he was born. And, somehow, Martin always knew how to handle her in a way that no one else in her life ever had. Her beautiful boy, now turning into a wonderful young man. Sarah could totally understand all those queens from history who stood behind their sons, proud to make them powerful.

'What is it, Mum?' Rose asked. She didn't make eye contact, but Sarah was used to that.

'I'd like you to keep the others busy, please. I need to talk to your father.'

Rose's eyes widened. She still wasn't looking directly at Sarah, but the surprise and resentment in her expression were evident nonetheless. There was something else, too, a self-consciousness. Sarah frowned: what was that about? She braced herself, expecting Rose to insist – as she had many times – that it wasn't fair to expect her to babysit the younger ones. But Rose said nothing. Instead a flicker of guilt crossed her face.

And in that moment Sarah was certain her daughter knew exactly what Iain had been up to.

Her stomach fell away. *How* could Rose know? *What* did she know? Sarah itched to ask questions, but she held herself back. It wasn't fair to drag Rose into her parents' drama.

'Thanks, Rose.'

Rose gave a quick nod and raced back upstairs.

Sarah took a deep breath and headed to the kitchen, where Iain was reading the paper.

The kitchen door was shut, but Rose – standing just outside – could hear the conversation clearly enough to tell that Mum was in tears and Dad was furious. She could picture them standing there – Mum's eyes all red, Dad crumpled and handsome in his grey suit, his olive skin so like Rose's own.

'Iain?' Mum's voice wavered as she spoke. 'Iain, please answer me.'

Silence.

Rose's heart beat hard. How much had Mum guessed? Thud. Thud. Thud.

'Was someone here ... with you ... yesterday?'

The silence grew deeper. Darker. Rose held her breath.

'No.' Her father's voice was low and cross. 'You're being stupid.'

'What about the hair I found? A long, red hair.'

An image flashed, unbidden, into Rose's head of that henna'd hair, so bright against the dark wood of the dressing table, of her father absorbed in his reflection in the mirror and of the woman's arched back, her white skin, her stretched-open mouth.

'Either one of us could have brought that in on our clothes,' Dad snapped. 'Come to that, so could any of the kids.'

'Iain, please, just tell me the truth—'

'I am fucking telling you the truth, you stupid, paranoid bitch.'

Rose's whole body froze. She had never heard her father speak with such contempt. Or lie so openly.

Inside the kitchen, Mum dissolved into sobs. Footsteps on the stairs sounded above Rose, first Martin's heavy tread, then Emily's light skip. Rose turned in alarm. What were they doing, coming downstairs? She'd left Martin reading to Emily in place of their mother. Her sister was really too old for such childish practices, in her first term at secondary school for goodness' sake. Still, as the baby of the family Emily was indulged in many things.

Whatever, Rose definitely didn't want her little sister

seeing their parents in the middle of a row, so as Martin and Emily walked along the narrow hall she put her finger to her lips, then made a movement to shoo them both away and back upstairs.

Martin made a face at her, then bent down and whispered something in Emily's ear that definitely included the words 'bossy Rose'. Emily grinned adoringly up at her brother. Rose frowned. How could Martin be so thick? At least there was no sound coming from the kitchen at the moment. Did that mean Mum had stopped crying? Or was she just sobbing too quietly for Rose to hear?

'We came down for chocolate,' Martin said.

Rose shook her head, barring the way to the kitchen with her arm.

A second later, Emily had ducked underneath and was opening the kitchen door. Rose watched her little sister as she scampered across the room to the store cupboard. As she hurried past Mum, Mum wiped her eyes and stood up, sniffing back her tears.

'Okay, Emily Sarah?' she asked.

Dad didn't turn around. He was gazing out through the kitchen window into the back garden.

Emily retrieved a bar of Galaxy from the cupboard. 'For me and Mart, bedtime snack.' Her dark eyes shone, all innocence and excitement. She strolled past Mum, clearly completely oblivious to Mum's distress.

Mum caught her arm and pulled her into a hug, stroking Emily's hair as she did so. 'Bedtime, yeah?'

'Okay.' Emily gave Mum a swift hug back. 'Night, Mum. Night, Daddy.' She hurried out of the room, leaving the door open.

Rose could hear her brother and sister going back up the stairs, but her eyes were focused on Mum's agonized face. She felt a surge of anger that Dad was denying his affair. It wasn't fair on Mum, on any of them.

Dad turned. Without looking at either of them, he swept past like a thunderstorm, grabbed his coat and slammed the front door shut behind him.

Mum sank into a chair, her face in her hands, her shoulders shaking with sobs. Rose fidgeted by the door. Should she say something to Mum about what she'd seen yesterday? At least then Mum would know the truth.

Except it wasn't Rose's job to sort out her parents' marriage. Resentment snaked through her. Some of this was Mum's fault too – she never made any effort with how she looked now and she was always nagging Dad about how little he did around the house.

Anyway, maybe if she said nothing, the whole situation would just go away. Casting a final look at her mother, still slumped over the kitchen table, Rose turned and went upstairs.

It was the last time she saw either of her parents.

August 2014

It's a near perfect day. Not that I appreciate it being near perfect at the time. In fact, after lunch I get a headache. It comes on suddenly, as we're walking up the endless series of steps and pathways of the citadel at Calvi. Jed, bless him, notices straight away. He pulls me back as the others dart past an oncoming Audi and through a dark tunnel.

'Are you okay?'

'I'm fine,' I say, though in fact the Corsican summer heat and the steep climb are making the tight band across the back of my head worse. I don't want to spoil the afternoon. Everything has been so blissful up to now – being here with all the people I love best in the world, secure in Jed's adoration, both of us looking forward to the rest of our lives together. 'It's just a bit of a headache.'

'Well, let me know if it gets worse.' Jed puts his arm around me as we head into the tunnel. We emerge into the bright light of the fierce August sun and Dee Dee hurls herself at me.

'Emily, Emily, come and look!' she says, grabbing my hand and tugging me away from her father.

'Gently,' Jed cautions.

But Dee Dee is so intent on showing me the view before anyone else gets a chance that I'm already halfway across the cobbles, Jed left several metres behind. This is typical Dee Dee. Caught almost exactly between child and adolescent, she was thirteen back in early June and is plumper than either she or her father would like. I've told Jed she isn't properly fat, just hormonal, a little lumpy and uncomfortable inside her own changing body, and he murmurs that I'm probably right, but I know he worries that she should be more in control of her eating – and of her behaviour. Dee Dee herself is certainly hard for any of us to get a handle on: one minute she's all excitable puppy, the next moody and withdrawn. At least she has seemed happy most of this holiday so far, enjoying the relative harmony of our extended family group – and away from her mother's histrionics. Right now she is pointing at the yachts moored in the bay, her thick dark hair – so like Jed's – shining in the sunshine.

'Is that Martin's boat?' she asks, indicating one of the larger motor launches that, like its neighbours, resembles a floating photocopier.

I shake my head, amused. My brother would be horrified if he could hear Dee Dee's question, but he's already around the next corner with Cameron. Their yacht – the *Maggie May* – is a far more elegant affair than the boats in the bay below. 'No, sweetheart, that's on the other side, near all the restaurants.'

'Oh.' Dee Dee rounds her eyes, making a little-girly face at me. 'Stupid, Dee Dee.' She gives her face a slap.

'Hey, no.' I'm shocked – and unsettled – by the gesture. As a primary school teacher I'm used to young kids showing off and acting out, but I'm finding it hard to keep up with Dee Dee's constantly changing attitudes. It's like she's whipping masks on and off her face so quickly that the real Dee Dee is a blur. Rose says such behaviour is normal, that – at thirteen – I was the same. But it still troubles me. After all, my relationship with Dee Dee has always been one of the bonuses of my time with Jed. Even when her older brother hated me and their mother stalked me to my school and shouted obscenities at me in the staff car park, Dee Dee and I have been close.

'Stupid, stupid Dee,' she says again, her voice even more little-girly than before though, thankfully, without the slap.

'You're not stupid.' I squeeze her shoulder and she flings her arms around me in a breath-defying hug. I hug her back, more gently. There's a desperation about Dee Dee sometimes – as if she is eager to please but knows she is no longer a cute little girl and hasn't worked out how to be appealing in a more adult way.

'Stop mauling Emily,' Jed orders, catching up with us. I know he doesn't mean to sound so brusque, it's just his manner, but his daughter lets go immediately, her head bowed. I sigh, feeling for her.

'I'm *fine*, Jed, seriously, Dee Dee's just being affectionate.' I hesitate. Everything I've been told about step-parenting stresses the importance of not interfering in parental discipline, especially in front of the child. Rose has told me time and again: 'never challenge them on their kids'. Trouble is, I worry Jed is getting it wrong. The very qualities that make him such a successful criminal lawyer – his quick, incisive mind and ruthless ability to sift facts, casting away whatever isn't needed – leave him ill-prepared to deal with his daughter's ever-changing emotions. Indeed, despite the fact that it means the world to him to have both his kids here on holiday, for most of the past week he has seemed at a loss with Dee Dee, with little understanding of the awkward teen she has become. Whereas I have every sympathy, remembering clearly how awful it felt to be thirteen and out of sorts with myself.

'I'm just worried about you.' Jed turns to his daughter. 'Emily isn't feeling well – be gentle, okay?'

Dee Dee nods.

'I'm going to tell Cam and Martin we need to go back to the yacht. I'll get the key to the main cabin off them,' Jed says, looking at me with concern.

'Can I come back with you, Daddy?' Dee Dee wheedles.

I open my mouth to say that of course she can, but before I can speak Jed laughs.

'Nice try, Dee Dee, but you'll be bored back on the boat. Anyway, a bit of exercise will do you good.' He grins, pats her arm, then strides off around the corner towards Martin and the others.

A tear leaks out of poor Dee Dee's eye. She keeps her head down.

'Oh, sweetie.' I give her shoulder another squeeze, unsure why the girl is so upset but Dee Dee is stiff with the desire to keep her pain to herself. 'How about we take a picture?' I suggest, hoping this will cheer her up.

'Okay.' Dee Dee offers me a weak smile. 'Just you though, not me.'

'No way.' I point to her phone. 'Go on, both of us.'

Grinning now, her mood altering with mind-bending swiftness, Dee Dee positions her iPhone in front of us. I move in close beside her. Dee Dee adjusts the angle, so the sea is visible behind us, then takes the photo. She peers at the screen and makes a face. 'I look fat.'

'I bet you don't.' I look over her shoulder. Unfortunately, the selfie has caught Dee Dee at a particularly unflattering angle. Plus, half my head is missing.

'One more, then,' I say. The band of tightness is starting to creep over one eye.

Dee Dee holds the phone out and positions it again. 'I've got a secret,' she says as she clicks.

'Oh?' I wonder what she means. Probably something about one of her friends, or a crush on some boy. I had millions when I was her age. 'What's that then?'

'It's something I saw.' Dee Dee hugs me again. Her gold bracelet is cool against my skin. I have one just like it; they were engagement presents from my brother and his boyfriend – a typically sweet and generous gesture to include Dee Dee in their gifts. She is still clinging to me. I feel horribly hot, but I don't want to push her away. Jed will be back any second and then it will only take ten minutes or so to get back to the cool of the boat.

'So what's this secret then?' I ask gently.

Dee Dee's body expands against mine as she takes a deep breath. 'It's—'

'For goodness' sake, let poor Emily be!' Jed's voice cracks like a whip through the air, making both of us jump. Dee Dee springs away from me, then sags down, her whole body collapsing into itself.

'I told you, Jed, she's *fine*.'

'Right, sorry.' Jed frowns. He pats his daughter's arm again. She shrinks back, like a cowed puppy. My heart goes out to her. Jed clears his throat. 'I didn't mean to shout,' he says. 'I'm just really worried about Emily. She might have heat stroke or—'

'It's just a bit of a headache,' I insist.

'Right, okay.' He turns to Dee Dee. 'Sorry, Dee Dee, now run and catch up with the others. Go on.'

Dee Dee glances at me, smiles ruefully, then turns and runs off. At least she isn't crying again. Yesterday she burst into tears because the strap broke on her new sandals.

'Probably collapsed under her weight,' Jed had joked in a side whisper to me. Dee Dee couldn't have heard him and the way he said it was light – an attempt at being funny – so I laughed to show him I knew he wasn't serious, but the truth is that we've both worried Dee Dee isn't coping well with her parents' break-up. Later I must take her to one side and remind her how much her dad loves her, how his bark – as the saying goes – is far worse than his bite. Jed's ex doesn't help matters, ranting whenever she gets a chance that he has ruined all their lives. She informed him accusingly the other day that Dee Dee had recently retreated into her shell, hardly ever going out or seeing her friends. I reminded Jed of what Dee Dee herself told me less than a month ago: that she'd had some problems with a few of the girls in her class, but her friends had rallied round and everything was okay now.

'Her mum is exaggerating,' I told him, 'making out Dee Dee's moods are *your* fault. When I was thirteen my life was dominated by my parents' deaths, but that wasn't why I was all over the place. *That* would have happened anyway. And Dee Dee would be hormonal right now whether you'd split up or not.'

Jed puts his arm around me as Dee Dee's thick white legs thud along the cobbles away from us. She is wearing shorts and a shapeless T-shirt that only emphasizes her bulk. That bushy hairdo doesn't help either. I wonder why her designer-loving mother doesn't give her some advice about how she looks.

'You were a bit hard on her just then,' I venture.

Jed sighs. 'I didn't mean to be,' he says. 'But she really needs to learn to think before she acts.'

'She's only thirteen, Jed.' I purse my lips. 'Do you think there's something bothering her? She told me she had a "secret" to tell, something she saw.'

Jed dismisses this with a weary wave. 'I'm sure it's just mood swings. She was fine this morning, bouncing about eating croissants. Anyway, what's she got to be "bothered" about?' His voice tightens and hardens. 'I pay her mother a fucking fortune so that *nothing* bothers *either* of them.'

'I know,' I say, wishing for the millionth time that Jed's ex wasn't still so angry about him leaving her. I understand, of course. But the fall-out on all of us, especially Dee Dee, is hard.

Jed sighs again, then steers me back along the path and through the tunnel. I fall silent, letting him take charge. As we walk along, my headache gets worse and worse. I'm concerned for Dee Dee still but also grateful – and not for the first time – that the full beam of Jed's forceful personality is focused on looking after me. After spending my twenties with a succession of irresponsible boy-men, I was single for nearly three years before meeting Jed last November. The experience has been like finding a port after years of storms. The fact that he is seventeen years older than me has never been an issue. My friend Laura was initially adamant that I'd only fallen for someone so much older because of my parents dying when I was eleven, but I think that's a cliché and that our ages are irrelevant. I just love the fact that, unlike all the younger men I've known, Jed knows exactly what he wants. And it still thrills me that what he wants is me. Jed asked me to marry him on my thirty-third birthday last month. We are planning a big wedding next year, probably in late spring.

'Let's do it properly: church service, a big party,' he said. 'It's your first time and it should be special.'

Frankly I'd happily marry him on a towpath, but I love

that he wants the best for us, that his view of marriage is still so positive even after the end of his relationship with his children's mother and – most of all – that despite having Dee Dee and Lish, he still wants kids with me.

Of course there is a voice in my head that says that if he could be unfaithful to his wife with me, then there's surely at least a chance he will one day be unfaithful to me with someone else – and that I wouldn't want him being as impatient with any children we might have, as he often is with his own daughter.

But it's only a small voice and, most of the time, I don't hear it at all.

OH. MY. DAYS.

So, like, I'd already decided to make a video diary for when I'm thirteen but I'm starting now, the day before my birthday, because the most AMAZING thing happened today and I HAVE to say about it. I can't BELIEVE it happened because I'd been thinking and thinking that I am going to be thirteen tomorrow and I haven't ever been kissed, like, properly, not pecks on the cheek or your mum but THAT kind of kissing and then I came out of school late after my piano lesson and Sam Edwards from year ten was round by the back exit near the Chapel just lounging about like he was waiting for something, a lift maybe, but no one else was there and when I went past he said hello and I, like, nearly DIED because everyone knows who he is and he has these big brown eyes and blond hair with bits of very blonde in it and did I say he's in year ten and he did a modelling job and everyone thinks he's really cool.

Anyway, he said hello and I stopped and said hello back and we just got talking and he was really nice, asking about where I'd been and how it was late to get out of prison (by which he meant school) and he said his dad had lost his job and was at home a lot at the moment which was a nightmare and he might even have to leave the school. So I told him how my dad wasn't at home AT ALL and that he'd moved out in February and gone to live with Emily and my mum was all upset and he said he was really sorry to hear that. Then he got a bit closer and said he'd noticed me before and he said I looked different than before half term and I asked what he meant and he looked at my coat, at the front of it, which was open, and he kept looking and the way he was staring made me feel a bit tingly and he touched my face and said I had very kissable lips. IMAGINE it, Sam Edwards from year ten actually thinking I was attractive and I couldn't speak and then he gave me a kiss and it made me feel all wobbly and even more tingly and he asked if I was in a hurry and I said no (because Mum wasn't even going to be home yet and I've been letting myself in on Tuesdays and Thursdays since September). So Sam put his arm around me and we started walking and somehow we ended up behind the Chapel just after the bit where the light comes on when you go past but there's just trees so it's all shadowy even when the light's shining. And he kissed me again. And at first it was lovely but then he put his hand on my school shirt, like, over my chest and he felt around a bit and I felt a bit uncomfortable but he was still kissing which I liked so I let him. Then he stopped kissing and tried to put his hand up my skirt and now I felt a bit scared but he said I was really hot and his breathing was all heavy and I liked that he was all looking in my eyes but not the touching. So I kind of wriggled back away from him and he asked what was I so worried about and I shrugged because really I wasn't sure.

And Sam said he wanted a feel for 'just a moment', that he

wasn't going to do anything, so I let him feel around a teeny bit more while I waited and I didn't like it – I mean I know that you can't get pregnant that way OBVIOUSLY, not unless they smear their stuff on their fingers first, I just didn't like it – but it was Sam Edwards and he looked so gorgeous in the shadowy trees and I didn't want him not to like me. Anyway, after it had been more than 'just a moment' I wriggled away again hoping he wouldn't be cross and he said 'all right then' and I thought maybe we'd do some more kissing but he started unbuttoning my school shirt and I REALLY did want to say no then but I'd already stopped him touching me so I let him and his eyes were like HUGE when he saw I hadn't put my bra on today because some days I do and some days I don't and today I didn't. And I felt REALLY self-conscious because there isn't much there and I didn't like him seeing so I pulled my shirt across me and he looked up and I said I should go and he said I was hot, AGAIN, and that we didn't have to do any more touching and what would I like to do and I sort of said ooh I like kissing, hoping he'd go back to that, but he just laughed and said they don't kiss in the films of it and I wasn't sure what he meant but I was feeling confused anyway – and a bit scared and a bit worried I should go so I'd get home before Mum.

And then he got out his phone and he said I was SO hot that he wanted a picture of my front, like I was a MODEL. And I wasn't sure but Sam said again that I was the hottest girl in the school and he was staring at my chest when he said that and I was AMAZED because to me they are just shapeless lumps so I said yes though I really don't know why except that he did ask all polite and his eyes were all sparkly and it seemed rude to say no and I know it's what

22

he expected and he was REALLY hot and I didn't want him to not like me. So he took a picture and it was so sweet because then he did kiss me a bit and he said the picture was just for him, he wouldn't show anyone, so he could remember them when he thought of me. And it was nice he liked them but I've never done any modelling OBVIOUSLY so I felt a bit embarrassed. But he said I was just like a model and then I said I really had to go and Sam said 'see you, Dee Dee' which means he wants to see me again. Oh my DAYS! So it was all worth it. And I buttoned up and came home. And like I said before it's AMAZING because yesterday NONE of those things had happened and now they have and just in time before I'm thirteen tomorrow.

August 2014

I feel better as soon as I'm on board, in the shade. Martin
has told Jed where to find the spare key – under the tarpaulin that covers the lifeboat in the stern of the boat.
Once we're inside the *Maggie May*'s main cabin, Jed tells me
to go and lie down while he looks for painkillers in the
bathroom.

I stretch out on the bed in Martin and Cameron's state-
room, pulling the blue silk throw over me. I smile to myself.
With its neutral tones and designer touches it is a far cry
from the decor in the terraced south London house where
we grew up. Martin has certainly landed on his feet when
it comes to his partner's finances. Cam is a trustafarian, in
his late thirties like Martin but with a massive monthly
income courtesy of the wealthy, land-owning Scottish
dynasty from which he is descended. Cameron neither has
nor needs a proper job, though I know he's involved in all
sorts of charitable projects. Martin could easily choose not
to work too if he wanted but, like me, he clings to the sense
of purpose his job gives him. At least he only works part-
time now.

Next door, Jed is rummaging through the bathroom cupboards, swearing under his breath that he can't find any painkillers.

'Martin said they'd be in here,' he calls out, clearly irritated.

'It's fine,' I call back, 'I just need to rest my eyes for a bit.'

Jed reappears. 'I'm ringing your brother.' He goes back to the main cabin. I close my eyes, not really listening as my fiancé, in characteristically direct fashion, demands to know where Mart and Cam keep their paracetamol and, on clearly being told by my laidback brother that if there isn't any in the bathroom, they must have run out, orders him to go to a pharmacy and buy some. 'Not anything with ibuprofen or codeine though,' Jed dictates. 'She shouldn't take that on an empty stomach.'

He's over-worrying but I kind of like it. I feel better now I'm lying down too. It's so wonderful that we are all together. This is a real family holiday of a sort I'm not used to, with Jed at the helm: guiding and managing and, of course, paying. Well, he isn't paying for Martin and Cameron. They aren't actually on the holiday with us, they've just pitched up in Cameron's yacht for a couple of days. We all went out in the boat yesterday and again this morning. It was lovely, though treacherously hot. That's probably why I have such a headache.

The crisp cotton pillow under my head is cool against my cheek, the waves outside soothing, like a whisper. Jed is making another call now, keeping his voice low so he doesn't disturb me. I lie, my head easing as I slide into sleep, grateful for Jed, for the air con, for my family around me.

When I wake up, Jed is sitting at the end of the bed, watching me. I'm used to this tic of his now, though the first few times it creeped me out. But then Jed explained and I just felt embarrassed. 'You look so beautiful asleep,' he said. 'Like a child. Which is how I love you, Em. Do you realize how extraordinary it is that I love you like my own children?'

I didn't. And don't. How can I? I'm not a mother yet – though soon, I hope, once we are married, babies will follow.

Right now, I'm yawning myself awake. Jed has pulled the blue silk throw up over my shoulders. I push it off and prop myself onto my elbow.

'How long have I been asleep?' I ask.

'Not long, baby,' Jed says. 'How's the head?'

I rub my eyes. 'Better, thanks.' I sit up properly. I do, indeed, feel fine. Perhaps I was just tired after last night's late barbecue to celebrate our first night in the villa. The strap of my dress falls off my shoulder. I scrape it back up, over my tan line. The porthole is closed, so all I can hear is the gentle slap of the water against the boat's hull. Music is playing from a distant café. It's strange to be so private, yet so close to so much life.

'Everyone's still on shore, baby. I called when you fell asleep to say there was no need for them to hurry back after all, give you some peace and quiet. Martin's taking them for cocktails in some bar in the citadel.' Jed holds out his hand. 'Come here.'

I wriggle closer. Jed pushes the silk throw completely away, then lifts the crisp cotton sheet off my legs. He takes my hand and kisses my fingers. 'Baby,' he groans. 'Oh, baby.'

He pulls me towards him and nuzzles into my neck, then presses me back down, onto the bed. I lie still, letting Jed move around my body, allowing myself to become slowly, sleepily aroused and trying to ignore the fact that I am making love on my brother's bed. Across the room I can see my tanned legs reflected in the mirrored wardrobe doors. Jed's paler-skinned bum rises and falls comically between them.

'Daddy loves you,' he croons in my ear.

I flush with self-consciousness, resisting the impulse to pull away. It's not a big deal, I remind myself; just Jed's way, though sometimes it still makes me feel uncomfortable. Has done from the start, if I'm honest. It was bad enough him calling me baby all the time, but when after our fifth or sixth time in bed he started making those occasional references to himself in the third person as 'daddy' I didn't know whether to laugh or feel grossed out.

But I'm used to it now. After all, everyone has their own style when it comes to sex. And Jed is, always, super-concerned that the sex should be good for me. I often feel daunted by his experience compared to my own: I've had precisely six sexual partners, only three of whom were really

boyfriends and only one of whom – the gorgeous but com-
mitment-phobic Dan Thackeray – lasted more than six
months. Jed, on the other hand, claims to have lost count.
Unsurprising, I suppose. He is fifty and I know there were
many lovers before his twenty-year marriage – plus the occasional one-night stand during. He says his restlessness ended
the day he saw me, that I meet his every need, that – now he
is older – he values our relationship in a more rounded way,
that sex is just a part of it, that he has slept with enough
women for the rest of his life, that I meet all his sexual needs
anyway. In fact he says I'm his fantasy, his ideal woman …

He is uninhibited in bed, too, though he doesn't particularly like it if I initiate the sex or try and take control at
any point. I have learned to let him lead me, trusting that
in this, as in everything Jed does, he has my best interests
at heart. The sex is good, too. The best I've had, apart from
with Dan – but then I was so infatuated with Dan I probably imagined half the orgasms.

We finish and Jed gives a contented sigh. I glance down
at the sheets. Just a small stain. I hurry to the bathroom
and dampen a flannel. Not that I think Martin would
mind – he's pretty easygoing – but it still seems rude.

I scrub at the stain while Jed's breathing grows deep and
steady. After a few minutes I'm satisfied that the mark
won't show once it's dry. I put my dress back on, then prod
Jed awake. While he tugs on his trousers I turn down the
white linen, smoothing the sheets over, then folding the
blue silk throw and laying it over the end of the bed.

'How's the headache now?' Jed asks, turning to me with a smug grin. 'Did we get rid of it?'

'Sure did,' I say, though in truth I can feel another band of pressure building at the back of my head. 'But it'll be good to take the painkillers anyway, make sure it doesn't come back.' I turn to leave the room but Jed catches my hand.

'I was thinking,' he says. 'When we get married, will you take my name?'

I bite my lip. It's not that I love my name – Campbell – so much, but it's all that is left of my parents and still a huge tie with Martin and Rose.

Jed senses my uncertainty. 'I don't mean give up yours,' he says, patting my hand. 'I know how important it is to you. I was thinking maybe we could do Campbell-Kennedy? What do you think?'

'I guess,' I say. 'Can I think about it?'

'Of course, baby, no pressure.' Jed smooths a stray hair from my cheek, then grins as he slaps me playfully on my behind. I grin back, feeling content. As we walk through to the living-room cabin, voices sound on deck. Martin is first through the door. He looks distracted but attempts a smile as he sees me.

'How you doing, Em?' he asks.

'Better,' I say for Jed's benefit, though my headache is now, in fact, definitely creeping back.

'Lish got you some headache pills,' Martin says.

'Actually they're powders,' Lish says, following Martin

through the door. 'It was a tiny chemist and the only *"anal-gésique"* they had without ibuprofen or codeine was a box of sachets that look a bit like Lemsip but they're called ExAche Powders.' He pushes back his long, greasy hair off his face and smiles, though the smile wavers slightly as he meets Jed's eye. Jed gives a brisk nod. He's trying not to show it but I can tell he's irritated that Lish didn't manage to find a better-known brand. And if *I* can tell then I'm guessing Lish can too. I know Jed wishes his son had more ambition, more drive, but Lish, despite his rather grungy appearance, seems fine to me. At least he's at college. Perhaps my feelings are over-shadowed because, after the first four months of complete stand-off between us, we now get on okay. It was hard at first, immediately after Jed left his wife back in the spring. Then Lish took his mother's side entirely but since Jed and I got engaged he seems to have accepted me.

'Pills … powders … so long as they work.' Martin punches Lish playfully on the arm. Lish pretends to reel back, his smile widening and deepening at the horseplay.

Martin has helped hugely to heal the rift between me and my stepson. But then, he has always been a peacemaker and one of the most emotionally intelligent men I know. When Mum and Dad died he was just a few weeks off his sixteenth birthday and while our older sister, Rose, looked after me in all the practical senses, it was Martin who stepped up as my protector – smoothing away Rose's rough edges when we clashed and as hard on my early boyfriends as any father could have been. My friends swooned before his handsome, square-jawed face and long, lean frame. They still do, if I'm honest, even though Martin came out many years ago. He told me first, even before Rose, knowing, or so he said, that I would never judge him. I didn't. Couldn't. Martin at almost thirty-eight is as charming as he ever was, and still boyish-looking, with that dimple in his chin and those big brown eyes. Lish has clearly fallen under his spell completely. I see him glancing from his own skinny arms to Martin's tanned and buff body in its white shirt and designer chinos. Is Lish just wishing he had some of Martin's style? Or might he be gay, too? He's never brought home a girlfriend nor, according to his dad, has he ever mentioned going out with anyone. I glance at Jed. Has this occurred to him? How would he react? I imagine he would be disappointed, not because he's openly homophobic – he treats Martin and Cameron with the greatest respect – but because homosexuality is not part of his vision for Lish.

Lish takes a small box and hands me a sachet of ExAche Powders from it.

'Apparently they're supposed to be good for headaches, that's what the pharmacist said, isn't it, Lish?' Martin asks. 'Lucky Lish's French was up to it.'

'Lucky for Lish he went to a good school where he had the chance to *learn* decent French,' Jed mutters with a wry chuckle.

There's an awkward silence.

31

'Thanks, Lish.' I walk over, take the sachet and reach up to peck his cheek.

Lish shrugs and blushes. He's as tall as his father now, but lanky and lolloping, without any of Jed's heft – or his forceful presence.

'I think I'll take one, make sure the head doesn't come back.'

Martin fetches me a glass of water and a spoon to stir in the sachet of powder. As he hands me the glass, Dee Dee rushes in and hurls herself at me. Water slops over the side of the glass. Out of the corner of my eye I can see Jed wincing at her clumsiness.

'Hey, Dee,' I say brightly before he can criticize her. 'How was it at the cocktail bar?'

'Brilliant,' she says, round-eyed. 'I had a mocktail.'

Not for the first time, I'm struck by how young Dee Dee sometimes seems. At thirteen I was driving Rose nuts, sneaking off to pubs with older kids from school. Martin was away at college so Rose bore the brunt of dealing with me then, explaining that the boys who bought me vodka Red Bulls and hot pink alcopops might have unscrupulous motives underpinning their generosity.

I stir the ExAche Powder into the water and look up. Where *is* my sister? There's no sign of her or Martin's boyfriend.

'What happened to Rose?' I ask. 'And where's Cameron?'

'Still on deck,' Martin says, sinking onto the nearest couch. 'They're dealing with the fish. We bought some sea bream from this private trader we met here before, plus a whole load of salad. Cameron thought it would be fun to eat on board.'

'I thought we were going to a restaurant?' Jed sits up. There's the tiniest edge to his voice. I imagine this is how he sounds with his staff of junior lawyers when they challenge him.'

Martin shrugs, unfazed. 'Sure, if you like,' he says, his face breaking into a disarming smile. 'Cameron just thought … if Emily wasn't feeling well … but we're easy, whatever you guys would like.'

'Of course.' Jed sits back, pacified at this show of consideration. He turns to me. 'Up to you, baby.'

They both look at me. I gaze down at Dee Dee. 'What do you think?'

Dee Dee hugs me, then puts on that little-girly voice again. 'Dee Dee doesn't like fish.'

'Don't be silly,' Jed says. 'Of course you like fish. Fish-finger sandwiches are your favourite meal.'

Dee Dee shrugs. Jed has a point: Dee Dee loves it when we stay in and do homemade fishburgers and pizzas, but there's a world of difference between a fish-finger sandwich and sautéed sea bream. I've never known Dee Dee to order fish when we go to nice restaurants. It's perfectly possible she doesn't like it and Jed would have no idea. I open my mouth to say that I didn't like fish dishes much when I was thirteen, and that I'm sure Cameron can find something else for Dee Dee to eat, but Jed is talking again.

'You're eating the fish,' he orders his daughter. 'Martin and Cameron went to a good deal of trouble to buy it and there's no good reason not to eat it. Plus Martin's right. If Emily isn't feeling too hot, then staying in is the best bet. We can always stop off for a drink on the way back to the villa later.'

And so it is decided.

The rest of the evening passes uneventfully. The ExAche tastes bitter, but my headache totally disappears. Rose makes a dressing for the salad while Cameron cooks the sea bream with a delicious lemon and caper sauce. I check with Dee Dee that she'll be okay eating it and she says she'll be fine. However when the time comes I can't help but notice that Dee Dee prods at her food and only actually eats the sea bream when Jed leans over and whispers something, stony-faced, in her ear.

Afterwards, Lish and his sister take themselves off to the cabin – Lish to play computer games on Martin and Cameron's massive, state-of-the-art TV and Dee Dee to make use of the onboard wi-fi to Skype with her friends back in Highgate. I'm glad she has such good mates. She told me a few weeks ago how supportive they'd been at the end of last term when a couple of girls at school were mean to her. Jed is always so dismissive of such upsets as 'teen nonsense' but I remember well myself how, at that age, even small conflicts can leave you reeling and desperate for days.

Rose, Jed, Martin, Cameron and I sit outside on the

Maggie May's rear deck, enjoying the warm breeze and the lights and bustle on the promenade beyond. While Jed tells the others about his latest court case – a high-profile acquittal of a government minister – I go inside to check on Dee Dee again; she seems fine, intent on something on her phone. She's probably finding out about the latest gossip back home or looking at pop bands. Back on deck, I'm pleased to see that Jed seems more relaxed than he has done all day. I settle down beside him with a glass of wine and he takes my hand. As dusk falls, the promenade lights twinkle and the bay hums with nightlife. Jed and I are inveterate people-watchers and tonight we're intrigued by an elderly couple eating across the jetty at the nearest – and one of the fanciest – restaurants along the quay. The woman has a leathery tan and a fabulously camp diamond tiara. I finger my own diamond – a huge oval set on a platinum ring that Jed chose and presented to me on my birthday last month. I said 'yes' and promptly burst into tears. For a fleeting moment I wanted to ask him how his wife reacted all those years ago when he proposed to her, but any such reference is liable to propel Jed into a bad mood and I didn't want to spoil the moment. Since then his ex has really faded from her dominant position in my thoughts. It's funny. Her shadow hovered over our first few months together, through our affair and Jed's decision, back in February, to leave her. I felt guilty – not so much about her, the stories Jed has told me make it clear she no longer loved or respected her husband – but over the kids. Still, they both seem to be doing okay now. Anyway, just after Jed proposed in July his ex pitched up at the school where I teach. She waited for me in the car park. It was almost the end of term and when I staggered outside that afternoon, laden with boxes and bags of files, she rounded on me, accusing me of being an evil-souled, husband-stealing, home-wrecking whore and insisting that I had tricked Jed into proposing in order to get my hands on his money. For the first couple of minutes I met her fury with denials and justifications. Then I realized that nothing I said would make a difference, that the woman would never listen to me anyway. Upset and humiliated, I got in my car and fled. I called Jed immediately and he was so outraged on my behalf and so furious with his ex that I actually started to feel sorry for her. And even though, since then, she does her best to tear into me verbally whenever she can, I find that most of the time I pity her: she might have been a bitch to Jed throughout their marriage, but she loved him, in her way, and now she has lost him.

Dusk turns to darkness, the promenade buzzes, music drifts towards us across the water and the five of us chat and laugh through the evening. It is this moment I will remember in the months to come, the way I am purely and perfectly content with the warm breeze on my skin, my fiancé holding my hand and my brother and sister at my side. Rose casts me occasional glances to make sure I'm really over my headache and I smile at her, happier than I can ever remember being before.

Cameron and Rose do most of the talking as Martin

opens another bottle of wine. Rose was recently dumped by her boyfriend, Simon – a work colleague of our brother's – and, though her tone is light as she refers to their split, I can see that underneath she is hurting. She's looking good on it though – 'yeah, that's the misery diet' she says with a wry laugh. But it's not just that she's shed a few pounds. The truth is that I can't remember her ever looking better than she has in the past few months. She's junked all her mumsy dresses and is wearing more fitted skirts, tops that show off her curves and even the occasional pair of heels. People say we're alike and we certainly share our olive skin and long dark hair, though Rose has a higher forehead and a snubbier nose, but our styles are very different. I like my clothes casual whereas Rose tends to wear more formal outfits, and makes sure she is fully accessorized at all times. Tonight she's in a smart linen sheath dress with a pash-mina over her shoulders and every time she leaves the deck to go to the bathroom, she returns with her nose neatly powdered and her lips a soft shade of pink.

We leave shortly after ten. Martin insists on me taking another sachet of ExAche Powders in case my headache comes back. I protest that I'm fine, but Lish has already fetched the box and found me a sachet. Martin hands it to me, then calls us a taxi and we go back to our villa, a few miles along the coast. The lights are on in the hall, the back door to the garden open. We all traipse through and find Jed's brother Gary and his girlfriend – who declined Martin's invite to spend the day based around the yacht – swimming naked in the pool. Jed tersely orders Lish and Dee Dee to bed, then insists Gary gets out. He is clearly drunk and, if Iveta's hints are anything to go by, they've been shagging all day – including in the water. Rose blinks at this, clearly horrified. My older sister has always been a bit of a prude compared to me though, frankly, I find the idea of Gary ejaculating into our holiday swimming pool fairly revolting myself.

Jed is back to being tense and irritated. I see him draw Gary to one side, a frown on his face, though I can't help but notice his eyes are fixed on Iveta, still naked in the pool as he speaks. She's gorgeous, all long slim legs and huge, high breasts that Rose and I have already decided are fakes.

Rose seems flustered by the situation and heads off to bed. I go to check on Dee Dee. She's sitting on her bed looking glum, her chubby legs startlingly white beneath her cotton pyjama shorts.

'What's up?' I ask.

'I can't find my phone and I turned off the locate app so I won't be able to work out where it is,' she says. 'I know I had it when we left the boat but . . .'

'Do you think you left it in the taxi?' I ask.

'Maybe,' Dee Dee says. 'Or maybe it fell out when we were walking to the taxi. That's the last time I remember seeing it.' Her lips tremble. 'I was sure I put it in my jacket pocket, but it is a bit loose and flappy . . . and it definitely wasn't in my pocket when we came into the house.' Her voice cracks.

'Oh, sweetheart.' I rush over and squeeze her hand. 'Listen, I'll go and get your dad to call the cab firm.' Dee Dee nods. I squeeze her hand again. 'It's horrible losing your phone,' I say. 'I've done it and it really sucks.'

Jed, already irritated by his brother, is predictably annoyed that Dee Dee has been careless over her mobile, especially when the cab company tell him it hasn't been handed in. I tell Jed that I'll break the news.

'Okay,' he says with a weary sigh. 'I'll probably just get it wrong if I speak to her anyway.'

I fetch a bottle of water and hurry up to Dee Dee.

'There's no sign so far,' I say, setting the bottle down beside her bed. 'But we can call again in the morning and if it hasn't turned up I promise we'll drive back down there tomorrow to where it might have fallen out and ask around.'

'Thanks, Emily.' Dee Dee reaches up to give me a hug.

'Get some sleep now.'

'Night, night, Emily,' she says in that little-girly voice. Did she speak like that the last time I saw her before our holiday? No, I'm pretty sure it's a new development. I let her go and she sits back, rubbing her forehead.

'Are you alright?' I ask.

She points at her forehead. 'Headache. Like you.' She gives me a wan smile. 'Hey, maybe it's catching.'

'Or maybe you haven't drunk enough water today,' I scold with a smile. 'You have to drink extra when it's this hot.' I point to the water bottle, then burrow in my bag for the ExAche sachet that Martin gave me. I check the back. It's fine for kids over twelve so I hand it over. 'Mix that in your water,' I say. 'There's a glass you can use in the bathroom. And I know it's got a bitter taste but make sure you drink it *all*.'

'Oh, thanks, Emily.' She lurches forward and almost crushes me with another hug.

'Night.' I peck her forehead. 'Don't stay up too late.'

'I won't.'

I yawn as I leave, climb the stairs to the round room at the top of the villa and clean my teeth. I'm just getting into bed when Jed arrives, still muttering about irresponsibility.

'She's a child, Jed,' I protest gently. 'And *anyone* can lose a phone.'

He starts unbuttoning his shirt. 'I don't mean Dee Dee, I mean Gary. He knew we'd be back around ten, he's so thoughtless. And, as you've just pointed out, Dee Dee's only a child, for goodness' sake.'

'She didn't see anything, they were in the water. Anyway, she's far more upset about her phone.' I yawn again as I stroke his face. 'So no harm done.'

'Mmmn,' Jed grunts, then disappears into the bathroom.

I'm asleep before he gets back, then I sleep deeply and dreamlessly the whole night. Sunlight is streaming into the room when I wake with a start the next morning. Beside me, Jed sits bolt upright.

Someone, downstairs, is screaming.

40

It takes a moment before I realize that it's Rose.

I'm out of bed in seconds, racing downstairs to her room next door to Dee Dee's.

Rose is standing on the landing, pointing in through Dee Dee's open door. A puddle of vomit lies on the wooden floor by the bed. Dee Dee is visible on top of the covers, face up, glassy-eyed. Her arm extends over the edge of the mattress, her bracelet dangling from her wrist.

I freeze, the room whirls around me. I think I might faint and clutch at Rose's arm. She is shaking. Now Jed is beside us.

'What the ...?' His mouth falls open as he sees his daughter. He rushes into the room. Rose and I follow. The August heat hangs heavily in the air. It's like a dream, a nightmare, as Jed feels Dee Dee's forehead, then presses his fingers against her wrist, her neck.

'Oh my God, oh my God.' Rose is whimpering. 'I just saw ... then ... then I came in ... found her like that, oh my God ...'

Jed turns to me, his eyes wide with shock. I'm expecting him to order me to call an ambulance and I'm already wracking my brains to remember the emergency number in France.

But instead Jed shakes his head. It's too late for an ambulance.

Sweet, plump, thirteen-year-old Dee Dee Kennedy is dead.

June 2014

So like today just sucked. TOTALLY sucked. And yesterday being so brilliant made it worse. And now it's actually my thirteenth birthday. TODAY! And I'm a teenager and I've been looking forward to it for SO long but now everything's AWFUL and RUINED. Firstly it was school . . . I didn't see Sam Edwards but some year ten girls giggled and pointed when I walked past and I wondered if it had got out that he liked me. Which would be bad OBVIOUSLY because I'm, like, two years below Sam and if his friends laugh at him it might put him off seeing me. So that's not a ruined thing yet, but with my luck I expect it will be and I kept hoping I'd bump into Sam but I didn't and then I had to come home cos Mum was picking me up early after school to go to tea at Craven's which we always do on family birthdays except we didn't for Dad's in April and Dad wasn't there for Lish's in May and so everything is different and THAT tradition is gone so I don't know why Mum still wants to do it.

Anyway, Lishy wasn't there because he's away at uni and I know Mum was sad about that. Then Daddy was supposed to come around in the evening to have dinner and cake with us and Mum was getting it ready for an hour and then he was late. Not that much late, just half an hour, and I wasn't worried because he always comes when he says and he's often late if it's after work and this was Friday when he's ALWAYS at his latest and I was watching an old Gossip Girl anyway. But Mum was angry. You could tell because she did that slitty thing with her eyes and her mouth when he arrived and she didn't smile AT ALL which I noticed because she had put lipstick on and her arms were folded and first off Daddy didn't see and he gave me a hug and my present which was a mini iPad which was OBVIOUSLY AMAZING. And Mum muttered something about 'buying her affection with gifts' and Daddy turned to look at her properly and saw she was angry and I was praying and praying he'd just smile and say let's have dinner and cake but instead he asked what her problem was and Mum exploded that he shouldn't keep me waiting, ESPECIALLY on my birthday, and Daddy said he hadn't been that late and it wasn't a fixed time and we weren't eating until eight anyway and he was sure I couldn't have been as upset as Mum said because I was thirteen now, not three. And then he looked at me and said 'are you, Dee Dee?' and Mum was looking at me too and I knew she wanted me to say I WAS upset. And I wasn't, but I didn't want her to be angry so I said nothing. Then Daddy got cross and he stood up. And suddenly they were shouting at each other. Which they haven't done the last three times and which I was hoping was over. And Mum was all red-faced and yelling he was a loser and put his whore before his family and Daddy was spitting tiny bits out of his mouth and YELLING 'Emily isn't a whore, how dare you say that, why are you shouting in front of Dee Dee, now she WILL get upset.'

Which was true, but again, I didn't want to show them so I just went out of the room and went upstairs and got under the duvet and next thing the front door slams and Mum says 'bastard' and I could hear her coming up the stairs so I pretended to be asleep under the duvet which OBVIOUSLY wasn't going to fool Mum.

She sat down beside me and pulled back the covers and said she was sorry but she meant sorry Daddy was a bastard, not sorry that she'd got angry with him. And I thought that but I didn't say it. Then she asked if I was okay and I could hear in her voice she really, REALLY wanted me to be okay so I said that I was and we went downstairs and she asked about my day and I said it had been cool at school (which wasn't true because of the year ten girls and not seeing Sam though at least Ava and Poppy who sometimes leave me out of things wanted to sit next to me in the canteen because it was my birthday). And after that Mum cheered up a bit and she and I ate the dinner and had the cake which was like a gigantic cupcake with thirteen candles and I blew them all out in one breath and I told Mum I didn't want any because I was fat but she said nonsense and gave me a huge slice and I ate it cos I did want it really and now I feel bad because eating it will make me fatter and I need EVERYTHING on my side to counteract the year ten girls knowing Sam likes me and Sam getting put off.

And now I'm upstairs and it's very quiet. And I feel SAD, SAD, SAD and everything's awful because it's my birthday and I didn't see Sam.

And Lish wasn't here.

And Mum is upset.

And Daddy has gone.

August 2014

I can't make sense of it, even after two hours. How can Dee Dee be dead? Gary's girlfriend, Iveta, is hysterical, her wails echoing around the house, but Rose and I are numb, unable to take it in. Jed is in shock too, white-faced with disbelief, virtually speechless. He brushes away my sympathy, saying he has to call Dee Dee's mother. I don't hear their conversation but afterwards Jed comments only that his ex will be here as soon as she can get a flight, then retreats into a tightly wound silence. I cannot imagine what this is like for him. Or for Lish, who withdraws to his bedroom and locks the door. Much to my amazement it is Gary who takes charge – and brilliantly. He manages to contact the emergency services and oversees first the doctor's visit then, immediately after, that of the local police. Inspecteur Chabrol is wiry, fox-faced and middle-aged, with greying sideburns and a sharply cut suit. He and his colleagues are soon questioning everyone in the house. They start with the most fluent French speakers: Gary and Lish. In among all this, Gary somehow manages to find time to console Iveta, who is still weeping, while Rose and

I sit huddled together. I call Martin but he and Cameron were leaving port at dawn and must be out at sea as both their phones are out of range.

'This is so terrible,' Rose whispers through her tears. 'Poor, poor Jed, to lose a child.'

And poor Dee Dee. It is incomprehensible that she isn't in the next room or out by the pool, her chubby legs tucked under her on a lounger. Rose and I sit in silence, waiting to be interviewed, while Jed talks to Inspecteur Chabrol. Lish is back in his bedroom.

'I keep thinking back to when I got the call from the hospital about Mum and Dad,' Rose says between sniffs.

I fall silent. I've heard Rose talk about this moment many times: how she was coming home from her gap-year waitressing job when she was summoned to the hospital and told our parents had been in a car accident, how she called the school to have Martin and I taken from our classes and asked one of Mum's friends to pick us up and bring us to meet her at the hospital.

Rose can describe everything that day in minute detail. My memories, on the other hand, are smudged. I was eleven, in my first term at secondary school. I remember I was in Maths and very bored and initially and self-importantly delighted to be called out of class. Then I remember the strained eyes of my head teacher and the sense that something must be very wrong for her to have softened her voice so much. Later, I remember Martin holding my hand as we walked into the hospital and Rose's tear-stained cheeks as she held out her arms to us and whispered the truth in our ears: that our parents had died in a side-on collision with a drunk driver.

I remember very little else from that time – the funeral is a blur, my memories of the next month consist of Rose in tears, Martin fighting someone at school, all the adults looking at me with pity and the many, many hushed conversations behind closed doors about who was to look after us in the absence of any directions from our parents. Rose insisted she could manage – that she would postpone uni for a couple of years. Mum and Dad's friends were worried that she was throwing her own chances away, but Rose insisted and, backed by me and Martin, was officially awarded guardianship of us both.

Looking back I think it was selfish to lay all that responsibility on an eighteen-year-old. I blame the friends of our parents who, seeing as we had no aunts and uncles, could have stepped in and offered themselves. But maybe looking after us was what Rose needed at the time. It was certainly what Martin and I wanted. Rose became a mother to me while Martin became – if not quite a father – then certainly my staunchest ally. Despite my being so young when I was orphaned, I feel now that I was sheltered from the worst of the trauma, that Rose suffered most, that in looking after me and, to a lesser extent, Martin, she was inevitably cut off from her own friends and opportunities. The two-year deferment of university turned into three, then five. In the end, she never went. Her entire twenties were devoted to my life and my chances. Perhaps the most remarkable thing is that I have never once heard her complain about any of it. She missed out on jobs and, despite being stunningly attractive, long-term boyfriends. No young man, it turned out, wanted to date a woman with a truculent teen in the house. Once I'd left home to go to teacher training college Rose carried on as before. I assumed that she would go to uni at last, but she didn't, saying to this day that she is happy in her job as manager of a local cookware shop. I also assumed she would find a man. After all, she wasn't yet thirty when I moved away. But Rose has never had anyone really significant in her life. I've met the few boyfriends she has gone out with and have no idea why none of them ever stuck. Rose has only ever given me edited versions of her relationships, no real details, nothing like the way I imagine sisters normally share information.

Right now we are leaning against each other. Rose sits in silence, twisting the hem of her top around her fingers. Jed is still in with the police. I'm just thinking that I should get up and go and check on Lish, when I'm called into the kitchen.

Inspecteur Chabrol is sitting at the table, his arms folded. A younger man in a black T-shirt sitting beside him smiles at me and says, in perfect English:

'Thank you for joining us, Emily, hopefully this won't take too long. I'm Charles Meunière, the translator.'

'Hello.' I sit down opposite Chabrol. His small, dark eyes study me intently.

Outside the kitchen door Jed and Gary are talking on

the patio. Jed turns and sees me sitting here. He takes a step towards the house but Gary puts a hand on his arm and he stops.

Chabrol speaks, a stream of rapid, intense French. Charles Meunière translates and in seconds I am forced to focus on the events of last night. It is clear that the inspector already knows Dee Dee wasn't on any medication or suffering from any illnesses. He asks me if I think it is possible she was taking recreational drugs of any kind.

'No,' I say emphatically. 'She was young for her age and anyway, *no*, there's no way Dee Dee would have taken *any* drugs ...' I stop, suddenly remembering the headache powders. My stomach lurches into my throat.

'*Qu'est-ce que c'est?*' Chabrol asks. He turns to Meunière, who places his hands on the table between us.

'What is it, Emily?'

I gulp. 'Some painkillers, she took them just before she went to bed, at least I assume she did.' I pause, trying to remember the exact sequence of events. 'She said she had a headache, so I gave the sachet to her, then I left. But ... but I took the same thing earlier on in the evening and I was fine.' I stop, my mind leaping and whirling at the thought that the ExAche powders could have had anything to do with Dee Dee's death.

Meunière translates and Chabrol leans forward. He asks me exactly when I left the sachet with Dee Dee. I tell him, then he asks me to explain everything I did that evening. I go over it again, describing how we ate our meal on the boat and how Dee Dee picked at her fish, then later said that she'd lost her phone. It's like I'm disconnected from myself as I speak. My mind is replaying the moment I handed the sachet to Dee Dee. Did she take the powders? Suppose she had an allergic reaction? Or suppose she was too young for them? I'm sure I checked the small print to make sure of the dosage. I remember because it was in English. Just like a Lemsip, okay to take for over twelves. I rub my forehead. I need to call Martin, tell him not to touch the rest of the powders. I break off to explain this to Chabrol. He barks something in French before Meunière has even finished translating.

Meunière frowns. 'He wants you to explain exactly what you did again?'

'Okay, but will you send someone to check about the powders?'

Chabrol speaks. Meunière translates. 'You don't need to worry, we will do our job.'

'I know,' I say, 'Of course. I just can't bear to think I might have misunderstood the dose or … or …' My stomach is twisted into hard, painful knots. I glance outside to where Jed is still talking with Gary. Our eyes meet. The pain in his expression is indescribable. Tears well up, my throat tight, my heart aching for him.

Jed strides to the French doors. As he opens them I can hear Gary protesting, telling him to come back, but Jed is stony-faced.

'What's going on?' he demands. 'Why is my fiancée looking so upset?'

'It's fine, Jed—' But before I can say more Chabrol is on his feet, gesticulating and speaking rapid-fire French. All of a sudden Jed is shouting in French, then Gary is by his side trying to calm him. Chabrol is talking over them both. All I can think is that upstairs, poor Dee Dee is lying dead, that she died alone, in her own vomit.

Meunière touches my arm. 'Go and call your brother,' he says quietly. I rush away, my tears now trickling down my cheek. Martin's phone is still out of range so I leave a hiccupy message, then go back to the kitchen. Gary is sitting at the table, his head in his hands.

'Where's Jed?' I ask.

'Up with the inspector, talking to Lish. They want to know where he bought the headache powders from.'

'So Dee Dee did take them?'

Gary nods. 'They've found the empty sachet by her glass, looks like she mixed it with some bottled water. They're taking the whole lot off to be analysed.'

I nod, numbly. It all still feels so unreal. Two long hours pass while the police officers cordon off Dee Dee's room. Her body has been superficially examined. There's no sign that she has been attacked, which leaves some kind of poisoning the most likely cause of death. As a result, the entire villa is thoroughly – and fruitlessly – searched for drugs while Chabrol questions and re-questions everyone. Jed stays upstairs with Lish. I haven't seen him since he harangued Chabrol. By midday the sun is scorching, high in the sky. Gary comes over and tells me in a solemn whisper that the body is about to be removed, that he and Jed will go with poor Dee Dee to the morgue. He asks me to keep Iveta and Rose outside by the swimming pool.

I go and sit with them, the three of us perched side by side on one of the loungers. Jed and Gary leave with the police officials and suddenly, after hours of frantic bustle and panic, the house falls silent. I head up to Lish's room but he doesn't answer my knock. As I pass the police tape across Dee Dee's door I suddenly remember the secret she hinted yesterday that she wanted to tell me, something she saw. Guilt wraps its cold fingers around my throat. I forgot all about it after Jed and I got back to the boat. Feeling sick, I seek out Rose and tell her how terrible I feel. She hugs me through her tears.

'It was probably nothing, you know what girls are like,' she soothes. 'Anyway, if it had been important, Dee Dee would have made sure she told someone.'

I pray that she is right.

Another hour passes. I try to call Jed, but his mobile goes to voice mail.

'Just calling to see how you're doing ...' I check myself. What a stupid question. How on earth do I think he will be doing? 'Just want you to know I love you.' I ring off.

I wander around the living room of the villa, still numb, lost. Absently I clear the wine glasses Gary and Iveta used last night. As I'm placing them in the sink, Martin calls at last.

'Oh, Emily.' The love and concern in his voice finally releases my own tears. I bawl my eyes out as I tell Martin everything. To my relief, he reassures me that neither he nor Cameron have touched the ExAche sachets which the police seem to think are the most likely cause of Dee Dee's death and that they are already on their way back to Calvi. They arrive a few hours later, shortly followed by yet another police officer who takes statements from them both. Rose insists that we all try to eat, though nobody has any appetite. All I can think is that Dee Dee is gone and that poor Jed must be hurting beyond anything I can imagine. He calls at last, shortly after nightfall. He is with Dee Dee's mother, Zoe, who has gone straight to the morgue and is sitting with their daughter's body. Jed sounds empty, wiped out.

'Zoe will have to stay with us at the villa,' he says.

'Oh.' I can't help the sharp intake of breath with which I receive this news. I understand, of course. But I cannot imagine what on earth it will be like to be under the same roof as a woman who has made it so clear she hates me. 'Do you want me and Rose to … to find a hotel?' I ask, thinking that maybe this will be easiest.

'I just want you to deal with it,' he says dully.

'Of course, of course.' My stomach churns with anxiety. 'I was just thinking of what would be easiest for Zoe.'

'She's lost her daughter,' he says, his voice strained to breaking point. 'It seriously won't make any difference where she sleeps.'

'I'll … I'll make up Lish's bed for her, he can take the sofa downstairs,' I say, eager to be helpful. 'I've seen where the linen cup—'

'She wants to sleep in Dee Dee's room.'

'But … but the police have put tape across the door.' This is not really my overriding concern, but saying it seems morbid to take the girl's bed seems unhelpful.

'That won't stop Zoe,' Jed says with a sigh. 'We'll be back in an hour or so.'

As soon as Rose hears about Zoe's imminent arrival she suggests that she should leave the villa with Martin and Cameron and spend the night on the *Maggie May*. 'So as not to be in the way,' she says, 'then Zoe can have my room, if she wants.'

I agree, not just for the room but because it seems best that there aren't too many people here when Jed and Zoe arrive.

After the others leave I check on Iveta, who is asleep, then on Lish, who appears to be drinking his way through the bottle of whisky that Gary bought the night we arrived. He receives the news that his parents are on their way with a miserable shrug. The stars and the moon light the sky. It feels like years since this morning. I am ridiculously nervous at the prospect of seeing Zoe again. Her angry rant in the school car park rings in my ears. Still, maybe losing Dee Dee will put all that in perspective. Most of all, I hope my presence here doesn't make this terrible evening any worse for her. I pour myself a glass of wine. My hands are shaking. I take a sip and then the front door key turns in the lock.

My legs carry me across the open-plan living room as the door opens and Jed and his ex walk in.

June 2014

My life is OVER. Seriously. I want to die. Everything is as bad as it could be. And I am SO stupid to have thought it would ever be any different. It started with those year ten girls giggling on Friday, then on Saturday Mum took me and Ava and Poppy and Marietta Hingis – who doesn't go to my school but who we have to include because she, like, thinks she's best friends with me though really it's Ava – to Pizza Paradise in Muswell Hill which is near where Daddy lives now with Emily but we didn't see them because Mum is still angry about Daddy coming late last Friday and anyway it isn't my weekend with him. So, like, everything was cool with Marietta but Ava and Poppy were REALLY weird, like they didn't want to be there, like they'd only ever been my friends because we got sat next to each other right at the start of the year and they'd been stuck with me ever since. They kept whispering to each other and shaking their heads like there was some BIG problem they couldn't tell me. They left early too, even though we were all supposed to be having a sleepover. Ava said she had to go home cos her cousins were visiting and Poppy said she wasn't feeling well though only after she'd eaten almost a whole pizza. In the end it was just me and Marietta which REALLY sucked. Though if that was the worst thing about it, I wouldn't care. But now I know. I know why the year ten girls were giggling and I know why Ava and Poppy didn't want to hang around with me.

I found out at school this morning. There was looking and pointing when I went into Form Room. People were saying things under their breath, things I couldn't hear. The girls were looking at me like I was a piece of dirt and the boys were laughing. I knew that it was about me, though I had no idea why. I wished I could see Sam, I'd been thinking about him all weekend, feeling sure we'd see each other this week. And then Georgia Dutton who's the prettiest girl in our year came over and there were four other girls right behind her including Ava and Poppy and they were all staring at me and Georgia said 'So do you think you're a model, Dee Dee-sy?' And the other girls giggled but I didn't understand. And then Georgia held up her phone. And it was a picture of me, the one Sam took with my shirt undone. And under there was a tag that said 'Dee D-Easy Tiny Tits'. My head spun and I kept staring, then Georgia whipped the phone away and I couldn't work out how she had seen the photo and I couldn't stop a tear coming out and Ava saw and said to Poppy 'she's only got herself to blame' in a loud voice and they wouldn't look at me. I ran away to the girls' toilets on the third floor and all I could think was that everyone had seen and Sam had shown and shared and my life, like I said, is OVER.

August 2014

Aside from the angry incident in the staff car park at school, Zoe and I have never met. But I've seen plenty of pictures, the most recent of which were from Dee Dee's thirteenth birthday in June when Zoe threw a visiting Jed out of the house in a totally unprompted rage. I know that Zoe is forty-seven, just a little younger than him, and that she looks good for her age. I know she has a heart-shaped face with a pointy chin, that she has blonde highlights and that she wears Prada perfume and designer dresses. I know that she has not found anyone since Jed left her, that she was brought up a Catholic and that she is a terrible snob and a dilettante who plays at fashion design but has never had a proper job. I also know that her favourite book is *Brideshead Revisited*, that she decided to become a designer after watching the famous 1980s TV series as a child and that she named both her children after the Flytes and – in Lish's case – a teddy bear: Sebastian Aloysius (known as Lish from day one, apparently) and Cordelia Julia (shortened to Dee Dee when she was little and couldn't quite manage her own full name). Most of all, I know that Zoe loathes me.

But none of these things I know prepare me for the sight that now meets my eyes. The only word I can use to describe her face is 'broken'. Jed is helping her to walk; she leans stiffly against him, her eyes red, her skin grey and drawn. Gary slips in after them, glances at me, then heads upstairs without a word.

The three of us are alone.

Zoe looks up, taking in the living area of the villa with blank, ghostly eyes, and I am suddenly aware that the pain I have felt over Dee Dee is nothing compared to this woman's, that there can, surely, be no greater agony for a mother than to lose her child. Overwhelmed with compassion for her, I move towards her, my hands clasped together.

'Zoe,' I say breathlessly, my heart feeling like it will burst, 'I am so, so sorry for your loss.'

Zoe gazes at me. She frowns as if confused. She turns to Jed. 'What?'

'I told you Emily would be here, remember?' He looks at me. 'The doctor gave her a sedative; she was literally tearing her hair out.'

'Oh, Jesus.' I stand, hovering, helpless, as Jed sets his ex onto the sofa. As he straightens, she clutches at his arm, pulling him down beside her. He sits hard, right next to her and she buries her face in his chest. She sobs, rocking backwards and forwards, murmuring things I can't quite catch. Jed holds her tightly. His eyes are closed but a tear trickles down his face. I stand watching them, an outsider to their shared grief. I feel empty, unneeded. Jealousy flashes through me, a hot wave. I turn away, embarrassed by my own selfishness. It is only natural Zoe and Jed would turn to each other at this time. I have no place here. I turn and walk out of the room.

Jed finds me in the kitchen, nursing a second glass of wine about fifteen minutes later.

'She's asleep,' he says, his voice thick with misery. 'Oh, baby.'

I'm in his arms as he reaches for me. And now he cries, the weight of his grief pulling him down to the floor. I sink down with him, holding him, stroking his hair as Rose used to stroke mine, as I dimly remember our mother stroking my hair long, long ago when I was very little.

I wake early, as the sun outside our window is just rising. The first thing I notice is that Jed is not in bed beside me. Then I remember Dee Dee. The pain of it is like a punch to the guts. It hurts so hard I gasp, then lie back, reeling. Grief is like this, I remember from the shock of losing Mum and Dad … those moments on waking before you remember, then the body blow of reality.

I must find Jed. I have no idea what I can do to make the pain he is feeling any less bearable, but I should be with him, letting him know he isn't alone. I pull on a cardigan and head downstairs. Whispers drift out from Dee Dee's room on the first floor. I pad across the landing. Jed and Zoe are sitting on either side of Dee Dee's bed. Zoe is holding

Jed's hand. Is she *praying*? Is *he*? I've never seen him do so or refer to doing so before. I can't help but feel another hot flash of jealousy, and I am, again, immediately ashamed. I hover in the doorway, waiting for her to finish. I can't hear a word, just the low rustle of her voice.

At last she sits up and releases his hand. I step forward, offering an apologetic cough for my presence. Jed and Zoe turn towards me. I'm struck by how good they look together. Jed might be fifty but could pass for a decade younger, while the few lines around his eyes and his greying temples confer a sense of authority rather than age. Zoe's skin looks fresher than it did last night and her blonde highlights – so messy before – now form a neat frame around her angular face. Close to, I'm fairly certain she's had some work done: botox and lip filler at least. I shake myself. What does any of that matter at a time like this? I remember how totally out of it Zoe was when she arrived, so I step forward and hold out my hand.

'Oh, Zoe,' I say, in an echo of last night. 'I loved Dee Dee very much. I'm so sorry for your loss.'

Zoe's dark blue eyes narrow as she takes me in. Her gaze runs over my entire body. I lower my arm and wait, dry-mouthed and self-conscious, wishing I had thought to put on more than a cardigan over my silk nightgown.

And then Zoe draws herself up. 'Get this fucking whore out of my sight,' she says.

I gasp. Jed is on his feet in an instant, ushering me away. My first instinct is to protest, to insist he tells her to take back what she just said, then I remind myself why she is here and I press my lips together.

I must let this go.

'Sorry, baby, sorry, sorry.' Jed leads me downstairs and into the kitchen. 'Sorry, sorry.' He paces across the room.

There's no sign that anyone else is up. Flustered, I fetch a pack of coffee from the fridge and set it down on the counter.

'Sorry,' Jed says again.

'It's fine,' I say, though it isn't at all.

But what else can I do? Under these circumstances the last thing Jed needs is for me to make a huge fuss. And what did I expect Zoe would say to me? *Hey, much-younger-woman-who-stole-my-husband-but-never-mind-that-now, thanks for offering your condolences.*

Jed rubs his hand over his forehead. He looks exhausted.

'Did you sleep at all?' I ask.

'Some, not much,' he says. 'The police were asking about Dee Dee's phone again. Did you tell them she lost it on the way back to the villa?'

I nod.

'They're testing those bloody powders today ... there's just no reason why it happened, I don't ... I can't ...' Jed sinks into a chair next to where I'm standing. 'I can't think straight, baby. But there are things we have to do, register-ing things ... telling people ... finding out how ... *when* we can take her, you know, home ...' His voice cracks.

I draw him towards me and press his face against my

61

stomach. He clings tightly to me for a moment, then pulls away. I can feel the damp of his tears through the silk of my nightgown.

'Gary and I can help with all the … the arrangements,' I say.

'Yes.' Jed nods, not looking at me, still completely distracted. 'Look, I need to go back to Zo and I have to deal with Lish too. He was asleep when I went in last night. How was he before we got back? Zo was asking.'

'He stayed in his room almost the entire time,' I explain. 'Look, I'll make us all some coffee, then Gary and I can start sorting out what needs to be done.'

'Okay, good,' Jed says, nodding again. He goes back upstairs. Gary appears as I make the coffee. We sit together and make a list of all the practical stuff that has to happen now. Iveta and I are dispatched for food which we dutifully buy and, later, cook and which no one really eats. Zoe remains in Dee Dee's bedroom the entire day, so – apart from a quick trip to fetch a sundress and sandals from our bedroom – I stay downstairs. I want to offer Zoe my sympathy again, but it's obvious she doesn't want to speak to me, that I'm the last person who can offer her any comfort. I feel stupid for caring, but her words last night still ring in my ears, as does the way Jed referred to her as 'Zo' earlier.

It's a hot, humid evening. I sit outside, staring at the still water of the pool. I can't believe that less than twenty-four hours ago Dee Dee was still alive. Gary and Iveta appear briefly to say that they're going out for a walk. Rose calls to check I'm okay. Lish, Jed and Zoe stay out of sight, upstairs. I'm torn between feeling I should leave them alone as a family and the desire to seek them out and ask if there's anything I can do for any of them.

Jed and Zoe appear as darkness envelops the villa and the heat fades and the lights around the pool cast long, thin shadows across the water. Zoe sits on a lounger on the other side of the pool. She doesn't look at me; her hands are trembling, twisting over and over in her lap. Jed takes the seat next to me.

'Are you all right?' he asks.

'Fine, just worried about you.' I hesitate. 'About you both.'

Zoe looks up at me. Her eyes are red-rimmed, her face pale in the pool lights. 'It's surreal, isn't it?' she says.

I nod, wary but hopeful this might be some kind of olive branch. 'I was just thinking how it's less than a day since she was here, since we all had dinner together.'

Zoe's eyes narrow. 'Not *all* of us,' she says slowly.

'No, I'm sorry, I didn't mean ...' I stop talking. My cheeks burn.

'This is your fault,' Zoe says. She's still looking straight at me.

'Zo,' Jed cautions. 'Come on.'

'No.' Zoe stands up. 'This is *your* fault, you little bitch.'

My breath catches in my throat.

'Dee Dee was safe at home,' Zoe hisses. 'She should never have come away. And the only reason she came here ... the only reason you *all* came here, where she *wasn't* safe, was because *he* …' She points at Jed. 'Because *he* wanted to impress *you*.'

I stare at her, unsure what to say. So much for an olive branch. My heart beats fast.

'Zoe, that's ridiculous,' Jed protests.

'Don't tell me I'm ridiculous.' She's shrieking now. 'You're the one who's made yourself ridiculous, bigging yourself up to your *whore*.' She spits out the last word, then bursts into tears and rushes back into the villa.

There's an uneasy silence. A dog barks in the distance.

'She doesn't know what she's saying,' Jed mutters. 'She's …'

'I know.' I reach across and lay my hand on his arm. 'It's fine.' I say. 'I can't imagine what this is like for her. I'm sure she'll calm down …'

Jed shakes his head. 'I don't think that's going to happen in the next day or two. In fact …' He pauses. 'Look, baby, I hate to suggest it but maybe you should think about going home early. Your brother and Cam have the boat nearby, your sister is already on board. You could go back with them … or …'

I swallow, hard. 'I wanted to be here for you, to help … to …'

'I know.' Jed pulls me to him, hugging me tight. 'I know, but Gary's dealing with all the practical stuff and I can't tell Zoe to leave, I think she might crack up totally. I know it's not fair and God knows it's not what I want, but …'

I disentangle myself from his arms, my emotions battling in my head. I hate the idea that Jed should be forced into being without me when he wants me here. And yet my leaving will make things easier for him – and therefore for Lish too – and he's right that Zoe will most likely crack up if he turfs her out. I take a deep breath. Going home right now is the right thing to do, the unselfish thing.

'Of course I will, if you really think it's best.'

'Thank you.' Jed hugs me again.

As I wrap my arms around him I look up at the villa. Up on the first floor all the lights are off except for the one in Dee Dee's room. For a second I think I see her outline at the window. Then I realize that it's Zoe, looking out at us. I shiver, though it's still warm, and bury my face in Jed's neck.

When I look up a moment later, Zoe is gone and the lights are out.

The next morning I leave and go home with Rose and Martin. A week passes. The date when Jed and the others were due to fly home from Corsica comes and goes. Jed calls every day. He is furious that so much time has passed and they still have no clue why Dee Dee died. From what he says, the police investigation sounds like it's run out of steam before it has properly begun.

'They say they're waiting on secondary reports but the post mortem was done days ago and we still don't really know what it says. They keep saying: "*peu concluant . . . peu concluant* ..." It's outrageous that they're keeping information from us.'

'Maybe tomorrow,' I suggest. 'When do you think they'll let you bring her home?'

'I don't know.' Jed sighs. 'How are you?'

'I'm fine,' I say. 'Actually school begins on Monday. I've got year two this time.'

'Christ, baby, I completely forgot. Are you sure you're up to it? Going back to work?'

'I'll be fine,' I reassure him. 'To be honest, it'll be good to have something to focus on.'

'Tell me about what you'll be doing. I could do with hearing about normal stuff.'

I chat for a while, explaining what my new role for this year as head of Key Stage One involves: mostly extra admin, as far as I can see. Jed listens but his mind isn't really focused on what I'm saying. It must be surreal for him to hear about medium-term topic planning and schemes of work while he's consumed with grief and dealing with frustrating officialdom in another country.

He murmurs something about it all sounding like hard work. I can hear plates and glasses being laid out in the background.

'Is that Iveta?' I ask lightly.

'No, Zoe,' Jed says. 'Gary and Iveta have gone out for dinner, er, they've taken Lish too, felt Zoe and I might like some time alone just ... I don't know ... personally I'd rather they were here, but Zo wanted to talk to me, so ...'

'Right.' Jealousy worms through me. I try to push it away. I mustn't be unreasonable.

There's an awkward silence, then Jed promises to call again when there is news on Dee Dee's post mortem. I want to tell him how much I'm hurting, how I think about her all the time, but it seems selfish to talk about my own pain when his – and Zoe's – is so much greater so instead I just say goodbye and head over to Rose's house.

Cameron is away on business for one of his charities and Rose has invited me and Martin over for the evening, as well as my old friend Laura from school who lives nearby. It's always a little strange being back on Ashley Avenue. I grew up in this house and have moved in and out of it many times since. Although technically Mum and Dad left it to all three of us, it has become Rose's house by default. Neither Martin nor I begrudge this. Rose deserves it. And, anyway, thanks to our partners, neither Martin nor I need the money.

Much like the entire house, this room is a slightly bizarre mix of the chrome and glass eighties furnishings from my early childhood and the pale wood and pastel colours that Rose has chosen in more recent years. I'm last to arrive and Martin and Laura are already ensconced on the sofa so I take the armchair by the fireplace.

'God, Emily, I can't believe it about Dee Dee, it's just *awful*.' Laura widens her dark eyes as she unfurls herself from Martin's side. My oldest friend is possibly the most tactile person I've ever met. She's not exactly beautiful – Jed described her as having a face like a pug when he met her – but there's something about the sensual way she behaves, particularly around men, that mostly has them falling at her feet. Gay men love her too. Martin has always found her great fun and Laura, like most of my friends, totally adores him.

'How are you doing, sweetie?' she asks.

'I'm okay,' I say. 'Worried about Jed.'

'Of course,' Rose says, bustling in with a bowl of crisps. 'It's the worst thing for a parent.'

We sit and talk. It's good to be here, surrounded by everyone and everything that roots me in my past. It's particularly nice to see Laura. Since I moved in with Jed and away from the area we've hardly spent any time together. She's full of concern for me tonight, asking about what happened to Dee Dee and how I have been coping with the shock and the loss. After a while, however, the conversation inevitably drifts away from my experiences and onto Laura's little girl and latest pregnancy. She's almost two months in and full of details about sore breasts and day-long nausea.

'Never mind morning sickness,' she says. 'I can't eat a thing until six p.m. Plus I want sex *all* the time.'

Martin laughs. Rose looks faintly appalled. I grin to myself. Laura has always been unashamed and open about her physical desires. She has a boyfriend, Jamie, whom she refuses to marry despite him asking her every few months, on the grounds that marriage – and indeed monogamy for life – are bourgeois fictions that prevent human beings from living full and natural lives.

I sometimes wonder how much of this philosophy Laura really believes. She has certainly held very liberal views ever since our secondary school days. And yet she seems happy enough with Jamie and has never, even in our most drunken moments together, expressed any serious desire to shag around. As she chatters on, Martin hanging on her every word, I catch sight of the photo of Jed, me, Dee Dee and Lish that Rose has thoughtfully placed on the sideboard and the pain of losing her fills me again.

'She was a sweet girl,' Rose says softly.

I look up. All three of them are gazing at me. Martin crosses the room and puts his arm around my shoulders. 'She was lovely, Emily, there was such an innocence about her. I'll never forget her eyes like saucers when we gave her that bracelet.'

I nod, remembering the engagement party back in July. 'She'd been picked on by some girls at school,' I say. 'She told me about it that night, said how her friends had rallied round.'

'She reminded me a bit of you as a young child, actually,' Rose says. 'Always surrounded by friends, loved by everyone.'

I shake my head. *Rose by name, rose-tinted by nature,* as our brother once said; my sister's version of my childhood before our parents' death has always been a little idealized. Still, she's right about Dee Dee. 'She did have good friends.'

My throat tightens. 'She was so lovely to me, no resentment over Jed at all.'

'Unlike that bitch of an ex-wife of his,' Rose says.

I stare at her. It's unlike Rose to sound so venomous.

'It's marriage as ownership,' Laura says. 'Zoe thinks she has some sort of permanent claim over Jed, just because they signed a bit of paper saying they would stay together.'

'And because they had two children,' I suggest gently.

'Emily's right.' Martin frowns. 'The poor woman's just lost her daughter. I think we should cut her some slack.'

Laura shrugs. 'I just mean that Zoe's feelings towards Emily are all about territory. I feel as sorry for her as you do.'

'I feel sorry for her too.' Rose sighs. 'I just can't stand how she's blaming Emily over Dee Dee. It's not fair.'

'Blames you over Dee Dee?' Laura turns to me. 'Jed's ex *blames* you? For what?'

I gulp. There's a hollow feeling in my chest: Dee Dee is gone and Jed is far away with Zoe and Zoe hates me. Talking about it is the last thing I want to do, but Laura is sitting forward, her hair hooked behind her ears, peering intently at me.

'She says Dee Dee died because we were in Corsica, and we were in Corsica because of me, because Jed wanted me to have a flashy holiday which I promise you I absolutely didn't. I just wanted us all to be together: Jed and me and ... and his kids.' My voice echoes in my ears: flat and sad.

'God, poor Jed,' Rose says.

'Poor Emily.' Laura reaches for my hand.

'How's Jed doing?' Martin asks.

'He's angry that they still don't have the results of the post mortem. I think knowing why she died would help maybe ... I don't know ...' Misery rises inside me. 'I don't know how he's doing really, he's so far away and having to deal with everything with Zoe and worrying about Lish, but he hasn't talked about his feelings so ...' I stop, the hitch in my voice threatening to turn to tears.

'Oh, sweetie.' Rose scuttles over and sits on my other side. Now she is holding one hand and Laura the other. 'Jed must be struggling, but you mean everything to him, I'm sure he'll open up more when he gets back.'

'She's right,' Laura adds. 'I mean I've only seen you guys together a couple of times but it's obvious he *adores* you.'

I nod, still trying not to cry. They've misunderstood me. I am not upset because Jed is withdrawn at the moment. What I can't bear is the knowledge that losing his daughter, just like losing Mum and Dad all those years ago, will never leave him, that the pain of it will shape his future forever. And that is a terrible burden for anyone to carry.

'It's tragic,' Martin says, leaning forward in his chair. I meet his eyes and I know that he understands. 'But Jed will survive it, he's strong.'

'Yes, and steady,' Rose adds.

'Yeah, the steadiest person you've ever been with,' Laura says, patting my hand. 'God and there were a few flakes back in the day.'

I smile at her.

'All charm and no substance,' Rose agrees. 'Like Dan Thackeray. D'you remember him, Mart?'

My brother nods. I look down at the carpet.

'Gosh, I haven't thought about Dan Thackeray in years,' Laura says. 'He was *gorgeous*. I'd have totally done him if you hadn't got there first, sweetie.'

I roll my eyes.

'Mmm.' Rose purses her lips. 'Gorgeous but unreliable. God, d'you remember how upset you were when he dumped you, Emily? Cried for nearly a week without stopping.' She tuts. 'I've never seen anyone so devastated.'

I look up to find everyone watching me.

'Yeah, Dan,' I say. 'That takes me back.'

It certainly does. Dan was the love of my life – at least he was before I fell in love with Jed. We met ten years ago at a party I hadn't really even wanted to go to. I was wearing a dress with thin straps and high, uncomfortable heels. I remember taking my shoes off to dance, feeling content and happy. I was delighted to be on my PGCE course, living away from home at last and enjoying being out with my friends. Love was the last thing on my mind. And then Dan walked over and without warning, my heart was racing and I was caught up in the spell of his sparkling eyes. Dan was twenty-three, like I was, and a journalist. He worked for a regional paper but was hungry for a job on one of the nationals 'before they go completely digital'. He spoke fast and intently and looked at me like I was the only person in the room. When he asked for my phone number, I punched it into his mobile with trembling fingers and when he called me the next day I, quite literally, jumped up and down for joy.

I meet Rose's eyes. She, more than anyone, bore the brunt of my misery when the relationship ended. Because Dan turned out to be a commitment-phobe who strung me along for nearly two years, then left me without a backward glance for a job in the States soon after we started living together.

I remember the agony that followed all too well, and how my ever-caring sister did her best to help, bringing me food for which I had no appetite and advice about pebbles and beaches from which I took no solace.

I loved Dan harder, but it's a better love with Jed: honest and solid and true. My phone rings into the silence. It's Jed himself. I take the call halfway up the stairs, a place I used to sit often when I was very little, watching and envying my older brother and sister allowed to stay up long after my own bedtime.

'The post mortem's in,' Jed says, his voice thick with tension. 'Dee Dee died from potassium cyanide poisoning.'

'What?' I'm jolted out of my nostalgic reverie. 'How on earth—?'

'It was in the ExAche powders you gave her,' Jed says flatly.

'Oh, God.' Guilt grips me like a fist. 'There was *poison* in the ExAche?'

'Potassium cyanide, yes. It's used in various plating industries and photographic processing. They found microscopic bits of it in the dregs of the powder left in the sachet.'

'But ... but ...' My mind whirls as I try to get my head around this news.

'If you're thinking the cyanide must have tasted horrible, you're right,' Jed goes on. 'But then according to your statement you'd already warned Dee Dee that the powders were bitter and told her to drink the whole glass.'

'Oh, God, Jed, I'm so sorry, I—'

'I don't mean it like that, baby.' Jed sucks in his breath. 'The police have gone back to the pharmacy where Lish bought the powders: they're testing all the stocks. The ones Martin brought back, too.'

'But how did ... how do they think the potassium cyanide got into the ExAche?'

'Either deliberately by an angry worker on the production line, which the manufacturers should have protected against, or because the manufacturers were careless, cutting corners on health and safety. Either way they're going to pay.'

'Pay?' I echo his words. He sounds furious and yet focused. Better than he has done all week.

'They'll have to close down the plant where they make the powders, get all stocks withdrawn. Then the French government will prosecute them for criminal negligence. At least I hope they will. Benecke Tricorp – that's the manufacturers – they're huge. Powerful. But ...' He hesitates.

'But what?'

'If we can't get a criminal case going then Zoe and I will take legal action ourselves, a civil case. Whatever it takes.'

'Jed, I feel awful about the powders. I mean I *gave* them to her.'

'Listen to me, baby, it's not your fault. It's the manu-facturer. And I know this is going to mean a court case and me and Zoe spending time on it together, but I need you more than ever. I can't get through this without you.' He lowers his voice. 'You are with me, baby? Aren't you? Whatever it takes? With this court case or whatever?'

'Of course I'm with you,' I say. 'I'm right here. Whatever happens. Always.'

We ring off and I stumble back downstairs and into the living room.

'What is it?' Rose is on her feet immediately, hurrying over. 'Jesus, you're white as a sheet, Emily.'

She sits me down in the armchair and perches beside me. I stare at the blank, dark TV screen opposite, unseeing.

Dee Dee was poisoned from the powders I gave her, because I told her to drink them.

It's unbearable.

'What's happened?' Martin crouches at my feet, trying to catch my eye.

I take his hand, then turn to my sister and take hers. Thank goodness I have them.

The others are as shocked as I am, though they refuse to accept that I'm guilty in any way. Rationally I know they are right, but I still feel terrible. I take myself off to the bathroom and weep. It's like the ten days or so since Dee Dee's death have been swallowed up. Her loss feels as raw right now as when it first happened.

I'm just blowing my nose and splashing some water on my face when my phone beeps. I glance down at the screen.

This is your fault. IT SHOULD HAVE BEEN YOU, WHORE.

I stare at the shouty capitals, fear tightening my throat. Zoe. It *has* to be.

IT SHOULD HAVE BEEN YOU, WHORE.

Part of me wants to call Jed straightaway, but what good would that do? Zoe must have just received the post mortem news too and be beside herself with fury. I open the bathroom door, intending to show my brother and sister. But as I cross the landing I realize that all that will achieve is to upset them – in Rose's case, probably make her worry that Zoe is planning another rant at me, an escalation of her car park performance from last month.

I look at the message again. It's the angry hurt of a devastated mother. I delete it and head downstairs, hoping that will be an end to it.

Little do I know, this moment is just the beginning.

PART TWO

November 1992

Rose felt like she had been thrown out of a plane with no parachute. The world seemed to be reeling around her. A car crash, the doctors were saying. Your father killed outright ... your mother unconscious at the scene, passing away in the ambulance on the way to the hospital ... we did everything we could ... truly sorry for your loss ... A nurse was still sitting beside her, her hand resting on Rose's arm. She had asked Rose who they needed to call. Rose gave her the number of Mum's friend Sally, then explained which school Martin and Emily went to.

They were all on their way here now. Sally would have warned them that there had been an accident but Rose had insisted she be the one to tell her brother and sister their parents were gone.

How on earth was she going to do that?

The minutes ticked away. The nurse was talking again, asking if she could fetch Rose anything. Rose shook her head. Panic filled her. She couldn't bear this. She couldn't face them: Martin, so private, so tightly wound into his own life, yet so close to Mum, and Emily, still

79

such a child, all smiles and sunshine. How could Rose obliterate their world?

'Would you like to see them later?' the nurse asked.

Rose stared at her blankly. Surely the nurse hadn't forgotten her siblings were already on their way here?

'Your parents,' the nurse explained.

'Oh,' Rose said. 'I don't know. No.'

She didn't know anything. Nothing made sense any more. She looked up. Martin and Emily were hurrying towards her through the long corridor, Sally just behind them. Martin was holding Emily's hand, almost pulling her along he was walking so fast. As they drew closer her eyes met his and Rose could see the shock of realization fill him. He stopped walking. Emily tugged at his hand.

'Come on.'

Her face was still so open, so light. She had no idea, Rose realized. For Emily it was simply inconceivable that the world could keep spinning without Mum flicking through a magazine or stroking Emily's hair to help her sleep or Dad grunting over his coffee and telling them to be quiet while he watched TV.

Martin began to cry, his arm over his face. Emily looked up at him, all concern. Rose hurried over. She was vaguely aware of the nurse beside her and of Sally hovering anxiously in the background. But she kept her gaze fixed on her brother and sister. She had to look after them. Yes. The thought fell like a drop of rain: single and clear. That was what she had to do: take care of Martin and Emily. Rose let the truth of it fill her, give her strength.

This truth would see her through.

Of course it wasn't that simple. Plenty of people told Rose that she was too young to take on a moody teen boy and a girl on the brink of adolescence. But Rose never wavered. It was what Emily and Martin wanted too. Martin – after that first cry – did not show his emotions again and only briefly, and very gruffly, said he didn't need looking after by anyone, that he and Rose would be fine taking care of Emily on their own. Emily was, in contrast, highly emotional, telling anyone who would listen that she wanted to stay in her home with her brother and sister and that she refused to consider moving to anyone else's house. She said so repeatedly and vociferously through floods of tears. She had turned to Rose immediately in a way that broke Rose's heart, yet helped mend it at the same time, asking her older sister to carry out all the little things Mum had used to do for her: from baking biscuits to reading to her at night, a habit that neither Emily nor their mother had wanted to give up.

Rose didn't really want to read the silly friendship stories that Emily devoured. She had never been much of a reader herself. But she sensed that what would help Emily most was routine. After almost a month of turmoil and endless conversations with family friends and distant relatives she'd never met before – neither Mum nor Dad had any living parents or siblings – it was decided. The house was Rose's – well, technically it had been left to all three of them, but Martin and Emily's shares were held in trust by Rose as their guardian. By the time of Martin's birthday at the very end of November, the three of them were living alone together. It was harder than Rose had expected. She had plenty of money now at least – from Dad's life insurance – so she had dropped her waitressing job and decided to defer her university place too. She had time to shop and to clean, and various friends of her parents brought round food twice a week, while Sally was lending them her cleaner on a regular basis too.

It wasn't the practical stuff that bothered Rose.

It was the guilt.

Every day that passed, Rose replayed what she knew of her parents' last hours over and over in her head. She had seen Dad with that woman, then she'd heard him deny the affair to Mum. And she had seen Mum sobbing because she didn't know what to believe.

Perhaps if Rose had spoken out and confirmed Mum's suspicions the crash might not have happened. An eye-witness had told the police that Mum and Dad had been arguing when the other car rammed into them. What else could they possibly have been rowing over than Dad's affair? Mum had almost certainly only got into the car in order to confront Dad – her shift hadn't been due to start until later so he couldn't have been giving her a lift to work or anything. Surely if Mum had known the truth already, she wouldn't have been in the car and Dad wouldn't have been distracted and so might have been able to avoid the crash.

Rose's thoughts careered from self-loathing to worry. Not over Emily, who was at least open in her grief. It was Martin. Rose couldn't reach him. His birthday was in two days' time and so far all he had done was bite her head off when she asked what he'd like to do to mark the occasion.

'Nothing,' he'd snapped. 'There's no fucking point.'

Rose didn't like him swearing. She knew Dad would have stopped him, but Martin seemed to think he was a law unto himself. He wasn't doing a stroke of work for his GCSE courses – understandable perhaps – but then he hadn't done much before the accident either. It was obvious that losing Mum and Dad would change him, but Rose was sure there was something else too, some deep anger in him that had been there long before their parents' death. The worst of it was that Martin rebuffed all her attempts to find out. He never spoke to her, hardly ever even looked at her. The last time they'd had a proper conversation had been weeks ago, on the day he'd got into a fight at school. Even then, all he'd said was that the other guy had deserved his beating.

Rose had no idea how to deal with him.

*

Martin Campbell looked at himself in the mirror. Sometimes these days he thought he was going mad. Even before Mum and Dad died there had been this weird distance between how he felt inside and how everyone else saw him. Mum had been the only person who'd sensed it. She had asked him, straight out, if he had feelings for Ben Bartholemew. Martin had said nothing at first, embarrassed. But Mum had drawn him out and reassured him, and now she was gone there was nobody he could talk to. So there was the Mum-shaped hole in his heart, plus the strangeness of the everyday reality of her and Dad just not being there any more, plus the burning desire for not just Ben but half of his friends and a million anonymous men plus this angry feeling that never ever seemed to go away. It was all Martin felt a lot of the time. Rose made it worse, hovering around him like *she* was his mother. She might be able to act like that around Emily but no way was Martin taking her being all Mum-ish over him. Rose had no idea. It was hard to believe they were related. For example, Martin liked the Stone Roses while Rose played bloody Take That over and over again in her bedroom. If he had to hear 'A Million Love Songs' one more time he would go insane.

Emily was the only person who didn't spin him into a rage, the only person in the world he felt calm around. He was never going to let anything bad happen to her. Rose might get all parental and on her case over piano practice and bedtimes but Martin was going to look after the important stuff and make sure nobody ever hurt her.

Martin ran his hand through his hair, smoothing the gel through to the ends so that it stood up in little peaks. He was too skinny and there were spots on his forehead but none of that mattered. In two days he would be sixteen and after that point he was never going to let anyone tell him what to do, ever again.

November 2014

The day of Dee Dee's funeral dawns bright and clear – a crisp autumn morning at the start of November. I'm hoping that this day will bring some kind of closure on Dee Dee's death – though obviously not her loss – so that our lives, Jed's especially, can start to settle around the new reality of life without her.

The funeral itself has been a long time coming. The French authorities kept the body for repeated tests, firstly for the police, then for the French government, then for the legal representatives. Jed and Zoe stayed in Corsica for nearly a month altogether, then brought Dee Dee home towards the end of September. They were just starting to plan a funeral for the following week, when yet more lawyers intervened and everything was delayed all over again.

Jed has been busy this whole time. This is partly, of course, because he is back to work, but even when he's at home he spends hours on the phone with Zoe or his brother, keeping them up to date with first the investigation into the manufacturers' production methods and then the attempts to get the French government to bring a negligence case.

Last week everything came to a head. Repeated inspections of the Benecke Tricorp factory had revealed no problem in working methods, which means the French government are unwilling to make a criminal negligence case against them. Jed, who is certain cross-contamination occurred, is determined to proceed with his civil suit.

'The company that makes ExAche has a bunch of processing plants in China that share equipment,' he tells me for the third time. 'The place where they make the powders is also used for electroplating which – because China postponed a ban on using it in 2013 – involves potassium cyanide.'

'So there's a chance it got into the powders.'

'A high chance,' Jed says. 'There's just no way to prove it.'

Matters are made worse by the fact that Benecke Tricorp have obeyed the letter of the law in everything: withdrawing stocks of ExAche all over Europe, launching a thorough internal investigation and cooperating with all the official enquiries that are thrown at them.

I watch Jed leave for the funeral, sombre in a dark suit. I ache to be with him – I took the day off work as soon as the date was fixed. But Jed points out that Zoe will not take it well if I show up. She has understandably gone to pieces since Dee Dee's death, spending her time either in floods of tears or furious rages, most of which are aimed either at me or Benecke Tricorp. She also spends hours listening to Jed talk about the civil suit. I resent the way she is suddenly so present in our lives again, though I try to keep my anger under wraps. The text I'm certain she sent me often floats to the surface of my mind:

IT SHOULD HAVE BEEN YOU, WHORE.

I've never told Jed. I've intended to do so a million times. But something has held me back. Apart from the fact I have no proof the sender was Zoe – though who else could it be? – it will only add to the burden on Jed's shoulders. He has aged enough as it is over the past few weeks and the more I think about it, the more certain I am that Zoe would like nothing better than to drive a wedge between us. She *wants* me to start complaining about her, to put Jed in the impossible position of choosing between cutting all ties with the mother of his children and living with a woman openly at war with his ex.

So I keep my counsel and trust that this time will pass. It's still hard to see Jed head off alone to his daughter's funeral.

'Hey, baby.' Hours later, Jed calls me from the wake at Zoe's house.

I've been on tenterhooks, my mind skittering over the Big Maths assessment sheets I've spent the morning trying to prepare.

'Oh, sweetheart.' I clutch my phone. 'How was it?'

'Terrible.' Jed's voice trembles. 'That is, the service was … was … like a standard thing, traditional Catholic mass. Impersonal, but it's what Zoe wanted.' He sighs.

I bite back the desire to point out that Jed's wishes should have been consulted too. 'How many people were there?' I ask.

'Loads. The church was packed out, full of girls from Dee Dee's school in tears.' He pauses. 'Zoe invited lots of our old friends too.'

'That must have been nice, at least?' I suggest. 'All those people offering support.'

'Mmn.' Jed's voice is low and unhappy. 'I don't know about that. It's just lots of people I haven't seen for ages. They keep coming up to me and there's this expression on their faces that they think I'm a bastard for leaving Zoe but they can't tell me because I've lost my daughter. Some of them won't even look me in the eye.'

'I'm sure you're imagining they think you're a bastard,' I say softly.

'I wish you were with me, baby.' A door opens behind Jed. I can hear the low hum of subdued chatter, the clink of glasses. Zoe's voice rises above the rest. 'It *had* to be Father Jim,' she is saying. The door shuts again. I push away the splinter of jealousy that pricks under my skin.

'How long do you think it will go on?'

'Not much longer, at least I hope not.' Jed sighs. 'I think it'll be okay for me to go in about half an hour or so.'

'I'll come and pick you up,' I say. Then, before Jed can make the suggestion himself, I quickly add: 'Don't worry, I'll wait outside.'

Jed agrees and thirty minutes later I park outside the

large detached brick house where he spent almost his entire marriage. It's a big house by London standards in a smart, leafy road; far more upmarket than the street where we live, nice though that is. I'm not going to do it, but I can't help feeling tempted to cross the carefully tended front lawn and ring on Zoe's doorbell. I would like Jed's old acquaintances to see that I am not the home-wrecking monster of their imaginations and that Jed and I truly love each other. But of course I stay put and simply send Jed a text to say that I'm outside. I sit and wait, fingering the delicate gold bracelet on my wrist. It's the one Martin and Cameron gave me on my engagement to Jed, identical to the one Dee Dee had on when she died. I've taken to wearing it a lot recently, it certainly seemed the right thing to do today. After a minute Jed texts back to say he needs to do a few quick goodbyes and won't be long. I get out of the car and walk around to the passenger seat. Jed hates to be in a car and not driving it himself. As I'm getting back in, Zoe's front door opens and a group of teenage girls tumble out. I stand by the car watching them chatter away as they cross the front lawn and turn onto the pavement. They must be Dee Dee's friends.

'Excuse me,' I say as they pass.

They stop and look up at me with the same wary expressions that I see in the older kids at my school. There's an entire generation we've brought up to fear adults and to suspect paedophiles are lurking on every corner. Their faces soften as they take in my relative youth and my gender.

'Are you ... were you friends of Dee Dee?' I ask.

The girls look at each other. There are four of them, all caught in the midst of adolescence. Two look a bit awkward and overweight, a third has terrible acne. Only the fourth carries herself with confidence. She is strikingly pretty too, a real Lolita with shiny blonde curls and full, Cupid's bow lips.

'I'm Emily Campbell,' I press on. 'I'm ... I'm Dee Dee's dad's girlfriend.'

The acne girl nods. The Lolita steps forward and offers her hand. 'Hello Emily, I'm Georgia.' Her accent is very upper-class, far posher than poor Dee Dee's was. Slightly taken aback, I shake hands. Georgia introduces the other girls. The acne-faced one is called Ava.

'Dee Dee was a really good friend of mine,' she says softly. Her lips tremble and one of the other girls puts her arm solicitously around her shoulders.

'We're all terribly, terribly upset,' Georgia says, tears welling in her eyes. 'We loved Dee Dee *so* much.'

My hand flies to my mouth, overcome by my own emotions. I stifle the sob that swells inside me. 'It's so nice that you came today, for Dee Dee,' I say, my voice breaking on her name.

The girls nod solemnly.

'I know how much your friendship meant to her,' I carry on, unable to stop a tear trickling down my cheek. 'She told me how she had some ... some problems at school last term and how her friends supported her. You should all be really proud of yourselves that you were there when she needed you.'

Ava is weeping openly now; the other girls look down at the ground. I've embarrassed them, bless them. Behind them the house front door opens and Jed appears in the doorway. Georgia follows my gaze and spots him too.

'It was nice to meet you, Emily,' she says, holding out her hand again for a final shake.

I give it a squeeze then raise my hand in a wave to the rest of them. 'Nice to meet you all as well.'

They troop off down the road, Ava being comforted by the girl next to her. I'm still watching them saunter away as Jed arrives at my side. He looks shattered.

'Thank you for being here, baby,' he says, pressing his lips swiftly against mine, then glancing back at the house as if to check no one has seen him.

'Are you okay?'

Jed ignores the question and gets into the car. As he revs the engine he glances at Dee Dee's friends, still just visible at the far end of the road.

'I see you met some of the girls from Dee Dee's class,' he says, his voice flat with misery.

'Yes.' I stroke his arm. 'She had some really good friends, and that's something to take comfort from. They are lovely girls. And they *really* cared about her.'

My brother's birthday falls at the end of the month. I haven't seen either him or Rose for weeks and I'm looking forward to the fancy do Cameron has planned in a Mayfair restaurant. It's a swanky affair, with a private dining room, expensive champagne flowing freely and gifts for all the guests. Martin greets me with a huge hug but then he whispers in my ear.

'Talk to Rosie, will you? She's upset about something, but she won't tell me what.'

I'm immediately concerned. For a start it's very unlike Rose to be down, she's usually so steady and sensible. It's even more peculiar that she won't confide in Martin. They've always been close, since the days immediately after our parents died when Martin's insistence that Rose should become our legal guardian made the difference to that decision. Of course it's true that they are very unalike: Martin is a free spirit whereas Rose likes to conform and it's also true that whereas Martin and I seem to 'get' each other without effort, Rose often seems puzzled by the way we think – and act.

I leave Jed chatting to Cameron and hurry to find my sister. She's in the ladies, applying some lipstick in the mirror. My mouth actually falls open as I clock what she's wearing: a short, fitted dress that shows off her long legs and high, thin stiletto heels. Her hair is different too: styled into a sweeping bob that suits her heart-shaped face rather than bundled into her usual ponytail. She's wearing eyeliner and if I'm not mistaken, a slash of Chanel's Rouge Noir on her lips. She might have restyled herself after her break-up with Simon but this is taking her look to a whole new level.

93

'Wow,' I say. 'You look *incredible*. Really glamorous.'

Rose smiles at me in the mirror. 'Just wanted to make the effort for the boy's birthday.'

I can't stop myself staring at her shoes. I've never seen Rose in anything so ... so sexy. Normally she wears flats or court shoes. 'Er, Mart seemed to think you were down about something. Is everything okay?'

Rose turns. Her bright expression falters. 'I keep thinking about Dee Dee,' she says. 'How she looked when I found her ... I ... it's just *so* upsetting to imagine her alone ... in pain ...'

'I know.' For some reason I wasn't expecting this to be the reason Rose is upset. A wave of grief washes over me. 'Still, all the post-mortem reports say she probably died very quickly, so ...' I hesitate. 'It's really hard but I think nights like tonight are important for Jed to have reminders that normal life is out there.'

Rose smoothes her hair self-consciously away from her face. 'Sometimes one loss triggers off another, like that day reminding me of Mum and Dad.' Her mouth trembles. 'And right now all I can think about is that I'm here on my own.'

'You mean without Simon?'

She nods.

'Oh.' Now I'm really flummoxed. Rose hasn't even mentioned Simon since the night before Dee Dee died when she joked sadly about being on the 'misery diet' since their break-up. And then I remember that Simon is a work colleague of Mart's and that this is Martin's birthday dinner. 'Oh my God, is Simon *here?*' I hiss.

'No.' Rose makes a face. 'Martin asked how I felt about inviting him and I said I'd rather not have him here so he isn't. It's just hard being here alone.'

She looks away, tears clearly pricking at her eyes. I rush over and give her a hug. It feels awkward. I'm not used to Rose opening up. She's always been very discreet about her relationships, at least around me. It's one of the many ways in which she's much more like a mother to me than a normal sister. Rose stiffens as I hug her and draws quickly away, wiping her eyes. She turns to check her make-up in the mirror.

'Sorry for being so emotional,' she mutters. 'I'm fine, really.'

A moment later we head back into the party. There are about twenty or thirty people here and I can see most of them doing a double-take as they catch sight of Rose. Several of Martin's friends comment on how good she looks but when I mention the fact to Jed he just nods, distracted. He's staring at the glass bar visible below us in the main part of the restaurant.

'You know what that takes me back to?' he murmurs.

I gaze at the bar and all the handsome people milling around it. 'What?'

'The night we met.' Jed draws closer.

I sigh. It's not really a memory I'm proud of, though Jed loves to remind me about it. I was on a spa weekend at a fancy hotel with a couple of girlfriends, Jed at a conference in the same place. He chatted me up in the bar. I was initially interested – charmed not just by his good looks but also his easy manner and fierce intelligence – but pulled back dramatically as soon as he mentioned he was married, about half an hour into our conversation.

'I'm telling you because I don't want it to be a secret,' he said, his eyes at once sorrowful and twinkling with devilment. 'I don't want to play games, so here it is: I'm unhappy in my marriage. Deeply unhappy and just hanging in there for the kids.'

I confessed I felt uncomfortable and Jed apologized.

'I would be lying if I said I didn't find you incredibly attractive,' he said, his hand a light pressure on my arm. 'But the last thing I want is to make you feel uncomfortable. Let's just finish our drinks, I'm enjoying your company so much.'

So we finished our drinks, then ordered two more ... the last two, I insisted. Jed nodded and asked me about my job. He listened attentively to everything I said. I told him about my work, how I loved the kids but was looking for more responsibility and hated the constant changes to the curriculum according to the whims of political fashion. More drinks appeared as if by magic while Jed hung on every word I uttered, before gradually steering the conversation onto my personal life. He expressed astonishment that I had no boyfriend and impressed me with his evident devotion to his children. Before I knew it, it was past midnight and we had been talking for almost three hours. I said I had to go to bed and he offered to escort me to my room, promising not to come inside.

At my door he asked, hesitantly, if he could see me again. I said no and he looked so upset that when he leaned forward to kiss me goodbye I let him find my lips rather than my cheek. Suddenly the kiss was properly passionate and Jed pressed me against the wall with a groan. I could feel him, hard, against me.

'Oh, Jesus,' he breathed in my ear. 'You are such a fucking turn-on.'

I only just managed not to sleep with him and spent the whole of the next morning in the hotel wondering if he would reappear. He didn't and I left the hotel unable to stop thinking about him. I knew that if he contacted me again I would surrender entirely but assumed that he wouldn't, that he was understandably a bit embarrassed he had come on to me so strongly and was now eager to get home to his family. Anyway, we had swapped neither email addresses nor phone numbers and though I had told him that I lived in south London and taught at a primary school near Oval, he didn't know any of the details.

Back at school, life seemed flat and dull, the men around me entirely lacking in charisma. I found my thoughts drifting to Jed over and over again, especially to our kiss. It had been months since I'd been on any kind of date and far longer than that since anyone had truly sparked my interest. I told Rose, of course, who made a face and told me I'd done the right thing in walking away.

I knew this was true, of course, but still I thought about him. And then, five days later, Jed sent flowers to me at school – a huge bunch of white roses. He included his phone number at the end of his note:

Thank you for an enchanting evening.

I phoned up, fully intending just to say thank you for the flowers. But Jed was so delighted to speak to me that I stayed on the call. Jed made it very easy, confessing with just the right balance of embarrassment and passion that he had been trying to track me down ever since he got back from his conference and that he couldn't stop thinking about me. He said (again) that his marriage was a sham and I said I would go for dinner with him. Later, we talked and talked over French langoustines and rack of lamb then he saw me all the way home, even though it was miles in the wrong direction and I had already told him my sister would be home and I wasn't going to invite him in. He kissed me at my door and left, having secured another date. This time we went for dinner in a Malaysian restaurant near Jed's offices in the City. Jed told me that he felt terrible about putting me in this position, but that he had fallen in love with me, that I was the one he had been waiting for all his life. Overwhelmed and totally in thrall, I gave myself up to him that night.

Jed pulls me closer now, his arm tight around my waist. He gazes across the room, at all of Martin and Cameron's good-looking friends.

'Do you realize how much every single man in this room envies me right now?' he whispers.

I snort, rolling my eyes. '*Please*, most of the men here are gay.'

Jed laughs and I smile with pleasure. It's been a long time since I heard him laugh. Then I look over and catch Rose staring miserably into her wine glass. I feel instantly guilty. Despite losing Dee Dee, I am so lucky to have found Jed, so lucky to be happily in love. All my petty insecurities over Zoe and concerns that Jed has withdrawn into a narrow focus on his case against Benecke Tricorp seem to melt away. Jed squeezes my hand.

'I spoke to my solicitor earlier,' he says. 'The decree nisi will be through any day and once it's issued I think we should start making definite wedding plans.'

I gaze at him. We haven't talked much about getting married since Dee Dee died. Somehow any kind of cele- bration has felt inappropriate.

'Are you sure you're ready to start thinking about that?' I ask.

Jed nods. 'If Dee Dee were here she'd be nagging me about it.'

I fall silent, remembering the conversation the three of us had just after the engagement party where Mart and Cameron gave Dee Dee and me our bracelets. Dee Dee had been keen to be a bridesmaid, though decidedly against any kind of frothy pink frock.

'I'd like to keep it small,' I say. 'It just seems wrong to do anything bigger without Dee Dee being here.'

'Whatever you want.' Jed smiles sadly.

'I love you,' I whisper.

Jed leans in, his breath hot on my ear. 'Good,' he says. 'Because I'm not letting you go. Ever.'

June 2014

SO I worked out how everyone has seen the photo Sam Edwards took of me. Basically he showed his friends and one of them is going out with Georgia Dutton in my class and she has made sure EVERYONE has seen. I don't know what is worst, that Sam broke his promise not to show anyone so he can't really like me even a little bit OR that EVERYONE at school has now seen and thinks I'm a slut AND ugly, including Ava and Poppy who haven't really spoken to me all week except to say things like 'I don't mean anything by it, but you were showing off for a boy.' Which I WASN'T.

It's not just the photo either. Sam has told people I let him touch me and that I was all hairy and now the boys in my class are calling me 'hairy Dee' then laughing like they've made the funniest joke in the world. I have been thinking that if I got all the hairs waxed off then maybe that would stop. I could casually just tell Ava or whoever that I'd done it, and then gradually everyone would find out and they'd think more of me. I don't know, I am so worried I just don't know but it has got to be worth a try.

I can hear Mum downstairs, she's had a few glasses of wine now so I'm going to go and ask her if I can go to her beauty place this weekend. I'm going to say I want to have my eyebrows plucked and *my legs waxed. I'm NOT going to say about the other bit, I'm not stupid and I know Mum wouldn't go for that OBVIOUSLY but once I'm in there I bet I could get the girl to do it.*

And then maybe Ava and the others would be my friends again.

December 2014

It's the first Friday in December. Jed is off at a conference on counterfeit medicines and won't be home until late. I'd been hoping that now the court case is properly lodged in the system, Jed's focus on Benecke Tricorp might ease up. But instead he has become interested in the many terrible stories his research into fake drugs has unearthed, from the diethylene glycol used as a substitute for glycerine in children's cough syrup to the leukaemia clinic in which patients were given false oncology drugs.

'There'll be sessions on lots of useful things including a seminar on international law,' he explains eagerly. 'There's even going to be a practical demo from the lab guys at the Campaign against Counterfeit and Substandard Pharmaceuticals; they're going to show how to use a spectrometer to analyse exactly what ingredients are inside fake drugs.' He pauses, his eyes glittering. 'Maybe it doesn't make sense to you, but I need to know that the law can and will change, that companies and dealers can and will be held to account.'

I nod. I understand better than Jed thinks that without

things changing in the future, it's as if the pain of the past has no point, no meaning. Unfortunately, I also understand that past pain *often* has no point and no meaning. My parents' death taught me that many years ago. You can rationalize and focus your ambitions all you like but, in the end, the dead stay dead and the agony of their loss must be absorbed, only transmuted in its own time, from within, and not through signing up to good causes or forming action plans to change the world.

My day at school is long and tiring. I hurry out to the school car park just before 5 p.m., two heavy bags in each hand. I'm planning to have a soak in the bath then head into town to meet Laura for a drink. I don't see her very often these days, not since the week after Dee Dee died. In fact, since I moved in with Jed I've hardly seen any of my old friends. It's not just that I'm preoccupied with my home life: my oldest friend, Moira, who I shared a flat with for several years, emigrated to New Zealand at the start of the year and most of my other friends – including Laura herself – have small children, which makes it far harder than it used to be to arrange to meet. On top of that, my new role as head of Key Stage One means I'm bogged down with admin and, like a total glutton for punishment, I have also taken on responsibility for the end of term production – coming up in just a few weeks now – which involves rehearsing the kids every other lunch hour.

As I reach my car and fumble in my bag for the key, my name echoes across the school car park. I look up. A man in a long, dark overcoat is walking towards me. The last time a stranger approached me in this car park it was Zoe, shrieking obscenities. I look more closely as the man draws nearer. This is not a stranger. It's my old boyfriend, Dan, who Laura herself mentioned the last time we met. I can't believe it and stare, stupidly, as he approaches. Dan has filled out a little since I last saw him and there are fine lines around his eyes, but otherwise it's the same face, the same disarming smile.

'Em?' he says again. Then he stops and stares at me.

I stare back, feeling my entire body flushing under his scrutiny. Seeing him is an electric shock to my system. My heart starts racing. My mouth falls open. I even forget that I have no make-up on and that there's a huge paint stain on my jacket.

'Dan?'

'Hello.' He grins. It's the same sexy smile that used to floor me ten years ago. My stomach cartwheels. I clutch at the car. What is going on? What is my ex-boyfriend doing here? Why is my body reacting like this? I haven't thought about him since that conversation three months ago and, before then, he hadn't crossed my mind in years. I realize my mouth is open and close it. I swallow, my throat too dry to speak.

'It's good to see you.' Dan moves closer, his hand resting on the bonnet of my car. I can see now that his coat and his haircut are both smart and expensive, that he has really grown into his looks: broad shoulders, full lips, a long, straight nose, cool, grey eyes and dark, wavy hair. My legs feel trembly and I have to lean against the car. I have no idea why my body is responding like this, but it's making me angry.

'How are you?' Dan asks.

'Fine.' The word sounds harsh as I say it, more harsh that I mean it to, but if Dan is fazed by this he doesn't show it.

'I came to find you,' he said. 'There's something I need to tell you.'

What the hell can he be talking about? It's eight years since he announced he was taking a job in New York and that it wasn't practical to think our twenty-month-long relationship would survive it. I was heartbroken for a long time. Dan, on the other hand, plunged into his new life with gusto, making little effort to stay in touch and stopping altogether within a matter of months.

What on earth could warrant this sudden reappearance out of the blue? Is he getting married? Becoming a father? No, surely neither of those things would bring him here, like this. Could he be dying? Or have some terrible disease which has lain dormant for ten years, which I might have caught from him?

I slam the car door shut. 'So why are you here? What do you want?'

Now Dan does look surprised. He raises his eyebrows, a smile curling around his lips.

'Not so pleased to see me, Emily Sarah?' he asks. Sarah

was my mother's name as well as my middle name; and as only my parents ever used the two names together it's disconcerting to hear them coming out of Dan's mouth.

Disconcerting, yet not unpleasant.

'No, I am, it's fine.' I'm still flustered but my body has, at least, calmed down. I don't know what that initial reaction was about, just shock I guess. 'How did you find me?'

'It wasn't that hard,' Dan says. 'I asked around. It's cool you've made it as a teacher.'

'Thanks.' How surreal is this? A group of other teachers cross the car park. They look over and wave. I can see them checking Dan out, wondering who he is. I say nothing, just wave back.

Dan clears his throat. 'Look, Em, I'm really sorry just to show up out of the blue.' He frowns, his forehead wrinkling, and I'm struck again by how he looks the same and yet different. The eight years that have passed have been good to him. I suddenly wonder how I look in his eyes. I stop leaning against the car roof, straighten my jacket and shake back my hair. Dan watches, still smiling. I have the uncanny sense that he can see exactly what I'm thinking.

'What is it?' I ask. 'What did you want to tell me?'

Dan's eyes flicker to my left hand. 'Nice ring,' he says. 'Er, congratulations.'

'You heard about that too?'

'About Jed?' He says the name as if it's italicized. 'I already knew. That's ... look, can we go somewhere? Get a coffee? There's a café over the road. I was waiting there earlier.'

I hesitate. Truth is, I'm equal parts intrigued and annoyed with him. Which is, I reflect, how it always used to be with Dan. I give myself a mental kick. Dan is old news, no longer part of my life. Still, Jed won't be back from his conference for hours and I have no plans. Plus, it will be interesting to catch up, to find out what he wants to tell me so badly that he's sought me out after eight years of silence.

'Fine.' I lock my car and we walk side by side to the café. Dan takes off his coat. He's wearing a navy suit, expensively cut. He shrugs off the jacket as we sit down. His pale blue shirt brings out the hint of blue in his grey eyes. I can see now that his new physique – that filled-out body – is partly muscle. I can just make out the cut of his biceps under the fine cotton of his shirt, though his height stops him from looking bulky or overdeveloped. Everything about him seems so much more manly than I remember. There is a faint rash of stubble on his chin which I'm certain he never had when he was younger. I check his hands. No rings, no jewellery of any kind. I wonder if he still has the swallow tattoo on his upper right arm. We were supposed to get them together, but I chickened out at the last moment.

I remove my jacket as the waitress comes over. We order coffees then I sit back. I gaze out of the window. I can almost see my car from here just beyond the edge of the school fence.

I can feel Dan's gaze lingering on my face.

'It's really good to see you, Em,' he says. 'It's been, what, eight years?'

'That's right.' I meet his eyes.

'Okay, I'll get to the point. Firstly, I'm still a journalist. After my job in the States I did a short stint in South Africa, then back to the States for the past six years. Now I've moved home and I'm freelancing. There's a story I started following a couple of weeks ago when I saw your ... when I saw about your stepdaughter, about what happened in Corsica.'

'You read about that?'

Dan nods. 'I'm so sorry, it must have been awful. You were there, weren't you?'

'Yes, but I don't understand, what's that—?'

'I noticed the article because Jed Kennedy was named in it.' He pauses. 'As you know, he was in the news back in the summer because he'd just got that minister off. I noticed him because of his connection to you.'

'How did you even know we were together?'

'I've known that for a while actually.' Dan smiles. 'I still see Charlie and he's still in touch with Ben who hears about you through Eve.' He rattles off the names of mutual friends from uni I haven't thought about in years. Eve and I used to be close, but now it's just the occasional drink. I thought everyone I knew back then had lost touch with Dan when he went to the States years ago. Eve certainly hasn't mentioned him in ages. Our coffees arrive and Dan takes a slurp then makes a face. 'I have to say this is not the greatest cup of coffee ever. The one I had earlier was better.'

'I've never been in here before,' I say, feeling stupidly defensive. 'I'm not in the habit of going out around here.'

'I just meant ... I'm sorry I suggested this place, it just seemed convenient.' Dan sets his cup down. He looks at me again, his eyes taking in my hair, my face. I start to blush over my unbrushed hair and paint stain. Then I shake myself. What does it matter how I look? I'm only here because Dan claims to have something to tell me. Nothing else is important.

'You were telling me that you saw an article about Dee Dee,' I prompt, hoping he can't see how flustered I'm feeling.

'Yes.' Dan says. 'Which must have been just the most terrible thing to go through.' He pushes his cup away from him. Mine still sits in front of me, untouched. 'The article I saw mentioned the fact that you'd all been on holiday, that you had a headache and Dee Dee's brother bought some painkillers from a local store that contained traces of potassium cyanide. Of course it said what happened to poor Dee Dee, then that Jed Kennedy had taken out a civil suit against the manufacturers Benecke Tricorp. I was already aware of a scandal from South Africa a few years back. Another powder-based painkiller. I used to know people who wrote stuff about faked and substandard drugs. They're more common than I realized.' Dan rubs the back of his head. It's a tiny gesture, but a terribly familiar one, transporting me straight back to our first proper date. How he took me to the pub, then dinner, eager to hear about my life, telling me about his job, then rubbing the back of his head in that vulnerable, slightly self-conscious way of his, as he confided his parents were getting divorced after years of growing apart from each other. Later, he drove me home where he followed me out of the car and kissed me on the street corner in a way that made my legs fold and my entire body tremble. It's pointless to make the comparison but with Jed I felt overpowered from day one, as if I'd been knocked off my feet by a tidal wave. Falling for Dan was more like a poison that coursed through my veins before I'd realized I was even under its influence, taking me over from the inside.

I pull myself together. 'So you saw a story about Dee Dee and . . .'

'And at first it looked pretty straightforward: some kind of accident at the factory, or some psycho employee adding potassium cyanide in order to kill people at random.' Dan pauses. 'But then I read up on the investigation and it was obvious that there was nothing, not one single shred of evidence that pointed to either of those possibilities. Plus, there have been no other cases of ExAche containing cyanide.'

'Well, that could be because they withdrew the powders from sale.' I frown. 'I don't see what you're getting at. There isn't another explanation. I handed Dee Dee the sachet myself and the cyanide was inside the sachet. There's no way it could have got there except when the powders were manufacturered.'

'Ah,' Dan says. 'You see, this is my point. No one found the top of the sachet, did they?'

'No, they think Dee Dee probably flushed it down the loo when she went to get a glass for her water, but it doesn't make any difference. I *gave* her the sachet. It was properly sealed. I would have noticed if it hadn't been.'

'Of course, but you wouldn't have been able to tell *how* it had been sealed,' Dan goes on. He leans forward, his eyes intent. 'Suppose the potassium cyanide was added after the ExAche sachet left the chemist where Jed's son bought it but *before* you gave it to Dee Dee?'

'I don't understand. What are you saying?'

'I'm saying that it's possible a tiny amount of potassium cyanide was added deliberately to the sachet then resealed so that no one would know. You just said yourself the top bit of the sachet was never found, so the seal can't be analysed.'

'That's crazy,' I say. 'Not one single person who has investigated has suggested that could possibly have happened.'

'Only because whoever added the potassium cyanide to the sachet knew what they were doing. They knew how to get hold of it for a start and they had enough expertise to reseal the sachet after adding the poison, so it looked just like all the others in the box. It's clever, almost a perfect crime.'

'But it doesn't make sense. That means it was someone on the holiday! Why would anyone in her family want to kill Dee Dee?' I ask. Anxiety swirls in my stomach. 'In fact, why would *anyone at all* want to kill her?' I stare at him. 'Why are you even interested in all this?'

'Because you're going to marry Jed Kennedy and ...' Dan lowers his voice '... and you have a right to know.'

'Know what?'

The chatter in the café fades as Dan lowers his voice further. 'It's Lish Kennedy, Jed's son. I dug around a bit and I found out that he was cautioned last year, when he was eighteen, for possession.'

'What ... *Lish*?' I shake my head. Jed has never mentioned this. '*Drugs?*'

'It happened a few months before you met Jed, when Lish was in his last term at school. Jed Kennedy is a lawyer with a lot of clever friends and the argument was that Lish was simply in possession of a bit of grass, a line of coke and a few E's – all for his own consumption. But as far as I can make out from the volumes and the drugs involved, he was actually supplying them to his classmates. Normally for Class A's it's a custodial sentence but, like I say, Lish just got a caution.'

'No,' I say. I can't believe this. Or that Jed wouldn't have told me something so serious.

'Okay, so that's in the past and obviously Lish didn't have drugs on him when Dee Dee died, or the police would have found them, but it's a drug connection so I get suspicious and I keep digging, which includes going to where the guy is at uni, and hey presto, when I ask around there

I'm told he's the go-to person for all sorts of illegal stuff: mostly pharmaceutical drugs, like Viagra and Vicodin. Basically, if it's chemicals you want, Lish Kennedy can get them for you at a knock-down price.'

'You're saying he's a drug dealer?' I stare at him, horrified.

'Exactly – specializing in illicit pharmaceuticals. He's known for it at his uni.'

No way. I can't believe it. Apart from anything else, Lish surely doesn't have the confidence to peddle drugs – and it would totally go against the way Jed has brought him up.

'It's a weird coincidence, don't you think?' Dan goes on. 'That some grungy posh boy who deals in pharmaceutical drugs at college is also the person who basically hands his sister a packet of ExAche containing potassium cyanide.'

'That's ridiculous. For a start, I took one sachet on the boat and I was fine, then it was my brother who gave me the second sachet to take away with me.'

'And who gave the second sachet to Martin? I bet it was Jed's son.'

I think back to the moment Martin had handed me the powder sachet. He hadn't taken it direct from the box of six. So who had? I frown, thinking back. It *was* Lish. I can see him in my mind's eye, taking the powder from its box and giving it to Martin to give to me. Is it really possible that he could have opened the sachet, added a few potassium cyanide crystals and resealed it while the rest of us were outside? He certainly had the time to do it; like his sister, Lish spent most of the evening after dinner inside the boat while everyone else was on deck.

'Okay but still, it's … it's totally random … *I* gave Dee Dee the sachet once we were back at the villa. It was *me* who had the headache.'

'I know,' Dan says, his voice heavy with emotion. 'That's why I had to find you.'

'What are you saying?'

'I don't think Dee Dee was the intended victim. Her dying was a mistake.'

'A mistake?'

'Yes.' Dan holds my gaze. 'But it was the *only* mistake. Everything else went exactly as planned: Lish could have made sure there wouldn't be any painkillers on your brother's boat to give him an excuse to buy more, thereby taking the focus away from any drugs that any of you already owned. Plus he could have easily made sure you got a headache so you needed painkillers by giving you something to bring one on. Then, having bought the powders, he was in the perfect position to add the potassium cyanide and reseal the sachet once he was back on the boat. He could have even researched where there would be a pharmacy that stocked ExAche.'

My mouth is gaping. 'You're saying … ?'

Dan nods. 'It all adds up, Em. From what I can see, I'm pretty certain that Jed's son meant to kill *you*.'

June 2014

SO I asked Mum about the waxing but she wouldn't listen. She said that I was being silly, that I hardly had any body hair and that I was too young to be worrying about it anyway, that 'there'll be time enough for that sort of carry-on when you're older, Jesus, you'll be bringing home a boyfriend next and I really don't need you acting out on top of everything else'.

I know what 'everything else' means. The divorce is going through. Mum signed the papers last night. Daddy came around again. He was really angry about what happened on my birthday which feels like SO much longer than a week ago. I was upstairs but I could hear Mum getting upset then Daddy put on his really stern voice and said she had to accept him being with Emily now and stop taking it out on me. And then Mum lost it completely and started shouting and she must have been waving papers about because she was saying 'what's written here DESTROYS us as a family, Jed, it's against EVERYTHING we've made together, and if I sign then your children will HATE you for what you are doing, your son already DESPISES you ... you AND your WHORE ... don't you understand how much I love you ...' and on and on like that.

After that there was silence for a bit, then she must have signed the divorce papers or whatever because next thing Daddy went – I heard the front door shut – and he hadn't even called up to me or come to see me even though he must have known I would be there and that made me feel like I used to when I would stay over with friends when I was little and miss being at home, a home-sickness-y sort of feeling.

And on top of all that I have to go to school tomorrow and like literally NO ONE wants to talk to me any more and Mum won't let me get waxed and I keep thinking about eating cake but my birthday cake is all used up so there are only chocolate chip biscuits which I don't even really like and they just make me fat but I ate them anyway.

December 2014

'No.' I frown at him. 'No, it's ridiculous.' But even as I'm speaking, I'm remembering ...

IT SHOULD HAVE BEEN YOU, WHORE.

Suppose that text was from Lish, not Zoe as I originally thought? Suppose 'should' was meant literally?

No. It's impossible.

Dan looks at me – an intense look full of sympathy. For a moment I feel totally connected to him, as if no time at all has passed since we broke up. But it has. Eight long years have gone by. We are both different people. Dan has no idea who I am now.

'Listen.' I lean forward. The lights flicker in the café as rain drums against the window. 'The idea that Lish might want to kill me is mad. Lish and I get on fine.'

'Do you?' Dan leans back and raises his eyebrows. God, I remember that quizzical expression of his only too well – part curiosity and part aloofness. It used to drive me mad.

'Yes,' I snap. I'm beginning to feel angry now. How dare Dan turn up like this out of the blue, peddling insane accusations, trying to unsettle me. What's he after anyway?

'Since when?' Dan asks. 'I mean, since when have you and Jed's son got on? Right from the start? Since you began your affair with his dad?'

God, so he knows about the affair. Of course he does. I feel my cheeks redden and look down at the bowl of sugar cubes on the table between us.

'I'm not judging you, Em.' Dan sounds uncertain.

I look up. 'Actually Lish was angry at first, but with his *dad*, not me. I mean, he didn't realize that his parents' marriage was already basically over before Jed met me, so of course he didn't particularly want to meet me for a few months, but that's understandable. He was upset for his mum; I know she leaned on him at the time and he was just starting at uni, only in his second term there when Jed moved out, which was bad timing. But things are different now. He's older, he's accepted me.'

'Or maybe he's just pretending to,' Dan suggests.

I take a sip of coffee. As Dan said, it tastes horrible. My hand shakes slightly as I hold the cup, though I don't know whether that's because I'm angry with Dan for being so self-assured or shocked to have this bolt from the blue hurled at me, or upset that it could, just possibly, be true.

'All I want is for you to have the information.' Dan says.

'Okay, then look at what you're saying.' I sit up straighter. 'Leaving aside the fact that Lish is a good kid and if he was mixed up in dealing illegal drugs, his parents would know, which I can promise you they emphatically

119

don't, why on earth would he be handling potassium cyanide? It doesn't fit with things like ... like Viagra and Vicodin that you mentioned earlier.'

'I know,' Dan concedes. 'I realize it's a stretch. I'm just concerned that he might have tried to hurt you.'

'It doesn't make any sense,' I persist. 'I've seen the info on Dee Dee and what ... what happened to her. Potassium cyanide is made for industrial use; it's one of the most dangerous chemicals in the world – a single teaspoon is enough to kill twelve fully grown men. Surely you'd only want to take it if you were suicidal? And if you're a student and you want to kill yourself, there have got to be easier ways. Anyway, I can't believe Lish would knowingly help someone commit suicide.'

Dan nods. 'I'm not saying I've got all the answers.' He hesitates. 'And I'm not trying to upset you either. I thought long and hard before doing *any* of this.'

'So why did you?' I look up.

Dan is silent for a moment. Then he sighs. 'At first I was just curious. You know, I'd heard you were getting married and ... I guess I wanted to know who to, that's why I read the article about Jed. Someone I work with remembered Jed's son being cautioned. I put two and two together, thought I'd do a little investigating and that's what I found ... then I got worried and ... and maybe I'm worrying over nothing, but I thought you should have all the facts.' He shrugs. 'If you're really sure everything's okay with Jed's son then obviously I'm wrong.'

IT SHOULD HAVE BEEN YOU, WHORE.

The words from the text circle my head like birds of prey. Dan is wrong. He *has* to be.

I push back my chair. The legs scrape noisily against the tiled café floor.

'I need to go.'

Dan's mouth tenses. It's a small gesture but another one I know well: Dan's 'tell' for when things aren't going to plan, though I can't imagine what he thought might happen. I must have spent hours ... days ... of my younger life absorbing his face to know it so well. What does he want from me now anyway?

We stand up. Dan slops both our coffees as he knocks against the table.

'You don't have to run off,' he says. 'I'm sorry if I've upset you. I'd like to help you find out the truth.' As he speaks his eyes flicker away from mine ... as if he can't make eye contact. Why? Because he's lying? Mistrust surges through me.

'No thanks,' I say. 'Bye.' I pick up my coat and walk away. Behind me I can hear Dan shoving money at the waitress. I don't look around. Outside, the rain is lashing down but I don't want to stop so I put my coat on as I walk. Dan catches me up on the other side of the road, just before the school entrance. He grabs my arm. 'Em, I'm so sorry about this, I'm—'

'Sorry for what?' I pull away. 'Throwing a grenade into my private life? Or treating me like shit eight years ago?'

Tears spring to my eyes. I blink them back, furious with myself for getting upset.

Dan looks stricken. He's holding something out to me. A business card. I don't want to take it, but he's pushing it into my hand. The rain is plastering his hair to his head, darkening the shoulders of his overcoat.

'Call me,' he says. 'Any time.'

I don't look back as I race through the school gates and across the car park to my car. My hands are still shaking as I start the engine and reverse out. I'm only upset because it was a shock to see him. There's no truth to what he's said. There *can't* be. I'm dreading finding Dan just outside the gates, but he has gone. Thank goodness. I stop to blow my nose. The business card he gave me sits in my lap. I pick it up. It's just Dan's name, along with the title freelance journalist, a mobile phone number and an email address. I tear it in two, then shove both bits in my jacket pocket. I drive home, take a hot bath and try to focus on some marking. Dan is wrong. He's put two and two together and made three hundred.

Later, I meet Laura, who is delighted now that the early stages of pregnancy have passed and she no longer feels sick all the time. She is in such a giddy mood, flirting with the waiters and full of excited baby talk. I can't bring myself to tell her about Dan's ludicrous accusation against Lish – and yet I can't quite push the thought of it away either. Dan's words echo in my head, and I'm actually grateful when Laura pleads exhaustion after just two (soft) drinks.

I head home. Somebody sent that nasty text. It could easily have been Lish.

IT SHOULD HAVE BEEN YOU, WHORE.

Were those vicious words a threat? I turn them over and over in my mind. Part of me wants to call Rose or Martin, tell them what Dan has claimed. But I know they will mistrust his motives. As I do. And yet why would Dan make up such a terrible story?

When the doorbell rings at eight thirty that evening, I half-expect it to be Dan on the doorstep. Instead I find Jed's brother Gary, all smiles and apologies for dropping by and with a bottle of Chateauneuf du Pape in his hand. I invite him in, explaining that Jed should be back within the next half-hour. Gary settles himself onto our living-room couch and asks if there's anything to eat. As I fetch a plate of left-over chicken from the fridge he launches into an elaborate story about how he was in the area for an after-works leaving do. Bearing in mind that he works in the City as a trader and normally drinks in the bars near his office, I'm highly sceptical that this is true. I think it's more likely he went for an after-work shag with some poor, easily flattered girl in his office who happens to live locally. He's certainly in a good mood, doing that classic Gary thing of flirting just enough to make you aware of it, but never so much that you think he might seriously be about to jump you.

'So how's Iveta?' I ask.

Gary's gaze gets a little shifty. 'Over.' He waves his hand.

'Oh?'

123

'She *was* a little old for me,' Gary says archly.

I roll my eyes. 'She was twenty-five, Gary.'

He grins. 'Like I say, a little old. I've just met someone new, actually, but it's early days, so no point talking about her yet.'

What is he like? Irritated and amused in equal measures, I let him change the subject and ask me about work. I talk about the end of term production I'm in charge of at school for a few minutes until Gary's eyes start glazing over, then ask him about the stock market. Gary says that some redundancies are in the offing, but he's confident he'll be safe. I find his breezy, cheery manner as annoying as his fixation on women with huge breasts. He's a classic younger brother, never happier than when he can poke fun at people who are more responsible and serious than he is. There is one moment where his jolly persona slips, for a second. I've just checked the cable box clock for the second time. It's well past nine, so Jed surely won't be too much longer.

'So how's my brother doing?' Gary asks suddenly, breaking off from an interminable tale about something called pork barrel packages. 'Is he okay? I've been really worried about him.'

I look up, surprised. Gary's not generally given to displays of concern. Then I remember how brilliantly he organized everything in the days following Dee Dee's death. Perhaps he's just not used to expressing his concern in words.

'I think he's doing all right,' I say, 'considering.'

'I'm just asking because I know he's not the easiest person, that he can be a bit intense, well, you know ... and this ... what happened to poor little Dee Dee must have put a huge strain on him, especially after everything he went through earlier in the year.'

He means Zoe's reaction to him leaving her.

'I think he's devastated, of course,' I say, choosing my words carefully. 'But we talk about it and I think that he's coping.'

'Good.' Gary looks genuinely relieved. 'And what about the civil suit? How's that going?'

'Slowly.'

'Right.' He hesitates. 'So are the manufacturers still refusing to accept responsibility? But it's definitely them who are at fault?'

I frown. Gary isn't normally this full of questions. Why the particular interest in the court case? Should I tell him what Dan has told me about Lish? Does Gary know that Lish was cautioned a year and a half ago? Does he suspect Lish himself?

I'm almost on the verge of asking, when Jed's key sounds in the door. In a flash, Gary reapplies his mask, ready to start with some affectionate needling. I can see as soon as he walks in that Jed is tired and irritated and really not in the mood for his younger brother, but he chats away while I pour him a whisky. Soon after, Gary heads home and Jed launches into a diatribe against the inadequacies of the international response to counterfeit drugs and the lack of the conference speakers' understanding of international law.

'That session was a joke. In fact the only bit that was any good was the session with the spectrometer, that was brilliant. This guy from the Campaign against Counterfeit and Substandard Pharmaceuticals – CASP – showed how you can assess the ingredients used in a range of drugs.' He pauses. 'And they also demonstrated these new, airtight boxes that you can hide drugs in so that sniffer dogs won't find them.'

'Airtight boxes?' I ask sceptically.

'Yeah, they're made from some special metallic compound, I can't remember what it's called.' Jed yawns. 'Anyway, apart from that it was rubbish. Plus Zoe was a total pain in the ass.'

'How so?'

'She kept banging on about me going round on Christmas Day, spending the entire thing with her and Lish,' he explains as he flops back, exhausted, onto the sofa.

'Oh,' I say, trying to gauge what Jed thinks of this idea before I respond. 'Er, what did you say?'

'I said that I would be spending Christmas with my fiancée but that I was sure you wouldn't mind me popping round to see Lish in the morning, if she liked.'

'Right.' Relief floods through me. 'Yes, of course, that would be fine.'

'You'd think so, wouldn't you?' Jed sighs. 'Unfortunately Zoe went ballistic, said no way was she entertaining me when I deigned to take a break from my "fucking whore" for five minutes.' Jed groans. 'I told her that she couldn't speak about you like that, that I understood she was still grieving for Dee Dee but that it was unacceptable to take it out on you.'

'You did?' I sit down beside him on the sofa.

'Course I did,' he says. 'Anyway, there's still a few weeks to sort it out. It's all made worse by the fact that Lish has decided to stay in his student flat in Southampton for most of the holidays. He's going back to Zoe's next weekend and for a few days over Christmas, but not the whole month that he has off uni. It's fair enough, really, he shouldn't feel he has to babysit his mum, but I don't think Zoe has taken it well.'

'No, I don't suppose that would be easy for her.' I choose my words carefully. Inside I'm itching to lambast Zoe for calling me a whore, but Jed has already defended me to her. I've got nothing to gain from lashing out at her myself.

'By the way, I asked Lish if he wanted to come for a visit on the Friday night of the weekend he's in London. Is that okay?'

'Sure.' Thoughts crowd through my head. Should I tell Jed about Dan's visit? No, there's no need to upset him. But what about Dan's claim that Lish is a dealer in pharmaceutical drugs? I still don't believe he can possibly be doing anything like that now – but what about the caution Lish supposedly received when he was at school? Jed has never mentioned it, but then I have never asked.

127

'We were doing this thing on drugs at school, you know, a discussion on how to approach the subject for year five and six, like a "don't go with strangers"-type thing and I wondered how they did it back in the day at Lish and Dee Dee's schools.'

Jed shrugs. 'No idea.'

I hold my breath. 'Did you ever worry about them taking drugs?' I ask. 'Maybe not Dee Dee yet, but Lish, when he was at school?'

A beat passes. Jed shifts in his seat. 'I suppose. He … I did think about it, but Lish only ever got up to the normal teenage stuff,' he says, not meeting my eyes. 'There was an incident before I met you when Lish was in the sixth form. Stupid boy got caught with some pot. Nothing major …'

I nod, my heart beating fast. This is exactly what Dan said had happened – well, the watered-down, covered-up version.

'That's all?' I ask.

'Yes.' Jed frowns. 'Why?'

'Nothing.' I lay my head on his chest. 'Do you still want kids with me?'

'Yes,' Jed says. 'Of course. There was a moment just after Dee Dee when I didn't, but now it seems like fate that I've met you, that I get the chance to be a parent again.'

'I used to want a big family,' I go on. 'Two boys and three girls.'

Jed laughs. 'And now?'

'I don't know,' I say. Jed falls silent and my thoughts

drift to what it must be like to be a parent of an adult child. I see lots of mums and dads at school, of course, but their children are younger. It never occurred to me before I met Jed that the worry of parenting doesn't stop just because your children grow up and leave home.

I glance at Jed, wondering if he's thinking about Lish and that drugs scare at school, but he looks so miserable that I'm suddenly sure he's remembering Dee Dee and my heart hurts for him so much I almost can't bear it.

I'm busy for the whole of the next week, preoccupied with the end of term production now, dizzyingly, less than a fortnight away. After that first evening I manage to put Dan's crazy claims out of my head, though I start dreaming of him. Bizarre dreams where I see him racing towards me, trying to save me from some unknown terror and I wake up with a start.

Lish is sullen and withdrawn when Jed picks him up from the tube and brings him home on the Friday night. He looks thinner too. Is that because of Dee Dee's death or because he's taking drugs? Or is it just a side effect of student life? He isn't exactly rude to me, though he doesn't make eye contact as he declines my offer to wash his bag of dirty laundry.

'Thanks, Emily, but I don't need anything right away and Mum likes to do it,' he says with a shrug.

'Sure,' I say. 'Of course. I understand.'

The next morning I pop to the shops. I'm supposed to

be going to the hairdresser too, but they've had to cancel so I'm back early. Jed has sent a text saying he's had to go into the office for a short meeting but will be back by 1 p.m., *so probably before my son gets up ...* he ends his text tersely.

Lish is famous for long lie-ins, so I am not expecting him to be awake when I let myself in through the front door soon after eleven. Much to my surprise he is sitting in front of his laptop at the kitchen table, talking on his iPhone. I haul my bags of food shopping onto the kitchen counter and, after a brief hello, start bustling about putting everything away. Lish acknowledges my arrival with a wave, then leaves the room to continue his call in private. I hear his heavy tread on the stairs and bend down to put a loaf of bread in the freezer. As I straighten up, Lish's laptop comes into my eyeline. It's on the table, still open. I hesitate, then scuttle over. I wouldn't normally dream of taking a peek at someone's computer, but Dan's words echo in my head: *maybe he's just pretending to accept you.* Could Lish intend me harm? Perhaps whatever he's looking at here will put my mind at rest. Anyway, it's not really snooping to glance at an open screen, is it? I'll probably just find porn or a YouTube video or an essay for college.

I press a key and the screen saver disappears. I see at once that Lish has about ten tabs going, but it's his Facebook page that is open. He has evidently been private messaging with someone. I hesitate. I know I shouldn't look at it, but I'm right here and he's upstairs and I'm not going to touch anything.

I peer at the screen. Lish is mid-message with someone called Ant.

Yeah so I is doing time @ me dads with him an his bimbo cunt bitch gf an is bare strain of the whole fuckin daze need sum shit put me right ...

I gasp. Is that *me* he's talking about? I close the Facebook page and back away from the laptop, horrified. I move around the cupboards on autopilot, putting the remaining food away. I'm just shoving the milk in the fridge as Lish comes back, his iPhone now in his pocket. He slouches over to the laptop and picks it up.

'I bought some quiche and salad for lunch,' I say, trying to sound normal. 'Your dad will be back at one, so I'm cooking for then. Would you like a jacket potato with yours?'

Lish gives a shrug. 'Yeah, er, thanks, Emily.' He doesn't meet my eyes.

The words on his Facebook message are burned against my retina: *bimbo cunt bitch*. A lump lodges itself in my throat. Is that *really* how he sees me?

'Er, Lish?'

He turns in the doorway, raising his eyebrows.

'Is everything okay?'

'Sure.' This time he does look at me. I stare into his eyes, trying to read his expression. It is blank. He's smiling, but not with his eyes.

bimbo cunt bitch

Does Jed know what Lish thinks of me?

I gulp.

'Was there anything else, Emily?'

'Er, no,' I say.

Lish turns and walks away, his laptop tucked under his arm. Again, I hear the thud of his footsteps on the stairs, then I cross the kitchen and sit carefully down in a chair. I'm dazed. I sit like that for a couple of minutes, letting what I saw on the Facebook page sink in.

Dan's words circle my mind: *maybe he's just pretending to accept you.*

I fetch my phone from my bag and turn to Jed's number. I know he will be deep in work mode, but I can't let this wait.

'Baby?' he answers straight away. 'What's up?'

I glance at the door. Lish is well out of the way, upstairs. Even so I speak quietly.

'I just caught sight of something Lish wrote. He basically said he hates being here and that he needs "some shit" – his words – to help him cope with it and … and he called me a bimbo and a … a bitch and worse.'

Silence on the other end. 'Lish just called you a bitch?' Jed sounds incredulous.

'No, he wrote it in a message on his Facebook.'

'What were you doing looking at his Facebook?'

This is not where I hoped Jed would go with what I'm telling him. 'I was just passing the screen,' I say. 'Jed, he *hates* me.'

'No, he doesn't.'

'He *does*. His exact words were that I was a "bimbo cunt bitch".'

A pause. 'Jesus.' Another pause. 'Whatever he wrote, I'm sure he doesn't mean that.'

'Then why write it?' I feel close to tears again.

'I don't know, baby, maybe he's just trying to sound important to his friends ...'

'*What*? Why would—?'

'I'm just saying that nothing Lish has said or done for the past few months makes me think he does anything but adore you.'

I hesitate. Part of me badly wants to tell Jed about Lish's alleged uni-based dealing activities, the possible link to Dee Dee's death and Dan's claim that this was really an attempted murder aimed at me. But what is the point? If *I* still don't believe any of that is true, Jed will certainly dismiss it out of hand, especially when he finds out the accusation comes from one of my ex-boyfriends.

'Look, baby, I'll have a word with Lish this afternoon. Asks if he minds being with us, get an update on his state of mind. Right now I've got to make one more call, then I should be free to leave.'

'Okay.'

'Love you, baby.'

Feeling numb, I end the call, then get up and make a cup of tea. I consider calling up to Lish to ask if he'd like one, but the ugly words he wrote about me still fill my head. In the end I drink my tea alone, then set about finishing off some bread I made earlier and preparing a salad for lunch. Lish doesn't reappear until Jed gets back and calls him down.

Lish avoids my gaze as he sits down. I bustle about, slicing the bread and putting the salad bowl on the table.

'So how's the course going?' Jed asks. He's referring to Lish's degree in Media, Communications and Culture, not a subject that Lish has ever been particularly forthcoming about.

Lish shrugs. 'Okay.'

Jed glances at me and rolls his eyes. 'Which module are you doing this term?'

'It's semesters, Dad,' Lish says. There's an edge to his voice. I sit down next to Jed, feeling troubled. Lish and his father have never had an easy relationship, at least not since I've known them, but it definitely seems to have got worse since Dee Dee's death. I watch Lish listlessly prodding a tomato. He doesn't really want to be here, that much is obvious. And he is angry too. I hadn't seen it before, but it's there in the clench of his jaw and the press of his lips.

'Okay, this semester,' Jed says with a sigh.

'Is it hard at the moment?' I ask, leaning forward and watching Lish intently. 'I mean, hard to deal with your course, after what happened to Dee Dee?'

Lish's head snaps up. There's real pain in his expression. Is that just grief? Or does guilt lurk behind it?

'Of course it's hard,' Lish says, his voice shaking slightly. 'But you just have to get on with things, don't you?'

There's an awkward silence. Jed clears his throat. 'So which module are you working on?'

Lish picks up his fork. 'Games Cultures,' he says.

'What does that involve then?' Jed asks with a grin. 'Playing *Call of Duty* then writing about its significance to our understanding of modern society?' He chuckles. 'I'd have thought "Games" and "Culture" was a bit of a contradiction in terms.'

I look down at my plate. Across the table, Lish is sullenly chewing at a mouthful of food, studiously ignoring his father. Can Jed not hear how disparaging he sounds when he makes jokes about Lish's degree choice? It would almost be better if he came right out and said he's disappointed his only son hasn't chosen something more academically challenging. I'm itching to tell Jed to ease off, but I'm wary of any perception that I'm interfering, especially in front of Lish. I recall Rose's wise words from just before my first meeting with Jed's children last March: *never challenge them on their kids*. Anyway, right now I'm more concerned about what Lish thinks of me, and that look on his face when I asked about Dee Dee.

Lish himself leaves the table as soon as possible, carrying his plate to the sink, then disappearing without a backward glance. Jed helps me load the dishwasher. He is adamant that we can't let on to Lish that I was snooping on his Facebook page, but – even though the past hour has shown me that Jed has no real idea how to talk to his son and despite the fact that he would clearly rather not engage him on such a potentially explosive issue – I insist that he talks to Lish about me.

Half an hour later Jed reappears. He shuts the living-room door and steers me onto the sofa.

'It's all good, baby,' he says with a relieved smile. 'I asked Lish how he felt about me being with you and he says that he's pleased I've found someone, that he thinks you're lovely. I pushed him about it, asked if he ever feels differently, if he ever feels resentful, and he said sometimes he makes out like it's a problem to his friends at college because lots of them moan about their family situations and he says it just makes sense to try and look like you're fitting in. I told him he should be his own man.'

'Right.' I can just imagine how such typically abrupt Jed advice will have gone down, but – again – I say nothing. What is far more important is the obvious point that Lish could be lying to his father and expressing the truth to his friends. However, before I can say anything else, Jed starts talking about a client at work. He couldn't be making it clearer that he wants this to be the end of the matter.

But how can it be?

'Jed, I'm still upset about what Lish wrote,' I persist.

'Okay, but just remember that the boy lost his sister only a few months ago. He inadvertently bought the very headache powders that killed her. He's allowed a little acting out, isn't he?'

I think of Lish's grief-stricken look again. Was there guilt in that look? If so, could such guilt simply be down to his purchase of the ExAche? Or to something more sinister? Of course he'd feel bad but I don't really see why being upset over Dee Dee's death would make him tell his friends he hates me. I hesitate. Now is the time for me to pass on to Jed what Dan has alleged. And yet it sounds so ludicrous to speak out loud:

I think your son who, by the way, may be a drug dealer, may also have been trying to kill me, but his sister died by mistake instead.

'Come on, baby, since those first few months has Lish once been rude to you? Or made you feel uncomfortable?'

'No,' I admit. 'But—'

'Well, doesn't that count for more than what he writes in a private message where he's trying to look the big man and thinks that slagging off his dad's fiancée is cool?'

At last I let it drop, but as the day passes I find myself thinking about Lish and those hateful words he wrote on Facebook more and more. The worm of doubt that Dan planted inside my head wriggles around, poking into all the dark crevices of my mind. In the end I creep up to our bedroom while Jed and Lish are watching football on TV. I have to speak to someone. But who? I could talk to Rose, of course, but I don't want to worry her. I know that if Martin found out what Lish wrote on his Facebook page he would call Jed immediately and insist that he takes his son in hand. Jed's own brother, Gary, would probably use the whole situation to get at Jed, who definitely wouldn't thank me for involving him. Which leaves friends: Moira in Australia is too far away and I can't call up Mel or Julie out of the blue and bombard them with such a melodramatic-sounding story. In the end I ring Laura. I saw her recently, and she's fully aware of both what happened to Dee Dee *and* how tricky things have been over the past year between me and Lish.

'But I thought he totally accepted you after the first few weeks?' she says, when I tell her about the Facebook entry. 'God, Emily, are you sure he was writing about *you*?'

'Yes,' I say. 'There's more.' I repeat a shortened version of the tale Dan told me, about Lish drug dealing – and his theory that the cyanide in the ExAche was added deliberately, then the sachet resealed.

'I know it sounds ridiculous, but I can't stop thinking about it.'

'Mmn,' Laura says. 'Even if Lish is peddling pharmaceuticals, it's still a massive leap from that to trying to deliberately poison you.' She sighs. 'Let's face it, Emily, lots of kids struggle with step-parents, I did myself. But that's a long way from trying to kill them. And anyway, it's all a bit elaborate: putting cyanide in a random sachet then going to all the trouble of resealing it.'

Everything Laura says is logical and sensible and yet I'm still feeling anxious when I get off the phone. It's dark when, several hours later, Lish appears downstairs, ready for Jed to drive him home to Zoe's house – just a short distance away in Highgate. There's a threat of snow and it's very cold. The heating has gone off, so I put it on again as Jed gives me a kiss and goes outside to scrape the ice off the car windscreen. A moment later Lish slopes up, his bag – still full of dirty laundry – clutched in his hand.

'Bye, Emily,' he says. He is smiling, making proper eye contact for the first time since this morning. Perhaps I have overreacted to his Facebook post after all, just like Jed suggested. I take a deep breath and walk right up to him. I put my arms around him.

'It's been lovely having you here,' I say, giving him a squeeze.

Lish hugs me back. A proper hug. I smile, relieved, and then I glance up. For a split second I see Lish's face in profile reflected in the hall mirror. He is looking away from the mirror, an expression of total disgust on his face. His eyes burn with it. As I look up he pulls away and forces his mouth into a smile again.

'Just going to the bathroom.' He disappears into the toilet by the front door.

I stand in the hall, frozen to the spot. Lish can lie to his dad all he likes, but I've seen the truth in his eyes. He *hates* me. I drop to my knees and yank at the straps of his bag. I don't know what I'm looking for, but I need to find out what Lish is carrying in here. The stench of his dirty laundry fills my nostrils. I plunge my hand into the bag, past T-shirts and boxers. My fingers circle something hard, like cardboard. I pull it out. It's a roll of twenty-pound notes. *Jesus*, there must be over five hundred pounds here. Where the hell did Lish get this? The answer flashes through my head: drugs, this must be drugs money.

IT SHOULD HAVE BEEN YOU, WHORE.

He *was* trying to get rid of me. And his poor sister died instead because I gave her my headache powders.

I have the text, I have Dan's claims, I have the ugly, angry way Lish just looked at me and I have his money.

But none of it is proof. And this is Jed's son. I can't go around making empty claims. I need proper evidence. Something I can take to Jed, not conjecture that Lish can easily wriggle out of. I'm certain if I ask about the cash he'll just say he's borrowed it, or taken it out of the account Jed set up for him to buy furniture or some such for the flat.

I shove the money back to the bottom of the bag and flip the top back over. I stand up as the toilet flushes and Lish reappears. He picks up his bag and slings it over his shoulder without looking at me.

'Thanks, Emily, it's been great.' He turns and goes.

I stare at the front door as it closes behind him, then I walk into the kitchen and sit down at the table. I am surprisingly calm, my hands resting on the warm wood. My bracelet, the same as Dee Dee's, rests on my wrist. This isn't just about me. I owe it to Dee Dee to find out the truth and to bring her killer to justice.

Whatever it takes.

PART THREE

February 1995

Rose picked up her phone. She knew what she had to do. But before she could even scroll to Andrew's number, Emily had stormed into the living room.

'I just found out Laura is going to FamFest as *well*,' Emily shouted, throwing herself down on the sofa. 'That means *all* my friends are. You *have* to let me go too.'

Rose gazed thoughtfully at her little sister. The past two years had been harder than she would have thought humanly possible. The immediate shock of losing Mum and Dad had given way first to the searing guilt that she could have prevented the accident that killed them, then, as she buried that particular agony deep in her soul, to the ongoing pain of being without them. Despite the fact that they'd rowed on an almost daily basis, she missed Mum terribly, her solid presence at the heart of the house. As for Dad, with his arched eyebrows and quick wit, in losing him she had lost the one person who always, unfailingly, made her feel special. But just as that loss became absorbed into everyday life, Emily had transformed before her eyes from a sweet-eyed little girl to a troublesome teen. Everyone had told her that once Emily hit adolescence things would get tricky, but Rose hadn't been prepared for the level of selfishness which her once thoughtful and generous sister would display. Rose was certain that she herself had never been so difficult. Ironically Emily still looked like a child: fairly late to develop, she only had small buds of breasts and her skin remained smooth and clear, not a spot in sight. The slight narrowing and lengthening of her face and those long, coltish legs were the only real indications of the beautiful young woman she promised to be.

'Rosie?' Emily's mouth wobbled and fat tears swelled in her eyes. '*Please*? It's just a two-day festival. Only *one* night's camping. And it's a *family* festival. Some of the parents will be there the *whole time*.'

'No,' Rose said. 'It's too far and it's not safe. There'll be drugs and alcohol and—'

'But I won't take them,' Emily persisted. 'I would *never* do that. Anyway, you'd be able to check I was all right if I had a phone.'

Not that again. Rose sighed.

'It's no good, Emily, it's not just *you* I'm worried about, there could be older boys trying to take advantage of you.' Rose shook her head. 'For goodness' sake, you're not even fourteen yet.' Why wouldn't Emily understand that all Rose wanted was to protect her? Couldn't she see that there was just no way Rose could risk losing her? That their parents dying so suddenly proved how fragile life was, how easily everything can be taken away from you?

'So *what*?' Emily was weeping now, tears streaming down her face. 'I won't *do* anything. I'm not *stupid*.'

'I know you're not.' Rose said. 'I just—'

'You just don't want me to have any fun.' Emily sprang to her feet, arms raised theatrically in the air. 'I *hate* you.'

She tore out of the living room, slamming the door behind her. Rose stood numbly for a second, then sank onto the arm of the chair behind her. The screen of her phone blurred as her own tears pricked at her eyes. She had been planning to spend the weekend hanging out with Andrew, but there was obviously no way she could do that now. Apart from anything else, she didn't trust Emily not to run off to bloody FamFest as soon as her back was turned.

Why was it so hard? Rose tried to imagine what Mum would have done. She would have been firm and consistent about the festival, Rose was certain of that. But how would she have dealt with Emily's hysteria? Her hate?

It wasn't fair. Rose was only trying to do the right thing. Had been trying to do it for over two years now. All her friends had gone off to uni. Rose planned to go herself, but not now. Not yet. She couldn't contemplate the upheaval of such a big life change while Emily was still such a problem, taking so much of Rose's time and attention.

None of Rose's friends had to deal with a difficult

teenager. Molly Gibson had a baby, which was a lot of work too, but at least babies were cute. Molly's friends doted on little Ayesha, cuddling her and buying her baby clothes and oohing and aahing whenever they went round. Nobody came round to Rose's house any more. Why would they? Emily was always stomping about and, while never openly rude to Rose's friends, she cast a pall over every room she entered. Anyway, the sort of late nights that her student friends enjoyed during the week were out for Rose, who was always in bed by boring o'clock to be ready for work and to get Emily up for school in the morning.

Rose's fingers hovered over Andrew's number. She didn't want to speak to him; she would text instead. With a sigh she wrote a short, polite message:

So sorry can't make next weekend after all.

This was the third date she'd had to skip in a month. She could sense Andrew growing impatient. If he loved her, he wouldn't mind, so if he did mind he didn't love her and wasn't worth hanging on to.

Rose told herself this, but it didn't make her feel any better.

She sent the text then set down her phone. There was no way she could take months more of Emily acting out without getting help. And there was only one person she could think of who could give her that help. He was out right now, of course. Martin spent most of his time going out these days. Rose had long given up nagging him over his A-levels. She suspected he was going to flunk the lot of them, though Martin himself seemed confident his grades would improve over the next few months.

Anyway, Emily adored him. And that made Martin Rose's best – perhaps her only – hope.

Martin knocked on Emily's door.

'Hello?'

'S'mee,' he said.

There was silence, which Martin took as permission to open the door. Emily was sitting on her bed, surrounded by school books.

'Pretending to be a workaholic, Flaky?' he asked with a grin.

His little sister grinned back. Martin sat on the edge of the bed. He didn't really see what the problem was. Emily was fine with him. In all honesty he thought Rose created half the difficulties herself. Stopping Emily from going to a family-oriented festival with a school friend and her parents was ridiculously overprotective, but it was more than that. Rose was hard on Emily without realizing it, forgetting to treat her with the little courtesies that were so important when you were trying to grow up. For instance, Martin was pretty certain that Rose wouldn't have bothered knocking on Emily's door just now, thereby setting up resentments before a conversation had even started.

Emily sat back against her pillows. Her room was a mix

of the little girl she was growing out of, revealed by the row of teddy bears under the window, and the adult she was eager to become, as evidenced by the large heap of make-up on the floor by the bed and the tiny-cupped bra draped over the back of the chair. Martin noticed the bra in passing. Some of his friends were obsessed with tits, but Martin didn't really see the point of them – sexually, that was.

'I hear you're upset,' Martin ventured, smoothing his hand over the duvet. 'What's wrong?'

'Just Rosie being mean.' Emily scowled. 'She thinks she knows how to be a mum but she's pants at it.'

Martin pursed his lips. If Rose were in the room, he was certain she would be urging him to defend her. But that was likely just to wind Emily up – and Martin didn't want a row. There was enough drama in his life without that. He thought of Mum. He missed her every day. In the two long years since she and Dad had died, Martin had often wished he could have talked to her again. He would have liked to have taken her out too, to her favourite restaurant, and made her laugh over wine and salad. She hadn't been happy with Dad – she'd more or less told Martin that. Not that he could tell anyone now.

But Mum was gone and no one else at home knew his secret. At school he was still pretending to like girls, to joke with the others about who he thought was hot – and not. But away from the sixth form and the need to fit in, Martin was starting to find himself. In bars and on the street looks would be exchanged and interest shown and felt – and sometimes acted on.

Martin knew who he was and he wasn't ashamed of it. But being open about it was another matter altogether. He wanted to talk. He was ready to talk. He was just waiting for the right moment.

'What's the matter?' Emily narrowed her eyes.

Martin cleared his throat, remembering why he was here. 'I know Rose can be a bit harsh.'

'Yeah, she's a fucking *fascist*.'

'Well, maybe you could show her how to deal with you better?'

'How?'

'Tell her how you feel, what you want.'

'I *do*.' Emily let out a low moan. 'She doesn't *listen*. She treats me like a baby.'

'You have to be honest about how you really feel …' Martin stopped. What was he doing? How could he lecture his sister on honesty, when he had been afraid for so long to tell her, to tell anyone he knew, who he really was.

He'd talked to Mum. And Mum had died, which had – he saw it now – totally freaked him out, like it was a jinx. But that was in the past. It was time to be open about the future. *His* future. And there was no one he trusted more to accept him as he was than his little sister.

'What is it?' Emily asked.

It was time. Martin took a deep breath and then he told her.

December 2014

Dan answers on the second ring.

'Em?' His voice is a mix of concern and delight. Something inside me shifts; I am reassured just by the familiarity of that deep, Essex-boy accent. Is it because Dan and I were so close once? Or just that Dan sounds like I do, unlike Jed, whose own accent is subtly but distinctly posher, so that when he says 'years' it sounds like 'yahs'.

'Em?' Dan falters slightly. 'Is that you?'

I hesitate. Dan's voice may sound familiar, but it's been a long time since I knew Dan himself. I have to keep remembering he is a stranger now.

'I . . . I've been thinking about what you told me,' I say. 'I'd like to meet up again.'

'Right.' There's a pause. 'Okay, that's good, Em.' Dan suggests a pub near King's Cross. I vaguely remember going with him there before, ten years ago. At the time Dan lived in a rundown house share on Caledonian Road, but when he and I moved in together we rented a flat south of the river, so I could stay closer to Rose. At first life in our one-bed flat in Camberwell was bliss, then Dan started staying out later and later in the evenings. Sometimes I'd join him, but mostly he was off with the lads, his east London friends, drinking pint after pint and rolling in drunk around midnight. He was always pleased to see me but I hated it. It was like he wanted me to be at home waiting for him, but didn't want to come back there himself until the evening was almost over. At first I tried to be patient, then I grew angry. We started arguing, which just led Dan to stay away even more often. Finally, I said I thought I should move back in with Rose, hoping it would be the moment he came to his senses but instead he nodded and said he'd been thinking the same thing. I moved out, deeply hurt, and the following week Dan announced he'd decided to take a new job in the States. There was never any talk that I might have gone with him. Or that we should keep the relationship going while he was away. My blood still chills at the memory of Dan telling me very matter-of-factly that his move offered us the chance of a natural break.

I am already dressed in jeans and a jumper. I consider changing tops, but I don't want Dan to think I'm dressing up for him, so I just tug on a jacket and some boots. I could wait for Jed to come home to explain what I'm doing, but Zoe will undoubtedly keep him talking when he drops Lish and, anyway, I don't want to mention I'm seeing Dan. Unlike other men I've known, Jed refuses to express any curiosity about my past: 'I'd rather imagine you were a

SOPHIE MCKENZIE

virgin when I met you,' he always says, and I've seen the flashes of jealousy on the few occasions when I've referred to my heartbreak over Dan. So I simply leave a note saying I've popped out to attempt some Christmas shopping. It's not much of a lie. Christmas Day is less than two weeks away and I have over half my presents still to buy.

I am wearing my engagement ring as I always do and I twist it around my finger as I hurry to the nearest underground. Dan could be married with a family now. Our last meeting was so short, so intense, there was no time for those kind of questions. It is freezing as I leave Caledonian Road tube station and scurry towards the pub where I'm meeting Dan. I can see him through the window as I approach, bent over his phone at a table in the corner. I take advantage of the fact that he hasn't noticed me yet to have a long look at him. The stubble on his chin is still there, but he is wearing more casual clothes than before: jeans and a cream and black-flecked woollen jumper. He looks perfectly relaxed.

I, on the other hand, am now feeling anxious. As I hesitate Dan looks up. He sees me and his face breaks into a huge smile. It lights up his entire face and leaves me with no choice but to go inside the pub.

'Hi.' Dan stands as I reach him. I sense he wants to kiss me on the cheek. He doesn't, however, simply asking: 'What can I get you?'

I hesitate again. Somehow asking for a drink would make this feel like an illicit date.

'Nothing.' I sit down opposite him, still wearing my jacket. Dan frowns, but sits down too.

The pub is half-empty; most of the customers are gathered around a TV at the far end watching a football match. Ten years ago, Dan's eyes would have wandered everywhere, checking out all the punters, the football score, the passersby outside. But right now he keeps his stone-grey eyes fixed on me.

'You look cold,' he says. 'Are you sure you don't want a drink?' He indicates the pint glass on the table in front of him. 'I'm on beer, but they do good coffee here if you're not ready for alcohol.'

I look around. The pub is barely recognizable from when we used to come here all those years ago; it's been redecorated with leather couches and rickety-looking reclaimed wood tables.

'D'you remember coming here?' Dan asks.

I nod. Dan is still watching me intently. His cool, appraising gaze unsettles me, as it always did. I look away. This is ridiculous. I shouldn't be here. I want to leave but I don't know how to tell Dan it has been a mistake. And then he reaches across the table and touches my shoulder.

'Relax,' he says. 'Breathe.'

I let out a sigh, releasing my tense shoulders. The radiator beside the table is blasting out heat. Maybe I should take my jacket off and just get on with this.

Dan sits back as I slide the jacket off and the barmaid slouches over. She's very young and rather pretty, with slanting eyes and a beauty spot on her cheek. She fixes her eyes on Dan and smiles.

'Hiya.'

Dan flashes a smile back and I swear the girl blushes. 'What can I get your, er, friend?' She's asking about me though so far she hasn't taken her eyes off Dan.

Dan looks across at me and raises his eyebrows.

'Coffee, please.' I glance at the board on the wall behind her. 'Flat white.'

'Thank you.' Dan grins at the girl again and she sashays off.

'Waitress service in a pub?' I comment, letting an acerbic note creep into my voice. 'Aren't *you* the valued customer?'

Dan shrugs. 'They're just not very busy. I've only been in here a couple of times since I got back from the States.'

Outside, the first few flakes of snow are floating through the air. A child in a passing pushchair is pointing into the sky. Dan sits, waiting. His stillness is somehow both calming and unnerving. I look down at the table. It's rough to the touch, with a panel in the middle painted a greeny-blue. The colour reminds me of our old kitchen table. Some of my earliest and happiest memories took place kneeling on a chair at that table: just my mother and I, baking cakes for Martin and Rose when they came home from school. I look up, into Dan's eyes. I see intelligence and compassion. And curiosity.

'I don't think Lish likes me as much as he pretends to.'

Dan nods. I'm dreading him asking me what makes me

think this; I really don't want to have to tell him about the Facebook entry or the *IT SHOULD HAVE BEEN YOU* text or the look Lish gave me earlier. Much to my relief Dan doesn't ask for explanations.

'What about drugs? Have you seen anything that makes you think he's using? Or selling?'

'No, well, no actual drugs, but I did see a roll of banknotes in his bag. Jed gives him plenty of money, but that was definitely more than you'd expect for a student.'

'Right.' Dan looks thoughtful. 'So it's worth investigating, d'you agree?'

I waver for a moment, then nod. 'I suppose, but I still think it's far-fetched that he could be involved in any major dealing, let alone have anything remotely to do with potassium cyanide.'

'Okay.'

There's a long pause, but not an uncomfortable one. The silence between us is not awkward at all, I realize, it's just the pace at which we're talking, the pace at which I'm adapting to the fact that we're talking. It's a pace which I'm setting and Dan is following.

He still hasn't taken his eyes off me. As I look up at him he smiles.

'You used to talk more,' I say.

'You used to be fairly chatty yourself.' He grins. 'The night I met you I couldn't shut you up. Now we've had two coffees together and you've got nothing to say. I must be losing my touch.'

I smile back and glance at the barmaid who is heading towards us, my coffee in her hand.

'I don't think so.' I watch the girl as she places the cup on the rough wood of the table, slopping it slightly in the process. She glances coyly at Dan as he pays, then says thank you and wiggles off again without looking once in my direction.

Dan keeps his eyes fixed on me. 'I'm a reporter, Em,' he says. 'Mostly it works to let the other person talk. In your case, I'm not quite sure what I should do.'

'You're doing fine.' As soon as I've spoken, I can feel my cheeks flush. I didn't mean to sound so encouraging. I hurry on. 'So what do you think we should do now?'

Dan lowers his voice. 'I'm going to go back to Lish's university campus. I already know he's dealing. Maybe now I can arrange a meeting, actually talk to him, find out exactly what he supplies.'

I stare at him, aghast. 'You're going to pretend you want to buy *drugs* from him?'

Dan shrugs. 'It's like an undercover investigation, a sting. No biggie.'

'Jesus.' I let out a sigh. 'Oh, but Lish isn't actually at uni this weekend. Jed's just dropping him at his mum's now in fact. He said his plan was to go back to college on Monday evening.'

Dan nods. He's silent for a moment, then he looks up at me. 'Em, I've got an idea,' he says, still keeping his voice low. 'You'll probably think it's mad, but have you ever been to Lish's college? Do any of his friends there know you?'

'No,' I say. 'Why?'

'Well, right now you only have my word that Lish is involved with any kind of illegal activity, so why don't you come to his uni with me on Monday morning before Lish goes back? That way you'll be able to see for yourself what he's up to.'

'What? I've got work, there's Jed. I *can't*.'

'Of course you can. Southampton is only a couple of hours away. We can be there and back before Jed's home from work. You can call in sick at school. Once we're there I can take you to the pub where he's known as a dealer. If you think there's enough to go on, I'll put you on a train home and I'll stay on into the evening and try to meet him direct on Monday night when he's back. What do you think?'

My heart races. 'Why are you doing this? Why do you want to help me?'

There's a long pause. When Dan finally speaks he picks his way carefully across the words. 'Because I'm worried that the son of the man you are going to marry has tried to kill you and may try again. Because I might have walked out of your life eight years ago, but I still care about you. And because I *can* help you so I *should*.'

'Right.' Hearing Dan spell out everything like that makes me feel lost. Everything I had thought was certain has been stood on its head. I suddenly wish Rose was here.

She has such a strong sense of what's right and wrong, a morality she got from our parents which she has always tried to instil into me.

'Just think about coming with me to Southampton.' Dan glugs down the rest of his beer then replaces the glass on the table. 'Would you like another drink?'

I shake my head. Dan stands up. 'I'm going for a pee then if you like I can drop you at home – or nearby, if you don't want to be seen getting out of my car,' he says. 'I've only had the one drink, by the way, just in case you were wondering.'

'Okay, er, thanks.' I put my jacket on and wait outside, shivering in the few flakes of snow that whirl through the air. It's the soft, wet kind, turning to slush as it hits the pavement. Dan's suggestion to go to Southampton on Monday is crazy. But I can't stop thinking about how Lish looked earlier, or the money I found or the things he wrote:

bimbo cunt bitch

IT SHOULD HAVE BEEN YOU

I shudder as Dan emerges from the pub. We walk around the corner to the side road where he is parked. I can feel Dan's gaze lingering on my face, but I resist the tempt-ation to meet his eye. The streetlights cast a soft glow around us, the pavements glisten. We reach Dan's car, a silver BMW. When I knew him eight years ago, he could barely afford a second-hand Ford Focus in dire need of a paint job. The car reminds me that I still know nothing about his personal life.

'Do you have a house that goes with this vehicle?' I ask lightly.

Dan clicks open the central lock, then raises an eyebrow. 'Why? Because you never imagined I'd be able to afford either?'

I blush, unable to deny it. Dan rounds his eyes with exaggerated shock. 'Are you possibly suggesting that the only way I could make money would be to marry it, Ms Campbell?'

'No,' I say. 'Um ... *are* you married?'

Dan chuckles. 'No, never been there. And I live alone before you ask. I'm renting a two-bed apartment in what is laughingly known as Hoxton borders.'

'What about, you know, er, dating?' I ask, hoping my question sounds light and casual. I don't want Dan to think I'm *that* interested in his answer.

'Whenever I can fit it in around my work.' Dan opens the passenger door for me and stands back to let me into the car. 'You know me.'

So he hasn't changed. Not really. I feel both a sense of relief and of disappointment as I get inside the car. Which is when I decide. I *will* go with Dan to Southampton. Because he's right: I need to know the truth about Lish for myself.

Of course, when Monday morning arrives I am wracked with guilt as I call in sick at school. I spent the whole of yesterday catching up with every single piece of outstanding marking and making detailed plans for the rest of the week. I will have to add an extra rehearsal for the school production at the end of the week but, other than that, I am well ahead of myself. The school secretary utters a weary sigh when I mutter I'm feeling flu-ey and think I should stay at home.

'You're the third sick call I've had in the past twenty minutes,' she says with a groan. 'Feel better by tomorrow. Please.'

Guilt twists in my guts. I apologize and ring off. Jed has already left for work, of course. He has no idea about any of this. No one does. I considered confiding in Laura, but the thought of her sceptical reaction to my suspicions about Lish, *sorry but that sounds really far-fetched*, holds me back. I will have to tell her and Jed in the end. I will have to tell Jed everything.

Just not yet.

Dan arrives, as arranged, at ten o'clock. It's a crisp, clear day and our journey to Southampton speeds by. After our long silences in the pub, we are chatting and laughing with surprising ease within minutes of setting off. Dan asks about Martin and Rose and a few old, mutual friends he has lost touch with. I, in turn, enquire about his work. It seems he's doing really well, a regular contributor to several nationals and blogs.

'And what about the rest of your life? You said you weren't married, but what about significant relationships?' I ask as casually as I can.

'No girlfriends as such.' Dan gives a shrug and it's there in the slight incline of his head: he's keeping something from me.

'You mean no one at the moment?' I press.

Dan concentrates on turning a corner. I'm almost certain he's buying himself time to think. But what does he need to think about? Why is my question so difficult for him?

'I broke up with someone in the States last year,' he says. 'Nice girl. Californian so almost as much of a foreigner in New York as I was. We worked in the same office. It was ...' He raises his hand from the steering wheel then carefully places it back. 'It was okay. Nothing major. She was the last person I dated for more than a few weeks.'

'I see.' I'm still sure there's something he's not saying, but before I can work out a way to phrase another question, Dan is speaking again.

'What about Jed and you?' he asks with a grin. 'I never imagined you'd end up with someone so much older.'

'You make him sound geriatric – he's only fifty,' I protest.

'Still, what are you doing with a fifty-year-old?' Dan winces. 'Sorry, that came out wrong. I'm just trying to understand how you two got together.'

'He swept me off my feet,' I say, trying – and failing – to resist the urge to impress Dan with Jed's romantic entry into my life. 'He knew what he wanted from the start.'

'Mmmn.' Dan nods, slowing to take a right turn. 'Good for Jed. I'm pleased he makes you happy.' He glances at my

161

bracelet. The gold is glinting in the sunlight. 'Did Jed give you that?'

'No, that was my brother and his boyfriend, an engagement present. They gave Dee Dee one identical.'

'Pretty,' Dan says. 'Your brother always had good taste.'

I nod, wondering what Martin would say if he knew I was seeing Dan today. He would understand my need to find out the truth about Lish, but he would also, I am sure, warn me that Dan Thackeray messed me around once before and I should think very carefully before trusting him.

Once in Southampton, Dan consults the GPS on his iPad then heads for what he tells me is the main student pub off campus. It's a spit and plywood sort of place with a few tatty Christmas decorations hanging limply from the wall above the bar. I gaze at a row of plastic Santas as Dan fetches us both an orange juice then peers around the room. Considering it's only just past midday, the pub is packed.

'It's good that the people I saw last time aren't here,' he says. 'Don't want anyone getting suspicious.'

A thrill wriggles through me. Despite the constant ache of losing Dee Dee, my anxieties about Lish, plus today's guilt over missing school and withholding information from Jed – I am enjoying myself here, with Dan. It feels like an adventure. It feels like fun.

More fun than maybe it should.

I push the thought away.

Dan's eyes alight on a young couple huddled in the corner. I have no idea why he thinks they might be in the know about who can supply anything illegal around here, but I let him lead me over. We sit at the table opposite. After a while, the guy looks up and notices Dan watching him. A moment later he whispers to his girlfriend, who gets up and leaves. As she passes our table, she nods swiftly at Dan. And that's all it takes.

'Come on.' Dan leads me over to the young guy. Close to, I can see that his fingernails are bitten and there's a rather fusty smell emanating from his grubby T-shirt. We sit down. The young guy looks from me to Dan.

'What do you need?' he asks quietly.

'Valium,' Dan says. 'Vicodin. Maybe other stuff too.'

The guy purses his lips. 'Not my scene.'

Dan nods. 'I heard there was a guy . . . weird name. Lesh or Losh or something?'

The guy studies him. 'You mean Lish?'

I hold my breath.

'That's it,' Dan says. 'Lish Kennedy.'

'Not around.' The guy sits back. 'I could probably fix you up with someone else.'

'I'd like Lish,' Dan says. 'He comes recommended.'

'I bet.' The guy smiles, revealing a set of surprisingly small white teeth. 'Lish can get his hands on anything chemical. Try here tomorrow night, after nine or so. He should be here then.'

'Thanks.' We pick up our orange juices and go back to our table where we finish the drinks in silence. My hand trembles on the glass. So it's true. Lish is trading in pharmaceutical drugs, just like Dan said. I drain the juice and set it down.

'Do you want me to ask anyone else?' Dan asks, putting his own glass on the table beside mine.

'No.' I can't quite take in that Dan was right about Lish's dealing. Not that peddling a bit of Valium and Vicodin connects him in any way to potassium cyanide, but still . . .

'Are you all right?' Dan asks. 'Do you want me to take you to the station?'

I shake my head. The truth is that the exchange with the guy in the grubby T-shirt has raised more questions than it has answered. Now I've had this fresh and disturbing insight into Lish's secret life I need to know more.

Beside me Dan watches and waits. I chew on my lip, an idea forming in my head. Then I turn to him, meeting the stone grey of his eyes full on.

'I want to look in Lish's room in his student flat,' I say. 'See if we can find out more about the stuff he's dealing in, maybe even get a hold of some of the illegal supplies. It'll be proof – well, a starting point for me to talk to Jed . . . maybe a proper police investigation.'

Dan blinks, startled. 'You're saying you want to break in to his home?'

'No. I don't know. I just . . .' I tail off, uncertain exactly what I *am* proposing.

Dan looks thoughtful. 'Does Lish live on his own?' he asks.

'No, Jed bought him a three-bed flat in Portswood.'

Dan raises his eyebrows. 'He bought his son an entire flat?'

I shrug. 'He said it would be cheaper in the end than rent for another two years. He pays for Lish's clothes, his iPhone, everything, he's very generous.' I stop, wondering why on earth I'm bigging Jed up so much. 'Anyway, Lish rents out the other two rooms to students, friends. I don't know if they'll be in or not.'

'Let's hope so.' Dan gives me a mischievous grin and stands up. 'I've got an idea. I'll explain on the way.'

I grin back, feeling suddenly reckless, then grab my jacket and follow him to the door. The freezing air outside stings my skin. The sky is still bright and clear. It's a beautiful afternoon. By the time we've reached the car our cheeks have a rosy glow and our noses are pink from the cold.

Dan finds Lish's road on his sat nav and we drive straight there while Dan explains his plan. It's almost 2 p.m., the sun about as high in the sky as it's going to get at this point in December. I stare at the light against the trees and go over what I'm going to have to say in order to get myself inside.

'So you're sure neither of the other tenants will recognize you?' Dan asks.

'Definitely not,' I say. 'I've never met them. I just know there's a girl and a boy.'

A moment later the sat nav tells us we have reached our destination. Dan slows and I peer out of the window, examining the buildings as we pass. I've seen pictures of Lish's modern apartment block and I know it's on the corner of a road with a large hedge in front, so I'm hopeful it won't be too hard to recognize.

Dan drives up and down. On the second pass I spot it.

'That's it.' I point.

Dan parks his car on the street opposite the hedge and stows his iPad in the glove compartment.

'How come you've never been here before?' he asks.

'Lish only moved in at the end of last term and Jed and Zoe brought him down together. I, er, I wasn't involved ...'

'... because the former Mrs Kennedy doesn't want anything to do with the soon-to-be?'

'She hates my guts for stealing her husband,' I say, then feel the urge to defend myself and the affair that led to Jed leaving his wife. 'Not that it was really like that. Jed and Zoe were virtually separated when I met him. I mean, it wasn't like I seduced him away from her. He just ... it just wasn't that simple.'

A beat passes. 'It never is.' Dan is still gazing at the drive beyond the hedge that leads to Lish's student flat.

I shoot a look at him. Is he being sarcastic? I can't read his expression.

'I'm just saying Jed was desperately unhappy in his marriage,' I go on, hating how defensive I sound but unable to stop myself. I don't want Dan to judge me harshly. Which is ridiculous. Of all people, Dan has absolutely no right to criticize me for anything I do in my personal life. And why should I care about his opinion anyway? 'Zoe treated him like shit,' I persist. 'She still does.'

Dan is still looking out of the car window. 'I'm sure it was complicated,' he says, his voice soft and low. 'Anyway, I can't blame him for falling in love with you ...' he turns and his eyes fix on mine '... having been there myself.'

For a second the air between us seems to crackle, as if all the oxygen is being sucked out of it. Then Dan turns away and opens his door and the cold air rushes in.

I follow him out of the car, feeling unsettled. I tug my jacket around me and we stand on the pavement, looking across at the apartment block.

'Which flat is it?' Dan asks.

'Ground floor, 1B.' I peer at the front of the ground floor. The curtains are drawn and there's no sign of anyone inside. 'Perhaps it's empty after all.'

'Let's hope not,' Dan says. He goes over the plan one last time. 'Okay?' he finishes.

I bite my lip, unsure now I'm here if I can really go as far as he's suggesting. And yet, if it works, I will get to explore Lish's room without the other residents even knowing I'm there.

The image of Lish's disgusted face in the hall mirror flashes before my mind's eye. I *have* to find out more about his drugs connection. If there's a stash in his room, I'll have something concrete to take to Jed.

Or the police.

I owe it to Dee Dee to try at least.

I shiver. I mustn't get ahead of myself.

'Let's go,' I say.

And together we cross the road.

June 2014

It's STILL going on at school. Not the pointing and talking so much, but the ignoring me, even though Sam happened around my birthday which was over three weeks ago. I was at Daddy and Emily's for the weekend and it's just like last weekend and the weekends before that ... nobody calls me or includes me in anything. Ava and Poppy have, like, decided they don't want to be friends since what happened with Sam, which doesn't even make sense. I've tried to tell them that I got all confused when I was with him but Ava said I had some serious thinking to do and Poppy said she thought I was maybe attention seeking because of my parents getting a divorce. It was weird, actually, because she acted all like she felt sorry for me – and I thought maybe she was, after all her parents split up too – but afterwards I saw her talking to Georgia Dutton who she's got REALLY friendly with now and they looked over at me like I was a disease they might catch.

I don't even feel anything about it now, like it's just the way things are. I'm doing my homework and paying attention in lessons and it's just during break time and after school that it's bad. Mum's still upset about the divorce. She keeps asking me how I feel about it. I know she wants me to say I'm really upset too and that

I hate Emily, but I don't like saying that because it feels mean to Daddy. Anyway, the truth is – and I can't tell Mum this OBVIOUSLY – but I like Emily. She's really pretty and she's fun and she makes Daddy laugh. She's cool, too. She teaches little kids who are, like, SO cute and she talks to me like she cares how I am but without pushing me into saying stuff or trying to be like she's all 'my mum'. She wears great make-up too and has awesome clothes. She lets me go through all her stuff and doesn't mind at all. I think she sees things in people too, not like being psychic but just understanding them. She knew I was upset soon as I arrived on Friday. I don't know how. She hadn't seen it the time before, but maybe I was trying harder to cover it up then. Anyway, earlier today when Daddy was up in his office and we were in the kitchen, I was checking my phone to see if Ava or Poppy had sent me a message which of course they hadn't and Emily was making bread in the breadmaker which is funny because I remember Mum saying she wanted one and Daddy saying 'women never use things like that, they just clutter up the kitchen' and here he is now and Emily has one and DOES use it.

So Emily looks over and asks if I'm all right and I say 'sure' and Emily says 'Ah, well, if you ever need to talk, if there's ever a problem . . .' and I didn't even look up but she carries on and says 'my parents died in a car crash when I was a bit younger than you so I know about problems'. And then I DID look up because I really wasn't expecting that, like Daddy never said a THING. And I said 'really, you mean in a car accident, all sudden?' and Emily looked sad and said 'yes, afterwards my sister looked after us, me and my brother, I'm the youngest like you'. And I didn't know what to say so I just looked at her and Emily went on and said her big sister was called Rose and was like half a mum and half a sister to her and her big brother was called Martin and he was five years older than her, like Lish is six years older than me so almost exactly the same. And then she said she hoped I'd meet Rose and Martin soon and I still didn't know what to say so I just nodded but when I left for Daddy to bring me home earlier I gave her a big hug.

December 2014

Dan and I reach the hedgerow that separates the front yard of the small apartment block from the street. 'Okay,' Dan says. 'Give me the ring.'

I tug my diamond engagement ring off my finger. Dan examines it for a moment. 'It's beautiful,' he says.

'Thanks,' I say, though in actual fact I had nothing to do with picking the thing out. Jed presented it to me on my birthday in July, eyes shining, irrepressible, irresistible. He told me how he'd already spoken to Dee Dee and Lish about his plan to propose, and how delighted they had been. Lish must have been lying about that. Oh, God, if Jed knew I was here – with Dan, spying on Lish – he would feel betrayed. I feel a deep twinge of guilt, then shake myself. This has to happen. And better that I spare Jed any details until I know beyond doubt the truth about Lish's drug dealing.

Dan crouches down and presses the ring into the crusty earth. The diamond sparkles in the bright sun.

'Will it be safe?' I ask.

'Yes, once we're past the next thirty seconds,' Dan says with a grin. 'Ready?'

I nod, then creep around the far side of the hedge. From here I can see the front door of the block. Dan crosses the front yard. Weeds poke up between the broken concrete slabs. I shiver as Dan reaches the door. He straightens his jumper, smooths his hair. He rings the doorbell.

A few moments later a girl – presumably Lish's female flatmate – opens it. She looks about his age, in skinny jeans and hot pink DM boots. Her long dark hair is dyed blue at the ends – a straight line, as if it's been dipped in ink. Dan immediately steps back, head down, slightly hunched.

'I'm sorry to bother you.' He offers up an anxious smile. The girl stares at him suspiciously.

My heart thuds.

'I was just passing. I'm in a bit of a rush, actually. I saw some jewellery over by the hedge. I wondered if someone here dropped it?'

'Not me.' The girl starts to shut the door, but Dan is talking again.

'Okay, look, I'm not usually such a good Samaritan, but it's a beautiful ring. I don't know much, but I can tell it's worth over ten grand. I'm in a crazy hurry to get to my mum in hospital, otherwise I'd take it to the police myself, but someone should look after it. The owner must be going mad.' Dan backs away, pointing to the hedge. 'It's just on the ground there.'

The girl is still looking at him suspiciously, but she is no longer shutting the door.

Dan reaches the hedge. He points to the ground where the ring is, then holds up his hands.

'I've got to go, do what you like, but it's there and someone should look after it.' Then he turns and crosses the road.

I watch the girl. She walks out of the building a little way so she can see Dan reach his car. He gets into it without looking around, revs the engine and drives away. I hold my breath. The girl glances back at the building. The front door is still open, but no one is around.

She strides purposefully over to the hedge. As she disappears from sight, I race across the yard. Not looking back I tear inside, carefully closing the front door behind me, as Dan instructed. The door to flat 1B is on my right, on the latch. I push it open, fly inside and shut the door. Dan said I could allow myself ten minutes. I need to make every second of each one count.

It's a small flat and I find Lish's bedroom in seconds. It's the largest of the three and easily identifiable from the photo of Dee Dee pinned to the wall above the desk, which is cluttered with text books and empty beer bottles.

I rummage through the books, pushing each one aside in turn. I open the drawers. They are stuffed with clothes apart from the bottom one, which contains a collection of hair gels and a pack of green condoms.

I get on my knees and peer under the bed. Two cans of Lynx and a sheaf of papers nestle beside a suitcase. I pull the papers out, they're just handouts from Lish's Media course.

I open the suitcase. More clothes.

I shove it all back under the bed and cast around the room. Outside the flat I can hear the dim buzz of a doorbell. Lish's flatmate has obviously returned and, as we planned, is locked out of the building. I'm guessing she is trying all the other flats, hoping someone will buzz her through. I gulp. I'm running out of time. Where else might Lish keep his drugs?

My eyes light on the wardrobe in the corner of the room. Clothes litter the floor around it. I race over and fling open the doors. It's a large closet with shelves on one side and a hanging rail across the other. I search the shelves methodically, pulling out the jumpers and socks randomly hurled inside. I come across sweet wrappers and two empty cans of beer. No drugs of any kind.

I sink to the floor to ransack the bottom shelf. I pull out two pairs of trainers. Outside in the hallway I can hear the girl's voice, loud and clear. Someone has obviously let her into the main building, though she is still locked out of the flat itself. She is swearing, angry that the latch must have slipped. She doesn't mention my ring to whoever she's talking to.

My heart drums against my ribs as my fingers fumble at the very back of the shelf. There's a piece of paper here. No, an envelope, addressed to Lish; something about the handwriting is familiar. I am shaking as I pull out the letter inside. It's dated 26 July, a few days after my birthday and Jed's proposal, and is written in elegant, spidery writing over two crisp white pages. My stomach clenches painfully as I read. The girl's voice in the hallway fades away.

Dearest Lishy

It is late. I am alone and unable to sleep. Your father's words are going around in my head. Earlier tonight he told me about his wedding plans with that whore of his. He said he has already given you his news. Stupid, stupid man, forcing you and poor Dee Dee to keep this ugly, horrible secret from me. I have been patient, waiting for the scales to lift from his eyes but they have not. So I must make sure, now, they do not fall on yours. Yes. It is time for you to know the truth about your father and his whore who, if we are not careful, may end up taking everything from us.

Firstly your dad: I hate to have to tell you this but he is a weak, stupid man who was unfaithful to me many times throughout your childhood. I stayed with him not just for your and Dee Dee's sake, but because I loved him and because none of the women he had his passing flings with actually threatened the heart of our marriage. That remained – and indeed remains – a pure and beautiful thing. My darling, I don't expect you to understand any of this, but you can and must know that despite his weakness your father never once thought of leaving us and his family home until that evil whore came into his life.

I shake my head. This isn't true. *Can't* be. Jed told me many times how the marriage had been over for years, how he had only stayed as long as he did for the children.

I know Emily Campbell has a pretty face and that she is
young and, as the saying has it, there is no fool like an old
fool, especially where middle-aged men and pretty girls are
concerned. But this one is a home-wrecker.

So . . . here it is, the reason why I am putting this in a
letter which I hope you will destroy, rather than an email
which will live online forever. The whore does not, I repeat
not, love your father. Her own parents died when she was
eleven years old – a drink driving incident, I believe – and
she is clearly looking for a father figure to look after her.

The first page of the letter ends. I force myself back to
the girl's voice in the hall.

'Yeah, I think Lish left it with 3A,' she is saying. 'I'd call
and ask him but my bloody mobile's locked in the flat with
everything else.' Footsteps on the stairs, then silence.

I look back down at the letter. Heart in my mouth, I turn
to the second and final page.

That whore just wants your father's attention. And his
money. I have spoken to people about this, my darling, and it
is painfully clear she is a gold digger, intent only on getting
hold of your father's money, of your rightful inheritance. She
will take it and spend it and there will be nothing left for you
and your sister. Oh Lish, I have no one to turn to except you,
my brave boy. I intend to challenge the whore myself, but I
suspect it will not be enough. I will need your help to get
through this. I'm sorry to ask anything of you, but there is no

choice. Your stupid father and that bitch of his have put us all in this position. It will only get worse. Your sister is miserable. She is comfort eating and withdrawn into herself, unwilling to talk to me about her feelings as she once did.

The whore must be stopped. And somehow you must help me stop her. It will be a liberation for us all, a good thing, an act of kindness to remove her and her evil from our lives. She is not human, no human could inflict this pain so callously, so happily. She cannot be allowed to get away with it, to take everything from us. She cannot be allowed.

I love you, my darling, more than I can say.

Mum xxx

I clutch the letter in my hand. Lines splash around my brain.

The whore must be stopped. And somehow you must help me stop her. She cannot be allowed.

With a jolt everything falls into place. Zoe *did* send me that text back in September: *IT SHOULD HAVE BEEN YOU, WHORE.* She has wanted me dead this whole time, since Jed left her in fact. And just as she has the motive, so Lish, through his drug dealing, has the means.

Not Zoe *or* Lish, but Zoe *and* Lish.

Together they tried to kill me and Dee Dee died instead.

My legs are trembling as I stand up. I shove the letter in my bag then hurry to the flat's front door. I open it carefully. Upstairs, I can hear the girl from this flat thanking whoever is in 3A for the spare key.

There's no time to get across the hallway and outside the building. Anyway, Dan insisted I should stay 'even if you feel like running, Em' – in order to get my ring back. Hands shaking, I close the flat's front door. A second later the girl reappears. She sees me loitering in the hall and slows her swift jog down the stairs.

'Can I help you?' she says, her voice as sullen as it is suspicious.

'Hi,' I say with an apologetic smile. I indicate the front door to the building. 'Sorry to barge in but it was open so I came through. I think I dropped my ring outside earlier. I was just calling by on the off-chance someone here picked it up.'

The girl's hand goes to the pocket of her skinny jeans. I follow her gaze. I'm betting that's where she's put my ring. Will she admit to it? Earlier, Dan had said we would be fine so long as the girl didn't either stop to think about how he had spotted the ring from his car or pretend to me that she hadn't found it.

'She'll take it in,' he had said. 'Either from greed or pity. But if she doesn't confess she's got it ...'

I look her in the eye. No way am I letting her keep the ring. 'Have you seen it?' I ask, a steely edge to my voice. 'I'm pretty certain it came off when I took off my gloves. It's a bit big, needs resizing.'

'A ring?' the girl asks.

'Yes,' I persist. I'm trying to focus but I keep thinking of the letter, stuffed in my handbag. *The whore must be stopped.*

And somehow you must help me stop her. She cannot *be allowed.* 'An oval-shaped diamond on a platinum band. Did you see it?'

There's a slight pause, then the girl digs the ring out of her pocket. She jogs down the remaining steps and hands it to me.

'Thank you.' My heart is still going at ninety miles an hour. 'Thanks so much.' I turn and walk quickly to the building's front door. Once outside, I have to stop myself from legging it until I'm on the pavement. I turn left and race to the end of the road. Dan is parked exactly where he said he would be, just around the corner. I open the passenger door of his car and he drives off. As I put my ring back on its finger I realize I'm still shaking.

Zoe wants me dead. I have proof that she has urged her son to kill me.

Dan glances down at the ring on my hand. 'You got it back. Did you get inside? Was it okay? What did you find?'

I shake my head.

'Are you all right, Em? You look white as a—'

'I'm okay,' I whisper. 'But ... but ...'

Dan frowns. 'Did you find drugs? Potassium cyanide? What happened?'

'No drugs,' I say. My throat is choked. Two fat tears trickle silently down my face. I am still trembling.

I'm certain now that Lish tried to kill me just like Dan said.

He did it for his mother. And his sister died instead.

A new thought punches me – a body blow on a bruise: if Lish and Zoe tried once, why haven't they tried again? Are they just waiting for the right time?

Dan pulls over and parks the car at the side of the road.

'Em?' He holds out his hand. I squeeze it. Then let go. I want, in this moment, to let him hold me and reassure me but I can't. What I should do is go back to Jed and tell him everything. Except I can't tell Jed because that means explaining that I came here with Dan and virtually broke into Lish's student flat. Or does what I found cancel out the crime I committed? I can't work it out.

'Em, I'm worried about you.' Dan leans forward and puts his arm around my shoulder.

His jumper smells of soap and bonfires. I'm transported back to our first proper date, at the Alexandra Palace fireworks display, ironically close to where I now live in Muswell Hill with Jed. We went to a party afterwards. There was a huge bonfire in a big shared house – lots of beer and dancing. Dan and I danced and kissed. He was the centre of the party, a magnet for both the other guys who were there – and plenty of the girls too. But wherever he went and whoever he spoke to, he introduced me proudly, barely leaving my side all evening.

I pull away. Dan looks down at me, his forehead creased with a concerned frown. 'I'm going to stay here, try and meet up with Lish tomorrow, like I said I would. You're sure there weren't any drugs in his flat?'

SOPHIE MCKENZIE

'I wasn't there long enough to be sure, but I didn't find anything like that in his bedroom.'

Dan looks at me curiously. I can see he knows I am hiding something from him and is holding himself back from pressing me about it with difficulty. I gaze into his anxious eyes. I have to get away from him. I need to clear my head. I will call Laura. Or my sister. Yes, it's Rose I need to see. I need to talk to my wise, caring big sister.

'*Em?*' Dan's eyes glisten with concern. I have a sudden and powerful desire to reach over and kiss him.

I resist, berating myself for such a stupid impulse. I'm just all jangled up. I need to get away from Dan and go to Rose.

The whore must be stopped. And somehow you must help me stop her. She cannot *be allowed.*

I need Rose.

June 2014

I hate my life. Hate it. HATE IT. Right now I'm in my room
hiding from Mum. Ever since I got back she's been asking and
asking about Emily, pushing me to say how rubbish it was being
with her and Daddy. I can't STAND it. I REALLY want to tell
Ava or Poppy just how bad it is, but I've been on everything and
they can see I'm online but they are all ignoring me and when I
join in a chat they just go somewhere else and I don't know where.
It's not fair. Mum is worse than EVER. I mean she always asks
about Emily but since I got home it's been, like, CONSTANT,
things like 'what did Emily cook?' and 'what was Emily wearing?'
and 'was Emily nice to you?' – all sneering – and I never know
what to say because if I say it was good and Emily – for instance –
had a really cool skirt on she gets all upset, things like: 'well of
course it's easy to look good in a mini when you're so young' in that
voice where she sounds like she's pinching it out of her throat even
though I NEVER said it was a miniskirt BUT if I say being with
Emily was bad though it isn't except when Daddy gets annoyed,
like when we go out to eat and he wants me to choose grown-up
things that I don't like or not have a pudding cos I'm so FAT, then
Mum gets upset anyway, about how awful it is Daddy's being so

183

selfish and what were they thinking taking me out on a Saturday night, 'your father seems to think he's twenty-one again'.

Anyway, here I am all alone. I can't tell Emily about everyone hating me at school because Mum would get upset and I can't tell Mum because she'd somehow find a way to blame Dad and Emily for it. Anyway, Mum wouldn't understand.

Nobody does.

December 2014

It takes me almost four hours to get to Rose's house. There's a delay on the main train to Waterloo, then engineering works on the slower line into south-east London. Rose is home from work when I let myself in. I can hear her upstairs in her room. I shout 'hello' and head into the living room where the fire is on and it's warm and cosy. It's reassuring, calming, to be here where everything is so familiar. In spite of this, Rose sees that I'm upset as soon as she walks into the room.

'What's wrong?' she asks.

'Oh, Rose.'

We sit down on the battered old couch opposite the TV. The latter is state-of-the-art, a present from Martin for Rose's birthday a couple of years ago. The sofa, on the other hand, is badly in need of re-covering. Rose has said, many times, that she will one day have it reupholstered but I know that she, like me, has a sentimental attachment to the threadbare blue chenille with its shiny patches from the many heads that have rested against its high back. As I sit there I think of Dad, where Rose is right now, watching

Match of the Day and Mum, in my seat, with her reading glasses on, legs tucked under her, flicking through a magazine. My memories are fuzzy – mostly, I suspect, arising from photos and videos rather than actual recollections. Of all the things I resent about my parents' death, the lack of real memories is one of the hardest to bear, especially as my brother and sister are so easily able to recount so many memories themselves.

'What's up?' Rose asks again.

I take a good look at my older sister. She's in casual clothes – jeans and a jumper – but there's that same highly groomed air about her that I noticed at Martin's birthday party. Her eyebrows look freshly plucked and her hair has been carefully teased into place. She's wearing full make-up again too. The overall effect is to make her look younger than she has done in years.

'You look lovely.' As I speak I wonder, not for the first time, what on earth would have become of me when our parents died if Rose hadn't taken me on. Martin might be my hero, but Rose is my lodestar.

'Thanks.' Rose smiles, then settles back on the couch. 'Now, spill.'

I take a breath, steady myself – then I tell her everything, starting with Dan's arrival in the staff car park at school earlier in the month. Rose sits forward, listening intently. As I come to my exploration of Lish's student flat, I take the letter Zoe sent him out of my bag and hand it over.

'I can't get what it says out of my head,' I explain. 'I really think Zoe wants me dead. I mean, her letter says she is going to come and see me, which she did, in the car park at school, remember? Exactly like she says there. And it *wasn't* enough to stop me and Jed, just like she predicts. Plus there was this text from a withheld number that I was sent just after they discovered the cyanide in the ExAche. It said: *IT SHOULD HAVE BEEN YOU, WHORE.* Which I'm *certain* was from Zoe. It all adds up. I really think she got Lish to try and kill me but Dee Dee died instead.' I pause. 'I'm scared, Rose.'

Rose nods. Her lips are pressed tightly together as she pores over the letter. I can't tell what she's thinking.

'D'you see what I mean?' I say at last. 'Zoe wants me dead.'

Rose looks up. 'I don't know that I'd read that into it.'

'Really?' I'm surprised. 'But she's telling Lish she wants him to help her "stop" me.'

'Exactly. "Stop" you, not "murder" you. She's just mouthing off ... asking for his support.'

'Oh.' There's a long pause. 'Do you think I should tell Jed?' I ask after a while.

Rose's eyes widen. 'God, no,' she says.

I'm surprised by how emphatic she sounds.

'But ... don't you think he'd *want* to know?'

'Want to know what?' Rose puts down the letter. 'That his adored fiancée thinks half his family are bent on murdering her? That you've snooped into private rooms, private homes ... Jesus, even private letters between a mother and a son?' She smiles, but there's a real edge to her voice as well as her words.

I gasp, bewildered. 'But I needed to know,' I protest. 'I was scared, I thought you'd understand.'

'I *do* understand. I get that you were scared. But all these bits and pieces of information you've been gathering don't add up in the way you think they do,' she says. 'I can't believe you've fallen for Dan Thackeray again, either.'

'I *haven't* fallen for him,' I insist. 'He hasn't tried anything on, he says he just wants to make sure I'm safe.'

'If you ask me, he wants to get back in your pants,' Rose says. 'He's spinning you a yarn.'

'I don't think so. It's not like he came to me with made-up facts, he just pointed out the connection between Dee Dee being poisoned and Lish selling drugs at his university.'

'What connection?' Rose asks. 'Even if Lish is really a dealer, he's hardly likely to be dealing in potassium cyanide.'

I gulp. 'What about that?' I point to the letter in her hand. 'Zoe wrote that I shouldn't "be allowed". Surely you can see why I'm disturbed? I mean she sounds so angry, like in the "should have been you" text.'

'Of course she sounds angry, but that doesn't mean she's making serious threats against your life. Come on, Emily. *You'd* be angry if some beautiful girl who has men falling at her feet decided to steal *your* husband.'

'It wasn't like that.' Tears spring to my eyes. 'You *know*

it wasn't. I never meant to hurt her or any of Jed's family.'

'I know.' Rose sighs. She reaches for my hand. 'I'm sorry, Em. I didn't mean to sound so harsh. I just think Dan's come along and planted some ridiculous idea in your head and you're letting him get you all carried away. Just like before.'

'Nothing's happened between me and Dan. And it's not going to. Anyway, I thought you *liked* Dan?'

'Back when you were both twenty-three, I did. He was fun. Charming. But I never trusted him to stick around. Which, you'll have noticed, he didn't.'

I stare at her. Irony is very much not Rose's style.

'And now he's back out of the blue,' she goes on. 'Winding you up and watching you go.'

'So ... so you don't think I should tell Jed?'

'Definitely not. Jed will just be hurt and upset. There's no point.'

'What about Lish? He hates me.'

Rose shrugs. 'You'll just have to give that time.'

'What about his dealing? He's trading in illegal pharmaceuticals. Should I give that "time"?'

'*Allegedly* trading. So far, all you know is that some guy in a pub mentioned his name. Dan could have set that up.'

I frown. 'Why would Dan do that?'

'To get you back, maybe?'

'That's crazy. Dan hadn't seen me for years before he told me what he's found out about Lish.'

'Believe me, I know how stupid men can be. Men like Dan are all about the chase. He'll have seen that you're getting married to someone more successful than he is, and he wants to put a spanner in the works because he thinks he can.' Rose sniffs. 'Don't give him the satisfaction.'

'I still think it's far-fetched to think Dan would get some guy to pretend Lish was a drug dealer.'

'Okay, but even if Lish *is* involved in something dodgy, so what? It's none of your business. I promise you that if you weigh in to tell Jed all about it, he won't thank you.'

I stare at her.

Rose bites her lip. 'As you know, I've had relationships with men who had kids from their marriages, including Simon. And what do I always say?'

'Never challenge them on their kids.'

'Exactly. Anyway, imagine the conversation if you do tell Jed any of this. You'll have to admit you went snooping around in Southampton then broke into Lish's flat. Jed will be devastated. Come on, Emily, he's *besotted* with you to the point where he doesn't even *look* at other women. How do you think he'll feel when he discovers how far behind his back you've gone?'

'I haven't . . . I just . . .' I'm reeling, too stunned to think properly. Have I been unfair on Jed? Everything has happened so fast today I haven't had a chance to think about it. 'I love Jed and I would *never* do anything to hurt him.'

'Good.' Rose pats my arm. 'That's good, Em. So apply that determined, rational voice you used there to all this nonsense about Lish hating you and Zoe wanting you dead. I mean, okay, so you've had a funny look from Lish and stumbled across a private outpouring of hurt and anger from Zoe ... but it's crazy to think that *she* would get him to kill you *or* that *he* would bungle it so badly that his own sister dies instead. It's ludicrous. Totally melodramatic.'

I pick at a loose thread on the sofa. Perhaps Rose is right. Shame flushes my cheeks.

'So you don't think I should worry?' I ask.

'Oh, sweetie.' Rose gathers me towards her in a hug. 'I really don't, and I don't think you should see Dan again either. Dee Dee was killed because Benecke Tricorp was negligent. That's what you need to remember.'

I pull away from her, keen to change the subject. 'You really are looking great. Is there someone new?'

'Not since Simon. Not that I'm still upset about that, but when he left me I realized that I'd maybe been a bit of a doormat around him, that I needed to go out and get a life. Then maybe someone will turn up ... you know, when I'm not expecting it. So I've decided to get my degree at last. Art History, something *interesting*.'

'That sounds brilliant,' I say, impressed. Rose has been talking about possibly doing a degree for as long as I can remember.

Rose shrugs and changes the subject to our brother and his relationship with Cameron. 'So there have definitely been hints from both of them about getting married,' she says. 'It came up several times at Mart's birthday do. All their friends think they'll say something soon.'

My stomach rumbles with hunger, reminding me that Jed will be expecting me home soon. It's a long trek from the house where I grew up all the way north to Muswell Hill. I stand up and ferry my mug to the kitchen sink. There are three dirty bowls and a plate waiting to be washed up. I clean them automatically. Rose might have looked after me when I was growing up, but she instilled a sense of personal responsibility into me too, always insisting I did my fair share of housework after Mum and Dad were gone.

As I finish, Rose's mobile rings from the kitchen table. Someone called Brian is calling. I pick the phone up and hurry back into the living room in time to hear the downstairs loo flushing.

'Hi,' I say into the phone.

'Hello, sexy girl.' The man's voice is a soft growl.

I'm thrown, beyond startled.

'Er, I'm not Rose,' I say quickly, feeling my cheeks burn. 'I'm her sister, she's just ... she should be back any second.'

Silence on the other end of the line.

'Er, hello?'

The line goes dead as Rose reappears.

I hand her the mobile. 'Someone called Brian just rang for you,' I say, still blushing.

'Right.' Rose takes the phone and settles herself back onto the sofa.

'So who's Brian?' I ask.

Rose's head shoots up. 'What did he say?'

'Enough to make me think there's something going on between the two of you.' I raise my eyebrows. 'How do you know him?'

Rose's gaze is level and cool. 'He's just a customer, comes into the shop sometimes. I think he has a bit of a crush on me.' She waves her hand dismissively. 'Nothing I can't deal with.'

'I see,' I say.

'Really, it's nothing,' Rose insists. She smiles. 'Now get home to your lovely man,' she says. 'And forget about Dan Thackeray and all his nonsense.'

It's eight thirty when I get home to find the kitchen warm and scented with garlic and herbs. Jed has made a real effort with dinner. He's defrosted and marinated some steaks ready to go under the grill, and made a huge salad which is already sitting on the kitchen table alongside a bottle of wine. He's even been outside and picked some sprigs of holly from our back garden. Their red berries catch the light from the candle he has set down beside the wine. I'm touched by his desire to make the evening special.

'What's all this in aid of?' I ask with a smile.

'Just wanted you to know how much I love you,' he says. 'Plus . . .' He points to a sheet of paper on the counter. 'We have something to celebrate: the decree nisi came through.'

I grin. 'That's wonderful.'

'I know. Only six more weeks and Zoe and I won't be married any more. Hey, come here.'

I shrug off my jacket and Jed draws me close. I relax into his hug then lift my face up to be kissed. It's impossible not to compare the ease of our intimacy with the awkwardness I felt when Dan put his arm around me earlier. Here I am truly at home. In every sense.

Jed groans softly as he hugs me, his hands running down, over my back, then lower.

'You have the world's best ass, baby.'

I laugh and he takes my face in his hands. 'I don't say it enough,' he says, his eyes intent on mine. 'But I do realize that I come with a *lot* of baggage and I am deeply grateful that you are so brilliant at coping with it all.'

Guilt sears through me. For a moment I'm overwhelmed with the desire to confess everything – then I remember Rose's advice to let it go, that there is no point upsetting him. Instead we talk a bit about the decree nisi, which leads to Jed reporting that Zoe called him earlier, ostensibly to ask about the case against Benecke Tricorp.

'Of course it turned into the usual nightmare within minutes,' he complains. 'I'm starting to think she's really only interested in the law suit so she can carry on berating me for everything I've ever done to her.' He sighs. 'She was talking about Dee Dee, how she'd been withdrawn and unhappy, how it was all down to my leaving home.'

'Oh, Jed,' I say. 'That's not fair. I told you already, Dee Dee was a bit down about some girly nonsense at school.

Of course she was upset about her parents breaking up, but it was Zoe who made things difficult. *You* never did.'

Jed gives me a wry smile. 'That's not how Zoe sees it. Not that she screams and shouts any more, not since Dee Dee ... but almost everything she says is so bloody passive-aggressive ...'

'Did she mention me?' I ask.

Jed shakes his head. 'Let's not talk about her.' He walks over to the grill and pops our steaks under the flame. 'I ... I was thinking. Now we've got the decree nisi, I think we should set a date for our wedding. If it's just a small do with close friends and family there's really no reason why it shouldn't be as soon as the decree absolute is given. That's going to happen in six weeks so we could easily bring forward the wedding to early Feb.' He turns to me with a mischievous smile. 'You could come off the pill, get pregnant ... we could have a kid of our own by this time next year. What do you think, baby?'

No.

My reaction is sudden and visceral. I stand, facing him, feeling the resistance through my whole body. I gulp, unsure why I should feel so strongly. It's not rational. I love Jed. I *want* to marry him and have his children. So why not agree to bring it forward to February?

'I guess, but that means getting everything sorted over the Christmas holiday,' I say, wrinkling my nose. 'Even if it's just a small wedding there's loads to arrange – licences, invites, booking a restaurant ...'

Jed checks the steaks. 'Okay,' he says.

I worry that he's hurt and hurry over. I put my arms around him.

'Don't you think it's a bit rushed, I mean … after Dee Dee?'

Jed leans his head close to mine. 'I just want to do whatever will make you happy,' he says softly. 'We'll do whatever you like, baby, I'm just telling you I'm ready. I don't want to wait. That's all. I want you to be my wife, for us to be married.'

'Me too.' I kiss his cheek. 'Let me get to the end of term then I can think about it. Maybe there's not so much to do as I think.'

'Sure.' Jed smiles and turns back to the grill. I trudge upstairs to change out of my boots. I sit on the bed and put my head in my hands. Rose was so, so right. Jed really does love me. And whatever Zoe put in an old text or a letter to her son from months ago, there's no way it's anything but madness to suspect her of using him to try and kill me. At best, Dan has got the wrong end of the stick. At worst, he is manipulating me for reasons that I don't understand – and definitely don't want to face.

I decide to ignore his next attempt to contact me.

The rest of the evening passes smoothly. Jed and I eat the steak and salad then watch a movie on TV. For once Jed resists the lure of his briefcase and emails and comes straight to bed. Dan sends me a text at eleven saying that

Lish is a no show at the pub. I delete it without replying. I don't want to think about Lish. His letter from Zoe is buried deep in the bottom of a drawer. I keep Rose's wise, tempered words in my head and do my best to forget all about Dan's claims.

In the end, after thinking I might not be able to get to sleep, I actually have a good night, waking to find Jed bringing me a cup of tea before leaving for work.

'I like this "showing me you love me" stuff,' I say, smiling up at him.

'I like your body in the morning, baby.'

I'm not really in the mood, but Jed is persuasive, though stressed afterwards and in a rush to get to work. I leave on time myself and have a busy day at school. The end of term production is on Friday and I rehearse the kids hard to assuage my feelings of guilt from taking yesterday off sick. I wonder several times if Dan will stick around in Southampton and try and hook up with Lish again. He said he was freelancing so presumably he can afford to take the time. But Dan doesn't contact me for the rest of the day – or indeed the rest of the week and, gradually, thoughts of Zoe's letter and Lish's illegal activities distil into three thoughts:

1. What Lish gets up to at uni is none of my business.
2. If either he or his mother wanted me dead back in the summer, surely they would have tried to kill me again by now.

3. They have both been recently and horribly bereaved and I should make allowance for that before rushing to any kind of judgement about them.

I try to put the whole thing out of my mind and yet it is impossible to remove a thought once it has occurred and as the days pass I am haunted by the image of Dee Dee smiling up at me as she asked to take that picture of us at the citadel in Calvi. If the ExAche powders were deliberately poisoned by a Benecke Tricorp employee or as part of some manufacturing accident, then Jed's case against the company *will* eventually achieve justice. But if the cyanide was deliberately added later then Dee Dee's death was a targeted murder, regardless of whether she or I was the target. Which means someone should pay.

At least I am distracted by my busy last week of term. The school production goes well: the kids do me proud and the head pronounces herself delighted. The day after term ends Jed and I take a walk along the river, then visit Gary in his designer flat near Canary Wharf. As he mentioned when he visited the other day, he's with a new girlfriend. Allia is slighter and shyer than Iveta – and seems much more in Gary's shadow. She runs around refusing all offers of help and making us Cosmopolitan cocktails and smoked salmon blinis while Gary interrogates Jed over the latest developments in the civil case against Benecke Tricorp. The whole thing is bogged down in incomprehensible (to me) legal details. As a trader I'm certain Gary has no greater understanding of the specifics than I do. I wonder again why he is so interested.

My answer comes about an hour after we arrive. Allia is pouring Jed a drink. She's bending over and her top has slipped, revealing the edge of a pink lace bra and the swell of her breasts. I can see Jed trying not to gawp at her cleavage and grin at his evident discomfort. She turns away to replenish her jug of Cosmopolitan and Jed busies himself with his phone. I wander out onto the balcony to take in the amazing view of the City. Canary Wharf looms up on the right with the expanse of south London spread out beyond.

'I'm telling you, Jed has no idea.' It's Gary speaking from the bedroom next door. His voice is low and tense, but it carries clearly through the crisp December air.

Jed has no idea about what?

I strain to hear more, unable to stop myself.

'He's still caught up in the case against Benecke Tricorp,' Gary hisses. 'Yes, I know, I know it's the wrong focus ... of course I know ...'

I freeze. What is Gary saying? What is 'wrong' with Jed's focus on Benecke Tricorp? Could he be saying that the drugs that killed Dee Dee have nothing to do with the company Jed is suing? Gary was there, at the villa, on holiday with us, after all. Might *he* suspect Lish of being involved? Or be involved in some way himself?

Gary moves out of earshot. I shake myself. I'm seeing conspiracies where there are none. Rose is right, I've let Dan get me all carried away.

Jed and I leave soon after Gary returns from his phone call, his usual ebullient self – full of backchat with his brother and low-level flirting with me. I can't believe he is aware of Lish's drug dealing – let alone involved in any way.

And then, on Monday everything changes.

July 2014

Oh. My. Days. Daddy just told me the most HUMUNGOUS secret before he dropped me off that it is Emily's birthday on Wednesday and he is going to propose to her and he thinks she will say 'yes' then they will get married. I have like rockets in my head going off bam bam bam because part of me thinks it is good because Emily is nice but part of me knows that it means Daddy will never come home which I didn't really think he would but this makes it for sure and Mum will be FURIOUS. There will be shouting and phone calls and I will have to pretend to be upset when I'm with her and NOT upset when I'm with him and EVERYTHING will get worse and worse.

At least it is the end of term on Tuesday. Ava has been talking to me again for the past few weeks but it's not like before. I have to sit alone in the canteen if I go in there and no one ever chooses me to do anything with. A few weeks ago I got Mum's razor and tried shaving down there to look more grown-up but it got all itchy and when I told Ava she gave me an odd look and I think she told other people because for a bit the looking and pointing started again so I let the hairs grow back and I think mine must be really ugly compared to other girls'.

The latest thing is drawing boobs on my text books which gets me into trouble because the teachers think it's me and I don't know which boy is doing it but they still call me 'tiny tits' or 'hairy Dee' almost the whole class so it could be any of them. Poppy blocks her number then sometimes sends me nasty messages like 'u r a slag' and 'skl d b better if u fkd of' and I know it is her because a) she won't look in my eyes and b) she is proper best friends with Georgia now. Georgia isn't even going out with Sam Edwards' friend any more. I've seen Sam lots of times now but he never looks at me either. But it's not like he's avoiding me like Ava and Poppy and the rest of my class do, I think he has just forgotten I exist.

Oh my days, I am HATING the thought of school tomorrow and Tuesday and then school being over for the holidays which is YAY obviously – but then Daddy telling Mum about marrying Emily. He talked to her earlier about going on holiday with me and Lish in the summer. He gets two weeks with me and he kept asking what we should do and saying it would be fun but all I could think was Mum would be SO upset all by herself and then I will feel bad if I am enjoying it because I will have to pretend to her that I'm not. Lish is back home from uni for a bit but he doesn't say much, just sits in his room, and I know he is going away with his friends soon and that Daddy has said he will only pay for that if Lish comes on our holiday too. When Mum heard that earlier she said Daddy was mean and 'you've obviously let that whore of yours spend all your money on new furniture' and then Daddy lost his temper and said 'it was one fucking sofa from John fucking Lewis' and I came upstairs so I didn't have to hear any more.

Emily says maybe her sister Rose and brother Martin can come on the holiday too. It must have been WEIRD Rose being like a mum to her when she was little and Martin is REALLY rich. He has a BOYFRIEND too. And a yacht. But Mum will still be all alone. I can hear her crying now and she doesn't even know about Daddy and Emily getting married yet. Lish knows about it but he hasn't said anything either. I wish we could tell Mum and get it over so she would be upset while I'm at school and I wouldn't have to feel so bad.

December 2014

On Monday morning Jed leaves me sleeping as he heads off to work. I wake alone at 9 a.m. with the sun shining in through the window. For a second I relish the space in the bed beside me and the day stretching ahead with no work, maybe just a little Christmas shopping later.

Then I remember Lish and Gary and Dee Dee, and anxiety twists in my chest. I potter downstairs and try to calm myself by making a cup of tea and reading the paper on Jed's iPad. It's no good. I can't stop thinking about it all. Hoping to clear my head, I decide to go for a run. I used to jog every morning but since moving in with Jed, it hasn't been easy to find the time. Plus Jed tends to poke fun at any exercise that doesn't involve highly competitive ball games. Ironically it was Dan who got me into running many years ago. He used to go out every morning before work. He said it kept his head clear and his body able to play the football that consumed his Saturday mornings. I went with him at first simply because I adored being around him so much, but after hating the initial few runs I grew to love it more and more. Right now it feels like just what I need. After the first five minutes when – as usual – I feel like I'm about to die, my body warms up. I run to Highgate Wood and do a couple of laps. The bright sunshine fades as I head home and it's just starting to drizzle as I turn onto our road. I'm a few metres from the house when I see Dan getting out of his car.

It is a total shock to my system. *Shit.* He must have been watching me running since I turned the corner. My first thought is that I'm sweaty, unmade-up and wearing old sweatpants with bleach stains on the legs. My second thought is that I'm an idiot for caring. What does it matter what Dan thinks of my appearance? He shouldn't have turned up here like this.

I slow to a walk as I reach the car.

'Hey, Em, good to see you in your element,' Dan says with a smile, closing the car door.

I stop, then release my hair from its ponytail and run my fingers through it self-consciously. Everything I had successfully pushed to the back of my mind during my run is flooding back.

Zoe's letter flashes through my head:

The whore must be stopped. And somehow you must help me stop her. She cannot be allowed.

'What's up?' I sound horribly abrupt. My cheeks burn.

The smile fades from Dan's face. 'Bad news.' He holds out a tiny notebook.

'What's this?' I flick through the pages. Each one is covered with lists of dates and initials in three columns. I can't make any sense of them. 'Dan?'

He points to the open page. 'It's an order book,' he says. 'I'm guessing Lish uses it to keep track of what he's selling and to whom. It's more secure than something electronic, plus it doesn't actually prove anything, but it's all there.' He indicates the top line, then reads the contents of each column. 'Va. - J.K. -30/11.'

'Which means?'

'My best guess is Va for Viagra sold to someone with the initials JK on the thirtieth of November. I've had a look through. There's Vic for Vicodin, plus Pro for propranolol, which is a beta blocker, and Stan for stanozolol – that's an anabolic steroid, Phen375, which I think is some kind of diet pill, and on and on, all the way to Z for Zoloft. You get the picture.'

I look up. 'Where the hell did you get this?'

Dan rubs the back of his head. 'I picked it from Lish Kennedy's jacket pocket.'

'You *stole* it?'

'Yes.' Dan holds up a paper bag. 'While I was buying these.' He opens the bag and shows me the contents: two small packets of Valium. 'From the look of the packaging, I'm guessing they're fakes rather than stolen, probably cut with chalk or talcum powder.'

Rain trickles down my face. This is proof, surely. *Real* proof against Lish.

'He's really doing it,' I whisper. 'He's really selling drugs.'

'I'm so sorry, Em,' Dan says. 'But there's something else. Something worse.' He turns the pages of the notebook. I wipe my damp hair off my face as he finds the place he's looking for and points to an entry halfway down. 'KCN - JL&LN -4/8.' He reads the entry out loud, then looks up. There is genuine anguish in his eyes.

'What is KCN?' I ask, though I have already guessed.

'Potassium cyanide.'

I stare at the entry. My mouth feels dry though the rest of me is damp from the rain and clammy with sweat from my run.

'I think it's for a couple of photography students. I checked the initials against the student year book for Lish's year and I'm guessing JL and LN are probably photography students James Leonard and Laurie Nolan.'

'Why does that fit?'

'Apparently you can use potassium cyanide as ... a sort of toner, to give a particular finish. It's a bit of a fad at the moment. And the cyanide isn't technically a banned drug though you're supposed to have a licence or something to buy it legally.'

The rain grows heavier, pounding on Dan's car roof. My hair is plastered to my face; I am soaked yet I barely feel it.

'Right,' I say. 'So Lish *did* mean to hurt me. But ... but ...'

'But then why only one murder attempt?' Dan asks. 'Why not try and poison you again, later?'

I nod.

'I don't know, I'm guessing that when Dee Dee died by mistake Lish must have felt terrible. He obviously got rid of his drugs before the police searched your villa so after that he would have needed to use something else, a different method, and perhaps he baulked at that. Or perhaps he just felt he needed to let things settle down a bit before he tried again and he's building up to another attempt now. Or perhaps he changed his mind when he saw how devastated his father was over losing Dee Dee and he's let go of the whole thing and ... and you're safe.'

I stare at him. He's in the navy suit he wore when I first saw him a few weeks ago. The shoulders are dark from the rain. His forehead is creased with concern, those fine lines around his eyes more obvious than on our previous meeting. I know before he opens his mouth that there is something weighing heavily on his mind, that he wants to confess it.

'There's something else.' Dan hesitates. 'I wasn't completely honest with you when I first met you again ... at the beginning of the month.'

I hold my breath. Is it what Rose thought? That he wants me back?

'I said ... I ... told you that I'd seen the story in the paper about Jed's daughter dying and I found out about his son's drug dealing and that I'd put it all together and was worried you might be in danger.'

The rain drives down. I am soaked through and shivering. All I can see are Dan's eyes, the colour of storms.

'The truth is that I didn't really think you were in danger at all. I thought what everyone else thinks, that Dee Dee died in a random accident and it didn't have anything to do with you. All I wanted was the story on Jed's son being a drug dealer. Jed Kennedy is a big-name lawyer who helped get a cabinet minister acquitted a few months ago. I thought you might get me to that story.'

For a second I am blank. Numb. Lost.

Dan doesn't want me. He wants a scoop on Jed's son, to discredit Jed.

'You used me?' As I speak, a riot of emotions tear through me: shame, humiliation, misery, anger.

Mostly anger.

'I'm so sorry, Em, I thought it would quickly be obvious that the idea Lish might want to hurt you was crazy. But I thought you'd tell Jed and he'd confess that Lish *is* drug dealing and then you'd tell me. It was only once I saw the state you were in after you went to Lish's flat which ... which was *not* my idea, you'll remember ... it was only then that I started to feel bad about what I'd done, determined to get the truth to show you you weren't really in danger. But ... but then I met Lish and got the drugs and this notebook and ...'

'You used me to get a story.' I wipe the rain off my face and take a step away from him.

Dan closes the gap. He touches my arm. It's like an electric current shooting through me. I shake his hand away. 'Get off me.'

'I'm so sorry, Em. I don't know what to say other than that I never meant to upset you and that I promise I'm not going to do a story now. I've destroyed all my notes, all the recordings, so there's nothing I can write.'

'Kind of you. Thanks.' The words spit from my mouth.

'But I think you should tell Jed everything. And I think you should take the drugs and the notebook to the police.' Dan turns back to his car and picks up the paper bag from the driver's seat. He holds it out to me. 'This is everything Lish sold me. I haven't kept anything back. And I'll support whatever you decide. There's just one thing.' He moves closer so we're only centimetres away from each other. Rain streams onto us, around us. 'I didn't realize how I was going to feel when I saw you again, how much you still matter to me.' He gazes down at me. We're too close to each other. I can see the longing in his eyes. For a split second I think he's going to close the tiny gap between us and kiss me. I break away, yanking the paper bag out of his hand.

'Don't call me.' Without looking at him I run across the road and into the house. I rush upstairs and peel off my wet clothes. I'm too angry to cry, too humiliated. I wrap a towel around me then peek out of the front window to make sure Dan has gone. He has. I shower myself warm and change into jeans and a sweater, Dan's words echoing around my head. He lied to me. He used me. He wants me. My mind jumps around, unable to process what has just happened. I'm only sure of one thing: that I was a fool to think that our past wouldn't cast a long shadow over anything we did in the present. And my past feelings for Dan were passionate in a way that my feelings for Jed have never been. But Jed is the better man. The stronger, steadier, man. I should never have listened to Dan.

Rose was right about him. She didn't guess the whole story, but she was fundamentally right: Dan Thackeray is not to be trusted.

I examine the contents of the paper bag. Two packs each containing three blister strips of little blue Valium pills. I don't know how Dan knows they are fakes; the only suspicious thing I can see is the slightly smudged print on the packets, though I've never seen Valium close to before so I have no idea what the genuine pills should look like. I breathe slowly out, trying to still my racing thoughts. Dan has gone. He has promised there will be no story. Which means there is no real harm done to Jed in terms of his job or his reputation. I think it through. I will show Jed the pills as soon as he's home, tell him everything that Dan and I have found out. It will be up to Jed what he does with the information, but I can't believe he won't act, that he won't want to protect me.

The rain continues to fall. I'm upstairs when Jed gets in from work, much earlier than usual. He calls up to say he's home. I should hear the heaviness in his voice, realize something's wrong, but I'm so intent on the conversation we're about to have that I just head downstairs, wondering how to begin. The bag Dan gave me is in my hand as I trudge into the living room. Jed is still in his jacket, sitting on the sofa to the right of the TV, staring out of the window. This is unusual in itself. Normally the first thing

Jed does when he gets in is shrug off his jacket and pour himself a drink.

I sit down opposite him, the paper bag in my lap. Jed turns and looks at me. He doesn't smile.

'There's something I need to tell you,' I say.

Jed nods his head. It's only now that I see how strained and miserable his expression is.

'What's the matter?' I ask.

'I don't know if you'll understand,' he says uncertainly. He looks away again.

'What's wrong?' I frown, trying to work out what on earth he can be referring to.

Jed sighs. 'I just realized that I didn't think about Dee Dee once, not the whole time I was at work *all day*. Not that there's any fucking point to thinking about her, but I feel so guilty that I actually didn't. It's the first day since . . .' His voice cracks and he puts his head in his hands.

I'm already across the room, my arms around him.

'Sorry,' he says.

'Don't apologize.' I lean closer. 'There's nothing to apologize for. I'm just so sorry too.'

Jed sits upright, shifting slightly away from me. I take the hint and remove my arms. I am getting used to this: when Jed feels unhappy, he often half opens up, then pulls away.

'So what did you want to tell me?' Jed asks.

I hesitate. I had been set to tell him about Dan's discoveries. The bag of drugs Lish sold him still lies in my lap. But it feels wrong to do so right now. How can I dis-illusion Jed about one child when he is in so much pain over the loss of the other? Except ... there's always going to be some reason not to tell him something so difficult: last night he was too tired, earlier today he was too busy ...

'What is it, Emily?' Jed points to the paper bag. 'Is it something to do with that?'

I take a deep breath and hand him the bag. 'This is fake Valium. At least I think it's fake.'

Jed takes the bag. Bemused, he peers inside. 'Where did you get these?'

God, this is so hard. 'Er, d'you remember me telling you about my ... my ex, Dan, the journalist who went to the States, from years back?'

'Dan the reporter?' Jed looks up, a wary expression on his face. 'Yes. Why?'

'Dan ... he approached me the other day,' I stammer. 'He said he'd been investigating fake drugs and had heard about what happened to Dee Dee and he found out some things about Lish and ... and ...' I'm condensing the truth wildly here, but I need to get the information out and Jed is already looking completely appalled.

'And *what*?' he demands.

'Dan said that Lish ... that ... at uni ... he sells phar-maceuticals, fake ones, stolen ones ... he's not sure.'

Jed stares at me, the colour draining from his face. I'm suddenly, horribly, taken back to the morning we found

213

Dee Dee, glassy-eyed and cold, and the look of horrified disbelief on Jed's face then.

'What's his evidence for this?' Jed asks coldly.

'He says Lish sold him the fake Valium. And he ... he took this off him too.' I hold up the little notebook. The cover feels clammy in my palm. Jed takes the book and flicks through the pages, a bemused expression on his face. 'It's lists of Lish's drug sales: what, who to, when delivered ...'

Jed sits in silence for a few moments, his jaw grinding as he pores over the neat entries. 'A journalist you used to go out with tells you my son is a drug dealer? And you automatically believe him? No questions asked?'

I stare at Jed. *Oh God.* 'Dan said he thought I might be in danger.'

'What? *How?*'

'One of the entries is for KCN, which is potassium cyanide. Jed, I'm so sorry but I think it's possible that Lish poisoned Dee Dee by mistake, meaning it to be me.'

Jed's mouth gapes.

'You heard how hateful he sounded on Facebook and there was an anonymous text too and I've seen how he looks at me and now Dan says he bought drugs—'

'Wait. Dan Thackeray told you this notebook and these drugs were from my son? That along with a few odd looks and comments they somehow add up to a belief that Lish wants to *kill* you?' Jed's eyes widen.

'I know it sounds mad, but it makes sense if you—'

'No, it *doesn't* make sense. None of it.' Jed blows out his

214

breath, clearly trying to gather his thoughts. '*Dammit,* baby, you are *so* naïve. The bastard just wants to set Lish up, probably as a way of getting to me: *privileged son of top London solicitor in drug scandal,* great story, well done Dan fucking Thackeray.'

I wince. 'Dan's admitted that he started out just wanting to find out about Lish, get a story on you having a drug-dealing son, but now he thinks maybe I really am in danger. When you link the potassium cyanide to the way Lish loathes me—'

'Stop.' Jed jumps up and paces across the room. 'Just fucking stop right there.'

I gulp. Jed's fury is palpable, he's literally shaking with it. He turns. Stops pacing. His eyes burn into me as he sits down. 'Tell me again, *exactly*, what Dan Thackeray has told you and what you've told him. Start from the beginning.'

Squirming under the ferocity of his glare, I explain how Dan sought me out in the car park and how I agreed to visit the student pub which Dan claimed Lish was dealing from.

'You went all the way to Southampton with your fucking ex and you didn't mention it?' Jed's voice rises. 'What else did you do with him?'

'Nothing.' I can feel my cheeks reddening. No way am I admitting to my illicit ransacking of Lish's student room, and the letter I found from Zoe. 'This isn't about me and Dan, it's about Lish. And the only reason I didn't tell you before was that I didn't want to worry you.'

'What . . . about the fact that my son was into drug dealing? Or that you were having a day out with your fucking ex-boyfriend so he could shaft me by writing a story about it?' Jed's voice is like ice.

'That's not fair,' I say, stung. 'I didn't know Dan wanted a story at first. He only told me that today *and* he promised he wouldn't write one. He's given us the proof against Lish.'

'These drugs and this notebook prove nothing, baby, except that Dan Thackeray tells lies and you are ridiculously gullible.' Jed sighs. 'I suppose he tried to fuck you while he was at it?'

My cheeks burn, remembering the longing in Dan's eyes earlier and how he said I still mattered to him. Rose's warning echoes in my ears: *Dan Thackeray wants to get back in your pants.*

'No, he didn't,' I say.

Jed snorts. I reach out my hand to him but he bats it away. I can't work out whether he's more angry that I'm accusing Lish of drug dealing and murder, or because I've inadvertently helped a journalist research (or in Jed's view, fabricate) a story about it or because I've seen an exboyfriend behind his back.

The last of these things is the one I latch onto, the one where I can at least offer Jed reassurance.

'I'm sorry I didn't tell you I saw Dan, but nothing happened between us.' I hesitate. 'If you think about it, I don't necessarily know about every time you see Zoe and she's *your* ex.'

'Zoe and I had children together, of course we still see each other. That's completely different. Anyway, I *do* tell you if I'm seeing her.' Jed looks at me, contempt in his eyes. 'Dammit, baby, how could you do this to me?'

I open my mouth to tell him, for the first time ever, not to call me 'baby', then I think better of it. Hard though it is, I should cut Jed a bit of slack – after all, it's only a few months since Dee Dee and he was almost in tears over her when he got in and here I am dropping a bombshell about Lish. It's understandable that he is upset.

It has turned dark outside while we've been talking. As I get up to close the curtains Jed scrunches the top of the bag over. The paper rustles in the silence.

'So what do you want to do now?' I ask.

'I'll talk to Lish,' Jed says. 'I don't believe these drugs or this notebook have anything to do with him.'

I turn around. 'Shouldn't we get the Valium tested at least? They have those specter-whatsits at the anti-fake and substandard drug organization where you went to that conference, don't they?'

'You mean the spectrometer at the Campaign ... at CASP? Yes, but ...' Jed stands up, the bag of drugs and the notebook in his hands. 'But finding out if this is fake Valium doesn't prove Lish had anything to do with selling it, does it? In fact taking it to be tested would just be playing into Dan bloody Thackeray's hands.'

'But suppose Lish lies to you when you ask him about it?' The words blurt out. 'He sold drugs at school so—'

'He never sold *anything* at school, he just had a little pot or whatever for his own use.' Jed narrows his eyes. 'Do you *really* think my son is capable of drug dealing, let alone wanting to murder you? It's ridiculous.' He sits forward. 'I need Thackeray's number.'

'Why?'

'Because I want to make it clear to him that if he tries writing a story about my son I will sue him into next year.'

I gulp. 'You don't need to worry, I told you. Dan promised me he'd drop the story, that he'd let us decide what to do with the drugs.'

'Did he?' Mistrust darkens Jed's eyes. 'I'm not sure that's enough of a guarantee for me. I want to talk to him, make sure.'

The memory of Dan's face – and my telling him that I never want to see him again – flashes before my mind's eye. 'I . . . I don't want to call him.'

'For fuck's sake, I don't want you to call him either. *I'm* going to do it.' Jed storms out to the hall.

I sit, frozen to the sofa. What a mess. I can hardly blame Jed for being angry, but how can he dismiss Dan's claims so completely out of hand? Is he not in the slightest bit concerned that Lish has been dealing? That he might have meant . . . still mean . . . me harm? That Dee Dee ended up the unwitting victim of his desire to hurt me? A second later I hear Jed rummaging through my handbag. Then the beep of a phone.

I jump up. 'What are you doing?' I run out into the hall.

Jed is standing, the paper bag of drugs in one hand, my phone in the other. He is hunched over the screen, scrolling through the contact list.

'Give that back!' I demand.

'Let me handle this.' Jed doesn't look around.

I launch myself at him, reaching for the mobile. Jed pushes me away. I stumble backwards and Jed bends over the phone again. I watch, helplessly, as he sends Dan's details to his own phone. I hear the trill as his mobile receives the message. Still clutching the paper bag, Jed puts down my phone, then picks up his own and heads into the kitchen.

We spend the rest of the evening apart. Jed is clearly still furious with me and I . . . well, I am not sure how I feel any more. Jed comes to bed late. I'm still awake, thoughts tumbling over and over inside my head.

'Did you speak to Lish?' I ask.

'He says it's a fit-up,' Jed says, not looking at me. 'As I expected he would.'

'What about Dan?'

'Left a message telling him to back off Lish and stay away from you,' Jed says curtly. He stalks off into the bathroom. When he returns he gets straight into bed and turns his back to me.

I lie awake for an hour. Beside me, my phone – on silent – registers that Dan is calling. I don't answer, then tiptoe downstairs to the kitchen to listen to Dan's voice mail. He sounds frantic.

'Em, your fiancé called me, I think the message was left a couple of hours ago. He's *furious.* Are you all right? I know you don't want to talk to me, but you've obviously told him what we found ... he doesn't sound like he believes *any* of it and I just need to know you're okay. I'm worried. *Please* let me know it's just me he's mad at and that you're all right.' There's a short pause, then Dan continues, a tremor in his voice. 'Everything I found out was true, Em. *True.* Not a set-up like Jed says. And I meant what I said, I had no idea how much it would mean to me when I saw you again. I've dropped the entire story because I don't want to make things difficult for you, because I care about you.'

I stand still, my phone in my hand, my feet cold on the kitchen floor. Instinct tells me Dan is telling the truth and I'm certain Jed is wrong to dismiss his claims. However, I'm painfully aware that it would be stupid to trust everything Dan says. Whatever I do now, I do alone.

I sleep badly and wake as Jed disappears into the shower. For a single, blissful second I am just warm and comfortable in my bed. Then it all floods back: Dee Dee's death, Zoe's desire to 'stop' me being with Jed, Lish's links to pharmaceutical drugs, including the very poison that killed his sister. And Jed's refusal to believe that there is any connection between these things.

In that moment I realize what I have to do now: I must go to the CASP offices in central London. I will take the drugs and the notebook to them and, with them, turn everything over to the police. Jed will hate it, but I don't have a choice. His daughter deserves justice, even if the price of that justice is her brother's freedom.

I hurry out of our bedroom, intent on looking inside Jed's briefcase. It's the only thing in the house that it's possible to lock and I'm sure it's where Jed will have put the bag of drugs and the notebook. As I pass the bathroom I can hear water running. Good. If Jed's still in the shower I should have at least ten minutes. I scurry downstairs. The briefcase is in its usual position beside the sofa. As I expect, it is locked, but I know the four-number combination: the date and month of my birthday, 22 July. I fumble as I rotate the lock to the correct numbers in turn: 2207. I open the lid. The inside is embossed with Jed's initials: JEK for his full name, James Edward Kennedy. Jed's files are loaded inside, along with his tablet. There's no sign of the drugs or the notebook. My fingers feel clammy against the leather as I close the lid and turn the numbers out of combination. Where has Jed hidden them? They must be in the house somewhere.

'What are you doing?' Jed's voice makes me jump.

I whip around, his briefcase still in my hand. Jed is in the living room doorway, a towel wrapped around his waist, water trickling from his damp hair.

'Nothing,' I lie, setting the briefcase down. 'Just looking for my phone.'

'On the counter by the toaster, charging?' he says suspiciously. 'Where it normally is overnight?'

I drift into the kitchen. My phone is, of course, exactly

where Jed has suggested. I can see immediately that Dan has called again. I pick up the phone and quickly delete the voice mail.

Jed follows me into the kitchen. He makes a show of fetching a juice from the fridge then goes back upstairs to change for work. I tiptoe around the kitchen. Has he thrown the drugs and the notebook in the bin? I rummage about. Nothing. I check all the cupboards, then go back to the living room and check underneath the TV stand, behind the bookcase and down the sides of the chairs and sofa.

Still nothing.

I hear Jed on the stairs and dart into the hall.

'Bye, darling,' I say breezily.

'Bye,' Jed grunts, deliberately not looking at me as he leaves.

I wait until he drives off then hurry upstairs and explore our bedroom, checking carefully in the wardrobe and all the drawers. A similar investigation of the spare room and the study reveals nothing. *Shit.* I get changed myself and wander back downstairs. Perhaps Jed has taken the drugs and the notebook with him in his jacket pocket. Or perhaps he put them in the car last night.

I decide to give the living room and kitchen another going over. An hour later I'm on the verge of giving up when I finally find the drugs, still inside their paper bag, wedged between the ironing board and a large box of washing powder at the very back of the utility room's most crowded cupboard. There's still no sign of the notebook but I don't want to waste any more time looking. The drugs in themselves along with everything else I know should be enough to open an investigation. Jed will surely be forced to hand over the notebook once the police are asking questions.

I fetch Zoe's letter to Lish from the bottom of my sweater drawer. I don't have to decide right now whether or not to hand it over along with the drugs to the police, but it is potential evidence and, unlike withheld texts and hearsay, it is at least tangible proof of her hatred for me.

Emotions career around my head as I leave the house. I shove the paper bag of drugs into my handbag and hurry off to Finsbury Park station. As I push my way onto the crowded train carriage the back of my neck prickles, as if I'm being watched. But when I look around I can't see anyone staring. I settle into a seat, desperately upset that Jed is so angry but also furious that he is refusing to believe Lish might have done something criminal.

I change trains at King's Cross and, as I walk along the Northern Line platform, my handbag clutched tightly under my arm, I can't help but remember that moment yesterday when Dan stood so close to me. I don't want to face it but I know that when I thought he might have kissed me, a big part of me wanted him to. Which is crazy. Dan *lied* to me, used me to get a story. Even if he's right about Lish I can't trust him. Not really. And I'm with Jed. No matter what is happening between us right now, it's Jed I want.

223

Is that true? Because last week, when he asked to bring the wedding forward, you didn't want to say 'yes'.

Rose said Dan Thackeray wants to get back in your pants.

Do you want to get in his?

Unhelpful thoughts battle each other in my head. The platform is packed. I am at the front, people jammed next to me on either side. I glance up. The next train is due in one minute. The air around me swirls, there's a low rumble in the distance. I stand, waiting. Dan's face in my mind's eye. People jostle, moving forward.

Out of nowhere, an agonizing pain rips through my right shoulder. My bag is ripped from my hand. I am spun sideways. I try to scream. I stumble, lose my footing. On the edge of the platform. The wind from the train whips my hair across my face as I fall.

Everything slows as the tracks rear up to meet me.

So the good news is school is finally over for the whole summer. Okay, so I'm still getting texts from Poppy and whatever other girls but I don't have to see them any more. The bad news is Mum has just told me Dad has asked if he can come around this evening. I've been waiting and waiting for this. Emily's birthday was FOUR WHOLE DAYS ago and Daddy sent me a text saying she said yes!!! But that was ALL and ever since I've been waiting for him to tell Mum and he hasn't and I keep going to tell her myself but then I can't because I KNOW she is going to TOTALLY freak when she hears. She has no idea. I mean LOOK at her. She is playing music in her room, changing her clothes and putting on make-up and perfume. I just went in and she had on a dress where you could actually see through the top bit to her bra. SO embarrassing. And she's doing it because Daddy's coming round when he wasn't expected and she thinks he's coming to see HER. Which he is, I guess, but not cos he wants to see her but to tell her he's marrying someone else and Mum is bound to shout at him again. She already had a go at him about the holiday, saying there was no way he could take me outside Europe. Daddy said fine, he was thinking about a villa in France somewhere. I could see Mum didn't know what to say. I know she doesn't really want me to go especially if Emily is there. I really think maybe she's hoping Daddy will come around tonight and ask her to come on holiday with us instead of Emily. AS IF.

December 2014

Someone yells a warning just above my head. Pain shoots through me again, this time in my forearm, the fierce grip of a strong hand. The world spins around me as I'm hauled up, onto the platform. The tube train rushes past. The man who has saved me is wearing builder's overalls. He looks terrified. The people around us avert their eyes.

The train stops. People are already pressed against us. They surge forward, ignoring us, not wanting to be late to get on board.

The man in the overalls releases me.

'Are you all right?' he asks.

'Yes,' I gasp. 'Thank you.'

He nods. Moves onto the train just like the other people. And that's when I realize my bag is gone. I turn to the woman next to me.

'I was pushed,' I say. 'Did you see who pushed me?' My whole body is tensed, my throat tight.

The woman frowns. 'No, pet,' she says. 'My, you look white as a sheet.'

People bustle around us. The woman is swept away from me.

'Please.' I reach out and grab her arm before she disappears. She turns, an expression of alarm on her face. 'Did you see *anyone*?' I persist.

The woman shakes her head. 'I'm sorry.'

The platform is emptying. Almost everyone is on the train. The woman gives me a rueful shrug, then gets on herself.

I stay where I am as the doors shut and the train zooms off. A new set of people have taken the place of the ones who just got on board. The platform is still packed. I back away, through the crowd, towards the stairs. My bag is gone. Whoever it was must have taken it, then tried to push me in front of the tube train.

I force myself to focus. I must report the bag, see if any of the tube officials noticed someone running out of the station carrying it, get the police to look at the CCTV. I head up the stairs to the ticket office. My whole body is shaking. Suppose whoever it was is still here, waiting for me.

I have nothing with me. No purse, no keys, no phone. The letter from Zoe to Lish is gone. So is the bag of drugs I was taking to the CASP lab to be analysed.

I lean on the handrail going up the short flight of stairs. As I step onto the escalator up to the ticket office my right arm begins to throb. My shoulder feels like it's been wrenched from its socket. I roll up my sleeve. There's a deep red mark where the man who saved me grabbed my arm.

I am still trembling all over as I look around. The escalator is empty, just two elderly ladies a few steps above me. A young couple get on below. I grip the side rail, feeling the warm rubber below my fingers.

Someone just tried to kill me. Why? To take the drugs? To shut me up?

Was it Lish?

I reach the ticket barriers as it sinks in. It *must* have been. It's too big a coincidence otherwise. Lish knew the drugs were at his dad's house because Jed phoned him about them last night. He must have waited for me outside the house, followed me when I left and mugged me on the tube platform where it was really crowded. I freeze as the reality hits home. Lish has tried to kill me. Again. A large, middle-aged guard is leaning against the widest gate, designed for suitcases and buggies. I stagger over to him. I can hardly breathe, barely focus. The guard sees me and raises his eyebrows.

'You all right, love?'

'I was just mugged,' I say. 'He took my bag, pushed me in front of the train. Someone grabbed me and saved me.' As I speak, tears spring from my eyes. I am crying and I can't stop.

The guard looks appalled.

'Here, love. Over here.' He ushers me through the wide gate. I'm still weeping uncontrollably. He's got his hand on my back: kind, fatherly. It makes me cry more. We stand by the ticket office to the side. People are swarming past. The man beckons a woman over. She is black and, like the man, middle-aged and plump.

I tell my story again, describing my handbag in detail. The woman is as kind as the man. They talk in quiet voices, then ask for a description of my attacker.

'I didn't see him.' I shake my head, repeating the words. 'I didn't see anything.'

The man goes inside the office. The woman offers me a tissue. She strokes my arm.

'Are you hurt?' she asks. 'Do you need an ambulance? Can I call someone for you?'

'Thank you, but I'm fine.' Jed and Rose and Martin would each want me to call them if they knew what had happened.

But it's not them I want to speak to.

After a minute, the man returns. He is holding something in his hand. My handbag. I stare at it, gasping with surprise as he lifts it up.

'This yours?' The man smiles. 'It was dropped just by the barriers. You're lucky I saw it. Two more minutes and someone would have cleared the station in case there was a bomb inside.' He hands it over and I take it and peer at the contents.

'Anything missing?' the man asks.

I'm still rummaging. My phone and my keys and my purse are still here, though the purse is open. But I can see at once the drugs are gone. More proof that the mugger was Lish.

'Check everything, love,' the woman urges.

I open up my purse. I can't remember exactly how much cash was in here, maybe thirty or forty pounds. All the notes are gone.

'Money's been taken.' I look in the side pockets of the purse. My cards are still in their places.

'Just cash?' the woman asks.

I nod.

'Well, it could have been worse.' She turns to the man. 'Any luck on the CCTV?'

'Yes, we just rewound the tape. There's someone in a cap and a grey sweatshirt with a hood. But you can't see the face. I checked the camera on the escalator and by the barriers. Clever little bugger, you can't tell anything: age, not even sex, though it isn't a hefty fella, that's for sure. I'd say around five foot eleven, but skinny.'

I gulp. That sounds like Lish. 'Can I see?' I ask.

The man makes a face. 'You have to put in a freedom of information request to do that. Best bet is to call the police and set the wheels in motion although ...' He sighs. 'I shouldn't say this, but I don't think there'll be much point. Whoever attacked you probably just wanted the cash. They've obviously kept their head down, so identification will be a nightmare, not to say impossible, and ... well, you've got your bag back, haven't you?'

I nod again. My arm and my shoulder still hurt, but I

seem to have stopped shaking. I need to get some air, then work out what on earth I do next.

The man and the woman are clearly waiting for me to speak. 'Thank you for your help,' I say, taking a step away.

The man frowns. 'You should make a report,' he says.

'I will,' I say. 'I just need to get outside and call ... call my boyfriend.'

'Of course, pet,' the woman says.

Clutching my bag I head upstairs. The cold air is soothing on my face. My arm aches badly. Around me, Euston Road is full of bustle. My mind is going at ninety miles an hour. I have to call the police, but I should tell Jed first. I should tell him what's just happened, that Lish has attacked me.

I take out my phone. But before I can open my *favourites* list to find Jed's number, it rings.

Dan calling.

I answer without stopping to think. 'Hello?'

'Em?' He sucks in his breath. 'What's wrong?'

I start gabbling an incoherent and slightly hysterical version of what has just happened, my voice breaking as I relive the moment when I almost fell onto the tracks. Dan listens, checks I'm not seriously hurt, then says he is coming straight over in a cab and that I should find somewhere nearby which is public, but safe, and stay put. I slump against the wall of the station, shivering in the cold air. I look around, half-expecting Lish to loom out of the surrounding crowd, but no one pays me any attention. It is an ordinary day. People are travelling, shopping, talking, working. Normality is all around me. But inside my head it is chaos. Jed. Zoe. Lish. Dan. Such a mess.

I should still call Jed, but Dan is coming. I need to deal with Dan first. I stumble along the road to St Pancras station and wait outside one of the shops. After about fifteen minutes Dan comes running into the station. He looks around for me, his hair falling over his eyes. He's wearing jeans and a black leather jacket. He looks, frankly, gorgeous, like a dishevelled movie star. People stare as he turns, desperate to find me. As I raise my hand to attract his attention, he sees me. His face floods with relief and he races over. He grabs me and hugs me. I fall into his arms.

'Oh, Em,' he murmurs, breathless in my ear. 'Thank God you're all right.' He pulls away, his grey eyes fixed on my face. He takes my cheeks in his hands. I close my eyes, letting the warmth of his fingers calm my skin, my nerves. He tilts my chin gently upwards. It's a fractional movement, but a clear one. *Yes.* I forget everything else and lean into him. His lips are soft on mine. My legs sag, my skin burns.

I kiss and I kiss and for a moment I forget everything. There is only Dan and me. There is only this kiss.

And then I realize what I'm doing. I wrench myself away.

Dan stands back too, eyes frantic. 'I'm sorry,' he whispers. 'I wasn't ... didn't ...'

Shit. Shit. Shit.

A sudden blast of cold air whips through the concourse, biting at my face. I shiver.

Dan takes my hand. 'Okay, let's get you inside somewhere warm, a cup of tea or something.'

I nod and let him lead me along the concourse and into a café. I look around me as we walk, wondering again if Lish could be here. Kissing Dan was stupid. *Speaking* to Dan was stupid. Why on earth didn't I just ignore his earlier call and ring Jed as I meant to. Dan sits me down and brings me a cup of strong, sweet tea. I put my hands around it, letting it warm me through.

'Tell me what happened,' Dan says softly.

I go through it again. After a few minutes I take off my jacket. I wince as I have to move my shoulder, still painful. The mark on my forearm is now a settled red bruise. Four fingertips are visible from where the man in the overalls grabbed me.

Dan looks down. I hear the breath catch in his throat.

'Did Lish do that when he pushed you?' he demands.

I shake my head.

'Was that *Jed* then? Last night?' His eyes blaze.

'No, no.' I quickly explain.

Dan sits back. 'You're not safe,' he says. 'We need to go to the police and tell them what's just happened. I'll fill them in about Lish selling me the drugs, you can show them the letter from Zoe—'

'Lish took that along with the fake Valium.' I gulp at my tea.

'Shit.' Dan rubs the back of his head. 'Okay, what about the notebook?'

'Jed has it.' I set my tea down. 'I'm going to go to his office now, tell him Lish pushed me. I'll make him give me the notebook.'

'Good.' Dan takes my hand. The memory of our kiss shoots through my head. 'I'll come with you if ... if you'll let me. Just to make sure you get there okay.'

We reach the lobby of Jed's office block. I indicate the lift opposite. 'I'll go up, but you should wait here. It'll just make things worse if Jed sees you.' As I finish speaking the lift doors open and Jed himself steps out.

He does a double take as he notices me and strides over. 'Emily?' He sees Dan and frowns.

'Er, this is Dan Thackeray.' I flush, covered in confusion. 'I was coming up to see you.'

Jed presses his lips together in a thin line. He says nothing. Two men in suits, intent on their conversation, pass close by.

'I was just attacked ... on the underground,' I stammer.

'What?' Jed's eyes fill with alarm. 'Are you all right, baby? What happened?'

'I'm okay,' I falter, the heat rising in my cheeks. 'But ... but they ... someone took my bag and tried to push me onto the tracks.'

Jed's face pales. 'Jesus, Emily. Did you see who it was?'

I take a deep breath. 'It was Lish.'

There's a long silence. A Tannoy announcement about a fire alarm test sounds overhead.

'You *saw* him? You saw Lish push you?'

'No,' I admit. 'I didn't actually see his face, but it had to be him.'

'I don't understand,' Jed says. 'What on earth makes you think my son would—?'

'Because he took the drugs I bought from him,' Dan interjects. 'Emily had them in her handbag. Lish took the bag then dumped it after he took out the drugs and some cash.'

Jed blinks rapidly. 'You took the Valium packs from the kitchen cupboard?' he demands, ignoring Dan.

'Yes,' I concede. 'I wanted them tested and . . . and, Jed, we really have to go to the police now, it's—'

'Stop.' Jed's voice is ice cold. He turns to Dan. 'I'd be grateful if you fucked off now.' He grips my arm and guides me towards the front door of the office building. He's pressing on the skin where the young man grabbed me earlier. I wince with the pain but Jed doesn't notice.

'Hey.' Dan is following us. Jed doesn't look around.

Out on the pavement he hurries me along the first turning, onto a small and deserted side street. He swings me around to face him as Dan pounds angrily up beside me.

'I'm not leaving until I know Emily is safe,' Dan says.

'I'm fine, Dan.' I turn to Jed. 'I'm sorry but we need the notebook and we need to go to the police. Now.'

'Don't you see you're playing right into his hands,' Jed snarls.

'She's not. Your son is a murderer. He's tried to kill Emily twice now and—'

'I told you to fuck off.' Jed draws himself up, fists clenched as he rounds on Dan. 'What the hell do you think you're doing, filling her head with lies about me and my family?' Spit flies from his mouth.

Dan looks almost as angry as Jed though he is obviously making a huge effort to control himself. 'No lies,' he says calmly. 'Your son sold me drugs. Emily's nearly been murdered. Twice.'

Jed's gaze swings round to me again. 'You have absolutely no proof it was Lish who mugged you,' he insists. 'For all you know it could have been him.' He jerks his thumb at Dan.

'Jed, *please*.'

'Think about it, Emily. Someone took your bag, okay. That kind of thing happens on the tube every day. It was probably an addict, a street criminal. Look at what they took … cash and Valium are the things *I'd* steal from a handbag if I'd just mugged someone in an underground station.'

'Jed …'

'You said you didn't see Lish's face so there's no evidence it was him who attacked you,' Jed goes on. 'Just like you only have Thackeray's word that the drugs and the notebook belong to Lish. It's sick and pathetic. And the sickest and most pathetic part is that you've fallen for it so easily.' He shoots the words at me, full of venom.

'Stop it.' Dan moves closer. He is breathing heavily,

pulsing with rage. 'How dare you talk like that to her, you hypocrite. You give all this time and help to CASP but when it's your own son you—'

'I told you to fuck off already.' Jed shoves him. Dan stumbles backwards. 'Stay away from me. Stay away from my fiancée.'

He grabs my arm, hard. Again his fingers press against my bruise.

'Ow,' I yelp.

'Let her go.' Dan pushes Jed away from me, squaring up to him.

'Stop it.' I pull Dan away. 'I just want the notebook, Jed. I know this is hard, but it's the right—'

'Enough.' Jed reaches for me again but I back away. 'I've destroyed the notebook.'

I gasp, horrified.

'It was a fake anyway. This whole thing is a fake. A set-up.' Jed points at Dan. 'He's already admitted he made up the drugs thing to get you to help him write a story about me.'

'I didn't make anything up,' Dan insists. 'And I've already told Emily I'm not going to be writing a story. But she's not safe. If you really cared about her, you'd see that.'

'That's ridiculous.' Jed turns to me. 'Come on, I'm going to take you home. I'll take the rest of the day off.'

'No.' I stare at him. I can't believe how he is acting, how much fury is in the way he is looking at me.

'I'm going home on my own.' I turn away.

238

'Come back here,' Jed orders.

But I keep on walking: back onto the main street, past Jed's high-rise office and down the next street towards the tube station, away from them both.

July 2014

So there is good news and bad news. The bad news is that as I predicted Mum went HYSTERICAL when Dad came round last night and told her about him and Emily being engaged. I KNEW she was thinking that he must be coming to see her specially because it wasn't his weekend to see me and that is why she got all dressed up. He didn't stay very long and afterwards Mum burst in and said 'You KNEW!' and I think she was cross I hadn't told her though she said she was just cross with Dad . . . 'so selfish to make you keep such an awful secret'. Mum asked how I felt about Dad and Emily getting married and I didn't know what to say and Mum went on and said it was a mistake and Dad would regret it and she couldn't let it happen and OH MY DAYS she actually went to Emily's work earlier to shout at her which is SO embarrassing. I can just imagine her TOTALLY losing it at Emily like she does at Daddy.

At least there is good news too.

REALLY good. I can't believe it but Ava has just sent a text. One actually from HER, not with the sender blocked. She has asked me to go to her house tomorrow night for a sleepover. I was supposed to see Marietta Hingis but OBVIOUSLY I cancelled that so I could see Ava. She was SO nice in her text, like saying she wished *we could be friends again and how it's been SUCH a long time since we hung out together.*

I am going to wear my skinny jeans and my black shiny top. The jeans are a bit tight but they are my newest thing – from March. I did get clothes on my birthday in June but Mum chose them and they were HIDEOUS. One of them was actually PINK. How could she think I would wear that? Mum said black doesn't suit me and that it was a nice pink, not little-girly at all.

She doesn't understand.

I have shaved 'down there' again too, in case we are in the bath-room or whatever and Ava sees. She has an older sister so she is BOUND to know how it's supposed to look. I am not going to eat while I'm there either, just to make sure Ava doesn't go back to thinking I'm all fat and stupid again.

I can't wait. I can't wait. I can't wait.

December 2014

I hurry home to pack a change of clothes. My phone lies, switched off, on the bed as I rifle through the chest of drawers. Both Jed and Dan called after I walked away, so I turned the mobile off but I need it now. I set my bag on the floor and power up. Ignoring the missed calls and messages from both men, I hover over my favourites lists. Part of me wants to call Laura, but if she was sceptical about Lish attempting to poison me, then she'll be even less willing to believe he pushed me in front of a train. I could call Rose, of course. She'd certainly be horrified about what happened at the tube station. No, I can't face my big sister. She predicted that seeing Dan would lead to trouble with Jed and I can just imagine the reproachful look on her face if I tell her about the kiss. Even if I don't, I know full well that as she's offering me a sympathetic hug, she will also sigh and shake her head and be unable to resist pointing out that she was right that I should have stayed away from Dan. In the end I call my brother at work and tell him Jed and I have had a row and that I need a place to stay tonight. He tells me to swing by his office and he'll give me his key.

I'm just adding my toothbrush to my bag when the door-bell rings – a long, continuous tone. Who on earth is that?

I pick up the bag and hurry downstairs.

I can't believe it. Standing outside in a pink coat, her hands twisting nervously, is Zoe.

'May I come in?' She sounds as anxious as she looks.

I step back, gesturing towards the living room. My heart is hammering. Does she mean me harm? There's nothing about the way she's holding herself that suggests she's about to whip out a knife. Anyway, surely that isn't Zoe's style. She's the sort of person who gets others to do her dirty work for her.

'Zoe?'

She's looking around the living room. 'Gosh, but it's *very* John Lewis,' she says, a note of tartness creeping into her voice. 'I'm astonished Jed let you pick out that sofa.'

I stare at the sofa. It is beige and chunky, a neutral part-ner to the larger, older couch which Jed brought with him when he bought the house for us in March. Stylish with-out being obviously designer, we did indeed buy it from John Lewis soon after moving in. Jed wanted me to have a say in picking out a new piece of furniture and the sofa was my choice. A cacophony of questions race through my head:

How does Zoe know I chose the sofa? Or where we bought it from?

Did Jed tell her?

What else has he told her about us?

I fold my arms. 'If you've come around to sneer at my home you can leave right now.'

Zoe meets my gaze. I haven't seen her properly since Dee Dee's death, though I've had reports of her rages and her upsets on an almost daily basis. There is something horribly defeated about her face, a sadness that underlies everything. She doesn't look like she intends to hurt me.

'I'm sorry,' she says. 'I didn't mean to be rude. This is just ... hard ...'

I sit on the arm of the sofa. Zoe lowers herself into the armchair. She has nude shoes and a Kate Spade handbag that accents the buttons on her coat perfectly. I tug at the arms of my jumper, trying not to feel intimidated.

'What's this about?' I demand.

'Lish,' she says. Her voice cracks slightly as she says his name. 'Jed's told me what you think he did ... at my behest.'

My breath hitches in my throat. Jed has confided in her? Why did he do that? And why didn't he tell me he had?

'Right,' I say.

Zoe leans forward, her face creased with anxiety. 'I've come round to tell you that there is no way I would *ever* try to hurt you. Not physically. I admit I was angry when Jed left me for you and there was a time after ... after Dee Dee when I fantasized about something bad happening to you. Lish knows how upset I was. He's an adult, I couldn't exactly hide it from him, but it's just *madness* to think—'

'He's dealing drugs, Zoe.' I meet her gaze head on. 'He had access to potassium cyanide in the summer.'

244

She looks away. 'It's not true,' she says. 'Jed says that reporter made everything up, invented a notebook and everything, got people to lie about Lish. He reckons that at first the guy was trying to get a story on him and that now he's after you. Jed says he's an ex of yours. Is that true?'

'Yes, he's an ex,' I admit. 'But I don't see how Dan could possibly have made up everything you think he has. The notebook was full of detail and I heard people in this student pub we went to give Lish's name.'

'I'm not saying drug dealing doesn't go on,' Zoe says earnestly. 'I'm just saying it's not Lish that's doing it. Jed went down to his uni and looked into it.'

I stare at her. Is that true? If so it's yet another thing Jed hasn't told me about.

'Jed questioned people all over campus,' Zoe goes on. '*No one* gave up Lish's name. Not one single person.'

'Well, they wouldn't, would they?' Not to a bloody lawyer in a pinstripe. I look down. All the evidence I have against Lish filters through my head: the bag of drugs, the notebook, the Facebook post, the money in his backpack, the furious look he gave me, the tube attack. It's all gone or too vague to be useful. There's nothing tangible I can present to prove my case. And yet I'm *sure* Lish is guilty.

'Your son hates me,' I say.

'Hating you doesn't make him a murderer or a drug dealer.'

There's a long pause. I shuffle, feeling self-conscious, on the arm of the sofa. 'There was this text, back when you were still in Corsica. It said "it should have been you". *Should* have been, as in literally was *meant* to be.'

Zoe bites her lip. 'That *was* me,' she confesses. 'I told you I was angry. Beside myself, in fact. But I didn't really mean . . . I was just lashing out.' She stands up. 'Look, I've said what I came here to say. I'm sorry I sent that text. But you have to understand it wasn't meant as a threat in any way. I'm just begging you not to cause any trouble for Lish. *Please.*'

'I can't promise anything,' I say.

'But you do believe I didn't tell him to hurt you?'

I think back to Rose's expression of disbelief when I told her I'd read Zoe's letter to her son as an open command to murder me. Zoe's eyes gleam with misery.

'Yes,' I say. And it's the truth.

Zoe nods, her expression easing a little. 'Good.' She gets up. 'So . . . well . . . just please think carefully before you do anything.'

The big graphics agency where Martin works part-time has its main office on the ground floor of a modern block. I'm sitting in reception waiting for Martin to appear, thinking about Zoe's visit, when Rose's ex, Simon, saunters out of a door marked IT Section A. In all the turmoil of the morning, I'd forgotten about him working here. Simon whistles as he walks towards the reception desk, picks up an envelope and turns to leave. I shrink down in my seat, hoping he won't notice me. A strained chat with a man who unceremoniously dumped my sister is the last thing I feel like dealing with at this point.

'Hi, Emily.'

Great.

I look up. Simon is beaming down at me. He has a doughy, comfortable face with hooded eyes and a seriously receding hairline. I force a smile onto my own face.

'Hi there.'

'You waiting for your brother?'

'Yes.'

There's an awkward pause. The clock over the reception desk ticks noisily into the silence. Somewhere in the distance a phone rings.

'Er, how's Rose?' A pink flush creeps over Simon's cheeks.

'Fine. Looking great, actually, and doing really, really well.' I sit up straighter, on my guard. I've got nothing against Simon himself, but family is family. Anyway I'm sure Rose wouldn't want me to give the impression she was still suffering from Simon breaking up with her more than six months after the event.

'Ah, well, Rose *always* looked great,' Simon says wistfully. He fidgets with the edge of the envelope in his hand. 'Is she, er, you know ... *with* anyone these days?'

I stare at him blankly. He's giving every indication of still holding a massive candle for my sister. Which makes no sense. He dumped *her*.

'It's just I was wondering about calling her,' Simon hurries on. 'But obviously, if she's seeing someone ...'

I clear my throat. 'Sorry,' I say. 'I'm not sure I follow.'

Simon looks around him. The reception area is empty, the receptionist behind the desk poring over a clipboard. He sits down next to me and lowers his voice.

'Do you think she would mind if I called? I mean, before, she said she needed space ... time ... but it's been a while and, if there isn't anyone serious ...?'

Another pause. 'Sorry, but it sounds like you're saying Rose broke up with you,' I venture eventually. 'And, maybe I've got it all wrong, but I thought *you* broke up with *her*.'

'No.' Simon's face is the colour of beetroot. I'm pretty certain mine is a similar shade. 'No, I don't know where you got that idea from but no, I didn't break up with her. She, er, she said she needed space ... like I said ...'

I have no idea what to say now. Thankfully Martin chooses this minute to appear, hurrying through the saloon doors which shut behind him with a whoosh. He nods, distracted, at Simon, who stands up, mumbles something that sounds roughly like 'tell her I said hello' and melts speedily away.

Martin rushes over to me, his face etched with concern. In an instant everything Simon just said goes out of my head. I'm back on the tube platform, reliving the shove and the grab. I shiver.

'Are you okay?'

'Yes,' I lie.

'Not buying it.' The kindness of his expression threatens to make me cry, so I press my lips together and attempt to smile at him. Out of the corner of my eye I can see the receptionist looking up. I flush, feeling self-conscious.

'Can we talk later?'

'Course, I'll be home as soon as I can.' Martin hands me his house key and asks the receptionist to call me a cab.

It's almost one thirty when I arrive at his and Cameron's elegant designer townhouse – whose most stunning feature is that it's located on the banks of the river near Twickenham. Their home is neat and stylish, full of angular furniture and several of the striking stone sculptures that Cameron collects. I wander around looking at the new pieces. The bottom level of the house is mostly a large open-plan kitchen/diner that leads onto the garden and the *Maggie May*'s mooring in the river beyond, but up the spiral staircase there are two large bedrooms, each with their own bathroom. The spare room is nominally Martin's den, but apart from some gym equipment and pictures of me and Rose and our parents, it's as bare – and styled – as the rest of the place. Martin and Cameron moved in here a couple of years ago. I have never stayed over – after all, both my old home with Rose and my home with Jed are less than a sixty-minute cab journey away – but now I test out the spare room's large double bed. It's firm and made up with crisp cotton sheets and an eiderdown. There are aluminium blinds at the window, a metal-tipped chest of drawers and a wooden dressing table that doesn't really fit with everything else. It used to belong to Mum, I think, though I don't remember it myself. Rose for some reason hated it and happily let Martin take it when he moved out years ago. Martin has lugged it around with him ever since.

Now I've stopped running I'm aware of how sore my arm is. I'm also extremely cold, in fact I can't stop shivering. Trying to warm up, I go into the spare room's en suite bathroom and run a bath. I soak and wash my hair, then dry myself with the soft white towel on the rail. There's a beautiful silk dressing gown on the back of the door, but I want something warmer and cosier, so I search the chest of drawers until I find a sweater. It's too big for me, of course, but I put it on anyway.

I think about going back down to make a cup of tea or find some painkillers to ease the dull ache in my shoulder, but I'm overwhelmed with tiredness so, instead, I crawl under the eiderdown and fall fast asleep.

The sound of a door opening makes me wake with a start. My eyes spring open. Martin is walking into the room. He sits on the end of the bed.

'So what's up, Flaky?' he asks, his concerned expression morphing into a sympathetic smile. 'Boy trouble, eh?' Flaky is his occasional pet name for me, a hangover from when he was a cool sixth former and I was his dizzy little sister.

I sit up, feeling disoriented. It takes a moment for everything to come back to me. Then I shudder, remembering the sensation of falling towards the track. I launch into my story, trying to tell everything as simply and clearly as I can.

When I get to this morning and my narrow escape from

Lish's attack on the tube platform I roll up the sleeve of his jumper and show him the dark bruise. 'This is from where a passer-by grabbed me and saved me.'

Martin lets out a low whistle. 'Whoa.' He frowns. 'That looks sore. Are you sure you're okay?'

I nod, though inside I am far from okay.

'I'm going to get some ice for that bruise. D'you want a paracetamol too?'

'Yes, thanks.' I still feel really cold. 'Would you mind putting on the heating too?'

'Sure.' Martin is already out of the door. He comes back a couple of minutes later with a tray containing water, pills and an icepack. I apply the pack to my sore skin and lie back on the pillows.

'Now go through what has happened again,' Martin says very seriously. 'Rose told me that Dan Thackeray turned up out of the blue peddling some line about Jed's son dealing drugs. She seems to think he's trying to get between you and Jed in order to get you back. Is that true?'

'No, well, yes ... a bit,' I explain. 'It's more complicated than that.'

'Go on.'

I take two paracetamol and tell him everything. I hesitate when I come to the recent part about kissing Dan, but then plunge ahead. Martin, like Rose, may not approve of Dan but unlike her he won't judge me for the kiss.

'Holy cow.' Martin's only interjection is heartfelt. I finish my tale, describing first the row between Dan and Jed, then

251

Zoe's visit. Martin gives me a brief, fierce hug, then shakes his head. 'I thought I was bad, but you're a bloody *disaster* magnet.'

We both laugh.

'I know,' I say with a rueful smile. Martin sighs and it strikes me that he looks tired and his suit is crumpled. There's a sprinkling of grey in his carefully gelled dark hair too. I'm sure that wasn't there in the summer. I wonder if he worries about getting older. Cameron is several years younger and arguably even better-looking than Martin.

I deepen my smile. 'At least I don't put too much wax in my hair.'

'You're not too old, young lady,' Martin jokes, echoing one of the lines our father used to say to Rose. The three of us often say the words to each other, part of the family tradition we have constructed in the absence of our parents. Of course I have no memory of the words ever actually being spoken, but Rose and Martin do and it helps all of us keep our awareness of Mum and Dad alive.

'What time is it?' I ask.

Martin checks his Rolex. I'm surprised when he says that it's only just gone three p.m.; it feels much later.

'You got away from work okay?' I say.

'Course. I was worried,' Martin says. 'Look, are you really sure you were deliberately pushed onto the tube track earlier?'

I close my eyes, recalling the blur of a memory that this morning has become. 'No,' I admit. 'I mean, I was definitely shoved but I couldn't say for sure that whoever did it meant me actually to fall off the platform. Anyway, there's no way of proving who it was. The guy at the ticket office said you couldn't see a face on the CCTV of him, just that whoever it was, was about five foot eleven and skinny. Which Lish is.'

Martin shrugs. 'So are lots of people. I mean it *could* just be a random mugger.'

I shiver, though the heating is on now and my limbs are warming up. I look down at the eiderdown between us and twist my still-damp hair around my fingers. I feel about fourteen years old again, on those occasions when Rose would get fed up with my behaviour and call on Martin to reason with me: *Please, Mart, Emily listens to you. Tell her that getting a navel piercing is a really bad idea.* It strikes me suddenly that poor Dee Dee never made it to fourteen.

'Jed was horrible earlier,' I say. 'He refused to listen to what Dan and I were saying. And he's been talking to Zoe about it too.'

'Well, it's got to be hard for him to hear,' Martin says softly. 'Not to mention to see you with Dan Thackeray. Word to the wise, don't tell him Dan kissed you. A guy like Jed doesn't take that sort of thing well.' He pauses. 'You know, when you first met him I thought he was a bit pompous and way, way too old for you, but the more times I've met him the more I think he's just what you need.'

'Meaning what?'

'Meaning that he's steady and he loves you as you are and he likes looking after you.'

'Mmmn,' I say. 'Maybe.'

'Relationships aren't easy,' Martin says. 'I'm just saying I wouldn't want you to split with Jed just because Dan's turned up and you're all overwhelmed because he's so hot . . .' He tilts his head to one side and gives me a camp smile. 'He *is* still hot, I assume?'

'Hotter.' I grimace, realizing the truth of this as I say it. 'Unfortunately.'

Martin makes a face back at me. 'Well, hot or not, I don't want to see you acting like Rose, sabotaging relationships because they're not exciting enough.'

'You think Rose does that?' What is he talking about? I suddenly remember my earlier conversation with Simon. I suck in my breath. 'She dumped Simon, didn't she? It wasn't the other way around at all, even though she said it was.'

'Never mind Rose, I shouldn't have brought her into this.'

'But you did,' I persist. 'What did you mean by her "sabotaging" relationships?'

'Forget it, I shouldn't have said anything.'

'Said *what*? What *are* you saying? Did Rose sabotage things with Simon?' I screw up my forehead, trying to think what this might mean in practice. 'He gave me the impression she dumped him, which is the opposite of what Rose said when it happened.'

Martin sighs. 'I can't, Emily. Rose spoke to me in confidence.'

'Please, Mart, I know she doesn't talk to me about stuff like that, but I half-know it now anyway. You might as well tell me the truth. Did she end it? Or did he? Because I thought she was gutted that he dumped her; she was always saying how nice he was.'

'Yeah, too nice for Rose.' Martin sighs again. 'It wasn't that simple. Look, for God's sake don't tell her I've told you, but the truth is that Rose had a fling with someone else while she was going out with Simon. He found out and, well, to be honest, I think he would have taken her back but Rose had fallen for this other guy quite hard, so she kind of did an "I'm confused about how I feel . . . I need time to think" number on him.'

My mouth gapes. 'Who was the guy she had the fling with?'

'I don't know,' Martin admits. 'She wouldn't say, but I think he was married.'

'*Rose* had an affair with a married man?'

'Rose isn't so perfect.' Martin shifts uncomfortably on the edge of the bed. 'I shouldn't have said anything, I just don't want you to go the same way, throwing away someone steady and reliable for a guy like Dan Thackeray.' He glances over at the dressing table in the corner. 'It was bad like that for Mum with Dad, you know. I remember her sitting there, in front of the mirror, telling me when I was thirteen or so.'

'Telling you what?'

'Dad having ... I think she called them "ladies" ... and being a bit unreliable, you know ... affairs ... well, maybe not full-on affairs but definitely flings ...'

I stare at him, open-mouthed, at this second bombshell. 'You're kidding, I thought Mum and Dad were happy together?'

'They were, in their way,' Martin insists. 'But I remember Mum being miserable that she'd chosen a bad boy. Not that she put it in those terms of course.'

'What terms *did* she put it in?' I lean forward, intent on Martin's reply. I have never heard our parents talked about like this before.

'I don't know, but that time I mentioned ... Rose was with her friends downstairs and you must have already been asleep. I was sitting on Mum and Dad's bed, watching Mum in front of that.' He points across the room to the elegant wooden dressing table. 'She was getting ready to go out, putting on make-up. She looked at me in the mirror and she said: "It's sad that I'm not enough for your dad, thank goodness I have you".'

'You're *kidding*?' This is so at odds with the perfect picture I've always had of our parents' marriage that I feel completely stunned.

Martin shrugs. 'Look, that's all ancient history. The important thing is what we do now after everything that's happened to you. With Lish. I'll come with you to the police if that's what you want, but I'm not sure they'll be able to make any more sense of it than I have. I mean it all rests on the fact that you think Lish tried to kill you back in Corsica because he and his mum were angry about you and Jed. Which doesn't tie up with Lish supposedly trying to kill you today because you had the fake drugs he supposedly supplied to Dan Thackeray. On top of which, *neither* attempt to kill you has worked. So you can't even point to an actual crime.'

'But poor Dee Dee *died*.'

'I know.'

'It all goes back to her and Lish.' I sit back. 'And Zoe. Except I believed her today, about not seriously wanting to hurt me.'

'Well, maybe she's got nothing to do with it,' Martin says with a sigh. 'Maybe it's just Lish. Except if he wasn't trying to kill you for his mother, what *was* his motive? It doesn't make sense. And why draw attention to his drug dealing anyway?'

I sit up. 'Maybe it's not just *his* drug dealing.' I blow out my breath, working it through. 'If Lish is dealing drugs at uni – and despite what Jed and Zoe think I don't believe Dan was lying about that – he can't be doing it in isolation. He'll have suppliers and clients, be part of a bigger operation.'

'I guess so,' Martin agrees. 'But that still doesn't explain why he wanted to kill you.'

'Suppose he *didn't*?' I think back to the day Dee Dee died, to that moment she told me she had a secret on the steps of the citadel at Calvi. 'Suppose Dee Dee saw her brother drug dealing while we were in France? She said there was something she wanted to tell me, something she'd seen. Maybe I wasn't the target after all. Not originally. Maybe Dee Dee was killed to stop her from talking.'

Martin frowns. 'You're saying Lish murdered his own sister on *purpose*?'

'Not necessarily *Lish*. Whoever he is working for. If they found out Dee Dee had witnessed them dealing, maybe *they* did it.' I get up and pace across the room. 'God, Martin, it's the only explanation that makes sense.'

'I still don't see how.'

'Okay, we know from the notebook that Lish was dealing in KCN - potassium cyanide. Well, suppose someone else in his gang or whatever had access to it too? They could have easily snuck into the villa, forced the cyanide down Dee Dee then put a few dregs in the ExAche powders, to make it look like it was a freak manufacturing accident. They murdered Dee Dee so she couldn't tell anyone what she'd seen.'

Martin's eyes widen. 'Leaving Lish too scared to speak out himself?'

'Exactly,' I say. 'The whole thing isn't some violent step-family melodrama, it's organized crime. Dee Dee just got in the way so they shut her up.'

'And now you and Dan Thackeray are getting in the way,' Martin adds. 'Which explains the attack on the tube. That probably wasn't Lish either but whoever he's working for.'

'You're right.' I reach for my clothes. 'Come on, we have to tell the police.'

'Are you sure, Emily? I mean, you don't have proof of any of this.' Martin points to the fingermarks on my arms. 'In fact the only physical evidence of you being hurt is from the guy who saved you.'

'Dan will back me up. At the very least, the police will have to investigate Lish's drug dealing properly, not just ask a few students like Jed did.'

'Jed will go ballistic.' Martin pauses. 'You could lose him forever.'

'I know, but the alternative is doing nothing. And I couldn't live with myself if I don't at least *try* to get justice.'

'Justice?'

'For Dee Dee,' I say. 'If her parents won't do it then it's up to me.'

PART FOUR

November 1997

Rose peered down at the UCAS application form. It made her feel old. The last time she'd applied to university the system had been different ... even the acronym had changed from the old UCCA. More significantly, Rose herself was not the same person. She sighed and picked up her pen. So far, all she'd managed to enter onto her form were the facts: her name and address, her date of birth and her GCSE and A-level qualifications. Now, somehow, she had to explain why she wanted to apply to do a Business Studies degree.

It shouldn't, surely, be this difficult. After all, she'd been planning to go to uni for years. Of course, when Mum and Dad died during her gap year she had turned down her original place to study History at Warwick. There was no way she could have left Martin and Emily then. But five years had passed – the fifth and, to Rose, highly significant, anniversary of their parents' death had been last week – and a lot had changed. Martin, who, against all predictions, had sailed through his A-levels, was studying International Relations at Durham while

Emily had just started in the sixth form at school. There was no reason why Rose shouldn't find somewhere in London to study part-time *and* still be at home for her sister. The longer she'd worked in the shop the more ridiculous the idea of her original degree in History seemed. Interesting, but irrelevant, was how she felt about it now. So she'd changed her mind and her sights were now set on studying Business. Though really, when she thought about it, Rose couldn't believe an academic course – even a good one – could prepare her for setting up and building her own business better than her job where she actually *managed* the store. Day in, day out. Ordering stock, dealing with staff, responding to customers. It wasn't easy. But Rose was good at it, at least she thought she was.

Her phone went. Martin. With a sigh, Rose picked up the mobile. Martin hardly ever called her, usually only to ask about something practical like when the next rent payment on his student house was due – Rose helped with all the financial arrangements – or how to get a wine stain out of a white shirt. Since he had come out two years ago, there had been less distance between them but Rose wouldn't describe their relationship as close. However, Martin definitely put a lot of effort into staying in touch with Emily – and for that, above everything, Rose forgave him all his self-absorbed ways.

'Hi, Mart,' she said.

'Rose?'

She could hear in his voice that something was terribly wrong.

'What is it?'

'I've been arrested,' he said. 'I'm not being charged but ...' His voice cracked. 'Could you come?'

Martin shucked off his jacket. Much to his relief the house was empty. Robbo was away visiting his parents, while Nathaniel and Dev, both of whom he sometimes slept with, were out. Rose followed him into the living room. She sat down on the edge of the couch, still in her coat. Martin glanced at her: she was tight-lipped, tense. Nothing unusual about that. Rose had been uptight for as long as he could remember. She was really the last person he'd wanted to turn to, but as she was also the only person he could turn to, there hadn't been much choice.

'I don't understand,' she said. 'It wasn't even on the anniversary.'

Martin frowned. Unlike his sister, to whom the anniversaries of their parents' deaths seemed incredibly important, he deliberately only allowed himself a vague idea of the date as having occurred in early November.

'Just promise me ...' Rose went on, now staring down at the threadbare carpet ... 'that it won't *ever* happen again. And that Emily will never know.'

Martin turned away from her and wandered over to the window. He wished, now, that he hadn't called her.

She was making too big a deal of it. All that had happened was that he'd been caught smoking some pot outside a student pub. It was hardly crime of the century. Just because Rose was so straitlaced that she had probably never even *seen* a joint, it wasn't fair to judge him. Cannabis was harmless, everyone said so. What would Rose say if she knew about the E's he took every weekend and sometimes during the week – or the regular lines of coke or the acid or the ketamine?

'Mart?'

He turned around. 'I won't tell Emily, I promise.'

'What about not *doing* it again.' Rose indicated the living room. 'And this place is filthy.'

'What's that got to—?' Martin stopped. This was typical Rose, he was starting to realize. Throwing two apparently unrelated comments at him to confuse him, but somehow connecting them in her head. He took a stab at the connection. 'If you are implying that I'm living in some kind of drugs den, then you've got it all wrong.'

'I just think you should take a bit of responsibility for yourself,' Rose went on. She folded her arms. 'It's not fair making *me* do it all.'

'Right.' Martin suddenly saw why Rose was so tight-lipped, so resentful.

She was talking about Emily.

Martin felt a wave of anger well inside him. Talk about 'not fair': Rose had *chosen* to take on their sister. She *lived* for Emily. And looking after her *suited* Rose. Not that Emily really needed that much looking after any more.

'Don't use Emily as an excuse,' he snapped. 'She's sixteen.'

Rose glared at him. 'What are you talking about?'

'I know what you're really saying: that you're Mrs Mature, staying at home and working and being a big sister and *I'm* just mucking about, having fun at uni, being lazy, having a laugh. Well, you know what, Rose? You should try laughing sometimes too, not to mention stopping hiding behind Emily as an excuse for not getting on with your own life—' Martin stopped in horror. Two fat tears were rolling down his sister's cheeks. Guilt seared him, swamping the fury. He stood, feeling awkward, while Rose wiped her eyes. She suddenly looked just like Mum, crying when Dad shouted at her.

'I'm just trying to do my best,' she muttered.

'I know.' Martin looked at the dirty floor. Rose was right, it was a bit of a tip in here – and he *was* a little lazy if truth be told. But he was right too. Rose was scared of life and taking care of their sister – for all it was a selfless, generous thing to do – was also a way of avoiding challenges. A way of staying stuck.

But it wasn't right to attack Rose about that. He wasn't going to be like Dad, making people he loved cry. Not ever. 'I'm sorry,' he said sheepishly. Then he took a deep breath. Better to lie and make things right between them, than tell the truth and hurt one of the only two

SOPHIE MCKENZIE

people in the world who he knew for sure had – and would always have – his back.

'I didn't mean any of that,' he said. 'You're a brilliant sister and the bravest person I know. That's why I called you when they arrested me.'

Rose looked up, mouth trembling. He held his breath, unsure why it was so desperately important that she stopped being upset.

And then, to his relief, his sister smiled.

DECEMBER 2014

Dan and I are outside the police station. Dan is checking his phone, dealing with a message from work. My heart is beating fast and hard. Can I really do this? It's one thing to suspect someone of a terrible crime, quite another to make a public accusation. And what about the fall-out on Jed? Will he ever forgive me for telling the police that I believe his son has tried to kill me twice – and that his daughter was the unintended victim of the first murder attempt?

The sun is shining, fierce and bright. I close my eyes, remembering the moment I felt that shove, then the fall through the air, the sudden pain in my arm when the young man gripped me and saved me.

I *am* doing the right thing. Because I have been lucky so far – but I may not be a third time. And because this is the only way to find justice for Dee Dee.

I open my eyes. Dan pockets his phone and turns to me. 'Ready?'

The young police officer listens as I repeat my story yet again. He takes some more notes, then asks me to wait. Dan has already been taken off into another interview room. I wonder if it looks the same as the one I'm in: beige walls, threadbare carpet, flimsy, plasticky chairs and tables. I feel sick to my stomach. All I can think is that Jed will never forgive me. I've told the police about everything, from Zoe's text and her letter to Lish to the drugs Lish sold Dan and the notebook containing details of his deals – and, of course, the tube platform attack. It's all out there now, in the open. And while it's a relief to have spoken, I'm also terrified about what will happen next. I feel like I've thrown my entire life up in the air and I'm now forced to stand, watching it spin and fall to the ground, wondering how things will settle.

The clock on the wall ticks slowly and loudly on. What are the police doing? I wait. And I wait. And I wait.

Eventually the young officer returns. 'I've got things moving,' he says.

'What does, er, that mean exactly?'

He clears his throat. 'We're looking into it,' he says. 'You'll probably be contacted again in the next few days.'

'Right.' Is it normal for the police to be so neutral? This guy seems almost wary of me.

'Where's Dan, the guy I came in with?'

'He's still talking to someone.' The officer studies me. 'But your fiancé is waiting for you outside. Jed Kennedy.'

A fist clutches my guts and squeezes hard. 'Jed?' I gasp. '*Here?* How did he know I was here?'

The officer frowns. 'Are you afraid for your safety, Emily? Because if you are, we can—'

'No.' I stand up. I can't believe Jed will hurt me. And I have to face him at some point. 'So you'll definitely investigate?'

The officer bristles slightly. 'As I said, we will look into everything you've told us.'

'Right,' I repeat, standing up. I follow the officer out of the room, along the corridor then back out past the duty sergeant's desk into the waiting room. My heart is thumping so hard I can only just hear the squeak of the officer's rubber soles on the linoleum floor. Any second I will have to face Jed. I cannot imagine how furious he will be. The room is crowded now. I glance around. Where is he?

'Emily?'

There. Jed is standing beside an empty seat. Lish is next to him. I gasp in horror. What is Lish doing here? The boy doesn't meet my eyes. He is looking at his dad who is looking at me: face drawn and exhausted, expression utterly miserable.

'Jed.' I am frozen to the spot. The officer has melted away. Lish moves out of my sight as Jed strides towards me.

'Oh, baby.' He lets out a strangled sob as he reaches me. There are tears in his eyes. 'Oh, baby, what have you done?'

'What are you doing here?' I can barely get the words out as Jed pulls me into a hug. I disentangle myself. 'How did you know I was here?'

'Your phone.' Jed points to my handbag. 'I switched your Apple ID to mine the other day after you told me ... what you'd been doing ... so I could see where you were.'

My mouth gapes. 'You've been *spying* on me?'

'No.' Jed looks horrified. 'Of course not, baby, I just wanted to make sure you were okay.'

'By *stalking* me?' I can't believe it.

'No, not at all. It's just you've been acting so weird, making all these claims against Lish.'

'They're *true*.' My breath catches in my throat. I can't believe Jed has actually gone into my phone and changed the settings. I glance around the room. No one is paying us any attention. All eyes are on an argument which has broken out across the waiting room. There is no sign of Lish.

'Where did Lish go?' I demand. 'Why is he here?'

'When I saw where you were, I called him,' Jed says, his voice tight with emotion. 'He agrees that making a statement is the best way to deal with false accusations, so he's here to do just that.'

I shake my head. 'I'm so sorry, Jed, but they're *not* false accusations. He's involved in drug dealing, using potassium cyanide ... my attack in the tube yesterday.'

'Lish has an alibi for yesterday morning,' Jed interrupts. 'He was in a lecture, there were lots of witnesses. He was *miles* away in Southampton.'

'Then I was pushed by someone he's working with ...'

'Please.' Jed bats this away. 'Lish says he's happy for the police to search his flat and he assures me they will find *nothing* there, no drugs, nothing suspicious.'

I'm sure this at least is true. After all, I searched his room myself and only found Zoe's letter.

Zoe. I suddenly remember yesterday's visit. 'You told Zoe everything – you went and told her what I was saying, you said you'd been down to Lish's university and—'

'I *have* been there. And of course I told Zoe.' Jed frowns. 'She's his mother.' He moves closer. '*Please*, baby, my son is *not* a drug dealer. Dan Thackeray has fabricated the whole story.'

'Dan *gave* me the fake Valium Lish sold him. I *saw* Lish's notebook.'

'Dan made those things up.' Jed takes my hand.

'No.' I pull it away. 'He recorded the meeting, he told me all about it.'

'He made it up,' Jed repeats. 'Think about it. Did you actually *hear* a recording?'

'No,' I admit. 'But that's because Dan destroyed it as … as a way of proving he wasn't going to use the story.'

'How convenient,' Jed sneers.

'I was still *attacked* yesterday, Jed.'

'I know, baby, and I'm so sorry that happened to you, but whoever did it must have been a common-or-garden mugger, probably just after your cash. Then they took the Valium too, because it was there. You said yourself the bruise on your arm was from where someone tried to save you. I understand it was upsetting, but I doubt if it was attempted murder. And it certainly didn't have anything to do with my son.'

My head spins. He's wrong. I *know* he is wrong.

'Please come home with me.' Jed's voice cracks. 'If you

don't love me any more then that's one thing, but if all this . . .' He waves his hand to indicate the police station. 'If being here is just because Dan Thackeray has filled your head with lies, then I'm not letting you go. I'm not letting the fucker win that easily.'

'Win?' A dull weight settles in my guts. 'Win what? I told you, Dan agreed to drop the story about you. He's just trying to help me.'

'Help himself, you mean.' Jed says. 'Dan Thackeray isn't doing all this to get a story on me. That's what I thought at first, but it isn't true, at least not any more. I've talked to your sister and she helped me see it. Dan Thackeray has made up all this stuff about Lish to get *you*.'

I stare at him, shocked that he has been speaking to Rose now, as well as Zoe. For a moment I waver. Could it really be true that Dan has made everything up to get me back? I think about our kiss and the look of longing in Dan's eyes. He has feelings for me, that's true, but he wouldn't fabricate an entire narrative about Lish just to prise me away from Jed. Apart from anything else, it's not Dan's style to be so calculating where his emotions are concerned.

Jed clenches his fists. 'Dan Thackeray is a first-class bastard. Rose filled me in on some of the details from your past: how he messed you around when you were younger. If I see him I'm not sure I'll be able to stop myself from hitting him. Not this time.' He pulls me towards him. 'Please come home, baby. I've taken the rest of the week off. I'm sorry, I know this is partly my fault. I've been distracted with the court case against Benecke Tricorp, preoccupied since losing Dee Dee.' His hand is strong and heavy on my arm. 'Please, I can't lose you too.'

I hesitate. Dan is still inside the station, talking to the police. I want to speak to him, to find out what he's said, what they've told him. But I also don't want Jed to carry out his threat. Better they don't meet right now. So I let Jed lead me out of the police station. I can call Dan later.

Our drive home is silent. Jed glances at me occasionally and there is such pain in his expression I can't meet his gaze.

'Oh, shit,' Jed says as we turn the corner into our road.

I look up. Zoe is standing outside the house, her arms folded. As Jed parks she starts pacing along the pavement towards us. Jed gives a weary sigh.

'Go in the house,' he says. 'I'll deal with her.'

As I get out Zoe lets rip. 'How could you do this, you whore?' she snarls, racing over in vertiginous heels. I hurry past her, taking in a flash of the apple green skirt poking out under the pink coat. 'You fucking cruel, stupid bitch.'

I keep going, head down. I can hear Jed behind us, ordering Zoe to stop, but Zoe stays beside me, her heels clacking against the pavement. 'I *told* you it was *me* who sent you that text,' she hisses under her breath. 'I totally humiliated myself so that you would fucking back off, and instead you've made things even worse.'

I reach the front door and turn to face her. Zoe's eyes

blaze, her mouth tight, everything tensed. Lines crease at her temples but her forehead is weirdly smooth. Definitely Botox then. I swallow the thought down.

'I told the *truth*,' I say quietly. 'I told the police what I honestly believe.'

Zoe stares at me. Before she can speak again, I hurry inside and shut the door. Outside I can hear her yelling at Jed now, his own voice taut with frustration as he tries to make her leave. As I slip off my jacket and hang it on the back of a kitchen chair my phone rings. The number is withheld. It could easily be Dan, calling from a landline at the police station. I take the call.

'Is that the little bird?' The voice is disguised, mechanical, but I'm certain it's male; the low growl is full of menace. 'The little bird who's been talking?'

I freeze, my hand resting on the kitchen table. 'Who is this?'

The line goes dead. I stare down at the phone. Was that Lish? His drug-dealing contact? I must know the caller. Why else would they disguise their voice? The front door opens and shuts behind me. A second later Jed stomps into the kitchen.

'Bloody woman,' he mutters. 'I was fucking dealing with it.'

I turn around to face him, barely registering that he is talking about Zoe.

'Someone just called me, they *threatened* me, Jed. At least . . .'

'Stop it,' he snaps. 'Seriously, enough with the melo-dramatics.'

'Jed, I'm not making this up.' I shove my phone under his nose. 'See? They withheld their number. They said something about a "little bird" who'd been talking.'

'And?'

'What d'you mean, "*and*"? It was a threat.'

'More likely it's fucking Thackeray again, setting you up.'

I shake my head. Why can't he see what's happening? Why won't he believe me? I take a deep breath.

'Jed, sweetheart, I can't begin to imagine how hard this is, having to deal with me and Zoe and everything you're hearing about Lish ... but don't you want justice for Dee Dee? Isn't her life worth as much as Lish's freedom?' I pause. 'Why are you so determined to believe Lish can't possibly have been drug dealing?'

Jed's mouth trembles, just a fraction. 'I admit that my starting point may be a bit biased about Lish, but I've seen absolutely no proof that he's done anything wrong. Anyway, can you not see that you're ten times more blink-ered about Dan Thackeray?'

'This isn't about Dan,' I insist. 'It's about your son. If Lish *is* mixed up in something bad, which I'm sure he is and that phone call I just had *proves* it, then don't you *want* to do something to stop that? Don't you *want* to help him?'

Jed's eyes fill with anger. 'Don't talk to me about my

277

children,' he snaps. 'You don't know anything about what I want for my children.'

I feel like he's just slapped my face. My phone rings again, blasting into the tense silence. I glance down at the screen. It's Dan. I rush past Jed and up to our bedroom, answering only when the door is closed.

'Hi.' I sit heavily on the bed, letting what happened downstairs sink in. Jed doesn't believe me, isn't ever going to believe me.

'Em?' Dan's voice is full of concern. 'Where are you? I just got out of the police station and you'd gone.'

'Jed turned up.' I'm struggling to stop my voice from shaking. 'He was angry, I didn't want him to see you so it was easier to leave.'

'Right.' There's a pause. 'Are you okay?'

'Yes but … but Jed says Lish has an alibi for when I was attacked on the tube and the police won't find anything at his flat and all the drugs and the notebook are gone so there's no proof so …'

'I know. And his dad is a top lawyer, et cetera, et cetera …' Dan's voice is bitter. There's another long pause. 'Are you really okay? With Jed, I mean?'

'I don't know,' I admit. 'He doesn't believe his son is guilty, but he loves me. And … and I love him.'

Despite the fact that he stalked me using my own phone.

'Okay.' Dan sucks in his breath. 'Listen, *I'm* not going to stop investigating, because what Lish Kennedy is doing is wrong and we both know it's linked to Dee Dee's death, but I'm not going to involve you any more. If you want to stay with Jed, you can't pursue his son.'

'But Dan, wait. Someone just called me. A man. He was threatening us.'

'All the more reason for you to stop being involved.' Dan sighs. 'So you won't get hurt.'

'I don't want *you* to get hurt either.'

'But you *do* want justice for Dee Dee,' he counters. 'And I'm going to help get it.'

I don't know what to say. I lie back on the bed.

'I think it's safest if I don't contact you for now,' Dan says carefully. 'But I will when I've got something . . . if you want me to.'

We say goodbye and ring off. I close my eyes, feeling lonelier than I can ever remember being in my life.

A long, miserable week passes. Jed reluctantly removes his Apple ID from my phone and I reset it with my own details. We speak mostly of meals and TV programmes, avoiding the topics of Lish and weddings altogether. I call the police to find out what's happening. It takes ages to get through to anyone who knows anything. Finally I speak to a liaison officer who tells me that, as Jed predicted, the police have been unable to unearth anyone on Lish's campus who is prepared to link him to any drug dealing. Though the officer doesn't say so directly, I can see the investigation is running out of steam already. It's a deeply depressing thought.

Christmas Day dawns crisp and sunny. Lish will not be

visiting, though Jed plans to slip out later and see him at his mother's house. The more time passes, the worse I feel: guilty to have caused Jed so much pain, of course, but also angry that he has not believed me. I'm fearful for Dan too. I've checked in a couple of times, just brief texts, to make sure he's okay. His replies are equally short, though he always asks how I'm doing. I feel as if I'm living with half the breath permanently squeezed out of my lungs. I have no appetite, no interest in anything. Sometimes I wake in the night and the mechanically disguised voice from the day I went to the police echoes in my ear: *the little bird who's been talking*.

How can Jed so wilfully ignore such a warning? How can he persist in thinking that Dan could terrorize me by setting up such a phone call? I am furious with Rose for reinforcing his suspicions about Dan with her own prejudices, ignoring her calls for a couple of days then having a huge row over the phone.

'Do you realize he *stalked* me to find out where I was?' I explain about Jed's manipulation of my mobile.

Rose gasps when she hears, but sticks to her guns over Dan: 'Jed shouldn't have done that, but just because he was in the wrong there doesn't put Dan in the right over everything else. I'm certain his main agenda is to get you back.'

'Okay, but now Jed thinks Dan's invented *everything* he's said in order to get me back. Which isn't true.'

'No, I see that. I'm sorry, Emily, I was just worried about

you when I talked to him.' Rose sniffs. She sounds close to tears. 'Things have just gone so far ... you going to the police and everything.' She hesitates. 'You *are* dropping this whole thing now, aren't you? For your own safety?'

'Yes,' I say. 'I am.' I don't tell her about Dan continuing with the investigation without me. She won't approve and she will worry. 'But it's hard that Jed doesn't believe me over Lish.'

'Well, Lish is his son,' Rose reasons. 'I guess it's a bit of a blind spot, but you shouldn't let it stop you being honest with him.'

I itch, suddenly, to point out that after lying about her break-up with Simon, Rose is hardly in a position to lecture me about being honest, but there's no point being antagonistic when we've only just made our peace over her talking to Jed. So I keep quiet.

Jed and I spend Christmas morning together at home, then drive to Rose's house just after midday. The place is beautifully decorated, with a slender Christmas tree in the living room covered in tiny silver lights that give that corner a glamorous feel to match the strings of baubles which Rose has hung around the room. I can just imagine how Dee Dee's big brown eyes would have wowed at the whole scene. A few weeks ago I would have said something to Jed; now the subject of his daughter feels taboo. Which cannot last. I chew on my lip. If today is hard for me, what on earth must Jed – and Zoe – be going through? My sister hands the carving knife to Martin and fetches the last dish – creamed potatoes – from the sideboard. Rose's hair is up today, just a few dark tresses escaping in loose curls around her neck. She's wearing black cut-offs with ankle boots and a low-cut fitted silk blouse. She looks amazing. Lunch is a triumph – a huge roast beef with all the trimmings, all expertly cooked and beautifully presented. Rose has invited Gary and Allia as well as Martin and Cameron – so it's a squeeze around the table, but everyone is good-humoured.

I'm wary of Gary. He says and does nothing that could remotely be construed as either suspicious or sinister, but I can't get the phone conversation I overheard at his flat the other day out of my head all through our lunch. In fact I'm so lost in my own thoughts that I don't hear my name being spoken until my brother, who I'm sitting next to, prods my arm.

'Wake up, Flaky.' There's a warning look in his eye as he indicates Cameron across the table. I brace myself for whatever my brother's boyfriend wants to say.

Cameron waves his fork in the air. 'I was asking how the wedding arrangements are coming on?' he says.

I gulp. Clearly Martin hasn't told him about my trip to the police and the strain it has put on my relationship with Jed.

'Oh, um …' I make a face. 'Haven't had a chance to do much, the end of term was crazy busy …' I tail off.

Jed shoots me a glance. 'We're thinking of going for

sometime in early February,' he says firmly. 'I'm expecting the decree absolute late January. There's no need to wait, is there, baby?'

I look down at my plate and give a small nod.

'Ooh, I don't know,' Gary says in that voice he uses to wind up his older brother. 'Sounds like you're rushing things a bit. Out of the Zoe frying pan, into the Emily fire, so to speak.' He glances at me, a big grin on his face. 'No offence.'

I smile wanly. At least this is business as usual from Gary. Watching him needle Jed, I wonder again about that overheard conversation. What did he mean when he said Jed's focus on the Benecke Tricorp case was 'wrong'? My earlier suspicions wash over me with greater force than before. Is it possible Gary's resentment of his brother goes deeper than I've ever realized? Is there any way he could be involved with Lish's drug deals – and the attack on my life at the tube station?

'Just because *you're* a commitment-phobe,' Jed snaps, rising to the bait.

'Fine, go right ahead,' Gary chortles. 'Just remember, every wedding takes you a step closer to your next divorce.'

At this, Cameron laughs and Martin suppresses a smile.

'For goodness' sake,' Rose scolds gently. She turns to Jed. 'It's none of my business, but how has your ex reacted to you saying you're getting married again so quickly?'

I stare at her, surprised at how direct she's being about Zoe. Jed just shrugs his shoulders. 'I'm deeply in love with Emily and she is with me,' he says grumpily.

I look down at the table. Is that true? Jed has spied on me and refuses to believe that I've been attacked and threatened. When it comes right down to it, he doesn't trust me. And I don't trust him. And where's love without trust?

'We want to be married,' Jed goes on. 'It's not really anyone else's business.'

'Well said,' Martin says, then deftly changes the subject to the holiday he and Cameron are leaving for the next day. I think that's the end of the matter so am surprised when Gary seeks me out later, while the others are gathered around the TV. I'm in the kitchen, unwrapping the bread I baked earlier and brought from home, ready to help Rose make some turkey sandwiches.

'Emily?'

I look up, startled by how close he's standing. My fears flood back. Is he about to threaten me? Worse?

'It's great you and my brother make each other happy,' Gary says, keeping his voice low. 'But don't let him push you on the wedding timing. He's a forceful guy.'

Is there some agenda behind what he's saying? I can't work it out. Gary gives me a wink then disappears back into the living room to ask Jed yet again about progress on his suit against Benecke Tricorp.

*

At home later, Jed is getting ready to go and see Lish. He's in a foul mood, stomping about the place and muttering under his breath.

'Gary asks a lot of questions about the case, doesn't he?' I mention, wondering if Jed has noticed. 'Does he have a particular reason?'

'Probably just trying to get insider info for his clients on what will happen to their share price,' Jed grunts.

'Oh.' This hadn't occurred to me. 'Are you still angry with him?' I ask. 'Because you know I think he only says that stuff about us to wind you up.'

'I know that,' Jed mutters. 'It's not Gary.'

He marches out of the living room. I follow him into the kitchen where he's pouring himself a glass of water.

'What is it then?'

Jed sets the glass down on the counter. He turns to face me. 'Do you still want to marry me?'

I stare at him. 'Yes, of course.'

Jed raises his eyebrows. 'Really? I saw the way you looked when the subject came up earlier.' He hesitates, his eyes boring through mine. 'Is it Dan? I know he wants you, but . . .'

I can feel my face flushing. Jed and I haven't spoken about Dan since the day of my police visit. But I've thought about him a lot. Every day, I've thought about Dan. 'What are you asking?' I stammer.

'Did you fuck Dan Thackeray?'

I wince. Jed is seething with repressed anger.

'I already told you I didn't and—'

'Do you wish you had?'

I suck in my breath. This is a question I have been trying not to answer myself.

'No,' I say. Though I'm not sure in my heart if it's the truth.

'Right.' Jed looks unconvinced. He takes a swig of water, then sets his glass down again. 'I'm going to see Lish then.'

He walks out.

I sink into a kitchen chair. I have to face it: something irretrievable has been lost between Jed and me since I went to the police, just as Martin predicted it would be. I sit, letting the realization flow through me. He can't get past Dan. And I can't get past the fact that he took his son's side over mine.

And above the need for justice for his daughter.

I can't stop thinking about that. In keeping silent I am letting poor Dee Dee down. And yet what choice is there?

I turn my phone over in my hand. I want to call Dan to see how he's getting on, to find out if he's uncovered anything useful, to make sure he's all right. Perhaps once Jed has gone.

'Bye,' Jed calls from the front door. A week ago he would have come back into the kitchen and kissed me goodbye.

'Bye.'

The door shuts. I sit, letting the silence of the house settle around me.

Outside, the car engine revs. I hear the tyres crunching

over the icy patch in the drive. A few seconds later the door-bell rings: long and persistent.

I look around. Is that Jed? Why is he ringing the bell?

I walk into the hall and peer through the spyhole. Nobody is there. My throat is tight as I open the front door. A single feather catches my eye, tumbling across the ground. I look across the small drive.

A sparrow lies by the hedge, its neck twisted at an unnatural angle.

Dead.

I stare at the tiny body. Is it road kill? Or something more deliberate? The disguised, mechanical voice echoes in my ears again.

The little bird who's been talking.

I slam the door shut, my whole body trembling.

AWFUL. AWFUL. I had to call Mum to fetch me home from Ava's earlier. It was the most humiliating experience of my LIFE. It wasn't just me and Ava after all, Poppy was there too and Georgia Dutton and a couple of other girls from our year. They were all dressed up in fancy outfits and they had been there for ages before I got there, doing each other's hair and fingernails. I just KNEW they had been talking about me. When I arrived they were like all gushy-gushy how nice it was to see me, then Georgia said something about Sam Edwards. I didn't even properly hear what and they ALL started laughing. And I felt really awkward. And then Poppy asked if I'd given Sam Edwards a feel recently. And they all laughed again. And Georgia asked 'have you started shaving yet, Dee Dee?' And she was all *innocent face* but I could see in her eyes she was laughing too. So I didn't know whether to say yes or no but I said 'yes' and Georgia said 'what, down there?' and I went red and nodded. And then they all wanted to see.

'Oh show us, Dee Dee, show us how it looks.'

And I didn't know what to do but I thought if I didn't show them they would just tease me some more, so I rolled down my jeans and I could see the girls across the room doubled over with

288

laughing I think cos my jeans were tight and I am so FAT. And I am all hot in my face to remember it but the other girls weren't laughing then, Ava was all serious asking if I'd cut myself shaving and if it was itchy and I said 'no' and 'no' and then Poppy ran out of the room and Ava followed. Which left just me and Georgia and the other girls and Georgia turned to me and said 'looks like you've still got a lot of problems, Dee D-easy' and they all laughed then Ava and Poppy came back in and Poppy looked all upset like she was close to tears and she said 'I'm really sorry, Dee Dee, but I don't feel comfortable being here with you showing off your minge to everyone so I think I'm going to have to go home.'

And I stared at her and I didn't know what to say. And the others all came round while I did up my jeans and Ava was upset cos Poppy was leaving and Poppy kept saying how she was upset because she liked me and I was obviously having problems, she meant like MENTAL problems, and she said that she'd feel better at home.

And then Georgia looked right over at me and said 'I don't see why it's POPPY who has to go home.' And Ava said quietly 'I know what you mean'. And they were both looking at me, then everyone was and I realized they wanted ME to go and I didn't know what to do, then Georgia rolled her eyes and said loudly that 'some people can't take a hint'.

And I wanted to cry then but I kept it back and just said I was sorry to Poppy. Then I got up and went downstairs and I told Ava's mum I had a tummy ache and wanted to go home.

And here I am and I don't see how my life could be any worse. And Mum just tutted when I opened a new packet of biscuits.

289

December 2014

'It was probably just hit by a car and knocked into the drive.' Jed rolls his eyes. As I'd feared, he is totally dismissive about the dead bird.

'No, I'm *sure* it's them, the people Lish is working with.'

'It's either nothing or it's Dan fucking Thackeray again.' Jed stalks out.

I hole up in our bedroom and call Dan.

'Em?' He answers immediately. 'What's up?'

My whole body releases with relief that he is all right. 'There was another threat, at least I think that's what it was.' I tell him about the sparrow.

'Why are they terrorizing *you*?' Dan demands. 'As far as they're concerned you've backed off.'

'I think they're just making sure,' I say, hoping this is true. 'Have you had anything weird happen?'

'No, and I'm being very discreet with my enquiries. I don't think they know what I'm looking into right now.' He pauses. 'So long as they don't find out what I'm doing we should be fine.'

'What *are* you doing?' I ask.

'Better you don't know. Better we don't have any contact for a bit . . . I couldn't bear it if anything happened to you.' He draws in his breath. 'But once I've got something I can take to the police, something concrete, I'd really like to see you. Would you . . . how would you feel about that?'

I hesitate. 'I'd like it,' I say. 'I'd like it very much.'

The next day is Boxing Day. Jed spends most of it taking Lish to a football match. I'm in bed, pretending to be asleep, when he gets back that evening. The next day he goes into his office. I leave before he gets home to meet Laura in town. We meet in a bar in the West End. It's usually full of office workers but tonight, in that limbo time between Christmas and New Year, there's hardly anyone around – just a group of guys by the bar who keep eyeing us up.

I fill Laura in on everything that has happened since we last spoke. She's full of concern, though whether because she genuinely thinks my life is in danger or because my relationship with Jed is under threat, I'm not sure.

'You just seemed so happy with Jed when I last saw you,' she muses.

'I know, but it's different now. I'm not sure Jed and I can get past all this,' I confess. 'I'm hurt that he doesn't believe me and he's furious that I don't believe him.'

Laura sips at her cranberry juice. She tilts her head to one side and considers me thoughtfully. 'Do you still love him?'

'I don't know any more.

Laura makes a face. 'Okay, this needs more wine . . . for you anyway. Jesus, I wish I could have a proper drink.' She gathers up her bag and heads for the bar. I watch her sashay towards the barman. Her pregnancy still isn't really showing, though knowing her as I do I can see that her waist has slightly thickened already and her breasts are at least a size bigger. The guys at the bar are watching her too. One of them – tall and in a pin-striped suit – wanders over as she waits to be served. I watch Laura lure him in, flirting like mad as the man leans towards her, clearly thinking he's in with a chance. Then she says something and the man draws back. Laura lifts her hand and wiggles her fingers at him in a little wave. The man retreats.

I smile to myself. Laura has always been a tease, some-how knowing exactly how to reel men in – and how to get rid of them – even when we were only teenagers.

A minute later she's setting our glasses down on the little metal table between us.

'Well hello there.' It's Gary, a bottle of beer in his hand.

I stare at him, shocked at seeing him in his suit, out of context.

'What are you doing here?' I ask, more rudely than I mean to.

'Drink after work,' Gary says. He turns to Laura. 'Do I know you?'

'Not yet.' Laura's eyes twinkle.

I sigh wearily to myself as Gary clearly senses he's in the

company of a woman who's as big a flirt as him and asks if he can buy either of us a drink.

'How are you, Gary?' I ask. If nothing else, this is a good opportunity to sound him out about his overt interest in Jed's case against Benecke Tricorp. 'Would you like to join us?'

'Thanks.' Gary settles himself beside Laura and takes a gulp of beer. 'So how's my brother doing? Court case keeping him busy?'

'Yes,' I say, my suspicions rearing up. Surely it can't be a coincidence that this is the very first thing Gary mentions? 'Jed's busy, the case takes a lot of his energy.'

Gary shakes his head. 'Lawyers,' he says. 'They'll bleed you dry every time.'

'Jed's a lawyer,' I point out.

'So you're Jed's brother.' Laura raises an eyebrow.

'*Younger* brother,' Gary says with a smarmy smile.

'Of course.' Laura virtually bats her eyelids at him.

Jesus.

'Er, anyway, the case is going fine, Gary,' I say but inside my head I'm remembering the disguised voice saying *little bird*. Could that have been Gary speaking? 'I was wondering . . .' I venture. 'I wondered why the interest? I mean, you ask about it a lot.'

Gary nods thoughtfully. 'Just don't want my brother losing all his money on a law suit that the chances are high he'll never win.'

'Makes sense,' Laura says.

'I suppose.' I sit back. Gary appears relaxed and laidback. Could he really only be interested in the financial aspect of the case? Does he truly have Jed's best interests at heart? Maybe he does – he certainly came into his own back in Corsica, taking charge of us all in the immediate aftermath of Dee Dee's death. And yet there's something phony about his concern too. I rack my brains trying to work out how to make him say more, but I can't think of a way of putting my questions that doesn't sound like a naked accusation and after a few minutes, Gary leaves to go back to his friends.

'Thinks he's a smooth operator, doesn't he?' Laura says disparagingly.

I grin at her unfailing ability to see through male charm.

'Just need the loo.' Laura hitches her bag back onto her shoulder and sashays off again, this time in the direction of the ladies, though still with plenty of admiring glances following her. I lean back in my chair and close my eyes.

What a mess. Never mind about Gary. Can Jed and I get through this? I'm really not sure that we can.

As I wait for Laura, my phone beeps. I glance down. It's a Snapchat, from Laura herself. What on earth has she seen in the ladies that she wants to show me so urgently?

I open the pic and the breath seems to leave my body.

It's a photo of the dead sparrow from two days ago, or else a different, similar bird, along with a two-line message:

Dan Thackeray will be dead soon. You're next.

I stare, horrified, at the screen as the picture disappears.

I jump up and look across at the ladies. Laura is just emerging. This came from her phone. Did *she* send it? Surely she *couldn't* have. *Wouldn't* have. Panic whirls inside me. Laura is staring at the floor; she bends down and picks something up. It's a phone. *Her* phone. She looks up at me, confusion written all over her face.

'Must have fallen out of my bag on the way into the loo,' she's saying as she walks towards me. 'Lucky no one pinched it.'

Reality hits like a punch. Lish's accomplice is here. Right now. I stare over at the bar. There's no sign of Gary. Has he left already? Could the Snapchat be from him? Surely it *has* to be. It must have been sent less than two minutes ago.

A shiver snakes down my spine as Laura slides back into her seat.

Dan Thackeray will be dead soon.

I have to warn him.

'I've got to go.' I pick up my jacket. 'Now.'

Laura frowns. 'But I just got the drinks in.'

I'm already out of the door, fumbling with my phone. I need to call Dan. I glance over my shoulder. Whoever took and used Laura's phone to send that Snapchat must have been watching us, is probably *still* watching.

The cold night air slaps at my face. Dan's number won't connect.

'Come on, come on,' I mutter into my mobile.

Laura stumbles out onto the pavement behind me. 'What's going on, Emily? What's the matter?'

SOPHIE MCKENZIE

I explain as I try Dan's number again. Laura's eyes widen with horror.

'You're saying someone in that bar deliberately took my phone from my bag, used it then left it on the floor for me?'

I nod.

'Fuck, Emily, this is mad. You should call the police.'

'No.' I point to her phone. 'It's a Snapchat. It's gone. There's no proof. There's never any proof. That's the point.'

I try Dan's number a third time. This time it rings, a long, continuous tone. My stomach lurches, bile rising into my throat.

'It's been disconnected.' I turn to Laura. 'Shit, this is bad.'

'What is?'

I shake my head. There's no time to explain it to her. I have to find Dan, make sure he's okay. I glance along the road. Three taxis with their lights on.

'I have to go.'

'You're not making any sense,' Laura protests. 'If some-one's threatening you, you need to tell the police.'

'No.' I grab her arm. 'No police. Promise me.'

'Okay.' Laura looks uncertain.

'*Promise* me.'

'I promise.'

I flag down one of the taxis. 'Get in,' I say.

Grumbling, Laura opens the door. 'Where are we going?'

'You're going home.' I slam the door shut, then give the driver Laura's street name in Kennington.

296

'Wait.' She grabs the handle, but the driver has already locked the door.

'Go,' I order.

Laura raises her hands in a gesture of annoyed impatience. 'Emily!'

'Go!' I repeat, more loudly.

The taxi pulls away.

I consult my phone again. Dan's number is my only way of contacting him. He said he had a flat in Hoxton, but I have no idea where and I can hardly start randomly knocking on doors in the area. I rack my brains. Who am I still in touch with who might know where he lives?

Eve. My friend from college. Dan mentioned her that first time we met, didn't he? I haven't seen her in months, since before I met Jed, but I do have her number. I scroll through my contacts with trembling fingers. Traffic rushes past. A group of women cross the road just ahead, all giggling hysterically.

'Eve?'

'Hey, Emily, how are you?' There's music in the background. People talking. Eve's voice is light, she's been laughing.

'I'm, er, fine.' I try and pull myself together. 'I'm sorry to call out of the blue, but I'm trying to track down Dan Thackeray. Do you remember him?'

'Course,' Eve giggles. Is she drunk? Tipsy, certainly. 'We used to call him Mr Hot. But I haven't seen him in a million years.'

My heart sinks. Behind Eve, the music pounds out – fast and loud. An intricate jazz track, very much to Eve's taste.

'Hey, Emily?' Eve slurs. 'You still there?'

'Yes.' My mind starts galloping over other options, other ways of tracking down Dan.

Suppose they've got to him already?

'I'm having people round, well, you can probably hear. Just moved in with my boyfriend. It's kind of turned into something bigger than planned. You know how I like spontaneous—'

'Eve, I'm sorry, but I'm just trying to find Dan Thackeray.'

'Yeah, I know, that's what I'm trying to say … Charlie Lewis will be here soon, d'you remember him? Maria Crowley went out with him, from our year? He knows Dan from their uni days so—'

'I remember Charlie Lewis,' I say. My mind fills with an image of Dan's friend from years ago: sandy-haired, broadshouldered and genial. 'Do you think he knows where Dan lives?'

'I'd imagine so, but I haven't seen him myself for—'

'When will Charlie be at your party?' I interrupt.

'Dunno, I don't have his number, but I'm guessing in the next hour or so. Come along, have a drink with us.'

'Thank you. Yes.' I look around, checking to see if anyone is standing close enough to overhear. But nobody appears to be watching me. 'What's the address?'

I make a note of it, then flag down a cab. My heart thuds

in my chest as I head towards Whitechapel. Not very far from Hoxton. So ... if Charlie turns up and if he knows where Dan lives I should be able to find Dan within the next couple of hours. That's if he is at home, of course. If he isn't already dead.

I try Dan's mobile again. Definitely disconnected. Surely he wouldn't have changed the number without telling me? My breath is coming in short, ragged gasps. I couldn't bear it if anything has happened to him.

Suddenly I remember Jed. I need to tell him where I'm going and what I'm doing.

He answers on the first ring. 'On your way home, baby?'

'No.' I gulp. 'I'm trying to find Dan, I think he's in danger.'

'What?' There's a sharp intake of breath. 'What the fuck are you talking about?'

I explain as quickly as I can about the Snapchat message. 'It adds up with the phone call and the dead bird outside our house. Don't you see? *Little bird.* It's another warning. *Dan Thackeray will be dead soon.*'

'I don't see that at all.' Jed's voice is taut with repressed fury. 'I've told you already, it must be Thackeray who's *sending* you this stuff.'

'No, if it was Dan I'd have seen him at the bar.'

'Then he got someone else to do it for him,' Jed insists. 'Come on, baby. You need to trust me on all this. Lish isn't drug dealing. Dee Dee was the victim of Benecke Tricorp's negligence. It's paranoid to believe a gang of organized criminals are after you.' He pauses. 'This is all down to Dan Thackeray ... he's *making* you paranoid.'

I grit my teeth. I have always hated not being believed. One of my strongest early memories is of playing ball with my brother and sister in the garden. I was about eight or nine, Martin and Rose in their early teens. We were supposed to only use tennis balls, but Martin had just got hold of a cricket ball. He mistimed his throw to Rose and broke a window. The two of them ganged up on me, told Mum and Dad that I'd picked up the cricket ball and thrown it at the window deliberately. My parents were furious, especially when I refused to admit that I'd done it.

'I'm not being paranoid and Dan isn't behind all the threats,' I say, struggling to keep my temper. How dare Jed still be patronizing me like this? Does he not understand how serious this is?

The taxi swerves around a corner and stops at a red light. I fidget in my seat. I'm still at least fifteen minutes away from Eve's flat in Whitechapel.

I take a deep breath. 'I have to warn Dan, I really think he's in danger.'

'Don't.' Jed's voice has a fierce edge. 'I'm telling you, *don't.*'

I hesitate. Outside the streetlights are flashing by, the buildings a blur as the taxi picks up speed along an empty road.

'Or what?' I ask.

Silence. 'You have to choose,' Jed says. 'Me or him.'

I sit, the phone pressed to my ear. 'I don't accept that,' I say.

'I don't care what you fucking accept.' Jed's voice rises.

And in that moment my choice is made.

'Bye, Jed,' I say. Then I ring off.

July 2014

Tonight was the engagement party at Daddy and Emily's house. I'd been dreading it, because Mum made comments ALL week about how I didn't have to go if I didn't want to, meaning that SHE didn't want me to go. But OBVIOUSLY I had to go as Daddy would have been SO MAD if I hadn't. But I was still dreading it because I wasn't going to know anyone and I am FAT and they'd all be grown-ups. Anyway, it started off actually quite nice. Daddy said my top was a pretty colour and Emily put on some cool music and her sister Rose and brother Martin came round and they were really sweet, especially Martin. And Lish was there too and he was really chatty for once because he was happy because he was about to go away to a festival with his friends that Daddy was paying for in order to get Lish to come on holiday with us in a few weeks. And Uncle Gary was there with his girlfriend who has, like, the BIGGEST boobs you've ever seen and she didn't say much and I got stuck with Uncle Gary for about ten minutes of 'so how is school?' and 'which subjects do you like best?' but then Martin's boyfriend Cameron turned up and he is TOTALLY cool and he and Martin gave me a bracelet. They had one for Emily too. It is gold and a bit big but REALLY pretty.

So they were all talking and getting ready for the other guests to come and Cameron asked if people my age still used Facebook and I said yeah, sort of, but there were other things and Martin asked 'like what?' and I told them a bit about things like Snapchat which they knew about and UFrenz and WeChat which they didn't. And Rose and Uncle Gary were all 'you have to be careful who you talk to online, there are paedophiles everywhere' blah blah like grown-ups do but Cameron said he thought people didn't give teenagers enough credit for telling the difference between a real friend and a paedo pretending to like you and then Uncle Gary started saying about how they needed to do more to prepare kids for the real world in schools and a minute later he was asking me about my school AGAIN. And Emily saw I looked sad and it was because talking to Uncle Gary about school had reminded me of everything that happened with Ava and Poppy and Georgia. And a bit later she asked me to help her in the kitchen and when we were on our own she asked if I was okay and I suddenly just told her how last term I got some nasty texts from a couple of girls at school. I said it was over now and that I'd deleted them so I couldn't show her, but that the girls had said mean things like I was ugly and stuff.

Emily was all shocked and upset for me. She asked what my friends thought when all this happened and I couldn't bring myself to explain that the girls sending the texts WERE my friends so I made out I had these whole other and imaginary girlfriends who had supported me and challenged the nasty girls until it stopped. Emily wanted to tell Daddy but I asked her not to but she said she really had to but I think she must have had a word with him first because he was really nice and didn't ask too many questions in that way he sometimes does. And he asked if he shouldn't get Mum to call the school or the mums of the girls who sent the texts but I said I didn't know exactly who the texts were from because the senders had blocked their names which is true though of course I know it's Poppy and Ava and probably Georgia Dutton too. Plus I said school was over for summer so there was no point raking it all up. And I definitely didn't want to tell Mum.

In the end I could see Daddy was relieved not to have to say anything and then the party started and it was all over. THANK GOODNESS because Mum had been on the phone to him earlier, getting all upset and angry about the engagement again. She EXPLODED when he told her last week. Even under two pillows and a duvet I could hear her yelling that he was a bastard. Earlier tonight I heard Daddy call her a bitch to Emily when he thought I couldn't hear. That made me feel all empty and I sneaked three whole chocolate cupcakes supposed to be for later out of the fridge.

Anyway, I don't know why I'm saying all this because none of it is the BIG news. That happened later, when the party was nearly over and I was going up to the top bathroom off Daddy and Emily's room and I got near their bedroom and I saw something between two people. And I don't want to say what they were saying or doing but I will say that it is a REALLY BAD secret and that they would be MAD AS HELL if they knew that I knew.

December 2014

Anxiety knots my stomach as I make my way into Eve's Whitechapel apartment. It's a beautiful flat full of her art dealer boyfriend's tasteful pieces and on another occasion I would have thoroughly enjoyed taking a proper look at all the abstract designs and elegant statues that decorate the two large reception rooms. Eve herself is delightfully pleased to see me, taking me straight over to a few uni friends. Charlie apparently isn't here yet so I stand and wait, an unwanted glass of white wine in my hand, trying to focus on what Keeley and Fran are saying about their respective toddlers.

I look over at the door every few moments. I last saw Charlie about eight and a half years ago. He can't have changed that much. A couple of the guys catch my eye and I immediately look down at the floor. After half an hour, I'm almost ready to break with the tension and Keeley and Fran are no longer even pretending to include me in their conversation, when Charlie walks in. He looks the same as I remember, just with shorter hair. He looks around, presumably for Eve. I set down my wine and start to head over.

But before I've taken two steps he laughs at something the person behind him has said, then he turns … and Dan himself is there.

I stop walking, partly from shock and partly with relief. He's here. He's all right. My whole body releases as I stare at him laughing with Charlie, then looking around the room. He's wearing a white shirt over dark blue jeans. His hair is scruffy and there's a hint of stubble on his chin. The tide of my relief washes away and is instantly replaced with a wave of lust. My face flushes as it fills me.

All this happens in a fraction, then Dan turns his head and before I can breathe our eyes lock. It's as if we're the only people in the room. In a second Dan is here, right in front of me, looking down at me, his grey eyes alive with delight and – unmistakably – desire. A delicious shiver wriggles through me.

'Are you okay?' I ask.

'Course. Charlie rang me, he said you were here, that you were asking Eve about me,' he says, moving closer, right into my space. Exquisitely close. He lowers his voice to a whisper and I have to lean in to hear him above the jazz that soars around us. 'Is something wrong?' He still hasn't taken his eyes off me. I can't look away, can't think, can't move.

'Yes.' I try to gather myself. 'I needed to see you.'

'Good. I'm … that's just so good.' Dan leans in closer. 'Em, I don't know how to say this but I can't stop thinking about you. I haven't called because it's what we agreed and anyway I know I fucked things up when I met you before, trying to get that story on Jed. But—'

'That doesn't matter now. Listen, Dan, you're in danger.'

'What?' Dan frowns. 'Come here.' He takes my hand and I let him hold it as he leads me through the living room and out into the corridor. He tries a couple of doors before we reach an empty room. It's a bedroom, a spare I'm guessing, littered with coats from the party guests – with what looks like a Picasso sketch above the bed.

Dan shuts the door and the music dulls to a soft lilt. 'Danger?' he says, still frowning. 'From who? Lish?'

'Yes, well, someone he works with, probably. It might even be Jed's brother, Gary.' I tell Dan everything that's happened since I saw him. Dan looks angry and horrified by turns. 'I tried to call you,' I finish, 'but it said the number was unobtainable.'

Dan nods. 'I switched to a new mobile number yesterday. I got tired of your fiancé harassing me.'

I stare at him. 'Harassing you?' Thoughts of Lish and the disguised voice on the phone fade from my mind. '*Jed* has been calling you?'

'Yes,' Dan says. 'Warning me to stay away from Lish, from you. Every effing day.'

Outside, a piano solo plays fast and intricate. A group of people are talking just beyond the door. One of them shrieks 'hey, no *way*' at the top of their voice. Dan still hasn't taken his eyes off me.

'Jed thinks you've made up the whole thing to get me back.'

'I know, it's—'

'It's not just that. He's been tracking where I go on my phone. That's how he knew I went to the police, but I think he also wanted to see if I'd go to you.'

'Jesus.' Dan shudders. I reach out and curl my fingers around his arm. In an instant Dan has closed the gap between us. He looks at me, his eyes glittering.

'I came here to warn you,' I say, struggling to keep my voice steady. 'I know you said you were going to investigate Lish on your own, but you can't. It's not safe. They know what you're doing and—'

Dan leans forward. His mouth presses against mine and I'm lost in the kiss, my whole body trembling.

'I'm not stopping, Em,' Dan whispers. 'Apart from the fact that what Jed's son is doing is illegal, it's also dangerous to hand out prescription drugs without a doctor or a proper medical assessment, and that's when the drugs are real brands. The Valium Lish sold me was fake, it could have contained anything.' He steps back, still staring intently at me. 'I don't mean to sound self-righteous about this, but I hate the way Jed is handling it: bullying you, haranguing me, all against fake drugs unless it's his own son who's peddling them. I'm not going to back off. It's what he wants. And it's wrong.'

'But you're not safe.'

'I've got a lead, something to look into tomorrow.' Dan

308

takes a deep breath. 'Look, I understand it's risky and that being connected to you involves you in that risk and that, more than anything, means that if you really want me to I'll stop. But not until I've followed this lead tomorrow.'

'No.' I shake my head for emphasis. 'If they haven't found you yet, it's just a matter of time. You can't go home, so—'

'Then I'll stay in a hotel. For tonight. After tomorrow I should have something to take to the police anyway.'

I chew on my lip. At least in a hotel Dan will be safe.

'Come with me, Em.'

I look up. Dan offers me a gentle smile. 'To the hotel . . . please? If I'm not safe, then you're not either, so come with me. You can stay in the hotel tonight and . . . and for as long as it takes until I've followed up this lead and told the police what I've found.'

'Stay in a hotel? With you?' I raise my eyebrows. 'Just because Jed is being an arse and I've kissed you once.'

'Twice,' he says.

'It doesn't mean I'm about to jump into bed with you in some seedy hotel.'

'It will be a nice hotel.' Dan grins. 'And we can have separate rooms, if you like. Please, Em. I need to know you're safe. Plus there's something I need to tell you. Nothing to do with this stuff, something personal.'

I should say 'no'; find my own hotel – or go to stay with Martin or Rose. It's completely fucked up to leave Jed and jump straight into bed with Dan, however much I'm attracted to him. Saying 'no' is the sensible choice.

I don't make it.

The hotel is warm after the cold December air. I know Jed will be calling me so I have switched off my phone. Neither Dan nor I have any luggage, of course, but the hotel manager is as smooth as he is professional and doesn't bat an eyelid. Our room is small but smart, with a great view over the streets of Covent Garden and elegant black and white tiles in the bathroom.

I sit down in the armchair next to the window and stare outside. What am I doing here?

'Have you eaten?' Dan asks.

'I'm not hungry.'

He walks over. I can feel him behind me, the heat of his body as he leans down, smoothes away my hair and kisses the back of my neck. 'I want you,' he whispers in my ear.

I turn around and look up. His eyes burn into me.

'I want you too.' The words slither out of me, under my breath. I don't even know I'm saying them. I can't think. Can't feel anything except the most overwhelming desire I've ever experienced in my life.

'How have you been?' I ask. 'Since I saw you?'

'Miserable,' he says. 'Missing you.'

Outside the streetlamps glimmer and traffic zooms past. I can still feel the imprint of Dan's lips on my neck.

'I don't just mean missing you recently. I realized when

I saw you at the beginning of the month that I've been missing you for eight years,' Dan goes on, his voice low. 'I was such an idiot when you knew me before ... I wanted travel, excitement, sex with every woman on the planet. A whole load of stupid, stupid stuff and I went and tried to get it and none of it made me happy because you and I were meant to be and I fucking threw it away eight years ago. And I didn't even realize until I saw you and at first I told myself it's just because you're so bloody gorgeous, but the more time I spent with you the more everything in my life made sense again and I don't know what I can do, what I can offer you, but I can't help how I feel. I love you. I've always loved you. I'm pretty certain that I'm always *going* to love you.'

My cheeks burn as he finishes. Dan backs away and sits on the end of the bed. 'So,' he says. 'This thing I need to tell you, it's—'

'Is it about Jed?'

'No.' Dan rubs his forehead. 'Christ. Shit. Is there anything in the minibar?'

'Wait.' I go over and sit beside him. I'm so close that I can feel the muscles under the thin cotton of his shirt. I'm suddenly certain that I know what he's going to tell me. And I know that if my guess is right, I will have to turn around and walk out of the door. 'Is it that you're married?' I ask, my guts twisting into a knot.

'No.' Dan frowns.

'But you're with someone?'

311

'No, of *course* not. I already told you I'm single. I'm in love with you.'

I stroke his cheek. He closes his eyes as my thumb traces the line of his lips. I want to kiss him, to touch him. I need to feel that he's real, that this is real.

'Then whatever it is that you want to tell me can wait,' I say.

Dan opens his eyes. He puts his hand on the wall above my head. He leans close, over my face, so that his lips are almost touching my skin.

'This is real,' he whispers, as if he heard my unspoken question.

My breath catches in my throat as his lips brush my nose, my cheeks, my mouth. Then I stop thinking and I give myself up to his kiss.

I wake up, wrapped in Dan's arms. I lie on the bed, my entire body heavy on the sheets. I focus on his hand. It rests on my arm, just above the elbow. Soft, warm, I can't tell where his skin ends and mine begins. I can feel his breath on my neck, slow and steady.

I know I should feel guilty about what I've just done. Not only am I still, technically at least, engaged to another man, by any measure it is crazy to dive into bed with Dan without stopping to think. Trouble is I don't feel guilty. I'm happy. Ridiculously happy. Dan wants me and I want him and right now I can't see beyond that.

He stirs, his arms pulling me back. I squirrel into his chest.

'I love you,' he whispers.

I turn around so we are facing. His face is soft with release, his wavy hair messy over his forehead. I reach up, sleepy-limbed, and stroke it back. The first time was fast and furious, all passion and lust. The second was calmer and quieter, just the sound of our breathing and our eyes never breaking contact and on and on. My fingers trail down to the swallow tattoo on Dan's upper right arm. I trace the outline.

'Do you remember when we went to get that done?' I ask.

Dan nods.

'And I chickened out?' I continue.

'I wanted to as well.' Dan grimaces. 'I mean, why a bloody swallow? I was too up my own arse to admit I'd changed my mind. I admired you so much for saying that you had.'

'Did you?' I prop myself up on my elbow. 'I thought you thought I was a coward.'

'Quite the opposite. It's funny, I remember most people who met you back then were fooled because you look so perfect, like a doll, and you're not loud and pushy. They thought you were – don't take this the wrong way – but they assumed you were a bit fragile. My friends teased me about wanting to be a "he-man", a cartoon hero, you know? As if what I wanted was to big myself up by protecting you. I think even your brother and sister thought you were like that – needing to be looked after. But I never saw you like

313

that. Right from the start I saw how strong you were. You would always do the right thing, even when it was hard; even when most people would have bluffed or lied or fudged their way out of a situation, you always faced everything head on.'

I stare at him. It's true that people have always seen me as fragile – a bit of a victim, even. And if I'm honest there have been times, as with Jed in our early days, when I have enjoyed people wanting to look after me, even *liked* being looked after. But in the end I always resent it.

'You never said any of that back then.'

'Didn't I?' Dan sighs. 'Well, as I say, I was so up my own arse I'm sure there were lots of things I didn't say or do that I should have done.' He kisses me gently on the lips then fixes me with a serious look. 'I don't want to push you, I don't want to pressure you, but I don't want to lose you again either. I'm not asking you to decide anything, not right now, but I'm serious about this, about us. Okay?'

I nod. 'Tell me about this lead you've got.'

'It came from the time I met Lish. I cloned his phone so I could track his texts and calls. He's pretty careful but there was one text yesterday about a meeting that I saw before he switched to a new phone.'

'What did it say?'

'Tomorrow's date then the word: *park*.'

'Park?' I frown at him. 'Which park? How do you know where he'll be? Or when?'

Dan smiles. 'Because there was another text to the same number about an hour later which said *3 p.m. RHG.*'

'Meaning?'

'I didn't know at first, but I Googled all the parks in London and the area around Southampton looking for something with those initials and I found it: Robin Hood Gate, in Richmond Park.'

'So you think Lish will be there at three p.m.?'

Dan nods. 'Er, d'you remember I said there was something I had to tell you?'

'Yes.' My stomach clenches with anxiety. What the hell is coming now?

'I really do need you to know this. I should have told you before; it makes a difference to us.'

'What is it?' I ask.

A look of anxiety fills Dan's eyes. He holds out his phone to me. 'It's this,' he says.

I take the phone and peer down at the text message on the screen. It was sent at 6 p.m. this evening:

Love you too, Lulu xxxxxx

I freeze. Who the hell is *Lulu*? Has everything Dan has just said and done been a lie? Am I, in fact, the most gullible person alive?

I look up at him. 'What is this?'

'Didn't you read the messages?'

I look back at the screen, at the previous part of the conversation:

Hope you had a fun day. See you on Saturday. Daddy x

Yes!!! Lulu xxxooxxx

Night night Lulu, love you, Daddy xxx

Love you too, Lulu xxxxxx

I stare up at him. 'You have a *daughter*?'

'Yes, she's nearly five.'

'Why didn't you say anything before?'

'I've wanted to but … but those times weren't about me.' Dan rubs his forehead. 'I'm sorry, I've really wanted to tell you but it's a complicated situation …' He tails off.

'Do you have a picture?' I say, feeling stunned.

'Sure.' Dan takes the phone from my hands, swipes the screen, then hands it back. The lock screen shows a little girl with blond hair in fine pigtails and a big grin. There's a touch of Dan about her grey eyes, though hers are bluer than his.

'She's gorgeous,' I say. I can't keep the sense of loss out of my voice. Dan has clearly had a serious relationship, maybe even a wife, though I'm sure he told me before that he hadn't. I look up. 'Where's her mother?' I ask.

'Okay, this is why I didn't just blurt it out.' He hesitates.

Oh, Jesus. What is he about to confess?

'You said you weren't married or with anyone.'

'I'm not,' Dan says quickly. 'I'm not. I'm single, just like I said.'

'So you're separated from the mother?'

'No,' Dan says. 'We were never together.'

'You mean a one-night stand?'

'Not even that.' Dan rubs his forehead again. 'Her

mother is a journo friend of mine who was out in the States same time I was. She wanted a baby, but also wanted to know the father, so—'

'So you shagged her?'

'No. Listen, Em. She's gay.'

I stare at him.

'Her name is Carrie. She was with someone, Gill, but obviously they couldn't have kids so they asked me and I said yes. The deal was always that I'd be involved – but not on an everyday basis. I agreed without really thinking about it, which was possibly the second most stupid thing I've ever done after leaving you. But once Lulu was born I fell head over heels with her. She's amazing, Em, just so smart and sweet. I can't wait for you to meet her, if … if that's what you want, if you decide you want to be with me.'

'Wait, slow down.' I look back at the screen, at the smiling Lulu. 'Are you telling me you are the father of a little girl, whose mum is a lesbian?'

'Yes. Well, she has two mums: Gill and Carrie. One of the reasons I'm here is because they came back to England because Carrie got a job on a national a few months ago. They live in Yorkshire now. That's why I left the States and came home too. I go up to visit every other weekend. I stay there, take Lulu out.'

We look at each other. Dan clears his throat. 'I realize this is a massive thing to throw at you, but it doesn't change how I feel … about us.'

I look away. I can't deal with this, not right now. 'What

about this meeting Lish is going to tomorrow?' I ask. 'What do we do about that?'

'I'm going to be there, at the park gate. I'll be able to see who he's meeting ... maybe even film what happens ...'

'I'm coming too,' I say.

'No—'

I press my finger over Dan's lips. 'I'm not asking permission, Dan. I'm coming.'

2 August

So like for a WHOLE DAY I kept thinking about what I saw at the party and should I tell Mum or Daddy even though they would both be SO MAD. In the end I went on UFrenz and the most AMAZING thing happened. It's funny cos Mum has been asking why I'm not seeing my friends over the holiday and I've said so and so is away or that I'd rather be on my own or whatever. And Mum said she'd get Marietta Hingis round for a playdate – like we were still FIVE YEARS OLD – and I told her NO and that I HATE MARIETTA HINGIS and Mum got all cross and said she was only trying to help. SO ... yesterday after we'd had a row AGAIN I came up here and went on UFrenz like I've done before only this time I met Bex on it. And she was SO lovely. And YES I KNOW that paedos and whatnot go to places like that like they were all saying at the party but Bex is real. I know she is who she says cos of the way she talks about her picture – you have to post a picture of your face and say your age and you're not ALLOWED to use it unless you're between thirteen and eighteen so it's supposed to be, like, TOTALLY safe.

I logged on as usual as Lia which is from my name Cordelia that no one calls me cos I'm stuck with stupid Dee Dee. So you see I was being careful and not using my name everyone knows me by. And Bex came and said hello and she is SO cool. REALLY nice and like pretty but not TOO much and she told me how she had these friends at school who had been mean and sent her texts saying it would be better if she wasn't at school at all JUST LIKE happened with me. And she's been SO nice, saying that it's not my fault those girls were mean, that we're better than girls like that and better off being friends with each other. And did I say she was pretty? She's got brown hair like mine but lighter and her nose and mouth are smaller and much, much nicer but she was complaining her hair gets all frizzed up just like mine does and how it's all thick and she HATES it and she said she thought looking at my picture that MY hair was nicer than hers so I said I thought HERS was nicer and she was SO pleased and said she was really glad she'd met me.

After we'd chatted for a while I told her what I saw at the party and she says maybe it was not what I thought and explained it in a different way so I feel better about it now. She really understands things and we both like cute kitten pictures and I know she lives MILES outside London so like there is NO chance we could meet up so I KNOW FOR SURE it's not some paedo like Mum would worry about.

December 2014

That night I lie awake for hours, until the sky outside the window turns from indigo to steel, spreading a grey light through the room. Dan and I spend the early part of the morning in the hotel room, ordering breakfast and making love. I switch on my phone to find several angry voice mails from Jed, plus a series of increasingly concerned texts from Laura, Rose and Martin. I reply to Laura and my siblings, reassuring them I'm fine. I can't face Jed's temper though. After a while I fall asleep again, this time properly. I'm out for several hours, waking as Dan shakes my arm. He is dressed, a worried look on his face.

'I've got the room for another night. I didn't want to wake you, but I didn't want you to be upset if you woke and I was gone.'

'I told you, I'm coming with you.' I swing my legs out of the bed and run my fingers through my hair. 'How are we getting there?'

'I hired a car while you were asleep.'

Half an hour later, we're on our way. The closer we get to Richmond Park, the more anxious I feel and the more tense Dan looks. I ask him about his daughter, hoping it will give him something else to focus on. His voice is full of emotion as he describes her and how open and affectionate she is.

'I look at Lulu with Gill and Carrie and … and … they're great. I love them both and they're super generous with me. But I realize how, I dunno, cavalier I was back then thinking I could have a child like an accessory or something. I was *such* a jerk. I remember thinking that I would never want a family of my own, so why not help someone else to have a kid, never thinking what an irresponsible shit I was being to the child herself … and with no idea of how much she would matter to me.'

'Show me some more pictures.'

Dan directs me to a video on his iPad of Lulu at her last birthday party. She is indeed a sweet-looking child. Carrie and Gill look nice too. I gaze at Dan, his whole face lit up as he glances across at the screen. It strikes me that he is a different man from the person I knew all those years ago.

We're almost at the park now.

'Are you sure this is what you want to do?' I ask.

'Yes,' Dan goes on. 'It's not just the drugs thing being wrong. I kept thinking about Jed's daughter, Dee Dee, how I'd feel if anyone did that to Lulu …'

Richmond Park appears on the left. Dan parks around the corner and shoves his iPad into the glove compartment. We walk to Robin Hood Gate. It is freezing, far colder than yesterday, the cold air made worse by a biting wind. I zip up my jacket, wishing I had a hat with me. I've left my handbag alongside the iPad in the glove compartment so that I'm unencumbered. My phone is in the shallow pocket of my jacket in case I need it later but I'm worried it might fall out if I have to run. I couldn't be worse prepared for what we are doing now though at least I didn't dress up to meet Laura last night and am still wearing jeans and low-heeled boots. I check the time as we position ourselves across the road from the gate, concealed by a van and a tree. It's twenty-five to three.

'Is your phone switched off?' Dan asks.

I check it then hand him the mobile. 'Would you keep this in your pocket? I'm worried it might fall out of mine.'

Dan pockets my phone and we stand in the cold watching out for Lish. After half an hour he still hasn't appeared and a light rain starts to drizzle from the dark clouds above.

'D'you think we misunderstood the text?' I ask.

'No, it's only five past.' Dan puts his arm around my shoulders and I lean towards him, lifting my face for a swift kiss. For a moment I experience the weirdest sensation, like I'm spinning through air, slightly out of control but full of joy. And then, out of the corner of my eye, I see Lish approaching the Robin Hood Gate carrying a small holdall in his hand.

I step back, feeling the cold, hard pavement beneath my feet again.

'Look.'

Dan turns and follows my gaze.

'What d'you think's inside the bag?'

'Drugs or money, I imagine,' Dan mutters.

An icy chill settles on my chest. 'That's good,' I say, trying to focus on what we need to do next. 'If it's drugs, we can film him selling them; if it's money, maybe he'll use it to pay for drugs *to* sell and we can film that. Then we take the film to the police.'

'Exactly.' Dan grits his teeth as we watch Lish arrive at the gate. He stops for a moment, glances around, then strides off, into the park. Dan and I look at each other. The drizzle settles like a mist on our faces.

'Come on.' Dan puts his arm around my shoulders and we hurry across the road and through the park gates. No one else is about; the only person I can see is Lish himself, up ahead. He is walking briskly along the path. Dan and I are too exposed here; if Lish turned he would see us. Dan has clearly had the same thought. He points to the trees.

'Let's go over there.'

We hurry from tree to tree, keeping Lish in our sights as he strides deeper into the park. The place is deserted, the rain still light and fine, the sky dark overhead. My heart pounds as we creep through the trees.

'This is like *The Inn of the Sixth Happiness*,' I whisper, 'you know, where Ingrid Bergman has to make her way to safety through the woods with a bunch of kids. It's one of my favourite movies.'

'I know,' Dan whispers back. 'You watched it with your

mum and her mum and Rose when you were little. It's one of your strongest memories of your mother and your gran.'

I glance at him, amazed he has remembered so accurately something I told him ten years ago. 'I can't—'

'Sssh.' Dan holds up his hand, then points through the trees. Lish has stopped walking. We are right in the heart of the park now, the lake just a few metres away. Lish is standing beside a bench that overlooks the water. After glancing around for a long, heart-stopping moment, he sits down, his bag in his lap.

'He's waiting for someone,' Dan whispers. 'Waiting to hand over whatever's in the bag.'

I look around. The park is silent, apart from the wind whistling through the trees and the soft patter of the rain on the leaves. It's unnerving. Soon it will be dark. I'm so cold now that my whole body is shivering.

I reach for Dan's hand, as much for warmth as for comfort.

But just as I touch Dan's fingertips, I am jerked back, a hand over my mouth. I try to turn, but only manage enough movement to see that Dan is being propelled to the ground by a huge guy wearing a thick, padded jacket and red cap. I can't see his face. Dan falls with a thud onto the damp earth. I give a muffled yell, then kick out. My hands are yanked painfully behind my back.

'Fucking quiet, please,' a low, male voice hisses in my ear. There's a slight accent. My insides contract with fear.

My arms are pulled tighter. A scarf is wrapped over my mouth. It smells sour.

'Fucking walk.' The voice is all menace.

I stumble forward. Dan is on his feet ahead of me, also gagged with his wrists tied. He is still struggling, trying to turn around, to get to me. I glance through the trees. Lish has vanished from the bench.

Are these men with him? Does he know we are here? Where are we being taken? What are they going to do with us? My heart drums loudly in my chest.

Dan and I are shoved through the woodland. The sky darkens overhead. The rain has stopped but the wind is raw in my eyes. I am trembling all over.

Out of the trees, across a patch of grass where two paths intersect. I look around. Surely someone is here, somebody will see us. But the park is utterly deserted. The two men shove us forward. They say nothing. We are pushed into another patch of woodland. Through more trees. After a minute or so we come to a gents toilets. We are forced inside. It's ice-cold and smells of stale pee and disinfectant. Across the room, Dan is shoved against the wall, his face pressed against the white tiles. My captor grips my wrist. He is much shorter and slighter than the other man. Like the bigger guy, his face is mostly covered with a cap. I can just make out his fleshy top lip and the stubble on his pale chin. I'm certain he's the guy who mugged me at the tube station. He's the same height, the same build as the figure the ticket officer described.

'You were there, on the platform,' I gasp. 'You—'

'Quiet.' The man whips a knife from his belt and presses it to my throat. The metal is cold against my skin.

I flinch. Across the room, Dan's captor is yanking on his arms, pulling them up behind his back.

'This. Last. Warning.' My guy speaks in a low, guttural voice. 'Stay. Away. Or end up like little girl. Understand?'

He means stay away from Lish, from investigating the drug dealing. Or end up like Dee Dee. *Fuck. Fuck.* My breath is coming in quick, shuddering rasps. Across the room, Dan is still being forced against the wall.

'Understand?' the man with me persists. He is only an inch or two taller than I am, but his fingers are like steel on my arm. 'Understand? Stay. Away.'

The menace in his voice is almost as terrifying as the knife at my throat.

'Yes,' I gasp. 'I understand.' For a split second I'm certain I'm about to die, that the stained, white-tiled wall in front of me is the last thing on earth that I will ever see. And then I'm spun around. The man lets go of my wrists, then slices through the rope that binds them. He pulls the scarf away from my mouth. I turn. Where is Dan?

He's being forced out of the door, held between the two men. The man who threatened me turns. 'Wait here. You don't try leave. We'll be back.'

'Emily!' Dan yells, the sound muted by his gag.

'Dan!' I run to the door. It slams shut in my face. Outside I can hear Dan's muffled shouts. I pull at the handle. But the door is locked. I hammer against the wood.

'Dan!' But my shout echoes off the bare walls into silence.

I stand at the door, the light fading around me as the full horror of the situation settles in my head.

Dan is gone and I am alone.

Trapped.

3 August

Oh, wow, Bex is SO amazing. She really understands my life. I went on UFrenz again today wondering if she'd be there again like she was yesterday and she WAS. And she asked how I felt about what I saw at the party now and I said much better thanks to her and she must have been right about me misunderstanding it and she asked if I'd talked to anyone else about it and I said no because I'd talked to HER. And she did an emoticon of 'embarrassed face' all bright red, JUST like I would have done if it had been me and I said I was glad I'd kept quiet because my whole family would be SO upset if I'd said anything but I was glad I'd told her and she said she was glad I had told her too and that it meant we were truly best friends and I said that I couldn't ask for a better friend and Bex said she felt the same.

December 2014

My legs give way and I sink to the cold, tiled floor. What are those men going to do with Dan? Oh God, why on earth did we come here? I can still hear my captor's harsh whisper:

'Wait here. You don't try leave. We'll be back.'

I run to the door. It's firmly locked and at least an inch thick. Bile fills my throat. Is Dan still out there? Have they killed him already? Or are they taking him somewhere else first? I press my ear to the door and listen hard, but the only sound I can hear is the swish of the wind in the trees. I feel for my phone but my jacket pocket is empty. Of course. Dan has my mobile. I gave it to him earlier.

'Help! Help!' My shout reverberates off the tiles. It's hopeless. Desperate. I already know the park is virtually empty and the light is fading fast. Nobody will come. I have to save myself. There is only one small window, above and to the left of the row of sinks. It's too high for me to see through it but if I could break the glass, I should be able to crawl through.

Even at full stretch, I can only just reach the bottom of the sill. There's no way I can pull myself up by my fingertips. I test the nearest sink. It seems solid enough. I clamber on top of it. There's a tiny ledge just above the row of sinks. I lean against it, trying to prevent all my weight being taken by the sink itself. I push at the window. The catch is stuck, the wood swollen. It's impossible to open; my only option is to break the glass.

'Shit, shit,' I mutter to myself. There's nothing in the room I can use. I jump down. Take off my boot. Up on the sink again I ram the boot against the glass. I almost fall off the sink with the effort but at least the glass cracks. Steadying myself against the wall, legs braced, I pound the glass again. This time it smashes. Loudly. I stop and hold my breath. If the men are just outside they will hear. But they have gone, Dan with them. What are they doing to him? Have they killed him?

I can't let myself think it.

Using the boot to cover my hand, I push out all the remaining shards of glass. An icy wind whistles straight in, nipping at my face. It is twilight outside, the nearby trees lost in a shadowy gloom.

'Come on.' I urge myself closer to the window. My foot slips against the sink. I jump down again. Put my boot back on. Then I climb up a third time. The sink creaks. With a groan it slips an inch down the wall. I lurch upwards, clinging to the window. I'm on one foot now, balancing awkwardly, trying to get my knee over the sill. But the window is too small. The sink creaks again. Last chance. Any second it will collapse. I strain upwards, balancing on the tip of one toe. I reach for the top of the window then turn so my fingers grip its outside edge. In a single movement, I push off from the sink and haul myself up with my arms. A second later the sink collapses with a crash and I am sitting on the window ledge, my arms and upper body outside, my legs from the knees down still inside. I wriggle back, bottom first. The ledge cuts into my fingers but I daren't loosen my grip. I clamber out so my feet are on the sill, then in one movement I let go and jump down. I land on the earth, knees bent to absorb the impact. My legs jar, my hands are sore and my arms are shaking, but I'm outside, I'm free.

I stand, trying to get my bearings. Which way is the fastest route out of the park? I have no idea, so I retrace my steps towards Robin Hood Gate. Night falls around me as I run, my breath coming in jagged gasps. The wind hisses through the bare branches of the trees. I have to get to a phone and call the police. Panic rises inside me. Suppose I'm not in time? Suppose Dan is already dead? He could be miles away by now.

Wait. I can work out where he is. The thought strikes me with such force I actually stop running for a second. Dan has my phone. Which means I can find him using the same app that Jed used to track me. Unless, that is, his captors find the phone and power it down. I start running again, head down against the wind, pounding across the grass. I reach the gates and hurl myself up and over them. There's nobody on the street, though a man walking his dog in the distance turns as I thud down onto the pavement. Ignoring him I hurry to Dan's car. To my relief it's still there.

I hesitate for a second, but I don't have a choice. There's no time to lose.

I wrap my hand in my jacket and punch the glass on the passenger side. The car alarm blares into the air. I reach in and open the glove compartment. Dan's iPad is wedged inside along with my handbag. I take them both out and set off again. Down the street. Around the corner. I don't stop until I reach the lights of the Kingston University campus. I take shelter under a tree and, with trembling fingers, turn the iPad on. It takes me a few minutes to piggyback someone's wi-fi, then another thirty anxious seconds to pull up the app and enter my details.

A map flashes up. Straightaway I can see my phone is on the move. Does that mean Dan is still alive? Or that they've killed him but haven't yet disposed of his body and everything in his pockets? My device is moving fast, they must be travelling by car. I peer more closely. The signal shows that Dan is now in Twickenham. I zoom in and stare at the screen. What road is that? *No.* I can't believe it. The signal stops. I switch to satellite view so I can see the individual buildings. My breath catches in my throat. There's no mistaking that flat modern roof set among all those old houses, with the river at the bottom of the garden.

My phone – and presumably Dan with it – are squarely positioned in the building. I blink, still unable to take it in.

This is my brother's house.

*

I realize I am holding my breath and take a deep lungful of cold air. I am standing opposite Martin and Cameron's modern townhouse. And here, on the screen in front of me, the icon for my phone shows that it is definitely still inside the building. It makes no sense. What have Martin and Cameron got to do with Lish's drug dealing? Or the men who took Dan? Apart from anything else, they were heading off on holiday on Boxing Day so I'm certain that neither of them can possibly be at home.

No lights are on in the house – at least not at the front. But someone must be inside. If not my brother and his boyfriend, then perhaps Lish's drug-dealing contacts. Perhaps Gary. I put down Dan's iPad and zip up my jacket. The curtains are drawn across the upstairs bedroom. Is Dan in there? No one is looking out. I creep across the road to the edge of the garage and reach for the top of the side gate. In seconds I'm over it and leaping down onto the paving beyond. After climbing the big gates in the park it's easy to land with the lightest of thuds. I still hold my breath, waiting to see if I've been heard. No one comes. I race along the passageway, creeping under the window of the kitchen wall as I pass. I stop to take my bearings. The only room downstairs at the back is the big kitchen/diner that leads out onto the garden. The lights *are* on in this room, casting shadows across the back lawn, right down to the water beyond. As I creep closer I catch sight of the river itself. Martin and Cameron's boat is moored at the end of the garden. It looms darkly out of the water. Lights are on in the central cabin.

I peer around the wall and look into the kitchen/diner. The room is empty. I stare in at the shadowy interior, at the familiar table and chairs, the designer sofa and the artwork on the walls. I have been here many times, hanging out with my brother and his boyfriend, laughing and joking with them. Is it possible that they've let Lish use their house? If it is, they must surely be ignorant of what he is doing here. And yet Martin knows most of what I know. Surely he would be suspicious? I turn again to the boat. The light from the cabin flickers, as if someone has walked past it.

Never mind what Martin and Cameron are aware of, I need to find Dan. The locator app tells me he is within a few metres of where I'm standing. Could he be on the boat? It's worth a look. Keeping to the cover of the trees on the right-hand side of the garden, I scurry down to the river's edge. Water slaps at the hull of the *Maggie May*. Again I'm thankful for my rubber-soled boots as I step gently on board. My heart hammers against my throat as I tiptoe along the cabin wall to the tiny window. Anyone looking out from the back of the house would be able to see me, but no one is looking. I creep up and peer into the cabin.

No sign of Dan, but Lish is in there. He looks smarter than when I last saw him, in skinny chinos and a zip-up wool jacket. His hair is carefully slicked back, making him look more like Jed than usual. He is peering into a tote bag, his hands dug deep into his pockets. He looks up. He's talking to someone I can't see across the room. Is that the guy who threatened me? Could it be Gary? A new possibility rushes through my head: perhaps Gary and Lish are making illicit use of my brother's house and boat while he and Cameron are away.

Lish reaches down, out of my eyeline. He straightens up, clutching a pile of cardboard packages bound together with cellophane. What's inside them? Drugs? I inch forward, trying to make out the markings on the packet but they are too small. A few more seconds and the last packet is in the bag. Lish says something I can't hear, then he picks up the bag and walks out of sight.

I duck down as the cabin door opens and footsteps sound across the deck. I wait, hidden from view, as agonizing seconds pass. Two light thuds signify Lish and whoever he's with have jumped onto the bank. I wait a few more long seconds, then peer around the cabin wall. I'm just in time to see two dark figures – once of which is definitely Lish – disappearing into the house.

Who is the other man? Surely it has to be Gary? And surely his and Lish's presence here proves they are using the place while Mart and Cameron are away? My heart thuds. And then I hear a muffled cry coming from inside the cabin.

Someone else is on the boat.

Dan.

I have to get inside. I look around, trying to work out how. I am standing on the sun deck where just a few months ago we all sat and ate that dinner in Corsica – the sea bream from a local trader – the night Dee Dee died. I touch the back of one of the chairs nailed to the deck. It is covered with canvas, protected from the winter weather. The fabric is rough to my touch. That holiday feels like another lifetime: when Jed and I were happy. We'd watched the people eating in that restaurant. An image of the elderly lady in the crazy tiara flashes into my mind's eye, then Jed insisting Dee Dee ate her fish – fish that Cameron had cooked – and my headache, which led to the original purchase of the ExAche powders. I suddenly remember how Jed and I came back to the boat early – and alone – that day in Corsica, and how we let ourselves into the cabin with the spare key.

I race to the tarpaulin that is fastened over the lifeboat at the far end of the yacht. This is where Jed found the spare key before. Do Martin and Cameron still keep it here? I lift up the edge of the tarp and feel along the side of the railings against which the lifeboat is secured. It smells of dust and damp and oil. I push aside the bollard that has been placed here and reach further back. A waterproof pack is taped to the deck floor behind the lifeboat. I peel up the first part of the tape and scrabble around. My fingers light on something small and curved. I tug the key away from its hiding place. Clutching the cold metal in my hand, I head back to the cabin door. A quick glance at the house – still in darkness – then the cabin door opens with a click.

I creep inside. I daren't put on the light but it's obvious

the main cabin is empty. Dan's muffled cries and thumps are coming from the bedroom, where Jed and I made love that same afternoon all those months ago. I hurry across and open the door.

Dan is sitting on the bed, his hands tightly bound by a chain and a gag around his mouth. His eyes widen as he sees me. I hurry over and pull the gag away.

'Em?' he breathes. 'What the fuck are you doing here?'

'I tracked the phone,' I whisper. 'I just saw Lish.'

'Is he here?' Dan grimaces. 'I haven't seen or heard anyone except those guys who took me in the park.'

'Are you all right?' I'm anxiously examining his face, his arms.

'They haven't hurt me ... yet.' Dan holds up the chain that is wound tightly around his wrists and padlocked to the bedpost. He indicates the padlock. 'There's a key for that. I heard one guy tell the other to put it in the knife box, whatever that means.'

I hurry back into the main cabin and along to the galley kitchen. I daren't turn on the light so I'm straining to see in the gloom as I pull open drawers and cupboards. What on earth is a 'knife box'? As far as I know, the only knives on board are stored along a magnetic strip above the galley counter – one of the *Maggie May*'s many neat space-saving devices. I rummage under the sink and through every cupboard in turn. Each compartment is tightly packed with all the paraphernalia of yachting life, from crockery to oil cans. No knife box as far as I can tell. I go back to the magnetic strip holding the knives against the wall as my eyes adjust properly to the dim light. There are just three knives, none of them particularly sharp. I reach out and pull them off the strip. I prod the empty strip. It doesn't budge. My heart beats loudly in the silence. I press the strip to the side and it gives, just slightly. I stare at it for a second, then shove it harder. With a judder the strip shifts to the left, revealing a gap in the wall behind. Holding my breath I reach inside. My fingers find a handle. I tug at it and the three rows of tiles below come away in my hands. Hidden in the wall is a metal box the size of a briefcase. With a jolt I remember Jed telling me about the airtight boxes that block the scent of the drugs so that customs officials and their dogs can't sniff them out.

I lay the box on the counter and lift the airtight lid. It gives way with a suck. A key that looks like it will fit Dan's padlock lies on top of a box covered in bubblewrap. A tight lump in my throat, I take out the box and unfurl the plastic covering.

Ten packs of Viagra, all wrapped up together, meet my eyes. I reach further and pull out another, similar bundle, this time of stanozolol. My fingers tremble as I undo the Viagra and remove a blister strip of pills. They look real enough. Stolen. No, *wait*. The 'g' on the back of the pack is out of sync with the others.

Fakes.

Is Lish storing his drugs on Martin and Cameron's boat too? Or is it possible that my brother is actually involved?

After all, surely Martin and Cameron would be aware of this hiding place set into the very wall of their boat? No. I can't believe that my brother knows about this. Gary *must* be behind it: he was on the holiday in Corsica and in the bar when the Snapchat from Laura's phone came through. He is Lish's uncle and he has shown an overt interest in Jed's case against Benecke Tricorp from the start. I even overheard him telling someone that Jed's desire to prosecute the company was the 'wrong focus', as if he knew they weren't responsible for Dee Dee's death.

I grab two packs of Viagra and shove them inside my jacket, then put the rest back in the box. As I reach for the key to Dan's padlock a fist grabs my arm. Wrenches me around. It's the smaller, wirier of the men from Richmond Park. His skin is pock-marked, his eyes pale and cold.

I open my mouth to scream.

'Shut mouth.' The man drags me out of the galley and pushes me against the wall. He grabs my bag and throws it to the floor. A second later his gun is out of his pocket and pressing against my forehead.

I stare at the metal barrel, shocked into silence.

'In there.' He indicates the bathroom.

'What are you going to do?'

'We said before: last chance.' The man shoves me towards the bathroom. 'This time, you die.'

'For fuck's sake, hold on, Bogdan.' It's Cameron's voice, a sharp hiss across the cabin.

I spin around. My brother's boyfriend is standing by the

340

open door, silhouetted against the light outside. He's dressed, as usual, in smart designer clothes: black jeans and a lemon yellow sweater. My first reaction is relief. If Cameron is here, I will be okay. Apart from anything else, Cameron is a trustafarian. He's already ridiculously rich, he can't possibly be involved in drug dealing for money. Plus, he is kind and thoughtful.

And then he switches on the cabin light and I see the scowl on his face and the fury in his eyes and my relief vanishes.

August 2014

So ... I've been chatting on UFrenz with Bex ALL WEEK and the holiday is coming up and I'm worried that I won't be able to go online and chat with Bex while we're away because Daddy was saying there might not be wi-fi in our villa and if I can't chat with Bex I will seriously DIE. I was on with her earlier and we were private chatting and she said how her mum was sick and how it was really, really upsetting and how the girls at school were so mean about it. Like they were hinting her mum getting sick was BEX'S fault. I told her that it wasn't, that it made me think how I should appreciate my mum, even though she is SO annoying, and Bex said I was very smart and kind for seeing that and that it upsets her because most of her friends moan about their mums and she'd give anything for hers to be well and getting cross with her again. I think it's worse because she has a stepdad who sounds horrible. He won't let her have a proper phone so she's got a really basic one just for texts and calls. She can only go on the internet on his computer and only when he can see what she's doing which is why she is mainly on UFrenz when he's visiting her mum in hospital. I think she's having chemotherapy for her cancer but Bex doesn't like to talk about it too much. It is SO sad. Poor Bex.

She should be online soon, I can't wait to chat with her again.

December 2014

Cameron and I stare at each other.

He raises his eyebrows. 'You *tracked* us?'

My heart thuds with fear.

'Emily!' Dan yells from the bedroom beyond the main cabin. 'What's happening? Are you all right?'

Cameron puts his finger to his lips. Bogdan disappears into the bedroom. I hold my breath as Dan's yell is muffled again. An instant later Bogdan reappears, shutting the bedroom door behind him.

'Bring her up to the house,' Cameron orders in a low voice. He turns and marches out of the cabin.

Bogdan grabs my arm. 'Not one word,' he hisses in my ear.

Panic grabs at my throat. 'Dan!' I call out.

A muffled yell is the only response I can hear, before I'm wrenched across the cabin and out into the chill night air. The *Maggie May* creaks as we jump off, onto the grass. Cameron is striding ahead, already almost at the house. My breath mists in front of my face. How can this be happening? Cameron is my brother's boyfriend. I've known

343

him for years. How can he be involved in Lish's drug deal-ing?

Could he be responsible for Dee Dee's death? What about Gary?

Could Martin be involved? Cameron disappears into the kitchen. I turn to Bogdan, still tightly gripping my arm.

'Where's Martin?' I ask. 'Where's my brother?'

Bogdan says nothing.

I am shaking as we reach the house. Across the kitchen/diner and up to the mezzanine living space with its surround-sound speakers and designer light fittings. Cameron is standing in front of the TV on the wall, its dark screen highlighting the yellow of his jumper. He looks so ridiculously preppy and respectable I am filled with doubt. Have I misunderstood everything?

'Why is Dan on your boat?' I demand. 'Where's Martin?'

Bogdan shoves me onto the sofa. I spring up. He forces me down again, his hands rough and strong on my arm. I have a sudden flashback to the tube attack. It was him, I'm more certain than ever. And he works for Cameron, which means . . .

'Thanks, Bogdan, you can go,' Cameron orders.

Without a word Bogdan slips out of the room and closes the door behind him.

'He's just outside,' Cameron says smoothly, 'so don't think about running.'

'He was the one who pushed me at the tube station.'

Cameron studies my face. 'That's right, he was, though

he wasn't supposed to hurt you, just take the drugs that were in your bag.'

My legs give way under me and I sink back onto the sofa. 'How did you know?'

'That you had the drugs Lish sold Dan?' Cameron sighs. 'Lish knew they were in your house because his father had told him the night before, so he and Bogdan waited outside. He was hoping to get a chance to go inside and look for them, but he saw you putting them into your handbag as you left the next morning. He got Bogdan to follow you.'

'And that was *you* calling me? Threatening me? Sending the ... the dead bird?'

Cameron gives me a curt nod.

I let this sink in. So Gary has nothing to do with the disguised voice. Jed's brother is not involved.

But what about mine?

Cameron sits down in the armchair next to the TV. 'I have done everything in my power not to hurt you, Emily, out of respect for your brother, but I have to say you have pushed me to the absolute—'

'Does Martin know?' The words shoot out of me. 'The drugs.' I feel for the boxes inside my jacket. 'The fake Viagra, the stanozolol ...' My stomach churns.

'No.' Cameron's green eyes meet mine. 'I promise you, Martin knows nothing about my business. He thinks I've just had to break into our holiday in order to deal with a crisis at one of my charities.

I stare at his yellow sweater, at the discreet designer logo over the right breast. And it suddenly falls into place. Cam doesn't have a trust fund at all. Drugs fund his expensive lifestyle.

'You lied about your family, didn't you? You just sail around picking up fake drugs in Africa or Asia or wherever, then selling them here. And Lish isn't the only dealer you use, either; you've probably got whole strings of them, all over the country.'

Cameron tilts his head to one side. 'Martin always said you were smarter than you come across on first meeting,' he says, a thin smile curling across his lips. '"That fragile, doe-eyed thing some straight men go mad for, don't let it fool you," Martin told me. "She might be a bit naïve about some things, but she's cleverer than the rest of us put together".'

'But Martin doesn't know?' I need to hear it again. The idea that my brother could be in any way involved in Cameron's crimes is too appalling to face.

'Martin has no idea.' I look into the hard green of his eyes. He's telling the truth. 'Before you judge me, I'd like you to listen,' Cameron goes on. 'What I do hurts nobody. I buy drugs made to more or less the same specifications as the patented brands and I sell them on to people who can't get a prescription or ... or are maybe just too embarrassed to ask their doctor for them. It's a necessary service. It's supply and demand. If *I* wasn't providing the drugs, some-one else would ... someone who might not be so scrupulous about their suppliers. With what I'm involved in, no one gets hurt.'

'What about Dee Dee?' I demand, a sob rising inside me as I picture her the day she died, all clumsy and affection-ate. 'She saw something, didn't she … like I saw you and Lish earlier? She found out what you were up to and you killed her to keep her quiet.'

'No,' Cameron says. 'Absolutely not. I'm not in the busi-ness of murder, especially not innocent children.'

We stare at each other.

'Seriously, Emily, that's not what happened. It's unthinkable. For a start, Lish may only be nineteen, but he would never have stood by while someone deliberately killed his own sister. Also Dee Dee was barely in her teens. I think we could have found a way to keep her quiet even if she'd known what we were doing, which she absolutely didn't.'

'Lish had access to potassium cyanide over the summer. I *know* he did.'

Cameron frowns. 'We let him have a tiny amount for some photography students and for a French dealer we'd arranged for him to meet in Calvi, but he got rid of all his drugs as soon as Dee Dee was found dead.'

'Don't you think that's a bit too much of a coincidence?' I ask.

'No,' Cameron says firmly. 'I've talked it all through with Lish. Firstly Dee Dee had no idea that Lish *had* the cyanide. Secondly, it was hidden in his bag in his room – neither of which were ever out of his sight and neither of which were in any way disturbed during the night before Dee Dee died, and thirdly – as I already pointed out – Lish had absolutely no motive for killing her.'

'Maybe she saw him with the drugs? Suppose she saw you giving Lish the cyanide?'

'We didn't "give" it to him. I told him the stocks were in and he took what he needed while the rest of us were on deck eating the sea bream that Rose and I cooked.'

'But Dee Dee told me she had a secret that afternoon; it *must* have been to do with her seeing something.'

'Except that, as I've just explained, Lish didn't *take* the drugs until we were all on the boat that evening, so whatever her secret was, it couldn't have been to do with that.'

I shake my head. There's no point arguing with him. Cameron is never going to admit the truth.

'Come on, Emily, you know it doesn't make sense. Think about it. Surely you can see that a lethal chemical mixed with a sachet of painkillers would be the last thing we'd use to kill anyone. Why on earth would we draw attention to *any* pharmaceuticals? Plus, there was no way either Lish or I could have known Dee Dee would end up taking that ExAche. It was given to *you*, remember? And we had no more reason to kill you than we did Dee Dee.'

All this is true, and yet I am more certain than ever that Dee Dee saw something, recorded it on her phone and was killed as a result.

'If you're not in the "business of murder", as you say, why did you tell me Dan was going to die?' I ask, my voice trembling. 'Why is he tied up on your boat?'

'I was trying to make you back away from all those bloody questions you were asking, you and Dan Thackeray.' Cameron slicks back his hair with his fingers. 'Clearly my threats didn't work so it was time to change tack.'

I press my lips together as Cameron sits forward, his face earnest. What is he going to threaten now?

'Listen, Emily, I'm giving you a choice,' he says softly. 'A choice which I wouldn't give you if you weren't Martin's sister. What I want you to do is call off Dan Thackeray, which means persuading him to leave London and stop looking into what Lish is doing, what I am doing.' He pauses. 'And that means you will have to cut all ties with him.'

Cut all ties. I gulp.

'Just to be clear: *you* I won't touch for Martin's sake, but Thackeray is on his last chance.' Cameron looks at me, his eyes intense. 'Do you understand?'

A shiver shudders through me. I nod slowly. 'You'll kill Dan if I don't get him to stop investigating you.'

'That's part of it, but what you also need to remember,' Cameron continues, 'is that if you and Dan *don't* stop and the police become involved, then your brother will inevitably end up in prison.'

My mouth falls open. 'But you said he wasn't part of the whole thing, you said—'

'Martin is an accessory after the fact,' Cameron says flatly. 'He doesn't know what I do, but I doubt a jury would believe that.'

'I thought you loved him,' I say.

'I do.' Cameron's eyes burn into me. 'Which is why my evidence won't count for very much … that and the fact that no one is likely to believe anything I say. I've been trading in fake pharma for twelve years and Martin has been living with me most of that time.'

He is right. And what's more, I'm certain that Martin must, at some level, know what's going on; that, after so much time, if he is truly ignorant, it's because he has chosen to turn a blind eye. Whatever. I don't care. All that matters is this: I must stop Dan from going to the police or writing a story or even carrying on investigating Lish's drug deals. If I fail, Dan will die and Martin's life will be destroyed.

'You may think what I'm doing is a crime,' Cameron goes on, his voice like steel, 'but it's a victimless one. I make sure what we supply won't hurt anyone – there'd be no sense in that anyway. We buy from suppliers who just water down what's in the brand-name drugs, not even by a huge amount. It works like that, *has* to work like that. If our product gets a bad reputation, no one will buy it.'

I don't bother to argue. All I can think is that I am going to have to lie … to Martin, to Dan, to the world. To lie and lie and lie again. Despite what Cameron says, I'm certain that Lish *must* have killed Dee Dee. And I will have to pretend he didn't in order to protect the people I love.

I stand up. Cameron stands too. I take a deep breath. There is no choice. 'I won't say anything to anyone, and I'll make Dan … back off.'

'Good.' Cameron takes something out of his pocket and holds it out to me. It's my phone. 'I'm going to let you go back to the cabin,' he says. 'Dan hasn't seen me, but he knows this is where Martin and I live. You need to persuade him that Lish was using our house, that he has let you go … is letting both of you go on the understanding that your investigations end right now. Keep your phone on and in your pocket. I will be listening in, so don't think about giving my name or trying to trick me in any way. Remember what will happen to Dan if you put a foot wrong. After you've told the lie once, it'll be easier to keep it going.'

I nod, my throat dry. I can see on the screen of my phone there are loads more missed calls, mostly from Jed. It feels like a million years ago since I spoke to him in the taxi yesterday. Cameron places a call to my phone. Once the line is open, he slips the handset into my pocket.

'Go,' he says.

Bogdan marches me down to the *Maggie May*. Suddenly I'm alone and inside the cabin, a small, sharp knife and the key to Dan's padlock in my hand. I hurry through to the bedroom. Dan is still tied up, his eyes wild with fear and fury over the gag around his mouth. I pull it down.

'Emily, are you okay? What's happening? Did they hurt you?' The words tumble out of him.

I hold up the key Cameron gave me. My phone weighs heavily in my pocket. Cameron is listening. Even if he wasn't, I wouldn't want Dan to know about his involvement. It's too risky. For Dan and for Martin.

'Hurry, Em,' Dan urges. 'Are you all right?'

'I'm fine,' I say, turning to the wall and fumbling with the padlock. 'Listen, Dan, it's Lish … he's involved with these people, he's just using Martin's house.'

I can feel my cheeks reddening. Thank goodness Dan can't see my face, I'm sure my deceit is written all over it.

'Who are the people he's with?' Dan asks. 'I only saw that Eastern European guy. Did you see someone else? Someone higher up?'

I shake my head.

'Did you see anyone? Someone you'd be able to recognize again?'

'No,' I say, opening the padlock and sliding the chain through. 'No. And I've promised Lish that I … that we … that we'll let the whole thing drop now.'

'What?' Dan shuffles around on the bed to face me. 'Are you serious?'

I can't look at him. Instead I focus on the binding around his wrist, slicing through it with my knife, then kneeling to free his ankles.

'I'm sorry, it's the safest thing to do.'

'Right.' I can hear the confusion in Dan's voice. 'What … *why*, Em? We have real proof now.'

'No we don't,' I say. 'We still have nothing concrete and we're in Martin's house, on his boat. If we go to the police Martin will be dragged into everything.' I hesitate. 'There's something else, Dan.'

'What?' He rubs his wrists then holds me as he stands

352

up. I hug him tightly, feeling the strength and warmth of his body against mine. My phone presses against my side, reminding me again that Cameron is listening. 'Lish's condition for sparing your life ... *our* lives ... is that you have to leave London. Right now. We ... we have to cut all ties.'

'No.' Dan pulls me closer. 'No, I'm not leaving you.'

I look up, into his eyes. Dan's gaze in the dim light is fierce. Any hopes I might have held that he would go along with me without a fuss fade away. I'm going to have to force the issue. 'It's what I want,' I say, meeting his gaze. 'Even if Lish wasn't threatening us, I ... I need some time, some space. Away from you.'

Dan looks at me. I can see he knows I'm holding something back. I reach into my pocket and silently hold up the phone so Dan can see it is on. His eyes widen with understanding as I put my finger to my lips.

'Okay,' Dan says. He takes my hand and we hurry silently through the main cabin, off the *Maggie May* and across the grass. The sliding doors to the kitchen/diner are open, though the room is still in darkness. I lead Dan through, out into the hall. The front door is locked. Fear rises inside me. I can't see a key.

Bogdan appears behind us. I shrink away. He glances at the phone in my pocket. Cameron is still listening. Of course he is. And Dan hasn't given me his word yet that he will back off.

'You have to promise, Dan,' I stammer, my throat

swollen with emotion. 'They don't want to kill us but they will if you don't leave London.'

'Leave tonight,' Bogdan growls.

Dan looks from me to Bogdan, then back again. 'I will leave tonight,' he says. 'To keep you safe, Em.'

Bogdan points to my phone and nods. Then he steps forward and unlocks the door. Dan and I hurry out onto the pavement. As we walk along the road, I switch off the phone call so Cameron can no longer hear us. Dan puts his arm around me.

'What the hell is going on, Em?'

I open my mouth to explain everything, then shut it again. There's no point me telling him about Cameron. It won't change the need for silence and it brings Martin closer to danger.

'I'm just scared for you and for my brother.' I pause. 'And for myself.'

'I get that, but it's wrong that Lish gets away with dealing, it's wrong that fake drugs exist. Watering down pharmaceuticals is dangerous, they don't work properly, they can be harmful . . . lethal. And it's wrong that we have to stay apart because of it.'

'I know, but that's how it has to be. *Please.*'

Another pause. 'Okay.' Dan clears his throat. 'But I don't want to leave you. I want to be sure you're safe.'

'I'll be fine.'

'Where will you go? To Rose's?'

'For a while, yes.' I reach my arm around his back. 'I

don't want you to go either. But we have to ... for now at least.'

Dan nods slowly. We make our way back to his car where the alarm is still blaring. As Dan finds his key and switches it off, I gaze up at the stars. In keeping silent, I'm covering up crimes including – I'm sure – that Cameron is responsible for murdering Dee Dee. I've lied to Dan, I must now lie to Martin. I must keep this terrible secret forever.

Dan drops me at Rose's house at about 10 p.m. I have already called and checked it's okay for me to stay. I haven't told her anything else, rebuffing all her questions over the phone. But I know that now I'm here I will have to deal with her curiosity – and confusion. And yet all my thoughts revolve around Dan and Martin – and keeping them both safe. Dan said very little on the drive here. We parted with a long, sad kiss. I promised him that I would call him soon. Cameron might be able to monitor Dan's investigations and check where he's living, but he can't control our conversations. For his part, Dan intends to stay with his daughter and her mothers for a while. 'Until I get my head around all this,' he says.

I'm certain he still senses that I haven't told him everything. And that he is holding back from pushing me. The knowledge makes me feel worse than ever. I let myself into Rose's house to find my sister on the living-room couch – at Dad's end, as usual – with a bottle of wine and two full glasses of Pinot Noir on the coffee table. She's dressed in silk pyjamas and a red satin dressing gown. Her hair is tousled, but her eyes are bright with curiosity.

'Thought you could use a drink,' she says, pushing one of the glasses in my direction.

'You thought right.' I sink into the sofa and take a long swig of wine. I'm praying Rose won't start asking questions, but of course she is itching to know why I'm here.

'What's going on, Emily? Jed called earlier. He was asking if I'd seen or heard from you all day which at the time I hadn't.' She sighs. 'He sounded desperately worried, but I haven't called him back even though I promised I would if I heard anything.' She pauses again and when she speaks, her voice is stretched thin with tension. 'I know he hasn't handled everything very well and that you're upset, but I don't think it's fair to just run out on him without any explanation. And ... I hate to sound judgmental but what the hell is going on with you and Dan Thackeray? I thought you were going to stay away from him?'

My relationship with Jed feels like the least of my problems right now. Still, I'm going to have to face up to it all sooner or later and I know Rose well ... she won't be put off if I try and play for time before answering her.

Not that I need any more time; I've made my choice.

'I'm going to leave Jed,' I say with a sigh. 'I've more or less told him already.'

'*What?* You *can't. Why?* For Dan bloody Thackeray? That's *mad.*'

'No it isn't.' I set down my glass. 'I'm sorry, but I don't want to talk about this.'

Rose tilts her head to one side and looks at me. I can see the exasperation in her eyes.

'Is this because Jed didn't believe you about his son and those stupid drugs?' she asks. 'Because if it is, I think you're being naïve. Of course Jed didn't believe you. He didn't *want* to believe you. Try and imagine this from his point of view: he loses his daughter and discovers his son may be involved with drug dealers. Now the woman he loves is telling him that the same son, his only remaining child, was responsible for his daughter's murder. It's just too hard for him to accept. I don't understand why you can't see that.'

I sit back, stung. 'I don't want to go over all that again.'

'You haven't told me the full story about you and Dan either, have you?' Rose persists. 'You might not be planning on going straight back out with him, but you've fallen in love again, haven't you?'

I can't meet her eyes.

'Oh my God, you've *slept* with him too!' Rose exclaims. 'I can *tell* you have. For goodness' sake, Emily, when are you going to get it through your head. Dan Thackeray is a chancer, a commitment-phobe. He didn't really care about you eight years ago. What makes you think it will be any different now?'

I look up at last. 'Dan's changed,' I say, feeling defensive. 'He's not the same person he was when he dumped me.'

Rose looks sceptical. 'Leopards, spots . . .'

'He's got a little girl.'

Rose's eyes widen. 'You're kidding.'

'No.' I explain the circumstances under which Dan became a father. 'He's changed, he's more responsible than he was eight years ago.'

'Humph.' Rose folds her arms. 'I'd say having a child in those circumstances rather speaks to his *lack* of responsibility. Anyway, what about Jed? Apart from him not wanting to believe you about Lish, I don't think he's put a foot wrong and he's going out of his mind worrying about you. What you're doing isn't fair on him.'

I open my mouth to protest. Jed is controlling and patronizing, I'd never realized how much until he admitted he'd tracked me using my phone, but now I see that's how it's been since the start. I don't know how to explain this to Rose, so I shut my mouth again. She pours herself some more wine. I watch her, feeling aggrieved, then she looks up and I see the concern in her eyes. My irritation evaporates. Rose is just worried for me, like a mother would be.

'I'm not going back out with Dan, at least not right now, but the truth is he makes me happy,' I say. 'Which isn't the case with Jed any more.'

'That's *crazy*,' Rose says. 'You've been in touch with Dan again for five minutes. And you *are* happy with Jed, at least you were before Dan showed up.'

I shrug. I don't know what to say to her, how to explain either the ways in which Jed has revealed his true colours, or the transformation that has taken place in my heart.

'Poor, poor Jed.' Rose shakes her head. 'I should call him, let him know that you're okay.'

'Please don't,' I say carefully. 'It's up to me to sort things out with him.'

'Okay,' Rose says reluctantly. 'You know I only want what's best for you.'

There's a long pause. 'I know,' I say with a sigh. 'But I don't think Jed is that ... not any more.'

Rose says nothing, just takes another sip of wine.

We go to bed soon after. I'm in my old room, where I always stay when I come back here. I think that with everything whirling about my head, I won't sleep a wink, like last night, but in fact I fall asleep as soon as my head hits the pillow.

It's still dark when I'm jolted awake. Someone is ringing and banging on the front door. I sit bolt upright. Is it Cameron's man Bodgan? Has Dan broken his word? Has he come after me? My heart hammers at my throat as Rose pads past my door, heading down the stairs. I switch on the bedside light – it's not quite 1 a.m. and pitch black outside in the back garden.

As I head onto the landing, Rose opens the front door.

'Where is she?' Jed hisses.

I freeze.

'When I told you she was here, I thought you were going to wait until morning,' Rose protests.

'It *is* fucking morning.' I can hear Jed stride past her, into the hall.

I back away from the stairs, trying to stay out of sight.

'Please, Jed, calm down,' Rose pleads.

'Don't tell me to calm down,' Jed roars. 'Now where is my fucking fiancée?'

August 2014

TERRIBLE news ... Bex's stepdad won't let her use his computer AT ALL and her phone is so basic all we can do is text. She wasn't online ALL DAY today and I nearly DIED as we are leaving for the holiday tomorrow morning. I thought perhaps she had forgotten about me or turned her back just like Ava and Poppy. I was REALLY upset, I couldn't even hide it from Mum. Of course Mum thought I was upset about the holiday. And I AM upset about that a bit because I look SO BAD in all my clothes but Lish will be there and Emily is nice and I liked her sister okay and her brother A LOT and we will be going on his YACHT which sounds super cool. Of course the two people I saw upstairs at the engagement party will both be there, but now I've done chats with Bex about them I'm sure she's right and I just misunderstood what was happening. So I'm not even worried about that, only that I might be WITH-OUT BEX for a whole fortnight!!!

Anyway, like I say, earlier I was SO upset when Bex hadn't been on UFrenz all day and then at last she was and I said I thought maybe she was mad with me and she said no never and then she explained about her stepdad. I think he sounds SO mean. Anyway, Bex said he had like grounded her from using his computer so

361

maybe we could text instead and she gave me her number. Of course she has such a bad phone that we can't even send pictures to each other but at least I know I will be able to be in touch with her when I'm on holiday and there's no wi-fi and Daddy makes me not go on the internet cos 'it's a waste'. I am SO relieved that Bex and I are best friends. I'm not even worrying about how fat I am for the holiday or if Daddy will be cross. I know he doesn't like me being fat – he makes remarks like he does about Lishy's course at uni, like jokey things that aren't jokey really. 'Do you really want that bar of chocolate?' and 'Maybe we should all pass on ice cream', meaning I should. Because obviously he doesn't mean Emily because she is REALLY slim, like an actual model. I love her hair too, it is so long and silky. I wish mine could be like that, all swishy instead of like a big ugly helmet plonked on my head.

Ooh, there's a text, I bet it's from Bex. Thank goodness she is my bestie, I don't know what I'd do without her.

December 2014

'I'll go and get Emily,' Rose says. 'You'll terrify her if you barge in like this.'

'Good, she deserves a fright after what she's put me through.'

I can hear Rose ushering Jed into the kitchen. I stand, frozen, on the landing. I can't believe Rose called him. Half-asleep, I run into my room and pull on a sweater over my nightdress. As I'm hitching up the sleeves, Rose appears in the doorway, anxiety etched on her face.

'Oh, you're awake.' She fidgets with the edge of her dressing gown. 'Did you hear Jed, he's—?'

'I expect half the bloody street heard him,' I hiss. 'I can't believe you told him I was here.'

'I'm sorry, I just knew how much he'd be worrying,' she says, her face wreathed in contrition. 'I thought he'd wait until morning. I'll tell him you're still asleep.'

I shake my head, flicking my hair out from where it's trapped under the sweater. 'He'll just barge up here if I don't go down. For God's sake, Rose.' I hurry past her, downstairs and into the kitchen. Rose follows. Jed has his back to us, looking out through the window at the dark garden beyond. My feet are cold on the tiled floor. Jed doesn't turn, but he must be able to see us both reflected in the window. Rose and I glance at each other, then Rose retreats to the hall. She shuts the door with a click. Jed straightens at the sound but still doesn't turn. He has taken off his overcoat which is draped on the chair opposite me.

I'm suddenly transported back to the day my parents died. The last time I remember seeing them my dad was standing exactly where Jed is now, with my mother on the other side of the table, just like I am. Mum hugged me and told me to run along, a bright, fixed smile on her face. Even though I was only eleven I sensed the smile was a fake, though I didn't – at the time – think to question why Mum might have been so sad. Because my dad was so cold? Because she had been unhappy in their marriage, like Martin said?

'Jed?'

He turns around at last. His body is stiff with fury, his eyes glinting in the low light.

'Would you mind telling me what the fuck exactly is going on with you?' he demands. 'You call me and tell me you're going to Dan, despite the fact that you *promised* you wouldn't see him.'

'I … I …'

'After which I get nothing. No call. No explanation. I've been going out of my *head* with worry,' he snarls. 'What happened, baby? Too busy *fucking*?'

'No.' I take a deep breath. This is it. 'I'm sorry I didn't call, but you told me to choose. And ... and I've chosen.'

Jed stares at me.

'It's not working,' I stammer, heart thumping. 'You and me, it just isn't working.'

'Not working?' Jed's voice is like ice. 'It was working until last night. What does *not working* mean exactly?'

'It means I ...' I hesitate. It's hard to say the words to his face. But I owe him that much at least. 'I can't be engaged to you – be with you – any more.'

The kitchen clock ticks loudly into the silence. Another reminder of my long-ago past. I meet his gaze as he crosses the space between us. Every step is careful and controlled. It feels like an eternity until he is standing in front of me, taller than I'm used to because he's in shoes and I have bare feet. Menacing. I hold my ground though inside I am shaking.

'You don't get to do this,' he says slowly, each word italicized. 'We're meant to be together. We're getting married.'

'No, Jed,' I say. 'You know I'm right. You must have felt it yourself. Everything's been wrong since ... well, definitely since I went to the police. Look at the way you traced me through my phone. That's not—'

'I did that because I *care* about you,' he says with self-righteous venom. 'I'm older than you and I *care* about you and you're sometimes deeply, disturbingly naïve as your ridiculous faith in Dan Thackeray's lies proves.'

'Dan hasn't lied,' I say. 'He told the truth about Lish. And you won't believe it. You don't trust me.'

365

Jed spreads his hands. 'Of course I trust you,' he says, his voice suddenly conciliatory. 'I was just upset. Okay, I was jealous, I admit it. But the ExAche was accidentally poisoned because Benecke Tricorp were negligent, which I am dealing with through the court case. It had nothing to do with Lish. Those are lies.'

'I haven't been lying about Lish,' I say with a sigh.

'I know. I don't think *you* were lying, just that Dan has conned you over him.' His eyes bore through me.

'You're wrong, Jed. I can't imagine how hard it must be to find out what ... what Lish is doing, what he's done. But the bottom line is he's breaking the law and you'd rather accuse me of being gullible and paranoid than face the truth.' I take a step away from him. 'So, I'm sorry that it hasn't worked out, but we can't be together any more.' Hands trembling, I pull my engagement ring off my finger and lay it on the table beside us. 'Here's the ring. Please take it back.'

Jed slowly picks it up and holds it out to me in his palm. 'I don't want it back,' he says fiercely. 'I want *you* back. God, don't you get it? I love you, baby,' he pleads, changing his entire demeanour so suddenly that I blink. '*Please* don't do this. Because I don't believe it's what you really truly want. I don't believe you've really stopped loving me.' He pauses. 'Think about it. Are you seriously saying you don't love me?'

Outside a police siren sounds into the darkness. I wonder if Rose is still next door, if she is listening to us. I lower my voice.

'I don't know exactly how I feel,' I say.

'So you're confused?' Jed pounces.

'Stop being such a lawyer,' I snap.

Jed holds up his hands in apology. 'Sorry, baby, sorry. Look, I get it now. We've been together over a year and it's not so exciting as it used to be. We've been through a lot: Dee Dee's death has put a big strain on us. Then Dan Thackeray and his lies.' He frowns sorrowfully. 'Oh, baby, perhaps it's also that you're just not coping very well with us settling down together. It would make sense. I mean, you've never lived for more than a month or two with anyone before.'

I grit my teeth, now irritated by how patronizing he is being.

'You're missing the point, Jed. I'm sorry it's not all sorted in my head. I just know I don't want to be with you any more.'

Jed's fist closes around the diamond ring in his outstretched hand. His knuckles are clenched so tightly they are white. In a stride he closes the gap between us. He looms over me, gripping my chin with his free hand and forcing me round to look at him. He is so close I can feel his breath on my skin. I stare into his eyes. He raises his clenched fist.

'Fuck you, Emily.' For a moment I think he's going to hit me. I flinch. But then he throws down the ring and storms out. I hear Rose murmur something as he walks through the living room. A second later the front door closes. I sink into a chair.

Rose appears in the doorway. Her face is ashen. 'I am so sorry,' she says. 'I didn't think he would be so ... so vicious. He must be really hurt.'

I turn on her, my whole body trembling. 'I know that you want to protect me, Rose, and I can never repay all the looking after me that you've done but you shouldn't have called Jed. You *have* to stop thinking you can run my life for me. Jed was a mistake. But he was *my* mistake. *My* responsibility, for me to deal with in my own time.'

Our eyes meet. I can't read Rose's expression at all.

'Okay,' she says. 'But I still think Jed is better for you than Dan Thackeray.'

'And what makes *you* so super-qualified to run my relationships?' I ask, my temper rising. 'From what I hear, you're not so great at managing your own. Simon more or less told me that you dumped him because you'd had a fling with someone else. What makes you think you're in any position to lecture me? At least I've made a decision about Jed *before* I've got involved with anyone else.'

'How *dare* you say that.' Rose's face drains of colour. 'And look, you're admitting you *want* to get involved with Dan. Even when Jed is a million times better for you.'

'Shut up about it, this is none of your business.'

Rose gasps. Immediately I feel desperately guilty. I haven't spoken like that to my sister since I was about sixteen.

'Sorry, I shouldn't have told you to shut—' Rose cuts me off with a wave of her hand.

'No,' she says, drawing away and wrapping her dressing gown around her. 'You're right, this is none of my business. I just care about you.'

There's a long pause. I don't know how to explain to Rose that caring about me can't mean telling me what to do. Not any more.

'I'm going to bed,' I say. I head upstairs and straight into my old room. I shut the door and sit on the bed. A few minutes later I hear the floorboards creak as Rose passes by on the landing. I wait for the sound of her bedroom door closing, then crawl under the duvet. Breaking up with Jed is a sideshow. The real, awful drama is what Cameron is doing; the secret I have to keep; the lies I must tell. I finger the gold bracelet on my wrist, then undo the clasp and take it off. I can't wear it any more. It represents everything that is wrong: it's a gift bought with drug money from a man who lies for a living, who has lied to my brother and is now forcing me to conspire in that lie. And it's the same gift that Dee Dee was wearing when she lost her life in a brutal murder that can never now be revealed ... that will never now be avenged.

PART FIVE

September 2004

'All packed?' Rose made sure there was a bright smile on her face. But inside she felt like crying.

'Yeah, I'm done.' Emily's eyes sparkled with excitement. 'There's a pool on the grounds so I've taken one of your swimsuits, is that okay?'

'Sure.' Rose gulped. 'But no late-night pool parties where you might drown and don't get too drunk and never walk home after midnight on your own and don't go on a first date without—'

'... without telling someone where you are, yeah, I *know*, Rosie.' Emily rolled her eyes and danced away, pirouetting across the living room.

Rose watched her spin. God, but she was pretty: her perfectly proportioned oval face animated by a vivacious personality; Emily exuded innocence and fun in equal measure. Rose had no doubt but that men would be all over her like a rash. And how was Rose supposed to protect her all the way from home? At least there probably wouldn't be that many guys on the teacher-training course. Why couldn't Emily have stayed at home to do it? She had been content to stay home through university but Rose had sensed her restlessness over the past year and knew Emily was at long last truly ready to leave.

Rose had dreaded this day for a long time but now it was here, it was far, far worse than she had expected.

'Okay, okay.' Rose forced another smile across her lips. 'Just remember you're not too old, young lady.'

Emily giggled and scampered off back up to her bedroom. She was acting like a ten-year-old, Rose reflected. No one who looked at her would believe she was twenty-three. At that age Rose herself had been working for five years, with sole responsibility for a truculent teenage girl. No, that wasn't fair. Emily's truculent years had been behind her by the time Rose had reached her mid-twenties. Since the sixth form Emily had been a delight to have around the house, doing the chores Rose set without complaint, always letting her sister know where she was and working hard to get through her A-levels and into uni.

'Any more bags?' Martin peered around the living-room door. He frowned as he caught sight of Rose, perched unhappily on the edge of the sofa. 'Hey, what's up?'

'Nothing, I'm fine.' She looked away, out of the window.

Martin sauntered over until he was standing directly in front of her. He was tall, now. And good-looking in a lean, rangy way. Since he'd got his marketing manager job two years ago he'd started spending more money on clothes. Right now he was wearing jeans with a zig-zag designer label Rose didn't recognize and a fine-knitted John Smedley jumper.

'Rosie?' Martin put his hands on his hips. 'Are you okay?'

Her lips trembled slightly. 'Course, it's just I'll miss her, that's all.'

Martin gathered her into a hug. Rose let him, though her arms remained stiffly by her sides. Both her brother and her sister had always been more tactile than she was. Martin in particular had become very affectionate in the past few years. They had been close since that time he was arrested at uni. Rose had driven up to see him and they'd talked for the first time about how resentful Rose sometimes felt looking after Emily on her own. For a few minutes, Martin had seemed to be accusing her of *using* Emily as a way of not getting on with her own life. Which was obviously nonsensical as proved by the fact that he had soon backed down and they'd ended up talking long into the night. Since then Martin had opened up about all sorts of things, mainly to do with his love life which seemed to involve shocking (to Rose) amounts of casual sex. At least he'd stopped taking drugs.

'Is it Mum and Dad?' he asked. 'I mean, does it bring back all that stuff?'

Rose shook her head though truthfully she knew that anticipating an Emily-sized hole in her life shone a light directly onto the loss of their parents.

'It would make sense if it was,' Martin continued, releasing her from the hug. 'She gave you a reason for living after. Now she's properly leaving home, maybe the grief can come through.'

Rose felt the familiar twitch of irritation she always did when Martin insisted on analysing her. He'd done two years of therapy while he was a student and ever since then he had a tendency to dissect people's motives, which Rose felt was as intrusive as it was pointless.

'I'm *fine*,' she persisted. 'It's just what it is. Emily's going and I have to adjust.'

'I'm ready!' Emily bounced into the living room. 'Family hug!' She bounded over and hurled herself between her siblings. For a second they stood there, each with their arms around the others. Feeling the press of her brother and sister's hands on her back, Rose suddenly wanted to cry. A huge sob grew inside her, but she pushed it back. She needed to put on a brave face for Emily. Anyway, she was only feeling emotional because Martin insisted on raking up all that history about Mum and Dad.

They drew apart. 'Mum would have been so proud of you, today, Flaky,' Martin said, his eyes glistening as he pulled Emily back for another hug.

Emily looked up at him adoringly. 'D'you really think so?'

'Course, she thought teaching was a brilliant career. I remember her saying once she wished she'd trained herself.'

Rose pursed her lips. She was quite certain that their mother had never said any such thing. Still, she couldn't fault Martin's desire to make Emily happy.

'Come on,' Martin went on. 'Let's go now. Beat the traffic.'

Emily turned away from him and put her arms around her sister.

'Bye, Rose.'

Rose's eyes filled with tears and this time she couldn't stop one from trickling down her cheek. She felt another twinge of irritation. *This* was why she hadn't wanted to go to Emily's halls with her, because she'd known she would just get all emotional. Yet here it was, happening in her own home anyway.

She disentangled herself from her sister and wiped her cheek as if brushing off a speck of dirt. 'Go on, get going. It's a long drive.'

Emily gave her a final kiss then skipped out of the door. Martin patted his pockets to make sure he had his car keys. It was a gesture that reminded Rose sharply of their father. He followed Emily to the door, turned and waved at Rose and disappeared.

The front door shut. Rose could hear Emily chattering down the path. Then silence. Terrible, oppressive, overwhelming silence. It filled the house. Rose's whole body tensed with fear. She shook herself. There was nothing to be afraid of. She was free to do whatever she liked. Maybe go to the shops or take in a movie. It was only Saturday morning. She had the whole weekend to fill and no plans.

She wandered over to the sofa. The cushions were both to one side on an arm, where Emily always put them when she was sitting there, legs tucked under her, elbow resting on the top cushion. Rose put the cushions in their proper places, separated and leaning against the back of the sofa. Then immediately changed them back to their Emily positions.

She sat at the other end of the sofa and stared at the cushions and the empty space beside them. A wave of desolation swept over her. She could call one of her friends, except most of Rose's friends were really just work acquaintances; her old friends had either dropped her years ago or were themselves now busy with young families. She could go on the internet and check out those uni courses she'd been thinking about, except she wasn't properly interested in any of them.

She glanced at the coffee table where her phone rested on top of one of Emily's magazines. This one was called *Heat* and carried the headline: '2004's Most Embarrassing Beach Pictures'. Rose occasionally flicked through its pages but she couldn't be bothered even to look at it today.

She picked up her phone instead. Her chest tightened. She hadn't spoken to Brian in more than a month. She'd told him after their weekend in Paris that it was over. They'd met when he came into the shop. She'd known he was married right from the start because his wife and two daughters had been in the shop with him. As they'd examined the novelty bake-ware, Brian had fixed Rose with the most intense, most sexual stare she'd ever seen in her life. Never mind that at forty-three he was many years older than her and that his muscles were soft and his belly more than a little flabby. He was a successful businessman who took her and her work seriously. He admired her, he said. And he fancied her rotten. If she called him, Rose was in no doubt that he would find a time to come over – either tonight or tomorrow. He would bring flowers and ador-ing words. They would have sex which would go on forever thanks to the Viagra she knew he would have popped beforehand.

Brian liked it best when she was on top, thrusting her breasts in his face. Ugh. Frankly the thought of the sex left Rose cold, but she liked performing for him, he was just so appreciative, so full of wonder at her body, so delighted at her attention.

Rose put down the phone. No, she shouldn't call. She didn't want to start all that up again.

On the other hand, the prospect of spending the entire weekend alone was more than she could bear. After all, it was a special case, this weekend, what with Emily leaving home. And her brother and sister need never know about the affair. *Would* never know.

It was a secret. Rose's secret. And afterwards, because no one else knew, she would be able to convince herself that it hadn't really happened at all.

Comforted by this thought, Rose picked up her phone again and made the call. Brian didn't answer so she left a brief, carefully casual message asking if he was around. She imagined him seeing her call, then making an excuse to his wife and creeping outside to call her back. Her phone rang and a smile curled around her lips. There he was.

'Hi there, lover boy,' she purred.

'God, I've been thinking about you *all the time*,' Brian said.

'Have you?'

'Can I see you later?' He let out a soft groan. 'God, I've missed you, sexy girl.'

Rose hesitated. 'Sure,' she said. 'When are you free?'

'I could get away early evening for a bit. Can't stay over, but I . . . I'll say I have to drop something off at the office, that'll give me a good few hours.' He paused. 'If I had had some notice I could get away for longer.'

Rose settled back on the sofa. Part of her hated the idea she was being fitted into Brian's busy life. On the other hand, Brian did tend to talk a lot about himself. A few hours of his company was, if she was honest, the perfect amount.

'That's fine, darling,' she said. 'That's just fine.'

*

Martin parked his car feeling satisfied with his day. Emily was safely settled in her lodgings. Unlike Rose, he had no doubt that she would sail through teacher-training college. She would certainly soon make friends, she was too bubbly and confident for any other outcome. Rose worried too much. The girl was twenty-three, for goodness' sake. Okay, she'd never lived away from home before, but that childlike manner of hers belied a genuine toughness. It was his older sister he fretted about. She had always over-protected Emily but the truth was that she probably needed Emily now far more than Emily needed her.

As Martin sauntered back into his rented flat, his mind drifted to tonight's party. Cameron would be there, and of all the guys Martin had ever met, Cameron was the only one he couldn't figure out.

He knew Cameron was attracted to him, but so were most of the gay men Martin met. He wasn't being big-headed about it, but he had a good body and a square jaw and, at nearly twenty-eight, knew he was the perfect blend of youth and experience.

Martin and Cameron had fucked on two occasions. Again, nothing special there. Martin had spent much of the past ten years having sex; he'd lost count of the number of partners he'd had. The first time, he and Cameron had barely spoken beforehand – they'd met through some mutual friends at a nightclub. The second time – months later – had been fast and furious and, if Martin was honest, a bit of an alcohol-fuelled blur.

Since then they'd bumped into each other three times. But no sex.

Martin wasn't sure why this was. All he knew was that, for some reason, Cameron was keeping his distance. And yet they'd talked and talked on each occasion. Cameron was like no one he'd ever met: beautiful, of course, with sea-green eyes and a slightly hooked nose that completely suited his strong, masculine face, but also mysterious. He came from an extremely wealthy family and exuded the confidence that Martin had learned to associate with the privately educated. He didn't have – or need – a proper job, but he worked as some sort of advertising-related freelancer, though he'd been so vague about the exact nature of his job that Martin didn't know if he was a planner, an account manager or a creative. What Martin did know was that Cameron had a dry sense of humour that matched his own and the same taste in music, delighting in the electronic garage anthems that Martin knew a lot of people found dull and soulless. But none of this summed him up. That was the thing, Martin reflected; there *was* no way of summing Cameron up.

Martin got ready for the party that evening with special care. He changed his top three times, settling eventually on a tight Hermès T-shirt that he knew showed off the cut of his upper arm muscles while also striking exactly the right balance between casual and making an effort. He and his flatmates arrived at the club shortly after midnight. Martin was instantly all eyes, looking around to work out who was there.

He didn't want to admit it to himself, but it was Cameron he was hoping to see. After ten minutes, however, it was obvious the man wasn't in any of the club's rooms so he went up to the party's host, a laidback guy called James, and shouted over the thump of the music:

'Is everyone here yet?'

'Yeah, think so.' James grinned at him. 'Were you expecting anyone else?'

Martin shrugged. 'I heard Cameron might be here.'

'No, he's away in the Far East. Something to do with a charity he's involved with, I think. Get on the floor, baby!' James danced away, across the room.

Martin didn't feel like following. He looked around again. There were plenty of guys in the room that he could easily end up with. There were obvious queens and muscle men, even a couple of throwbacks with biker jackets and handlebar moustaches. There were preppy gays and arty gays in mismatched colours that made them look like peacocks let loose in a paint factory. But Martin didn't want any of them.

There would be drugs on offer too. But Martin had stopped doing all of that about two years ago. It was more trouble than it was worth to come down the next morning *and* put in a full day at work.

As Martin stood in the middle of the room with the music throbbing and the dancers gyrating and the atmosphere building, it suddenly struck him that if Cameron wasn't there, he didn't want to be there either.

He turned on the spot and left the nightclub. Outside he found Cameron's number on his phone and sent a text.

am @ James party. He sez you're away. Let me know when you're back. We should hook up.

He pressed send, then leaned back against the wall by the fire door, the music a dull vibration at his back. He felt better for having done something. His interest was out there now, it was up to Cameron what to do about it. A very drunk couple stumbled past, nearly knocking him over. Martin stepped neatly aside then turned and headed for the tube station. If he hurried, he might just make the last train. His phone beeped, loud in the night air.

His breath misted as he read the text.

Don't tell J but I'm at home, couldn't face yet another club. Come over if you like.

Cameron's address followed – a penthouse apartment in the City near the Barbican. Less than a mile away from where Martin stood right now. Grinning, he jumped into a cab. Ten minutes later he was standing outside Cameron's front door, more nervous than he had ever been in his life. And then the door opened and those green eyes met his and they both smiled and in that moment Martin knew, he just *knew*, that this was it, the real thing, the love of his life, the one he'd been waiting for. And all the fun and the fucks in the world didn't matter any more. Because he'd found Cameron and he could see already in Cameron's eyes that Cameron had found him.

January 2015

Two long days pass. Rose and I don't talk again about her calling Jed and she makes no further mention of her belief that I should go back to him. As a result the ice between us thaws and our quiet evening in on New Year's Eve turns into a marathon movie watch, taking in all our favourite films from *Dirty Dancing* to *The Inn of the Sixth Happiness*. There's no one else in the world I can share these stories with who understands my take on them like Rose does – from the inside.

I haven't gone outside the house since my showdown with Jed. This suits me fine. For the moment I'm wearing Rose's old sweatpants and T-shirts, while I wait for Jed to send over my own clothes. He keeps promising he will – then they don't arrive. I would go around there and pick them up myself, but I don't want to risk bumping into him. He calls me on a daily basis and has rung Rose on at least two occasions to plead with her to make a case for him. She still, clearly, thinks I would be better off going back to him but she has learned to stay quiet on the subject.

Dan keeps his promise to leave London but is also calling me every day. I'm aware this is not the total cutting of ties that Cameron insisted on, but I can't see how he can either find out or prevent us speaking. Dan still doesn't know about Cam's involvement though he must surely suspect it. He says he has stopped investigating Lish's drug dealing and I believe him, though the fact brings me as much misery as it does relief. How can I keep my terrible secret from my brother? I keep thinking that if I were Martin I would want to know. But fear for Dan keeps me silent.

A fresh January begins with the threat of snow. I suggest cancelling our planned New Year's Day lunch at Martin and Cameron's. It is really the last thing I feel like facing now – but Rose insists we can't let them down. I know I will have to see Cameron at some point anyway; the thought fills me with horror. As for Martin, the prospect of being with him and having to pretend everything is fine is almost as bad. Rose lends me a dress for the occasion as my clothes from my home with Jed still haven't turned up. She's slightly taller and bigger-chested than I am, but the dress fits well enough. I team it with a pair of her boots that she has always complained pinch a little at the toes but, again, fit fine on me. I don't much care what I wear to be honest. This time twelve months ago I spent hours picking out lace and satin lingerie to impress Jed as we holed up for a few stolen hours in some fancy hotel overlooking the Thames. We were six weeks into our affair and had hardly seen each other over Christmas. Of course as soon as we met we were tearing each other's clothes off. I can still remember his gasp as he saw me naked. And yet, despite the lust and the long loved-up conversation that followed it, there was a sadness to our time together too. I think I had just begun to realize how lonely being a mistress was, how I was setting myself up – in the short term at least – for an uncertain future of Jed's family time taking precedence and me just waiting for his call. At that point I hadn't told a soul about the affair, yet I was already convinced that Jed was the love of my life. I can't believe how wrong I was. All the things I was so sure of back then, how much I felt for him and how strongly I believed that our feelings for each other justified all the hurt that would result if our affair became known. All these things seem false to me now –an illusion created by the drama of our being together through those snatched evenings and hurried afternoons.

My phone rings. It's Jed's brother. I stare at the screen. Why is he calling me? Jed insisted his brother and I swapped numbers in case of emergencies, but Gary has never called me before.

The phone rings again, too loud in the silence.

'Hello?'

'Emily.' Gary's voice is every bit as posh as Jed's but with a lighter, more arch tone to it. 'Thanks for speaking to me.'

I peer outside the window where the clouds are dark and heavy. Two of the streetlamps are already on, even though it's not quite eleven. It seems strange that just a few days ago, as I crossed Martin's back lawn, I could have seriously thought that Gary was behind Lish's drug-dealing operation.

'Hi, Gary, sorry, but this isn't a good time.'

'No, of course not.' He hesitates. 'Okay, I'll get right to the point. I'm calling to put in a good word for Jed. He's told me you've dumped him and God knows we both know he isn't the easiest person in the world.' He chuckles. 'Made my life a misery for large parts of my childhood, but he absolutely adores you. *Crazy* about you, like I've never seen. He's going to pieces at the thought that he's lost you.'

My mouth feels dry. 'Gary, it's not that simple and this really isn't a—'

'Yeah, I know. You've let that sleazy journo ... er, look, believe me, I'm not judging you and I told Jed he shouldn't judge you either. He and I ...' Another chuckle. 'We've both been there, as in "where we shouldn't" but—'

'That's not what I mean, I—'

'Just let me finish.' Gary sighs. 'Jesus, this is hard. Look, I promised Jed I would say something. He's basically a decent guy and he's given up *everything* to be with you. Bloody Zoe's fleecing him for every penny, he's totally caught up in the court case.'

This reference to Benecke Tricorp reminds me of that overheard conversation. 'Why *are* you so interested in that?' I blurt out.

'Sorry?'

'I overheard you, in your flat the other day. You were on the phone, it sounded like you thought Jed was going down the wrong path in suing Benecke Tricorp, that it was the wrong focus.'

Gary clears his throat. 'That was about money,' he confesses. 'I'm in debt and I was on the phone to my accountant who wants me to go to Jed for a loan which would be tricky so long as Jed was focusing on – and using all his money paying for - the law suit.'

'Right,' I say, the overheard conversation making sense at last.

'That's a good example of how great Jed is, actually,' Gary goes on. 'You see, Jed would loan me the money if he had it. He would *do* that for me. That's what I'm telling you. Jed's a decent bloke. And he's lost Dee Dee. I seriously don't know how much more he can take.'

I'm suddenly very weary. 'I appreciate you sticking up for him, Gary,' I say, 'and I am *really* sorry how things ended with Jed, but it's over and I don't want to talk about it any more.'

I switch off the call before he can start speaking again, then power down my phone. Pocketing my mobile, I hurry down to Rose. The sky clears as we drive to Martin and Cameron's house, though Rose is sure this means the threatened snow is all the more likely. Dreading the day to come, I peer through the window. The sun has burned away most of the earlier clouds and the sky that I can see is clear and bright and blue – a Simpsons' sky, Martin used to call it when we were kids, after the opening credits of *The Simpsons*. A dull, dead feeling creeps over me.

'Are you okay, Emily?' Rose glances across from the driver's seat, her kindly face wreathed in a frown.

'I'm fine,' I say. But even as I'm speaking the words, a sob swells inside me, breaking my voice. Tears leak from my eyes and I turn my face away, not wanting Rose to see.

But of course she does see. And, being Rose, a few moments later she pulls over and puts her warm arms around me. Her soft skin presses against mine, her soothing voice whispering reassurance in my ear, taking me back to the many, many times I cried on her shoulder as a teenager, full of insecurities, hurt by perceived slights. How Janine-Marie Walsh had told Lily Tomkins that I was fat in Biology, how I was ugly and nobody would ever go out with me, how my hair was too flat and my nose too large and my breasts had failed the 'pencil' test.

'I'm sure it's not too late,' Rose says, pulling away.

'Too late for what?' I wipe my eyes.

'To repair the damage.' Rose sighs. She is wearing a dark blue pencil skirt with an angora sweater. Unlike me, she has applied eyeliner and lipstick and brushed her hair.

'Did I tell you how nice you look, Rosie?'

'Thanks, but don't change the subject. I'm saying that I don't think it's too late for you and Jed.'

'Me and Jed?' I frown. My thoughts have been on Martin and Cameron, and how Dan is so far away. Jed was the last thing on my mind. 'What do you mean?'

'Jed *really* wants to be with you,' Rose says softly. 'He called me again this morning and I think he's honestly sorry for being so angry when you broke up the other day. He can see that tracking you on your phone was invasive, but he only did it because he cares about you. He's obsessed with the idea that Dan Thackeray has somehow tricked you away from him, that if he can just get you to see—'

'Stop, Rose, *please*,' I say, wiping away my tears. 'I'm not upset because of *Jed*. That's *over*. I … I …' I cast wildly around for a reason to explain my evident misery. 'I guess it's just the upheaval …' I finish lamely.

Rose narrows her eyes. 'What about Dan? Are you crying for him?'

'*No.*' I turn away. I should have realized Rose, who knows me so well and who has the persistence of a wasp, wouldn't let me alone over this. She's so used to me telling her everything. I gulp, steeling myself for the silence I know I have to sustain. 'I'm sorry, Rose, it was nothing, just all the stress coming out.'

'Right.' Rose starts the engine and we drive off. The sun disappears again behind a cloud. The sky darkens. 'Listen, Emily. I'm sure you *think* you're right, but *I* think you're being really stupid over Jed.'

I stare at her, shocked by the vehemence with which she's speaking.

'Do you *really* not love him?' she goes on. 'Because you did up until a few weeks ago and … and look, you're all upset now and I can't see what else it can be *other* than splitting up with Jed.'

I bite my lip, turning again to stare out of the window.

Streets flash past in a blur. Irritation rises inside me. How typical of Rose this is, I realize, to treat me like a child who doesn't know her own mind.

'Talk to me, Emily,' Rose scolds.

I shake my head, still staring out of the window. There's no way I can tell Rose about Cameron's drug running. It would devastate her. She is so fond of him and, of course, adores our brother.

'Emily, come on,' Rose persists. 'You tell me everything. *Talk.*'

Suddenly I see it all so clearly. Rose loves me, yes, but her being 'half a mum, half a sister to me' – as I once described it to Dee Dee – has to develop into something more grown-up. There are things I can't tell her for her own sake – and ties that have bound us for a long time which I must now break.

'I'm really fine,' I say. 'And it's not Jed. And I don't want to talk.'

Rose purses her lips. I see the hurt on her face and flush with guilt. 'I'm sorry, Rose, I—'

'It's fine.' Rose holds up her hand, waving away my apology. 'I just care about you, *so* much, you've got no idea …'

'I do, I know,' I say, feeling awkward.

The rest of our journey passes in silence. There's not much traffic on the roads and we arrive at my brother's house in good time. It seems weird to be back here so soon after my last, awful visit and weirder still to have to go inside and pretend to smile and laugh with Martin and Cameron. They have cooked a roast duck with lots of intricate side dishes. It's all delicious but I can only pick at the food. Seeing the two of them together – affectionate and full of gentle teasing – only makes it harder to bear the deceit that is being practised on my brother, especially now that I am complicit in the lie. Every now and then I glance at Cameron. He is playing his part to perfection. How I loathe his mean, foxy little face and the way that Martin and Rose both dote on him. I do my best to chat and grin and act as if nothing is wrong.

Cameron gives absolutely no indication that anything passed between us earlier in the week. We make our way through the better part of two bottles of wine. Cameron is just opening a third when I traipse upstairs to the bathroom. I pee and flush, certain that I've succeeded in fooling both my brother and sister. Then I leave the room, to find Martin waiting for me.

I raise my eyebrows as Martin ushers me back into the bathroom.

'What's the matter?' he asks.

I stare at him. I should have known my sensitive, intuitive brother would see through my efforts to appear happy and relaxed.

'Nothing,' I say, attempting to fix a bright smile on my face.

'Not buying "nothing",' Martin says, folding his arms. 'Is this about Jed? Because for what it's worth I think you've done the right thing leaving him.'

Exasperation pulses through me. 'Oh, for goodness'

sake. Why does everybody feel it's okay for them to comment on me and Jed breaking up?' I snap.

'I'm not "everybody". I'm just asking why you're upset. I'm *guessing* it's because you've split with your fiancé, but I don't know because you haven't said two words since you got here.'

'Sorry ... I'm fine. I guess I am sad that things didn't work out but I'm okay, honestly ...' My heart thuds against my ribs. How can I lie to my brother? How can I *live* with the knowledge of my lies? It is *wrong*, against everything my parents and then Rose brought me up to believe in.

'Hey, where's your bracelet?' Martin asks, looking at my wrist.

'I, er, broke it,' I say quickly. 'I'm getting it mended.'

There's a pause. Downstairs I can hear the clatter of plates. Is that Rose and Cameron clearing the crockery away?

'What's really going on, Emily?' Martin asks. 'What aren't you saying?'

I'm itching to tell him. Surely I owe him the truth?

'I can see that you want to tell me,' Martin says softly. 'You'll feel better when you do.'

He's right. The thought of the coming months and years and me keeping this terrible secret from him fills me with horror. Suddenly I wonder if it wouldn't be better just to make a clean breast of it after all. However hard it is for Martin to hear, whatever the risk to Dan, surely anything is better than living a terrible lie?

'It's difficult,' I begin. 'But it all started last summer when—'

The bathroom door swings open, stopping me in my tracks. Cameron stands in the doorway, his emerald eyes glittering dangerously. 'Is there a problem?' he asks.

Fear freezes my face. 'No, not at all,' I stammer. 'I just had a bit of a tummy ache.'

Cameron holds my gaze. Out of the corner of my eye I can see Martin frowning.

'Nothing you ate here, I hope?' Cameron asks. He's smiling, but there's a menacing edge to his voice.

'No, I've had it all day,' I say. 'It's just stress.'

'Well, come back down,' Cameron says, putting his arm around me and ushering me out of the bathroom. 'I just remembered we have some Christmas crackers. I got the same as last year, with proper jewellery inside.'

I can't look at Martin as I head down the stairs. He makes no further attempt to ask me what's wrong and I make a superhuman effort to look like I'm enjoying the crackers and the rest of the meal. Cameron says nothing either but his gaze is never far away: hard and sinister, casting a shadow over my heart.

August 2014

I am whispering because it is very, very early and my bedroom in the villa is right next to Rose's and along the corridor from Lish's. Tonight is our first night in the villa and OH MY DAYS this place is SO cool. There is FREE WI-FI so Daddy can't moan at me going online AND a HUGE pool out the back. There are so many rooms and corridors I lost count!!!! But there are three of us on this floor like I said plus a big, white bathroom and my room is SO pretty with green shutters and a low couch like a proper sitting room and a four-poster, not all Barbie and pink but really elegant with satiny sheets. Daddy and Emily are upstairs and Uncle Gary and Iveta down in the room behind the kitchen and they each have their own bathrooms too.

It is hot here but not like it was in the south of France when Daddy kept dragging us to CULTURE and MUSEUMS and GALLERIES. He says we have to go into Calvi to see the cita-something, whatever that is, tomorrow, which sounds REALLY boring BUT at least we will see Martin and Cameron again. We met up with them on our way here yesterday and we went on the boat and it was SO amazing and Emily says we are going to go out in the boat again because they are sailing here. IMAGINE, sleeping on a boat, I wish

I could do that, all under the stars. SO romantic. Tomorrow they will be in the harbour at Calvi, Daddy says with all the 'super-rich buggers', and we are going to meet them and go out on the boat.

So . . . well . . . that is something to look forward to but there have been some bad things too like Lish hardly speaks to me, mostly just to Martin and Cameron. Actually they are great and Rose is nice too, though not fun like Martin and not cool like Emily, like she's trying to be friends but she doesn't really know what to say. BUT Dad gets cross all the time, he doesn't like me to have puddings and he always says 'go on then, let her have what she wants' with a sigh if Rose or Emily ask what I'd like off the menu and I know he thinks I am too fat and clumsy. He got snarky yesterday when I broke my sandal then a bit later I overheard him saying to Emily it was cos I was FAT, but it wasn't my fault, the strap just came off. At least Emily always asks if I need anything and if I want to call Mum but not like I HAVE to. Which I don't want except Daddy makes me every other night and Mum is all 'I hope you're having a lovely time' in a voice which means she doesn't want me to be having one at all, like I've done something wrong. But if I moan to her then Daddy hears and gets cross and says I'm wasting the education he's paying for though I don't see what school has to do with it. I don't want to think about going back to school. I've been texting and texting with Bex and she always texts back, she is SO lovely but SO sad about her mum I am worried she will hurt herself, she says she has cut herself which I don't know what to say to. Like on her legs where no one will see.

Oh my days I am not sleepy at all but I am fed up of whispering.

Ooh, wait, I just heard a noise. I'm going to take the phone in case I need a light though there is a big moon outside . . .

I am shaking. I can't believe it. It's like what I saw at the engagement party but WORSE. Much worse. I am going to text Bex RIGHT NOW and tell her.

January 2015

Rose's birthday is on the second Sunday in January. She doesn't want a big fuss but I rouse myself sufficiently from my unhappy thoughts about the secret I am keeping from my brother – and my enforced absence from Dan – to make her a cake and invite a few of her friends over. I don't know any of them very well. Mostly they're colleagues – and ex-co-workers – from Rose's many years as a shop manager. Unlike Martin and me, Rose doesn't have friends from her childhood which, considering she still lives in the same neighbourhood, is a bit strange, though I guess looking after me must have made it difficult to sustain friendships.

I invite Martin and Cameron too, of course. I am going to have to steel myself better for these encounters. I don't know which is worse: anticipating the menacing glint in Cameron's eye or my brother's kindness and trust. At least my clothes and other belongings have finally arrived from Jed. I check everything through; nothing of mine is missing while most of our shared stuff was paid for by Jed and I don't want it anyway. I brace myself for a note or some other kind of message tucked in among the dresses and books but, much to my relief, there is nothing. Perhaps Jed is, at last, moving on.

Rose's birthday begins with a strange visit: a man – well-preserved, probably in his fifties – turns up at the door, a huge bunch of lilies in his hand. He looks startled to see me, just shoving the lilies in my hand and muttering that they're for Rose before hurrying back to his Audi and zooming away.

I sneak a look at the card before Rose comes down.

Still a babe! Happy Birthday, Brian.

My mind goes back to the 'hello, sexy girl' phone call I intercepted last month. My curiosity roused, I push Rose to tell me who he is but she is as cagey as she was before, simply repeating her claim that Brian is nothing more than a customer with a crush.

'Twenty arum lilies delivered in person to your door suggests a bit more than a crush,' I argue. 'Have you been on a date?'

'Course not.' Rose wrinkles her nose. 'Brian is *so* not my type.' And she refuses to say anything further.

Later the party guests arrive and our dinner gets underway. We order a Thai takeaway, Rose's favourite, which Martin and Cameron pay for. I tuck in hungrily, until it occurs to me that the meal is being bought with drugs money and my red curry and jasmine rice turn to bile in my throat. I force down a few more mouthfuls, then scurry into the kitchen when Mart's back is turned. I don't want him to see that I'm not eating properly. He seems distracted

401

tonight. Troubled even. Looking over at me from time to time with a worried frown. He's been asked if he's okay and he is claiming he has a headache, but I'm certain he's still wondering if I've told him the truth about what is wrong with me. Rose's friends leave soon after the cake, pleading an early start at work the next day.

It's almost eleven and Cameron and Martin are the only people left in the house. Much to my relief Cameron announces they should leave in a minute and pops upstairs to the bathroom. The doorbell rings.

Rose makes a face. 'God, that's probably Jenny come back. I bet she left her phone here, she's always losing it.' She stands up and saunters out into the hall leaving Martin and me alone at the kitchen table.

'I know what Cameron's been doing,' Martin says in a low voice. 'I know about the drugs.'

My head jerks up. My brother's expression is one of utter misery.

'I know everything,' Martin goes on, through gritted teeth. 'I could see something was up with you last week, more than the Jed thing, so I snooped a bit, found some texts. I thought it was an affair at first. Then I followed him, saw him with Lish, a couple of other guys . . .'

'Mart . . .' My heart races.

'Let me get this out: I *knew* something was wrong. I've known it for a long time, but I didn't want to face it.' His mouth trembles.

I reach for his hand and he lets me take it and squeeze it.

'I am facing it now,' he says. 'I called Lish, demanded answers, but he refused to talk to me, then I tried Jed. I told him I was going to come and see you tonight, that I was starting to think all your suspicions about Lish and the drug dealing were right. Jed hung up so I tracked down Dan Thackeray through his work. We spoke just before Cam and I left the house earlier; Dan filled me in on what he knew. He sounded scared, Emily, for himself and for you.' Martin pauses. 'I'm scared too. I talked to Cam on the way over here. He's admitted ... well, enough. I know about ... about the drugs, how he makes so much money, and I know that he threatened you ... and Dan Thackeray. I can't believe what he's been doing.' Martin's voice cracks. 'And that poor little girl ... he says it was an accident and maybe it was, but ...'

My blood freezes. 'He admits Dee Dee died from the potassium cyanide Lish was selling?'

'He admits it's too big a coincidence to explain logically,' Martin goes on. 'Whatever he's said to you, he knows in his heart there must be some connection.'

I stare at him, feeling sick. Outside in the hall I hear Rose speaking in low, urgent tones. A man is talking back to her. I can't make out what he's saying, but I recognize the voice. My stomach cartwheels. I stand up, almost knocking over my chair in my hurry, just as Dan rushes into the kitchen.

There are dark shadows under his eyes. He takes in Martin in an instant, then strides over to me. For a second

SOPHIE MCKENZIE

I give myself up to the relief of his hug. Then I remember Cameron is upstairs – a danger to Dan – and I pull away.

'What are you doing here?' I ask.

'I knew Martin was going to talk to Cameron about what he'd found out and that both of them were coming here, to see you and Rose. I was worried about you.' Dan envelops me in another hug.

'You can't just barge in here,' Rose snaps from the doorway.

'Dan, you said this wouldn't be safe.' Martin's voice is full of concern.

Ignoring them both, Dan strokes my cheek. 'I'm not running away from this any more,' he says, looking into my eyes. 'We're going back to the police. Martin too. If Martin gives evidence against Cameron, he'll be—'

'He'll be what?' Cameron's voice from the doorway is ice cold.

Dan and I turn to look at him.

'What the hell is going on?' Rose demands.

Dan draws me closer to him. Across the table, Martin puts his head in his hands.

'We're not keeping your secret any more,' Dan says, looking at Cameron.

'What secret?' Rose asks, looking baffled.

Cameron takes a step towards Dan. His eyes are filled with hate. 'You talked to Martin.' It's a statement, not a question. 'You were told to keep quiet. And you talked.'

'What are you—?' Rose starts.

404

'So fucking what,' Martin protests, jumping up from the table. 'You've been lying to me since I fucking met you, Cameron. You—'

The doorbell rings again.

'Did you call the police?' Cameron's eyes widen. He stares at Dan.

Dan shakes his head.

Rose rushes out of the room. There's a split second where we can all hear her fling open the front door and I'm hoping against hope that Dan *did* call the police. And then Jed's voice fills the air.

'Is Cameron still here? Martin said they'd be here.' He storms into the kitchen, his fists clenched. He barely notices me or Dan or Martin. His eyes bulge as he focuses on Cameron, standing in front of the counter.

'You fucking bastard.' Jed hurls himself forward, shoving Cameron against the wall. Cameron rams into it hard, gasping for breath. Jed swings a punch into Cameron's gut. With a groan, Cameron doubles over. It all happens in a flash. I stand next to Dan, unable to move. Across the kitchen my brother and sister watch with open mouths.

'You dragged my son down into your fucking *hellhole*,' Jed roars, ramming Cameron against the wall again. 'After Martin called me I spoke to Lish again. He's admitted everything. He was crying his eyes out like a baby, telling me how you tricked him into running drugs, how you're a fucking *criminal*, a *drug dealer*, you *bastard*.' Jed gives

Cameron another shove. Cameron reels back, hands flailing for purchase on the kitchen counter beside him.

Jed shoves his arm up against Cameron's throat. He presses the windpipe, fury in his eyes. 'You killed my daughter.' His chest heaves, the words rasp out of him. He forces his arm against Cameron's neck. I'm frozen to the spot, unable to move. Martin is standing beside me. I can feel the terror coming off him in waves.

Cameron's hand is now reaching along the counter, searching for something he can use to push Jed away.

'Lish admitted he had potassium cyanide,' Jed spits. 'Which means you must have found a way of giving it to Dee Dee.'

'No,' Cameron gasps, wild-eyed with fear.

'I'm going to fucking kill you,' Jed growls.

'Jed.' I'm barely aware I'm speaking. I have no idea what to say. 'Jed, stop, please.'

Jed glances over, his arm still pressing against Cameron's skin. He sees me properly for the first time and his gaze softens.

'You're right to be angry, Jed,' I say. 'But let's call the police. Dan and I can give statements. And Cameron's told Martin everything. We've got enough to send him to jail. For a long, long time.'

Jed nods and, for a second, I think it will be all right, that he will stop. Then Jed's eyes shift to Dan beside me, to Dan's arm, protective, around my shoulder. His expression hardens again and he turns back to Cameron.

'*You bastard,*' he snarls, his hands now tightening around Cameron's throat. Cameron lets out a terrible gasp. The colour is draining from his face. He can't breathe. His hand is still reaching, straining across the counter.

He lights on the knife block. His fingers claw around the handle of the long, sharp carving knife in the centre.

As he pulls out the knife, Martin lurches across the room. And then everything happens so fast it's a blur. As Martin grabs Jed's arm, pulling him away, Cameron lunges forward. The knife gleams under the light, then disappears as Martin and Cameron cling to each other. An eternity passes in a second as Martin staggers back, the knife in his chest. He falls to his knees, then slumps to the floor. Cameron lets out a roar. He flings himself onto the floor beside Martin. Jed backs away, his mouth wide open in shock. I wrench myself out of Dan's grasp and race over to my brother. I kneel down on the other side of him from Cameron, who has taken Martin's hand and is moaning under his breath. 'Please, no, please . . .'

Martin looks at him for a second, then turns his head towards me. Blood is pouring from his chest. Rose stands in the doorway, her hands over her mouth. Behind me I can hear Jed suck in his breath. But I keep my eyes on my brother's face. Martin's gaze meets mine: soft, fearful, full of love. For a moment I think he's going to speak then the bright of his eye fades to nothing. Rose gasps and Cameron bows his head and the room fills with silence. I feel for Martin's pulse, on his neck, on his wrist. I can't find it. *No.*

I won't believe it, *can't* believe it. Dan comes over. He bends over Martin and presses his neck, a firmer, more expert touch than mine. He looks up and shakes his head and the truth shifts the world on its axis, changing everything forever.

August 2014

So I texted Bex straight after I saw what I saw this morning and said she had to text me back URGENTLY and I was going MAD waiting for her to text. I kept thinking about what I had seen them do and what it meant. It is wrong, REALLY wrong and I don't know what to do. I WASN'T misunderstanding AFTER ALL. It REALLY happened. In fact it was much WORSE this time – I actually filmed a bit by accident on my phone but I couldn't bear to look at it.

I was still waiting for Bex to text back and thinking that I HAD to tell someone. In fact I was waiting for Emily to wake up but then OH THANK GOD Bex sent me a text asking what was wrong and I told her and she was REALLY shocked and sad and said there isn't anyone you can trust and grown-ups will always let you down and to be honest she made me feel a bit like it was scary inside me and I said I was going to tell someone, Emily probably, and Bex texted back in like two seconds saying NO!!!! and I asked her why and she said it would just mess everything up for my whole family and get everyone upset and I texted saying I was ALREADY UPSET and Bex said she knew and of course but I could tell her all about it. And I said I thought I should tell a grown-up and she *said what was the point, grown-ups don't have all the answers you know, and THAT surprised me because she sounded a bit cross and it didn't feel good so I said Emily was different and I would just tell her and it wasn't about having answers. And Bex did a sad face emoticon and said she would be upset if I told Emily my secret and I said why and Bex asked why wasn't she enough of a friend for me to share my secret with just her. So I said she was my bestie and that wasn't the point but she said she was REALLY upset because I don't trust her and I am her only friend and her mum is really ill and her stepdad is so mean and she started talking about cutting herself again, she was so upset, and I felt REALLY bad. And she sent text after text saying she was crying and SO upset and so I promised I wouldn't tell anyone after all.*

January 2015

A day passes. Two. Dan and I give long interviews to the police, telling them everything. Cameron and Lish are arrested.

Jed doesn't call me, for which I'm thankful. Neither does Zoe. I spend my time with Dan, when he is free from police questioning, and with Rose. We cry together for our brother. For the fresh gash splitting our family. For the fact that our lives have been turned upside down. Again.

Bogdan is caught trying to leave the country. He gives evidence against Cameron and Lish. Then Lish gives evidence against Cameron. None of it seems to matter. Martin is gone. I feel nothing, only a dull, numb sense of loss, punctuated by terrible flashbacks to the moment Martin fell backwards, the knife in his chest.

Two more weeks pass. Martin's funeral takes place. Rose has people back to the house afterwards. I think this is morbid – it's where he died. I can't bear to sleep here and am staying with Laura. I spend most of the wake out in the garden, even though it is freezing.

As the light fades from the day I sit on the swing at the

far end of the lawn. I remember my dad installing it for me on my seventh birthday, soon after we moved here. Despite my desire to create a different, more grown-up, relationship with Rose I can't deny that it's a huge comfort to be here, surrounded by the strong sense of my parents that this house provides, a testament to their love for us. Dan seeks me out and holds me. I love his silence, his understanding that there are no words for my grief.

'Come home with me?' he asks gruffly. 'I want you to meet Lulu, move in with me, please?'

I shake my head. 'I just can't rush from Jed to you, not after everything that's happened, not after Martin. There's got to be a bit of space.'

Dan nods, his storm-coloured eyes reflecting the dying light of the clouds overhead. 'Okay,' he says softly. 'We'll do whatever you want.'

'This is so hard,' I say. 'I keep reliving the knife in his chest, I see it over and over again. Rose says I should talk to someone, but ...'

'You're not ready?' Dan asks.

'No.' I lean against him. 'Not for any of it, but soon maybe, soon.'

'Soon,' he says.

He goes and I return to the wake. Only a few people are left, mostly old acquaintances of our parents that I'm no longer properly in touch with. Rose is talking intently to a couple in the living room. I head to the kitchen and start clearing the dirty plates and glasses. As I work, a thousand thoughts crowd my head. I think of Dan, of course, but mostly of Martin, how impossible it seems that he is gone. I know that the full pain of being without him hasn't even begun to hit me yet, that the flashbacks are only the start of my grieving. I think of Cameron and Lish and the court case that lies ahead. I wipe the counter tops. I have a book somewhere on helping people deal with trauma. I read the chapter on children for a course I did during teacher training. There were exercises for helping you get past a terrible shock. I can't remember the details, but maybe one of them might help me process what is happening. I fold the dishcloth, frowning. Where on earth is that book? It's so long since I read it, I can't even remember the title, but I know it was a seminal work.

The lawyers are confident that the combination of Bogdan's testimony and the statements that Dan and I have each given, plus the ongoing police investigation, will enable them to build a strong case when it comes to the drug dealing. It's a different story when it comes to finding out who killed Dee Dee. It's ironic that the only mystery that remains unsolved is the one that began everything. There is absolutely nothing, it seems, to link either Cameron or Lish to her death and without proof that Lish was actually in possession of any potassium cyanide at the time (and Lish and Cameron have both sworn to the police that he wasn't), the lawyers have been unable to bring a murder charge against them.

The last few guests leave and Rose and I work in silence

together for a while longer. At last it is done. As Rose lugs a bag out to the rubbish bin, I slip away, avoiding looking at the patch of kitchen floor where Martin died. Rose insists we have to get past the fact that his life ended in this room, that our positive memories must be allowed to outweigh the negative ones – but I'm not sure I will ever be able to feel comfortable in the house again. Thank goodness I can go back to Laura's later.

I'm determined to find the trauma book. I know it isn't in my bedroom, or in any of the unopened bags and boxes I brought back from Jed's house which are currently stored in Martin's old room.

I stand on the landing, trying to think where it might be. Outside, I can hear Rose clanking the bin lid down and walking back along the path. She pushes open the front door and sees me at the top of the stairs.

'Cup of tea?' she asks.

'Thanks. I'm just looking for something, then I'll be down.'

Rose disappears into the kitchen and I go into her bedroom. It's large and airy, Mum and Dad's old room, with the bed at one end, a chest of drawers between the two windows and a long fitted wardrobe along the far wall. As I flick through the clothes on its rail, I'm struck again by how smart and sophisticated Rose's outfits have become. This closet used to be crammed with shapeless tops and trousers going back twenty years but they're all gone and a neat row of simple, well-designed suits and dresses – similar to the grey silk shift she is wearing today – hang in their place.

I rifle past these to the other end of the wardrobe which is stacked with shoes and old cardboard boxes. If my old text book is anywhere in this room, it will be here. I open a box that looks likely and find myself faced with Martin's collection of football annuals from when he was ten or eleven. Tears fill my eyes as I put the lid back on and reach for the next box. It just contains old clothes. As I pull it away from the wall to get a purchase on the next box along, something wedged behind falls to the floor with a light thud.

It's a phone. An iPhone, similar to my own.

What the hell is this doing here? It's clearly not Rose's normal phone, which has a silvery cover and is with her downstairs. Even odder, this iPhone is still attached to its charger. There's a plug socket right next to the wardrobe. Heart suddenly beating fast, I shove the charger into the socket. The phone whirs into life. I see the Apple icon, then the lock screen appears.

I gasp. The screen shows a photo of myself and Dee Dee. It's sunny and we're smiling, the sea sparkling behind us. All at once I'm back in Corsica, standing with Dee Dee as she took our picture while Jed went to tell Martin and Cameron that he and I needed to go back early to the yacht.

This is Dee Dee's missing phone.

August 2014

Everyone else is outside on the deck except Lish who is in the kitchen which they call the galley. I thought it would be fun being on Martin and Cameron's yacht but so far I've HATED it. It's all because of what I saw this morning. I've been thinking about it all day. It's like in my head ALL the time. I can't stop seeing it. And I know that it's wrong that no one knows and they're outside LYING and I really want to tell someone though it would be SO hard to talk about it so I'm glad I made that promise to Bex not to say anything but now I feel all dead inside, like there's a stone pressing down on my chest squeezing all the breath out and it hurts and I just want it to go away but it goes on and on and I'm scream-ing inside my head and nobody else can hear.

I nearly told Emily earlier, when we were on that ruins bit up that hill that Daddy made us climb and I took a picture and made it my lock screen. Emily got a headache and now I've got one too. I just sent Bex a text saying I really think I should tell Emily, that maybe they don't need to know it's me, that I could just leave a clue somewhere for her when we're back in the villa.

It's not fair Daddy made me eat that fish for dinner just now. It was RANK. He doesn't like chocolate with nuts in and nobody *makes him eat THAT. I hate him, I hate him. They think I'm in here Skype-ing with my friends but I only have one friend and thanks to HER stupid dad she can't go online AT ALL. I HATE both of our dads. Oh, come ON, Bex. Text me back.*

There, it's her. Back in a sec.

Oh, now I feel worse than ever. I can't BELIEVE what Bex has texted, she says I am evil for wanting to mess up people's lives and I shouldn't need to tell anyone other than her anything because she is supposed to be my best friend and she swears that if I talk to Emily she will never be my friend again. I don't know what to do, I can't believe it, Bex HATES me and I thought she was like my blood sister and now the weight on my chest is like filling my whole body SO dragging and heavy and I want to DIE because it is ALWAYS like this, that people I think will be my friends turn away and NOBODY cares.

I just went into the kitchen-galley bit of the boat to see Lish. I thought maybe I could tell him, but he was by the sink scooping stuff like tiny crystals out of a jar and putting them in a little packet and when I said his name he jumped and shouted at me. And I said I wanted to talk and he held up the packet and he said 'get out of here, you silly little bitch, this stuff is fucking LETHAL, what are you doing in here' and I said I didn't know and he called me 'a useless little' then the c-word which I don't like saying. And he told me to go away and I did but when he didn't know I was looking I saw him put the packet in his bag and I wanted to get it and throw it in his face but instead I came back in here. They've all been talking outside all evening. Except Rose once came in to the bathroom and she smiled at me and Emily came to see how I was and I would have told her but she was in a hurry and saying how much fun they were having outside.

Okay, there is another text.

It is Bex again, she says she is SO upset and PLEASE not to tell anyone else what I saw or it will prove I'm not her friend and she will CUT herself.

Inside me it is all dead and cold and it just made me realize Bex isn't really a friend, she just wants me to do what she says. Who was I kidding that she would really like me for me? I am totally alone.

I am not going to reply to her text except to say don't hurt yourself love DD x. I don't know what to do about what I saw, maybe it is best just to keep it to myself but not because Bex says and I still want us to be friends but because it would be too hard to say anything and I will keep their secret and just hate them forever. My head is hurting. I just don't know, I just don't know.

January 2015

What the hell is Dee Dee's missing phone doing in my sister's wardrobe? I stare at the picture on the screen. I look happy and relaxed, though you can see the tension behind my eyes from the headache I had that afternoon. Beside me Dee Dee is smiling, yet I can't help but notice the look of desperation on her face. How did I miss that at the time? For a moment I'm transported back to the citadel at Calvi, the sun beating down, the band of pressure across the back of my head and Jed, striding over, irritated with his daughter, ordering her away and leading me back to the yacht.

What is Rose doing with this? Where did she get it? Why hasn't she said anything? My mind flashes back to the morning Dee Dee died. Other than my sister's terrified face as she stood outside Dee Dee's door when Jed and I came downstairs I have no memory of her involvement. She left, of course, to go to Martin and Cameron's boat. Could Rose have picked up Dee Dee's phone without realizing what it was? It seems unthinkable. Even more so that she wouldn't have mentioned it, knowing that – for a while at least – the police were actively looking all over the villa for it.

Downstairs I hear the kettle coming to the boil. Rose is making tea. Soon she will call up the stairs and tell me it is ready and I will have to go down and face her and ask her what possible reason she has had for keeping and hiding this phone. An image of Dee Dee's anxious face flashes into my head again: 'I've got a secret ... It's something I saw ...'

Suppose Dan and I were right? Suppose there is something on Dee Dee's phone that explains who killed her? A cold hand circles its fingers around my heart. Suspicions press at my brain, demanding to be let in, but I won't give them access. I still believe there must be a logical explanation for why the phone is here, wedged behind this box in my loving, caring sister's house.

Numb, I swipe the screen, opening it up. I turn to the call log ... there are nine or ten missed calls from Jed's phone here, all placed when we were searching for the mobile. I remember the dead look in Jed's eyes as he handed Gary his phone and let him make call after call, each one ringing into silence. I scroll up, but see no names other than 'Mum' and 'Dad'. I turn to the messages. The last set of texts are from someone called Bex, sent on the evening Dee Dee died, the evening she was made to eat fish to please her father. I scan the converstion:

I want 2 tell Emily, or myb get her 2 fnd out smhw. She shd no, D xxxx

U r selfish and evil messing up ppls lives, I thought I ws ur best frind so y do u want 2 tell Emily? If u tell I wont spk to u EVER agn Bex

The blood thunders in my temples.

*If u want b my frend, jst dnt tlk 2 any1 else, or I wl CUT myslf
Bex*

Don't hurt urslf, love DD x

That's the final text. I frown. Who is Bex? What did she
(or he) not want Dee Dee to tell me? Was this about some
drug deal? I don't see how it can be, unless Rose has somehow found the phone and hidden it so as not to implicate
Martin ... but Martin didn't *know* about the drug dealing
until just before he died.

'Emily, tea's made!' Rose calls out. Downstairs in the
hallway she is humming to herself, completely unaware of
what I've discovered.

With trembling hands I open the email then the
FaceTime apps. Nothing. I turn to the photos. I can see at
a glance that there are pictures here from our holiday.
There's the selfie Dee Dee took of me and her again. But
there's also a series of videos. The start points are all close-
ups of Dee Dee's face, except one towards the very end of
the final row. The two figures in the frame are blurry,
entwined. I peer closer. Are they *kissing*?

I forget Rose downstairs or the bedroom around me and
press play.

The film starts. The two figures *are* kissing. They pull
apart and my brain registers in slow motion what my eyes
have just seen.

Jed and Rose.

'Please don't go,' on-screen Rose is pleading. 'Just one
more time.'

'I want to but …' Jed holds her away from him. She is wearing a sheer black slip, her breasts clearly visible underneath. 'God, you're fucking gorgeous.'

The video ends abruptly.

I stare at the final image on the screen, my sister a blur with her hands in the air.

'What are you doing?' Rose's voice from across the room makes me jump.

I turn, scrambling to my feet. Dee Dee's phone, still in my hands, is ripped out of the charger.

Rose's eyes widen as she sees it.

'You …' My voice sounds strange, hoarse, to my ears. 'You … and Jed …'

I see the acknowledgement in Rose's eyes.

'I did it for you,' she says quietly. 'I've always done everything for you.'

'What?' There's a long silence as we stare at each other.

'Emily, you need to—'

'No. Wait. How can you … you and Jed … how can you have slept with my fiancé? How can that have been *for me*?'

Rose sits down on her bed. She pats the mattress beside her, just as she used to years ago when I had a problem I needed to share as a teenager.

I stay where I am.

Rose sighs. 'Okay, the truth is that Jed was drawn to me. We had a few nights together in the early days of your relationship, then he pulled away, for your sake,' she says matter-of-factly. 'I let him go, for your sake.'

The room is silent. I am frozen. The bed that Mum and Dad slept in, that I remember coming to when I was ill or on cold mornings, resting my feet against Mum's legs, my head on her chest … and then Rose, thinner and harder than Mum, no substitute for the hugs and cuddles I still sometimes wanted, but always there, always offering help, always in my corner.

I stare at her. I can see no contrition in her eyes.

'Jed told me back in March, just after you moved in together, that he wanted to marry you, to look after you as I had done for so many years, that part of his reason was to help *me*, to let me be free of all the responsib—'

'Wait,' I butt in, unable to stop myself. 'You're talking as if I'm a child. Neither of you need to "look after" me or "take responsibility".'

Rose shakes her head. 'You don't understand, Emily. I sacrificed Jed for you, because I wanted you to have him, just as I gave up my late teens and twenties to look after you and—'

'I didn't ask you to give up anything. You can't have an affair with my boyfriend and make out you were doing me a good turn. How many times did it happen? When did it start?'

'The first time was in March, just before you moved in together,' Rose confesses, her cheeks flushing pink. 'Jed came around to pick you up, but you were doing a parents' evening and you'd forgotten to tell him you'd be late. I had to get out of the shower to answer the door and I guess my robe slipped off my shoulder and I saw him looking at the bare skin and I offered him a drink while he waited for you to get back ...'

I frown, trying to remember the evening she's talking about. I did come home one night, exhausted, not really in the mood for dinner with Jed, but guilty that I was late. He was waiting in the living room, sipping at a white wine, and brushed away my apologies, saying how wonderful it was that I did something so worthwhile as a job, unlike Zoe who had managed to run the business he'd bought her into the ground.

I don't remember Rose from that evening at all; she must have gone upstairs before I came back.

'You had sex with him? In this room?'

Rose nods, her face suddenly radiant. 'It was wonderful,' she breathes. 'He's an amazing lover, so powerful ...'

I feel sick. 'And what about afterwards?'

'Not for ages.' Rose grimaces. 'I felt terrible. I knew it was wrong, that he had chosen you. But the heart wants what the heart wants and there were a few times when we just couldn't help ourselves.' She pauses. 'You see the thing was that I knew it was wrong, but it felt so *right*. It gave me a new lease of life ... it still does, even though it's been over for a long time. I can't explain it, but I feel better about myself than I have done in years.'

I stare at her, unsure whether to believe her, uncertain whether it matters either way. Why did I never pick up on any chemistry between them? And yet, it kind of explains the new glow Rose developed around that time, the way she lost weight and smartened up, all the new dresses hanging in the wardrobe. And then I remember Martin's revelation from before Christmas. 'So *Jed* was the married man you had the affair with?'

'I think affair is putting it too strongly. It wasn't a proper sneaking-around relationship, just a few disconnected episodes. Seriously, Emily, we couldn't help ourselves ...' she half-smiles and the sick feeling inside me gives way to a pulsing fury '... it was like we turned into *animals*, and it wasn't really anyone's fault. Jed just couldn't keep away, he told me I was amazing, an amazing person.' Rose looks down at the carpet.

I clench my jaw. 'Did it happen in Corsica?'

Rose gives a swift nod. 'Yes. Once. But that was the very last time. Jed said it had to be, that we couldn't keep doing what we were doing, it was wrong and ... and sooner or later someone would find out. I'm not sure if we would have been able to stop, though I swear we both meant to ... but then Dee Dee died and ...' She sighs. 'Honestly, Emily, I *never* wanted to take him away from you, I just wanted him to want me.' Her voice cracks. 'You've got no idea what it meant to me, such a handsome, powerful man hungry for *me*. He was like the perfect version of Brian ... what I thought Brian was when I met him.'

'Brian?' I think of the harassed-looking man who dropped off the big bunch of arum lilies on Rose's birthday. 'So you've secretly being going out with this Brian as well?'

'No.' Rose frowns. 'Well, we see each other from time to time, but it's nothing serious. And Jed wasn't serious either – at least, not a serious threat to you. Anyway, you didn't really want him, did you?'

'Don't try and fucking justify it.' Fury fills me. Before I know what I'm doing I'm across the room, facing Rose down. She shrinks away. I can't believe it. My own sister.

Dee Dee's phone is clammy in my hand. And, suddenly, the whole horrific picture falls into place.

'Dee Dee saw!' I gasp. *Dee Dee found out.*

'Yes,' Rose admits. 'The silly girl saw us upstairs at your engagement party. She must have come up to use the bathroom. She can't have seen much, but probably enough to make her a bit confused. I saw her walking away and I wanted to make sure she was clear that there was nothing going on between me and her father. So ... I debated telling Jed but I thought it would freak him out too much and then I thought about having a word with Dee Dee myself. But I knew I couldn't compete with you in getting "down with the youth" so I decided it was best to pretend to be one myself.'

I hold up the phone. My hand is shaking. 'You're "Bex"?'

'I made friends with her, convinced her she must have misunderstood what she'd seen. Of course when Jed came to my room on our holiday and she saw us together it was impossible to pretend any longer.' Rose sighs. 'I couldn't believe it when I found the phone and saw she'd filmed our kiss, not that I think she meant to, but still ...' Her eyes grow soft, almost dreamy.

I stare at her in horror. 'You kept the phone so you'd have the texts safe – and the video as ... as a *memento* of you and Jed?'

Rose nods again.

My stomach lurches, bile rising into my throat. 'So it wasn't Lish or Cameron. *You* killed her, just to stop her telling me about you and Jed.'

Rose looks up, her expression hardening as it meets mine. '*Kill* her? No, of course I didn't *kill* her.'

'I don't believe you,' I say.

Rose's mouth gapes as I head for the door. 'You think I'm capable of *murder*?' She looks horrified.

'You're capable of sleeping with my fiancé,' I counter. 'I don't know what else you'd do. I don't know who you are any more.'

'Emily, I'm—'

'Shut up.' My heart thuds, fast and painful, in my chest. Sickened, I push past her into my room. I grab my bag.

'Where are you going?' Rose is on the landing.

'I need to tell Jed what you've done to Dee Dee,' I say. 'I need to call the police.'

'No, Emily.' Rose's lip trembles. 'I didn't touch her, I just told her that I was really Bex, and that she'd regret it if she said anything to you about me and Jed kissing, that she was too young to understand that it really wasn't something to be talking about. I kept her phone after she died because you all thought it was missing anyway and I saw that Dee Dee had retrieved all the stuff I'd deleted and there was Jed and me on the film and I couldn't bear to get rid of it all over again, especially once I realized it ... him and me ... was never going to happen again ... but it had to be a secret. Anyway, that doesn't matter. What counts is that I tried to make sure you'd never know. Don't you see? I was trying to protect you.'

I push past her again and walk to the stairs, my eyes blurring with tears. I don't know any longer what is true and what isn't or how to work it out. Everything that I thought was certain has been thrown into the air.

'I didn't hurt Dee Dee,' Rose says. 'You'll see the truth on her phone. And when you do, if you have any scrap of humanity in your soul, if you care about *any* of us you will let this go.'

Ignoring her, I hurry down the stairs.

Rose's voice echoes after me. 'I sacrificed everything for you, Emily, and never asked for a thing in return. I gave up a career, a love life, I even gave up Jed. I have suffered for you. Lost *everything*.'

I reach the front door. I turn. I look up at her. 'I didn't know you felt like that,' I say, trying to keep my voice steady. 'But Dee Dee still died. And someone has to pay.'

I shut the door, but I can still hear Rose storming down the stairs.

'I haven't breathed a word about Dee Dee for *his* sake. I'm just asking you to do the same. *Please,* Emily.' Her voice fades as I reach the pavement.

I dart inside my car and slam shut the door so I can't

hear her any more. Without looking around, I quickly put a couple of streets between us, then I park. I am tempted just to go straight to the police, tell them what I know. But maybe I should look at Dee Dee's phone first, to see what Rose was saying.

I switch it on. Whatever it tells me, somebody is guilty. Somebody should pay.

August 2014

I can't believe it. I can't take it in. My friend Bex wasn't real. She was Rose, Emily's sister who I saw with Daddy. She came into my room in the villa here after Emily went and she told me that she had been pretending to be Bex with a fake photo and made-up stories and now the pretending needed to stop. She said that it was really important I didn't tell Emily I saw her kissing Daddy. And I didn't know what to say so I just looked at the bed and Rose sat beside me and said though she didn't have her own children she looked after Emily when she was my age and that there were things you think you understand when you're thirteen that you don't really.

And in my head I was thinking that what I did understand was that everyone had been lying to everyone else. But I didn't say anything. So Rose leaned in and said all softly that if I told Emily, Emily would just hate me EVEN MORE. I looked up then because I was surprised Rose was saying Emily hated me AT ALL because Emily is always so nice and Rose said that just today Emily was saying how fat I looked and how embarrassing it was for Jed to have such a fat child. And Rose said that if I told Emily then 'all hell would break loose' and Mum and Daddy would resent me more than they do and I still didn't say anything but I couldn't stop tears itching in my eyes. And Rose saw and said she understood how hard it was but it was obvious that Daddy found me irritating and Mum had complained I was withdrawn, then she said if I talked to Mum she would be upset 'and you don't want to upset your mother, do you?' and if Daddy knew what I'd seen he would hate me for ruining things with Emily. So Rose went on that I needed to think about other people and not be selfish and that I needed to keep the secret.

Then she gave me my phone which I'd lost a bit earlier and she said SHE had taken it and she'd deleted our texts and my film of her and Daddy and that if I promised not to say anything I could have it back. She asked if I would promise and I said nothing so she asked again and I nodded though I still hadn't looked up properly because my eyes were still all prickly with tears. And she asked a third time and this time I looked up and I whispered 'yes' and Rose said 'good girl' and she left.

Once she went I thought I would cry but in fact I didn't, I just lay in the dark on my pillow with my phone and I got back the texts and the film of Rose and Daddy because Rose had just put them in the trash and it was easy to get them back and I needed to see they were real but in the end what was the point because I looked at all the texts from Bex who WASN'T real and WASN'T really my friend though I thought she was my ONLY friend, and I remembered all the giggling and pointing and picking on me from everyone at school and how that would start again soon in just a week or so when we were back from holiday and the new term started.

And I thought about Emily and how nice she'd been before, then what Rose said about what she really thought of me. And I wondered for a minute if Rose was making it up, then I remembered hearing Daddy say yesterday to Emily in one of his loud supposed-to-be-funny whispers that maybe I broke the strap on my sandals because I was too heavy for them and how she laughed and then, this afternoon, when I was taking pictures of her and me up at that citad-thingy place where you can see the sea I said I should take a second photo because I looked so terrible in the first one and Emily agreed and I realize that she thinks I'm fat and stupid, just like everyone else. And anyway, in the end Mummy's right:

Emily took Daddy away from us.

And that's when everything started to go wrong.

I went over to the window where outside everything is hot and dark and I knew I didn't want to go back to school and I knew I couldn't explain to anyone why and that's when I decided.

So I tore the top off the headache powders and scrunched it up and put it down the loo and got a glass then I went along the corridor to Lish's room where he was asleep and I found his bag under the bed and I got out the packet he took before with the crystals that he said were 'f-word lethal' and I tipped a teeny tiny bit, less than a quarter of a teaspoon, of the crystals into the headache powders Emily gave me then I put the crystals packet back exactly where I found it in Lish's bag so Lish wouldn't know and get mad, then I picked up my glass and came back in here. I put in some water from my bottle and mixed in the headache powders that contained the teeny bit of crystals and sat on the bed.

So here is the drink and I am going to have it now. I don't know what it will do, maybe just give me stomach cramps and I'll be sick.

Or maybe it will be enough and in the morning they'll find me.

Then the pain will stop.

Then it will all be over.

Then they'll all be sorry.

March 2015

Two months to the day since Martin's funeral I take the recording to Zoe and Jed. Why have I waited so long? Partly because I wanted to spare them the knowledge that their daughter died so pointlessly, in so much anguish. Partly because it can't change anything.

And partly because of the deep guilt I feel that I was so blind to Dee Dee's unhappiness, that among all the adults who failed her, I have to count myself.

Rose, of course, is totally against them seeing the recordings. But I don't care what Rose thinks. I haven't spoken to her for weeks. Straight after I'd watched Dee Dee's diaries I took all my things from the house and stored them in Laura and Jamie's attic, directly above their tiny spare room where I'm still sleeping. I know I'm in the way here, with the new baby due soon, but I keep to myself as much as possible and babysit for them twice a week, so for the time being it's okay. They don't know what I've found out. The only person I've told is Dan and it's him, as much as anything, who persuades me at last that Dee Dee's parents deserve to know how she died.

'However painful it is,' he says. 'Just think about it. You'd want to know if she was your daughter, wouldn't you?'

I would. Dan still wants me to come and live with him. After initially hating the idea of leaving London, he's found himself a great job on a regional paper in Yorkshire where he can see Lulu every weekend. I've been up to stay and met her and Carrie and Gill. I like them all but it seems like a huge upheaval to move there myself. If I'm going to hand in my notice at work, I'll have to decide soon. But not yet. First I have to pass on what I know about Dee Dee's death: before I can allow myself a future, I have to deal with the lies of the past.

I park outside Zoe's house. Jed's car is in the drive. Well, that's no surprise. I'd assumed they would both be here. I just hope Jed isn't proposing to ambush me while I'm here, to press me to go back to him. I can't think he will, not after not contacting me for all these weeks, not after the whole horrendous business with Martin. I haven't heard from Jed at all in fact, though I have heard that the case against Benecke Tricorp has been dropped. I swing between hating him for pushing Cameron into reaching for that knife and rationalizing that Jed's fury was understandable and that everything that happened afterwards was a terrible accident.

I check my bag for Dee Dee's phone and walk steadily up the path to Zoe's front door. The last time I was here was when I waited outside after Dee Dee's funeral. That feels like a million years ago. I take a deep breath as I ring the doorbell, bracing myself. I have no idea how Zoe will react to me. She sounded okay on the phone, but I know how deeply she loathes me, though perhaps she has calmed down a bit now it seems Lish is unlikely to serve a custodial sentence. As the lawyers prepare for the court case, everything I hear about it suggests he has given the police masses of information they can use against Cameron. Not that Cameron has been hard to crack. He is, by all accounts, clinically depressed, mourning my brother. Under other circumstances I would have shared my grief with him and my sister. But now I mourn alone.

The door opens. Zoe appears, smart and slim in beige cut-offs and an open-necked powder-blue shirt.

'Come in.' I follow her into the nearest room. It's a dining room, dominated by a big polished wood table with old-fashioned dark wood cabinets across one wall. It is far more formal and expensive-looking than anything in my home with Jed was. Jed himself is sitting at the table. He looks up as I walk in and I'm shocked to see how old and tired he seems, the grey hairs outnumbering the brown, his face lined and sagging with grief.

'Hello, Emily.' His face is a blank. Of all the states he might have been in, this dull, unhappy disengagement is the last one I expected.

'Hi.' I sit down opposite him, feeling flustered. 'How are you?'

'Okay,' Jed says non-committally. 'People have been kind.'

'Gary?'

Across the room, Zoe snorts at the mention of Gary's name.

Jed shrugs. 'My brother has debts and he's busy dealing with those.'

So much for sibling loyalty.

Zoe walks around the table to take the seat next to Jed. She lays her hand on his arm and I suddenly realize that Jed hasn't just driven over, that they are together. Zoe has taken him back and he is living here with her again. I search myself and feel no jealousy, nor even any surprise. If anything, I'm pleased for him – for them – that they have each other.

'So ...' Jed says. 'Why are you here? What do you want?' His face is entirely without expression.

I gulp, remembering the bombshell I am about to drop. I take Dee Dee's phone and place it on the table between us.

'I found this,' I say. 'My sister was hiding it.'

Zoe looks up at me, her eyes wide with shock. 'That's Dee Dee's.'

I nod. 'It explains everything,' I say. 'It wasn't Cameron. Or Lish. Not exactly. It ... it was no one. And everyone.'

I show them the texts from Bex, then the series of video diaries. I force myself to sit still while they watch. Zoe cries openly, her hand over her mouth. Jed's eyes are dark with their pain.

They play each video in turn, right through to the end.

As Dee Dee's voice fades for the final time, Zoe takes her hand from Jed's arm and shrinks back in her chair. The agony in her eyes is unbearable, yet I force myself to look at her.

'I'm so sorry,' I say.

Jed clears his throat. He doesn't look up at either of us and when he speaks, his voice is suffused with shame.

'What are you going to do with this video?' he asks. 'This last one, I mean.'

'Nothing,' I say. 'No one is going to suffer for anything they didn't do. And all of us are paying the price of what we did do.'

Jed nods slowly.

'I think you should show Lish,' I go on. 'He should know how Dee Dee got hold of the potassium cyanide. He must have guessed even if he's never said. It must have eaten away at him.'

'He hasn't said anything,' Jed says, staring down at the table.

'Other than that, it's up to you what you do. She was your daughter.'

As I speak I meet Jed's eyes at last.

'I'm sorry,' he says. He means about Rose.

Zoe pushes her chair back and leaves the room.

I nod, accepting the apology, then stand up. I expected to feel more angry ... about Rose, about Martin, but now I'm here and the explanation is done, mostly I just feel relief.

As I leave the house I can hear Zoe crying. Then I shut the front door and the sound vanishes. I drive slowly back to Laura's, aware that something has been lifted from me, some terrible weight I've been carrying since Martin died, maybe even since Dee Dee.

And it occurs to me that there is nothing to keep me here, in London ... in the past.

I check the time. It's not yet midday and the rest of the weekend stretches ahead. But I know now where I should go, where I should be. There's no need to agonize over it any longer. Laura and her family are out, so I scribble a note, pack a small bag then get back in my car and set off. I stop on the way to lay flowers on Martin's grave. The sun shines on the headstone and across the grass as I make my way to the car, to Dan and to the future.

Acknowledgements

Here We Lie began as a conversation with my brother, the economist Roger Bate, about his work investigating the world of counterfeit drugs. The references to drug cases in my story are taken from the real life cases in his book, *Phake: the deadly world of falsified and substandard medicines* and I am deeply grateful to him for his advice and his feedback as well as to Lorraine Mooney who worked with him. I'm also grateful to Ramez Hamade who filled in some of the many gaps in my knowledge about both primary school teaching and boats.